FANTASY ADVENTURE

THE Silent Blade

R. A. Salvatore

THE SILENT BLADE

Distributed to the book trade in the United States by Random House, Inc. and in Canada by Random House of Canada, Ltd.

Distributed to the hobby, toy, and comic trade in the United States and Canada by regional distributors.

Distributed worldwide by Wizards of the Coast, Inc. and regional distributors.

Cover art by Todd Lockwood

ISBN: 0-7869-1180-8

U.S., CANADA,
ASIA, PACIFIC, & LATIN AMERICA
Wizards of the Coast, Inc.
P.O. Box 707
Renton, WA 98057-0707

+1-800-324-6496

EUROPEAN HEADQUARTERS
Wizards of the Coast, Belgium
P.B. 34
2300 Turnhout
Belgium

+32-14-44-30-44

FANTASY ADVENTURE

Books by R.A. Salvatore

The Icewind Dale Trilogy
The Crystal Shard
Streams of Silver
The Halfling's Gem

The Dark Elf Trilogy
Homeland
Exile
Sojourn
The Dark Elf Trilogy Collector's Edition

The Cleric Quintet
Canticle
In Sylvan Shadows
Night Masks
The Fallen Fortress
The Chaos Curse
The Cleric Quintet Collector's Edition
(Available January 1999)

The Legacy
Starless Night
Siege of Darkness
Passage to Dawn
The Silent Blade

PROLOGUE

ulfgar lay back in his bed, pondering, trying to come to terms with the abrupt changes that had come over his life. Rescued from the demon Errtu and his hellish prison in the Abyss, the proud barbarian found himself once again among friends and allies. Bruenor, his adopted dwarven father, was here, and so was Drizzt, his dark elven mentor and dearest friend. Wulfgar could tell from the snoring that Regis, the chubby halfling, was sleeping contentedly in the next room.

And Catti-brie, dear Catti-brie, the woman Wulfgar had come to love those years before, the woman whom he had planned to marry seven years previously in Mithral Hall. They were all here at their home in Icewind Dale, reunited and presumably at peace, through the heroic efforts of these wonderful friends.

Wulfgar did not know what that meant.

Wulfgar, who had been through such a terrible ordeal over six years of torture at the clawed hands of the demon Errtu, did not understand.

The huge man crossed his arms over his chest. Sheer exhaustion put him here in bed, forced him down, for he would not willingly choose sleep. Errtu found him in his dreams.

And so it was this night. Wulfgar, though deep in thought and deep in turmoil, succumbed to his exhaustion and fell into a peaceful blackness that soon turned again into the images of the swirling gray mists that were the Abyss. There sat the gigantic, bat-winged Errtu, perched upon his carved mushroom throne, laughing. Always laughing that hideous croaking chuckle. That laugh was borne not out of joy, but was rather a mocking thing, an insult to those the demon chose to torture. Now the beast aimed that unending wickedness at Wulfgar, as was aimed the huge pincer of Bizmatec, another demon, minion of Errtu. With strength beyond the bounds of almost any other human, Wulfgar ferociously wrestled Bizmatec. The barbarian batted aside the huge humanlike arms and the two other upper-body appendages, the pincer arms, for a long while, slapping and punching desperately.

But too many flailing limbs came at him. Bizmatec was too large and too strong, and the mighty barbarian eventually began to tire.

It ended—always it ended—with one of Bizmatec's pincers around Wulfgar's throat, the demon's other pincer arm and its two humanlike arms holding the defeated human steady. Expert in this, his favorite torturing technique, Bizmatec pressed oh so subtly on Wulfgar's throat, took away the air, then gave it back, over and over, leaving the man weak in the legs, gasping and gasping as minutes, then hours, slipped past.

Wulfgar sat up straight in his bed, clutching at his throat, clawing a scratch down one side of it before he realized that the demon was not there, that he was safe in his bed in the land he called home, surrounded by his friends.

Friends . . .

What did that word mean? What could they know of his torment? How could they help him chase away the enduring nightmare that was Errtu?

The haunted man did not sleep the rest of the night, and when Drizzt came to rouse him, well before the dawn, the dark elf found Wulfgar already dressed for the road. They were to leave this day, all five, bearing the artifact Crenshinibon far, far to the south and west. They were bound for Caradoon on the banks of Impresk Lake, and then into the Snowflake Mountains to a great monastery called Spirit Soaring where a priest named Cadderly would destroy the wicked relic.

Crenshinibon. Drizzt had it with him when he came to get Wulfgar that morning. The drow didn't wear it openly, but Wulfgar knew it was there. He could sense it, could feel its vile presence. For Crenshinibon remained linked to its last master, the demon Errtu. It tingled with the energy of the demon, and because Drizzt had it on him and was standing so close, Errtu, too, remained close to Wulfgar.

"A fine day for the road," the drow remarked lightheartedly, but his tone was strained, condescending, Wulfgar noted. With more than a little difficulty, Wulfgar resisted the urge to punch Drizzt in the face.

Instead, he grunted in reply and strode past the deceptively small dark elf. Drizzt was but a few inches over five feet, while Wulfgar towered closer to seven feet than to six, and carried fully twice the weight of the drow. The barbarian's thigh was thicker than Drizzt's waist, and yet, if it came to blows between them, wise bettors would favor the drow.

"I have not yet wakened Catti-brie," Drizzt explained.

Wulfgar turned fast at the mention of the name. He stared hard into the drow's lavender eyes, his own blue orbs matching the intensity that always seemed to be there.

"But Regis is already awake and at his morning meal—he is hoping to get two or three breakfasts in before we leave, no doubt," Drizzt added with a chuckle, one that Wulfgar did not share. "And Bruenor will meet us on the field beyond Bryn Shander's eastern gate. He is with his own folk, preparing the priestess Stumpet to lead the clan in his absence."

Wulfgar only half heard the words. They meant nothing to him. All the world meant nothing to him.

3

"Shall we rouse Catti-brie?" the drow asked.

"I will," Wulfgar answered gruffly. "You see to Regis. If he gets a belly full of food, he will surely slow us down, and I mean to be quick to your friend Cadderly, that we might be rid of Crenshinibon."

Drizzt started to answer, but Wulfgar turned away, moving down the hall to Catti-brie's door. He gave a single, thunderous knock, then pushed right through. Drizzt moved a step in that direction to scold the barbarian for his rude behavior—the woman had not even acknowledged his knock, after all—but he let it go. Of all the humans the drow had ever met, Catti-brie ranked as the most capable at defending herself from insult or violence.

Besides, Drizzt knew that his desire to go and scold Wulfgar was wrought more than a bit by his jealousy of the man who once was, and perhaps was soon again, to be Catti-brie's husband.

The drow stroked a hand over his handsome face and turned to find Regis.

* * * * *

Wearing only a slight undergarment and with her pants half pulled up, the startled Catti-brie turned a surprised look on Wulfgar as he strode into her room. "Ye might've waited for an answer," she said dryly, brushing away her embarrassment and pulling her pants up, then going to retrieve her tunic.

Wulfgar nodded and held up his hands—only half an apology, perhaps, but a half more than Catti-brie had expected. She saw the pain in the man's sky blue eyes and the emptiness of his occasional strained smiles. She had talked with Drizzt about it at length, and with Bruenor and Regis, and they had all decided to be patient. Time alone could heal Wulfgar's wounds.

"The drow has prepared a morning meal for us all," Wulfgar explained. "We should eat well before we start on the long road."

4

" 'The drow'? " Catti-brie echoed. She hadn't meant to speak it aloud, but so dumbfounded was she by Wulfgar's distant reference to Drizzt that the words just slipped out. Would Wulfgar call Bruenor "the dwarf"? And how long would it be before she became simply "the girl"? Catti-brie blew a deep sigh and pulled her tunic over her shoulders, reminding herself pointedly that Wulfgar had been through hell—literally. She looked at him now, studying those eyes, and saw a hint of embarrassment there, as though her echo of his callous reference to Drizzt had indeed struck him in the heart. That was a good sign.

He turned to leave her room, but she moved to him, reaching up to gently stroke the side of his face, her hand running down his smooth cheek to the scratchy beard that he had either decided to grow or simply hadn't been motivated enough to shave.

Wulfgar looked down at her, at the tenderness in her eyes, and for the first time since the fight on the ice floe when he and his friends had dispatched wicked Errtu, there came a measure of honesty in his slight smile.

* * * * *

Regis did get his three meals, and he grumbled about it all that morning as the five friends started out from Bryn Shander, the largest of the villages in the region called Ten Towns in forlorn Icewind Dale. Their course was north at first, moving to easier ground, and then turning due west. To the north, far in the distance, they saw the high structures of Targos, second city of the region, and beyond the city's roofs could be seen shining waters of Maer Dualdon.

By mid-afternoon, with more than a dozen miles behind them, they came to the banks of the Shaengarne, the great river swollen and running fast with the spring melt. They followed it north, back to Maer Dualdon, to the town of Bremen and a waiting boat Regis had arranged.

Gently refusing the many offers from townsfolk to remain in the village for supper and a warm bed, and over the many protests of Regis, who claimed that he was famished and ready to lay down and die, the friends were soon west of the river, running on again, leaving the towns, their home, behind.

Drizzt could hardly believe that they had set out so soon. Wulfgar had only recently been returned to them. All of them were together once more in the land they called their home, at peace, and yet, here they were, heeding again the call of duty and running down the road to adventure. The drow had the cowl of his traveling cloak pulled low about his face, shielding his sensitive eyes from the stinging sun.

Thus his friends could not see his wide smile.

Part 1

APATHY

ften I sit and ponder the turmoil I feel when my blades are at rest, when all the world around me seems at peace. This is the supposed ideal for which I strive, the calm that we all hope will eventually return to us when we are at war, and yet, in these peaceful times—and they have been rare occurrences indeed in the more than seven decades of my life—I do not feel as if I have found perfection, but, rather, as if something is missing from my life.

It seems such an incongruous notion, and yet I have come to know that I am a warrior, a creature of action. In those times when there is no pressing need for action, I am not at ease. Not at all.

When the road is not filled with adventure, when there are no monsters to battle and no mountains to climb, boredom finds me. I have come to accept this truth of my life, this truth about who I am, and so, on those rare, empty occasions I can find a way to defeat the boredom. I can find a mountain peak higher than the last I climbed.

I see many of the same symptoms now in Wulfgar, returned to us from the grave, from the swirling darkness that was Errtu's corner of the Abyss. But I fear that Wulfgar's state has transcended simple boredom, spilling into the realm of apathy. Wulfgar, too, was a creature of action, but that doesn't seem to be the cure for his lethargy or his apathy. His own people now call out to him, begging action. They have asked him to assume leadership of the tribes. Even stubborn Berkthgar, who would have to give up that coveted position of rulership, supports Wulfgar. He and all the rest of them know, at this tenuous time, that above all others Wulfgar, son

9

of Beornegar, could bring great gains to the nomadic barbarians of Icewind Dale.

Wulfgar will not heed that call. It is neither humility nor weariness stopping him, I recognize, nor any fears that he cannot handle the position or live up to the expectations of those begging him. Any of those problems could be overcome, could be reasoned through or supported by Wulfgar's friends, myself included. But, no, it is none of those rectifiable things.

It is simply that he does not care.

Could it be that his own agonies at the clawed hands of Errtu were so great and so enduring that he has lost his ability to empathize with the pain of others? Has he seen too much horror, too much agony, to hear their cries?

I fear this above all else, for it is a loss that knows no precise cure. And yet, to be honest, I see it clearly etched in Wulfgar's features, a state of self-absorption where too many memories of his own recent horrors cloud his vision. Perhaps he does not even recognize someone else's pain. Or perhaps, if he does see it, he dismisses it as trivial next to the monumental trials he suffered for those six years as Errtu's prisoner. Loss of empathy might well be the most enduring and deep-cutting scar of all, the silent blade of an unseen enemy, tearing at our hearts and stealing more than our strength. Stealing our will, for what are we without empathy? What manner of joy might we find in our lives if we cannot understand the joys and pains of those around us, if we cannot share in a greater community? I remember my years in the Underdark after I ran out of Menzoberranzan. Alone, save the occasional visits from Guenhwyvar, I survived those long years through my own imagination.

I am not certain that Wulfgar even has that capacity left to him, for imagination requires introspection, a reaching within one's thoughts, and I fear that every time my friend so looks inward, all he sees are the minions of Errtu, the sludge and horrors of the Abyss.

He is surrounded by friends, who love him and will try with all their hearts to support him and help him climb out

*of Errtu's emotional dungeon. Perhaps Catti-brie, the
woman he once loved (and perhaps still does love) so
deeply, will prove pivotal to his recovery. It pains me to
watch them together, I admit. She treats Wulfgar with such
tenderness and compassion, but I know that he feels not her
gentle touch. Better that she slap his face, eye him sternly,
and show him the truth of his lethargy. I know this and yet
I cannot tell her to do so, for their relationship is much
more complicated than that. I have nothing but Wulfgar's
best interests in my mind and my heart now, and yet, if
I showed Catti-brie a way that seemed less than compassionate, it could be, and would be—by Wulfgar at least, in
his present state of mind—construed as the interference of
a jealous suitor.*

*Not true. For though I do not know Catti-brie's honest
feelings toward this man who once was to be her husband—for she has become quite guarded with her feelings
of late—I do recognize that Wulfgar is not capable of love at
this time.*

*Not capable of love . . . are there any sadder words to
describe a man? I think not, and wish that I could now
assess Wulfgar's state of mind differently. But love, honest
love, requires empathy. It is a sharing—of joy, of pain, of
laughter, of tears. Honest love makes one's soul a reflection
of the partner's moods. And as a room seems larger when it
is lined with mirrors, so do the joys become amplified. And
as the individual items within the mirrored room seem less
acute, so does pain diminish and fade, stretched thin by
the sharing.*

*That is the beauty of love, whether in passion or friend-
ship. A sharing that multiplies the joys and thins the pains.
Wulfgar is surrounded now by friends, all willing to engage
in such sharing, as it once was between us. Yet he cannot so
engage us, cannot let loose those guards that he necessarily
put in place when surrounded by the likes of Errtu.*

*He has lost his empathy. I can only pray that he will find
it again, that time will allow him to open his heart and
soul to those deserving, for without empathy he will find no*

purpose. Without purpose, he will find no satisfaction. Without satisfaction, he will find no contentment, and without contentment, he will find no joy.

And we, all of us, will have no way to help him.

—Drizzt Do'Urden

Chapter 1

A STRANGER AT HOME

rtemis Entreri stood on a rocky hill overlooking the vast, dusty city, trying to sort through the myriad feelings that swirled within him. He reached up to wipe the blowing dust and sand from his lips and from the hairs of his newly grown goatee. Only as he wiped it did he realize that he hadn't shaved the rest of his face in several days, for now the small beard, instead of standing distinct upon his face, fell to ragged edges across his cheeks.

Entreri didn't care.

The wind pulled many strands of his long hair from the tie at the back of his head, the wayward lengths slapping across his face, stinging his dark eyes.

Entreri didn't care.

He just stared down at Calimport and tried hard to stare inside himself. The man had lived nearly two-thirds of his life in the sprawling city on the southern coast, had come to prominence as a warrior and a killer there. It was the only place that he could ever really call home. Looking down on it now, brown and dusty, the relentless desert sun flashed brilliantly off the white marble of the greater homes. It also illuminated the many hovels, shacks, and torn tents set along roads—muddy roads only because they had no proper sewers for drainage. Looking down on Calimport now, the returning assassin didn't know how to feel. Once, he had known his place in the world. He had reached the pinnacle of his nefarious profession, and any who spoke his name did so with reverence and fear. When a pasha hired Artemis Entreri to kill a man, that man was soon dead. Without exception. And despite the many enemies he had obviously made, the assassin had been able to walk the streets of Calimport openly, not from shadow to shadow, in all confidence that none would be bold enough to act against him.

No one would dare shoot an arrow at Artemis Entreri, for they would know that the single shot must be perfect, must finish this man who seemed above the antics of mere mortals, else he would then come looking for them. And he would find them, and he would kill them.

A movement to the side, the slight shift of a shadow, caught Entreri's attention. He shook his head and sighed, not really surprised, when a cloaked figure leaped out from the rocks, some twenty feet ahead of him and stood blocking the path, arms crossed over his burly chest.

"Going to Calimport?" the man asked, his voice thick with a southern accent.

Entreri didn't answer, just kept his head straight ahead, though his eyes darted to the many rocks lining both sides of the trail.

"You must pay for the passage," the burly man went on. "I am your guide." With that he bowed and came up showing a toothless grin.

Entreri had heard many tales of this common game of money through intimidation, though never before had one been bold enough to block his way. Yes, indeed, he realized, he had been gone a long time. Still he didn't answer, and the burly man shifted, throwing wide his cloak to reveal a sword under his belt.

"How many coins do you offer?" the man asked.

Entreri started to tell him to move aside but changed his mind and only sighed again.

"Deaf?" said the man, and he drew out his sword and advanced yet another step. "You pay me, or me and my friends will take the coins from your torn body."

Entreri didn't reply, didn't move, didn't draw his jeweled dagger, his only weapon. He just stood there, and his ambivalence seemed to anger the burly man all the more.

The man glanced to the side—to Entreri's left—just slightly, but the assassin caught the look clearly. He followed it to one of the robber's companions, holding a bow in the shadows between two huge rocks.

"Now," said the burly man. "Last chance for you."

Entreri quietly hooked his toe under a rock, but made no movement other than that. He stood waiting, staring at the burly man, but with the archer on the edge of his vision. So well could the assassin read the movements of men, the slightest muscle twitch, the blink of an eye, that it was he who moved first. Entreri leaped out diagonally, ahead and to the left, rolling over and kicking out with his right foot. He launched the stone the archer's way, not to hit the man—that would have been above the skill even of Artemis Entreri—but in the hopes of distracting him. As he came over into the somersault, the assassin let his cloak fly wildly, hoping it might catch and slow the arrow.

He needn't have worried, for the archer missed badly and would have even if Entreri hadn't moved at all.

Coming up from the roll, Entreri set his feet and squared himself to the charging swordsmen, aware also that two other men were coming over the rocks at either side of the trail.

Still showing no weapon, Entreri unexpectedly charged ahead, ducking the swipe of the sword at the last possible instant, then came up hard behind the swishing blade, one hand catching the attacker's chin, the other snapping behind the man's head, grabbing his hair. A twist and turn flipped the swordsman on the ground. Entreri let go, running his hand up the man's weapon arm to fend off any

15

attempted attacks. The man went down on his back hard. At that moment Entreri stomped down on his throat. The man's grasp on the sword weakened, almost as if he were handing the weapon to Entreri.

The assassin leaped away, not wanting to get his feet tangled as the other two came in, one straight ahead, the other from behind. Out flashed Entreri's sword, a straight left-handed thrust, followed by a dazzling, rolling stab. The man easily stepped back out of Entreri's reach, but the attack hadn't been designed to score a hit anyway. Entreri flipped the sword to his right hand, an overhand grip, then stepped back suddenly, so suddenly, turning his hand and the blade. He brought it across his body, then stabbed it out behind him. The assassin felt the tip enter the man's chest and heard the gasp of air as he sliced a lung.

Instinct alone had Entreri spinning, turning to the right and keeping the attacker impaled. He brought the man about as a shield against the archer, who did indeed fire again. But again, the man missed badly, and this time the arrow burrowed into the ground several feet in front of Entreri.

"Idiot," the assassin muttered, and with a sudden jerk, he dropped his latest victim to the dirt, bringing the sword about in the same fluid movement. So brilliantly had he executed the maneuver that the remaining swordsman finally understood his folly, turned about, and fled.

Entreri spun again, threw the sword in the general direction of the archer, and bolted for cover.

A long moment slipped past.

Where is he?" the archer called out, obvious fear and frustration in his voice. "Merk, do you see him?"

Another long moment passed.

"Where is he?" the archer cried again, growing frantic. "Merk, where is he?"

"Right behind you," came a whisper. A jeweled dagger flashed, slicing the bowstring and then, before the stunned man could begin to react, resting against the front of his throat.

"Please," the man stammered, trembling so badly that his movements, not Entreri's, caused the first nick from that fine blade. "I have children, yes. Many, many children. Seventeen . . ."

He ended in a gurgle as Entreri cut him from ear to ear, bringing his foot up against the man's back even as he did, then kicking him facedown to the ground.

"Then you should have chosen a safer career," Entreri answered, though the man could not hear.

Peering out from the rocks, the assassin soon spotted the fourth of the group, moving from shadow to shadow across the way. The man was obviously heading for Calimport but was simply too scared to jump out and run in the open. Entreri knew that he could catch the man, or perhaps re-string the bow and take him down from this spot. But he didn't, for he hardly cared. Not even bothering to search the bodies for loot, Entreri wiped and sheathed his magical dagger and moved back onto the road. Yes, he had been gone a long, long time.

Before he had left this city, Artemis Entreri had known his place in the world and in Calimport. He thought of that now, staring at the city after an absence of several years. He understood the shadowy world he had inhabited and realized that many changes had likely taken place in those alleys. Old associates would be gone, and his reputation would not likely carry him through the initial meetings with the new, often self-proclaimed leaders of the various guilds and sects.

"What have you done to me, Drizzt Do'Urden?" he asked with a chuckle, for this great change in the life of Artemis Entreri had begun when a certain Pasha Pook had sent him on a mission to retrieve a magical ruby pendant from a runaway halfling. An easy enough task, Entreri had believed. The halfling, Regis, was known to the assassin and should not have proven a difficult adversary.

Little did Entreri know at that time that Regis had done a marvelously cunning job of surrounding himself with powerful allies, particularly the dark elf. How many years had it been, Entreri pondered, since he had first encountered Drizzt Do'Urden? Since he had first met his warrior equal, who could rightly hold a mirror up to Entreri and show the lie that was his existence? Nearly a decade, he realized, and while he had grown older and perhaps a bit slower, the drow elf, who might live six centuries, had aged not at all.

Yes, Drizzt had started Entreri on a path of dangerous introspection. The blackness had only been amplified when Entreri had gone after Drizzt again, along with the remnants of the drow's family. Drizzt had beaten Entreri on a high ledge outside Mithral Hall, and the assassin would have died, except that an opportunistic dark elf by the name of Jarlaxle had rescued him. Jarlaxle had then taken him to Menzoberranzan, the vast city of the drow, the stronghold of Lolth, Demon Queen of Chaos. The human assassin had found a different standing down there in a city of intrigue and brutality. There, everyone was an assassin, and Entreri, despite his tremendous talents at the murderous art, was only human, a fact that relegated him to the bottom of the social ladder.

But it was more than simple perceptual standing that had struck the assassin profoundly during his stay in the city of drow. It was the realization of the emptiness of his existence. There, in a city full of Entreris, he had come to recognize the folly of his confidence, of his ridiculous notion that his passionless dedication to pure fighting skill had somehow elevated him above the rabble. He knew that now, looking down at Calimport, at the city he had known as a home, at his last refuge, it seemed, in all the world.

In dark and mysterious Menzoberranzan, Artemis Entreri had been humbled.

As he made his way to the distant city, Entreri wondered many times if he truly desired this return. His first days would be perilous, he knew, but it was not fear for the end of his life that brought a hesitance to his normally cocky stride. It was fear of continuing his life.

Outwardly, little had changed in Calimport—the town of a million beggars, Entreri liked to call it. True to form, he passed by dozens of pitiful wretches, lying in rags, or naked, along the sides of the road, most of them likely in the same spot the city guards had thrown them that morning, clearing the way for the golden-gilded carriages of the important merchants. They reached toward Entreri with trembling, bony fingers, arms so weak and emaciated that they could not hold them up for even the few seconds it took the heartless man to stride past them.

Where to go? he wondered. His old employer, Pasha Pook, was long dead, the victim of Drizzt's powerful panther companion after Entreri had done as the man had bade him and returned Regis and the ruby pendant. Entreri had not remained in the city for long after that unfortunate incident, for he had brought Regis in and that had led to the demise of a powerful figure, ultimately a black stain on Entreri's record among his less-than-merciful associates. He could have mended the situation, probably quite easily, by simply offering his normally invaluable services to another powerful guildmaster or pasha, but he had chosen the road. Entreri had been bent on revenge against Drizzt, not for the killing of Pook—the assassin cared little about that—but because he and Drizzt had battled fiercely without conclusion in the city's sewers, a fight that Entreri still believed he should have won.

Walking along the dirty streets of Calimport now, he had to wonder what reputation he had left behind. Certainly many other assassins would have spoken ill of him in his absence, would have exaggerated Entreri's failure in the Regis incident in order to strengthen their own positions within the gutter pecking order.

Entreri smiled as he considered the fact, and he knew it to be fact, that those ill words against him would have been spoken in whispers only. Even in his absence, those other killers would fear retribution. Perhaps he didn't know his place in the world any longer. Perhaps Menzoberranzan had held a dark . . . no, not dark, but merely empty mirror before his eyes, but he could not deny that he still enjoyed the respect.

Respect he might have to earn yet again, he pointedly reminded himself.

As he moved along the familiar streets, more and more memories came back to him. He knew where most of the guild houses had been located, and suspected that, unless there had been some ambitious purge by the lawful leaders of the city, many still stood intact, and probably brimming with the associates he had once known. Pook's house had been shaken to the core by the killing of the wretched pasha and, subsequently, by the appointment of the lazy halfling Regis as Pook's successor. Entreri had taken care of that minor problem by taking care of Regis, and yet, despite the chaos imposed upon that house, when Entreri had gone north with the halfling in tow, the house of Pook had survived. Perhaps it still stood, though the assassin could only guess as to who might be ruling it now.

That would have been a logical place for Entreri to go and rebuild his base of power within the city, but he simply shrugged and walked past the side avenue that would lead to it. He thought he was merely wandering aimlessly, but soon enough he came to another familiar region and realized that he had subconsciously aimed for this area, perhaps in an effort to regain his heart.

These were the streets where a young Artemis Entreri first made his mark in Calimport, where he, barely a teenager, had defeated all challengers to his supremacy, where he had battled the man sent by Theebles Royuset, the lieutenant in powerful Pasha Basadoni's guild. Entreri had killed that thug and had later killed ugly Theebles, the clever murder moving him into Basadoni's generous favor. He had become a lieutenant in one of the most powerful guilds of Calimport, of all of Calimshan, at the tender age of fourteen.

But now he hardly cared, and recalling the story did not even bring the slightest hint of a smile to his face.

He thought back further, to the torment that had landed him here in the first place, trials too great for a boy to overcome, deception and betrayal by everyone he had known and trusted, most pointedly his own father. Still, he didn't care, couldn't even feel the pain any longer. It was meaningless, emptiness, without merit or point.

He saw a woman in the shadows of one hovel, hanging washed clothes to dry. She shifted deeper into the shadows, obviously wary. He understood her concern, for he was a stranger here, dressed too richly with his thick, well-stitched traveling cloak to belong in the shanty town. Strangers in these brutal places usually brought danger.

"From there to there," came a call, the voice of a young man, full of pride and edged with fear. Entreri turned slowly to see the youth, a tall and gangly lad, holding a club laced with spikes, swinging it nervously.

Entreri stared at him hard, seeing himself in the boy's face. No, not himself, he realized, for this one was too obviously nervous. This one would likely not survive for long.

"From there to there!" the boy said more loudly, pointing with his free hand to the end of the street where Entreri had entered, to the far end, where the assassin had been going.

"Your pardon, young master," Entreri said, dipping a slight bow, and feeling, as he did, his jeweled dagger, set on his belt under the folds of his cloak. A flick of his wrist could easily propel that dagger the fifteen feet, past the awkward youth's defenses and deep into his throat.

"Master," the lad echoed, his tone as much that of an incredulous question as an assertion. "Yes, master," he decided, apparently liking the title. "Master of this street, of all these streets, and none walk them without the permission of Taddio." As he finished, he prodded his thumb repeatedly into his chest.

Entreri straightened, and for just an instant, death flashed across his black eyes and the words "dead master" echoed through his thoughts. The lad had just challenged him, and the Artemis Entreri of a few years previous, a man who accepted and conquered all challenges, would have simply destroyed the youth where he stood.

But now that flash of pride whisked by, leaving Entreri unfazed and uninsulted. He gave a resigned sigh, wondering if he would find yet another stupid fight this day. And for what? he wondered, facing this pitiful, confused little boy on an empty street over which no rational person would even deign to claim ownership. "I begged you pardon, young master," he said calmly. "I did not know, for I am new to the region and ignorant of your customs."

"Then you should learn!" the lad replied angrily, gaining courage in Entreri's submissive response and coming forward a couple of strong strides.

Entreri shook his head, his hand starting for the dagger, but going, instead to his belt purse. He pulled out a gold coin and tossed it to the feet of the strutting youth.

The boy, who drank from sewers and ate the scraps he could rummage from the alleys behind the merchant houses, could not hide his surprise and awe at such a treasure. He regained his composure a moment later, though, and looked back at Entreri with a superior posture. "It is not enough," he said.

Entreri threw out another gold coin, and a silver. "That is all that I have, young master," he said, holding his hands out wide.

"If I search you and learn differently. . . ." the lad threatened.

Entreri sighed again, and decided that if the youth approached he would kill him quickly and mercifully.

The boy bent and scooped up the three coins. "If you come back to the domain of Taddio, have with you more coins," he declared. "I warn you. Now begone! Out the same end of the street you entered!"

Entreri looked back the way he had come. In truth, one direction seemed as good as any other to him at that time, so he gave a slight bow and walked back, out of the domain of Taddio, who had no idea how lucky he had been this day.

* * * * *

The building stood three full stories and, decorated with elaborate sculptures and shining marble, was truly the most impressive abode of all the thieving guilds. Normally such shadowy figures tried to keep a low profile, living in houses that seemed unremarkable from the outside, though they were, in truth, palatial within. Not so with the house of Pasha Basadoni. The old man—and he was ancient now, closer to ninety than to eighty—enjoyed his luxuries, and enjoyed showing the power and splendor of his guild to all who would look.

In a large chamber in the middle of the second floor, the gathering room for Basadoni's principle commanders, the two men and one woman who truly operated the day-to-day activities of the extensive guild entertained a young street thug. He was more a boy than a man, an unimpressive figure held in power by the backing of Pasha Basadoni and surely not by his own wiles.

"At least he is loyal," remarked Hand, a quiet and subtle thief, the master of shadows, when Taddio left them. "Two gold pieces and one silver—no small take for one working that gutter section."

"If that is all he received from his visitor," Sharlotta Vespers answered with a dismissive chuckle. Sharlotta stood tallest of the three captains, an inch above six feet, her body slender, her movements graceful—so graceful that Pasha Basadoni had nicknamed her his "Willow Tree." It was no secret that Basadoni had taken Sharlotta as his lover and still used her in that manner on those rare occasions when his old body was up to the task. It was common knowledge that Sharlotta had used those liaisons to her benefit and had climbed the ranks through Basadoni's bed. She willingly admitted as much, usually just before she killed the man or woman who had complained about it. A shake of her head sent waist-length black hair flipping back over one shoulder, so that Hand could see her wry expression clearly.

"If Taddio had received more, then he would have delivered more," Hand assured her, his tone, despite his anger, revealing that hint of frustration he and their other companion, Kadran Gordeon, always felt when dealing with the condescending Sharlotta. Hand ruled the quiet services of Basadoni's operation, the pickpockets and the prostitutes who worked the market, while Kadran Gordeon dealt with the soldiers of the street army. But Sharlotta, the Willow Tree, had Basadoni's ear above them all. She served as the principal attendant of the Pasha and as the voice of the now little seen old man.

When Basadoni finally died, these three would fight for control, no doubt, and while those who understood only the peripheral truths of the guild would likely favor the brash and loud Kadran Gordeon, those, such as Hand, who had a better feeling for the true inner workings, understood that Sharlotta Vespers had already taken many, many steps to secure and strengthen her position with or without the specter of Basadoni looming over them.

"How many words will we waste on the workings of a boy?" Kadran Gordeon complained. "Three new merchants have set up kiosks in the market a stone's throw from our house without our permission. That is the more important matter, the one requiring our full attention."

"We have already talked it through," Sharlotta replied. "You want us to give you permission to send out your soldiers, perhaps even a battle-mage, to teach the merchants better. You will not get that from us at this time."

"If we wait for Pasha Basadoni to finally speak on this matter, other merchants will come to the belief that they, too, need not pay us for the privilege of operating within the boundaries of our protective zone." He turned to Hand, the small man often his ally in arguments with Sharlotta. But the thief was obviously distracted, staring down at one of the coins the boy Taddio had given to him. Sensing that he was being watched, Hand looked up at the other two.

"What is it?" Kadran prompted.

"I've not seen one like this," Hand explained, flipping the coin to the burly man.

Kadran caught it and quickly examined it, then, with a surprised expression, handed it over to Sharlotta. "Nor have I seen one with this stamp," he admitted. "Not of the city, I believe, nor of anywhere in Calimshan."

Sharlotta studied the coin carefully, a flicker of recognition coming to her striking light green eyes. "The crescent moon," she remarked, then flipped it over. "Profile of a unicorn. This is a coin from the region of Silverymoon."

The other two looked to each, surprised, as was Sharlotta, by the revelation. "Silverymoon?" Kadran echoed incredulously.

"A city far to the north, east of Waterdeep," Sharlotta replied.

"I know where Silverymoon lies," Kadran replied dryly. "The domain of Lady Alustriel, I believe. That is not what I find surprising."

"Why would a merchant, if it was a merchant, of Silverymoon find himself walking in Taddio's worthless shanty town?" Hand asked, echoing Kadran's suspicions perfectly.

"Indeed, I thought it curious that anyone carrying such a treasure of more than two gold pieces would be in that region," Kadran agreed, pursing his lips and twisting his mouth in his customary manner that sent one side of his long and curvy mustache up far higher than the other, giving his whole dark face an unbalanced appearance. "Now it seems to have become more curious by far."

"A man who wandered into Calimport probably came in through the docks," Hand reasoned, "and found himself lost in the myriad of streets and smells. So much of the city looks the same, after all. It would not be difficult for a foreigner to wander wayward."

"I do not believe in coincidences," Sharlotta replied. She tossed the coin back to Hand. "Take it to one of our wizard associates—Giunta the Diviner will suffice. Perhaps there remains enough of a trace of the previous owner's identity upon the coins that Giunta can locate him."

"It seems a tremendous effort for one too afraid of the boy to even refuse payment," Hand replied.

"I do not believe in coincidences," Sharlotta repeated. "I do not believe that anyone could be so intimidated by that pitiful Taddio, unless it is someone who knows that he works as a front for Pasha Basadoni. And I do not like the idea that one so knowledgeable of our operation took it upon himself to wander into our territory unannounced. Was he, perhaps, looking for something? Seeking a weakness?"

"You presume much," Kadran put in.

"Only where danger is concerned," Sharlotta retorted. "I consider every person an enemy until he has proven himself differently, and I find that in knowing my enemies, I can prepare against anything they might send against me."

There was little mistaking the irony of her words, aimed as they were at Kadran Gordeon, but even the dangerous soldier had to nod his agreement with Sharlotta's perception and precaution. It wasn't every day that a merchant bearing coins from far away Silverymoon wandered into one of Calimport's desolate shanty towns.

* * * * *

He knew this house better than any in all the city. Within those brown, unremarkable walls, within the wrapper of a common warehouse, hung golden-stitched tapestries and magnificent weapons. Beyond the always barred side door, where an old beggar now huddled for meager shelter, lay a room of beautiful dancing ladies, all swirling veils and alluring perfumes, warm baths in scented water, and cuisine delicacies from every corner of the Realms.

This house had belonged to Pasha Pook. After his demise, it had been given by Entreri's archenemy to Regis the halfling, who had ruled briefly, until Entreri had decided the little fool had ruled long enough. When Entreri had left Calimport with Regis, the last time he had seen the dusty city, the house was in disarray, with several factions fighting for power. He suspected that Quentin Bodeau, a veteran burglar with more than twenty years' experience in the guild, had won the fight. What he didn't know, given the confusion and outrage within the ranks, was whether the fight had been worth winning. Perhaps another guild had moved into the territory. Perhaps the inside of this brown warehouse was now as unremarkable as the outside.

Entreri chuckled at the possibilities, but they could not find any lasting hold within his thoughts. Perhaps he would eventually sneak into the place, just to satisfy his mild curiosity. Perhaps not.

He lingered by the side door, moving close enough past the apparently one-legged beggar, to recognize the cunning tie that bound his second leg up tight against the back of his thigh. The man was a sentry, obviously, and most of the few copper coins that Entreri saw within the opened sack before him had been placed there by the man, salting the purse and heightening the disguise.

No matter, the assassin thought. Playing the part of an ignorant visitor to Calimport, he walked up before the man and reached into his own purse, producing a silver coin and dropping it in the sack. He noted the not-really-old man's eyes flicker open a bit wider when he pulled back his cloak to go to his purse, revealing the hilt of his unique jeweled dagger, a weapon well known in the alleys and shadows of Calimport.

Had he been foolish in showing that weapon? Entreri wondered as he walked away. He hadn't any intention of revealing himself when he came to this place, but also, he had no intention of not revealing himself. The question and the worry, like his musing on the fate of Pook's house, found no hold in his wandering thoughts. Perhaps he had erred. Perhaps he had shown the dagger in a desperate bid for some excitement. And perhaps the man had recognized it as the mark of Entreri, or possibly he had noticed it only because it was indeed a truly beautiful weapon.

It didn't matter.

* * * * *

LaValle worked very hard to keep his breathing steady and to ignore the murmurs of those nervous associates beside him as he peered deeply into the crystal ball later that same night. The agitated sentry had reported the incident outside, a gift of a strange coin from a man walking

27

with the quiet and confident gait of a warrior and wearing a dagger befitting the captain of a king's guard.

The description of that dagger had sent the more veteran members of the house, the wizard LaValle included, into a frenzy. Now LaValle, a longtime associate of the deadly Artemis Entreri, who had seen that dagger many times and uncomfortably close far too often had used that prior knowl-edge and his crystal ball to seek out the stranger. His magi-cal eyes combed the streets of Calimport, sifting from shadow to shadow, and then he felt the growing image and knew indeed that the dagger, Entreri's dagger, was back in the city. Now as the image began to take shape, the wizard and those standing beside him, a very nervous Quentin Bodeau and two younger cocky killers, would learn if it was indeed the deadliest of assassins who carried it.

A small bedroom drifted into focus.

"That is Tomnoddy's Inn," explained Dog Perry, who called himself Dog Perry the Heart because of his practice of cutting out a victim's heart fast enough that the dying man could witness its last beats (though none other than Dog Perry himself had ever actually seen this feat performed).

LaValle held up a hand to silence the man as the image became sharper, focusing on the belt looped over the bottom post of the bed, a belt that included the telltale dagger.

"It is Entreri's," Quentin Bodeau said with a groan.

A man walked past the belt, stripped to the waist, reveal-ing a body honed by years and years of hard practice, muscles twitching with every movement. Quentin put on a quizzical expression, studying the man, the long hair, the goatee and scratchy, unkempt beard. He had always known Entreri to be meticulous in every detail, a perfectionist to the extreme. He looked to LaValle for an answer.

"It is he," the wizard, who knew Artemis Entreri perhaps better than anyone else in all the city, answered grimly.

"What does that mean?" Quentin asked. "Has he returned as friend or foe?"

"Indifferent, more likely," LaValle replied. "Artemis Entreri has always been a free spirit, never showing allegiance too greatly to any particular guild. He wanders through the treasuries of each, hiring to the highest bidder for his exemplary services." As he spoke, the wizard glanced over at the two younger killers, neither of whom knew Entreri other than by reputation. Chalsee Anguaine, the younger, tittered nervously—and wisely, LaValle knew—but Dog Perry squinted his eyes as he considered the man in the crystal ball. He was jealous, LaValle understood, for Dog Perry wanted, above all else, that which Entreri possessed: the supreme reputation as the deadliest of assassins.

"Perhaps we should find a need for his services quickly," Quentin Bodeau reasoned, obviously trying hard not to sound nervous, for in the dangerous world of Calimport's thieving guilds, nervousness equalled weakness. "In that way we might better learn the man's intentions and purpose in returning to Calimport."

"Or we could just kill him," Dog Perry put in, and LaValle bit back a chuckle at the so-predictable viewpoint and also at his knowledge that Dog Perry simply did not understand the truth of Artemis Entreri. No friend or fan of the brash young thug, LaValle almost hoped that Quentin would give Dog Perry his wish and send him right out after Entreri.

But Quentin, though he had never dealt with Entreri personally, remembered well the many, many stories of the assassin's handiwork, and the expression the guildmaster directed at Dog Perry was purely incredulous.

"Hire him if you need him," said LaValle. "Or if not, then merely watch him without threat."

"He is one man, and we are a guild of a hundred," Dog Perry protested, but no one was listening to him anymore.

Quentin started to reply, but stopped short, though his expression told LaValle exactly what he was thinking. He feared that Entreri had come back to take the guild, obviously, and not without some rationale. Certainly the deadliest of assassins still had many powerful connections within the city, enough for Entreri, with his own amazing skills, to topple the likes of Quentin Bodeau. But LaValle did not think Quentin's fears well-founded, for the wizard

understood Entreri enough to realize that the man had
never craved such a position of responsibility. Entreri was a
loner, not a guildmaster. After he had deposed the halfling
Regis from his short rein as guildmaster, the place had been
Entreri's for the taking, and yet he had walked away, just
walked out of Calimport altogether, leaving all of the others
to fight it out.

No, LaValle did not believe that Entreri had come back to
take this guild or any other, and he did well to silently con-
vey that to the nervous Quentin. "Whatever our ultimate
choices, it seems obvious to me that we should first merely
observe our dangerous friend," the wizard said, for the benefit of the two younger lieutenants, "to learn if he is friend,
foe, or indifferent. It makes no sense to go against one as
strong as Entreri until we have determined that we must,
and that, I do not believe to be the case."

Quentin nodded, happy to hear the confirmation, and
with a bow LaValle took his leave, the others following suit.

"If Entreri is a threat, then Entreri should be eliminated,"
Dog Perry said to the wizard, catching up to him in the corridor outside his room. "Master Bodeau would have seen
that truth had your advice been different."

LaValle stared long and hard at the upstart, not appreci-
ating being talked to in that manner from one half his age
and with so little experience in such matters, for LaValle
had been dealing with dangerous killers such as Artemis
Entreri before Dog Perry was even born. "I'll not say that
I disagree with you," he said to the man.

"Then why your counsel to Bodeau?"

"If Entreri has come into Calimport at the request of
another guild, then any move by Master Bodeau could bring
dire consequences to our guild," the wizard replied, improvising as he went, for he didn't believe a word of what he
was saying. "You know that Artemis Entreri learned his
trade under Pasha Basadoni himself, of course."

"Of course," Dog Perry lied.

LaValle struck a pensive pose, tapping one finger across
his pursed lips. "It may prove to be no problem at all to us,"

he explained. "Surely when news of Entreri's return—an older and slower Entreri, you see, and one, perhaps, with few connections left within the city—spreads across the streets, the dangerous man will himself be marked."

"He has made many enemies," Dog Perry reasoned eagerly, seeming quite intrigued by LaValle's words and tone.

LaValle shook his head. "Most enemies of the Artemis Entreri who left Calimport those years ago are dead," the wizard explained. "No, not enemies, but rivals. How many young and cunning assassins crave the power that they might find with a single stroke of the blade?"

Dog Perry narrowed his eyes, just beginning to catch on.

"One who kills Entreri, in essence, claims credit for killing all of those whom Entreri killed," LaValle went on. "With a single stroke of the blade might such a reputation be earned. The killer of Entreri will almost instantly become the highest priced assassin in all the city." He shrugged and held up his hands, then pushed through his door, leaving an obviously intrigued Dog Perry standing in the hallway with the echoes of his words.

In truth, LaValle hardly cared whether the young troublemaker took those words to heart or not, but he was indeed concerned about the return of the assassin. Entreri unnerved the wizard, more so than all the other dangerous characters that LaValle had worked beside over the many years. LaValle had survived by posing a threat to no one, by serving without judgment whomever it was that had come to power in the guild. He had served Pasha Pook admirably, and when Pook had been disposed, he had switched his allegiance easily and completely to Regis, convincing even Regis's protective dark elf and dwarven friends that he was no threat. Similarly, when Entreri had gone against Regis, LaValle had stepped back and let the two decide the issue (though, of course, there had never been any doubt whatsoever in LaValle's mind as to which of those two would triumph), then throwing his loyalty to the victor. And so it had gone, down the line, master after master during the tumult immediately following Entreri's departure, to the present incarnation of guildmaster, Quentin Bodeau.

Concerning Entreri, though, there remained one subtle difference. Over the decades, LaValle had built a considerable insulating defense about him. He worked very hard to make no enemies in a world where everyone seemed to be in deadly competition, but he also understood that even a benign bystander could get caught and slaughtered in the common battles. Thus he had built a defense of powerful magic and felt that if one such as Dog Perry decided, for whatever reason, that he would be better off without LaValle around, he would find the wizard more than ready and able to defend himself. Not so with Entreri, LaValle knew, and that is why even the sight of the man so unnerved him. In watching the assassin over the years, LaValle had come to know that where Entreri was concerned, there simply weren't enough defenses.

He sat on his bed until very late that night, trying to remember every detail of every dealing he had ever had with the assassin and trying to figure out what, if anything in particular, had brought Entreri back to Calimport.

Chapter 2
RUNNING THE HORSE

heir pace held slow but steady. The springtime tundra, the hardening grasp of ice dissipating, had become like a great sponge, swelling in places to create mounds higher even than Wulfgar. The ground was sucking at their boots with every step, as if it were trying desperately to hold them. Drizzt, the lightest on his feet, had the easiest time of it—of those walking, at least. Regis, sitting comfortably up high on the shoulders of an uncomplaining Wulfgar, felt no muddy wetness in his warm boots. Still, the other three, who had spent so many years in Icewind Dale and were accustomed to the troubles of springtime travel, plodded on without complaint. They knew from the outset that the slowest and most tiresome part of their journey would be the first leg, until they got around the western edges of the Spine of the World and out of Icewind Dale.

Every now and then they found patches of great stones, the remnants of a road built long ago from Ten Towns to the western pass, but these did little more than assure them that they were on the right path, something that seemed of little importance in the vast open stretches of the tundra.

33

All they really had to do was keep the towering mountains to the south, and they would not lose their way.

Drizzt led them and tried to pick a course that followed the thickest regions of sprouting yellow grass, for this, at least, afforded some stability atop the slurpy ground. Of course—and the drow and his friends knew it—tall grass might also serve as camouflage for the dangerous tundra yetis, always hungry beasts that often feasted on unwary travelers.

With Drizzt Do'Urden leading them, though, the friends did not consider themselves unwary.

They put the river far behind them and found yet another stretch of that ancient road when the sun was halfway to the western horizon. There, just beyond one long rock slab, they also came upon some recent tracks.

"Wagon," Catti-brie remarked, seeing the long lines of deep grooves.

"Two," Regis commented, noting the twin lines at each groove.

Catti-brie shook her head. "One," she corrected, following the tracks, noting how they sometimes joined and other times separated, and always with a wider track as they moved apart. "Sliding in the mud as it rolled along, its back end often unaligned with the front."

"Well done," Drizzt congratulated her, for he, too, had come to the same conclusion. "A single wagon traveling east and not more than a day ahead of us."

"A merchant wagon left Bremen three days before we arrived there," Regis, always current on the goings-on of Ten Towns, commented.

"Then it would seem they are having great difficulty navigating the marshy ground," Drizzt replied.

"And might be other troubles they're findin'," came Bruenor's call from a short distance to the side, the dwarf stooping low over a small hump of grass.

The friends moved to join him and saw immediately his cause for concern: several tracks pressed deep into the mud.

"Yetis," the dwarf said distastefully. "And they came right to the wagon tracks and then went back. They're knowin' this for a used trail or I'm a bearded gnome."

"And the yeti tracks are more recent," Catti-brie remarked, noting the water still within them.

Up on Wulfgar's shoulders, Regis glanced around nervously, as if he expected a hundred of the shaggy beasts to leap out at them.

Drizzt, too, bent low to study the depressions and began to shake his head.

"They are recent," Catti-brie insisted.

"I do not disagree with your assessment of the time," the drow explained. "Only with the identification of the creature."

"Not a horse," Bruenor said with a grunt. "Unless that horse's lost two legs. A yeti, and a damned big one."

"Too big," the drow explained. "Not a yeti, but a giant."

"Giant?" the dwarf echoed skeptically. "We're ten miles from the mountains. What's a giant doing out here?"

"What indeed?" the drow answered, his grim tone giving the answer clear enough. Giants rarely came out of the Spine of the World Mountains, and then only to cause mischief. Perhaps this was a single rogue—that would be the best scenario—or perhaps it was an advanced scout for a larger and more dangerous group.

Bruenor cursed and dropped the head of his many-notched axe hard into the soft turf. "If ye're thinkin' o' walking all the way back to the durned towns, then be thinkin' again, elf," he said. "Sooner I'm outta this mud, the better. The towns've been livin' well enough without our help all these years. They're not needin' us to turn back now!"

"But if they are giants—" Catti-brie started to argue, but Drizzt cut her short.

"I've no intention of turning back," he said. "Not yet. Not until we have proof that these tracks foretell a greater disaster than one, or even a handful, of giants could perpetrate. No, our road remains east, and all the quicker because I now hope to catch that lone wagon before the fall of darkness, or soon after if we must continue on. If the giant is part of a rogue hunting group and it knows of the wagon's recent passage, then the Bremen merchants might soon be in dire need of our help."

They set off at a swifter pace, following the wagon tracks, and within a couple of hours they saw the merchants struggling with a loose and wobbly wagon wheel. Two of the five men, obviously the hired guards, pulled hard to try and lift the carriage while a third, a young and strong merchant whom Regis identified as Master Camlaine the scrimshaw trader, worked hard, though hardly successfully, to realign the tilted wheel. Both the guards had sunk past their ankles into the mud, and though they struggled mightily, they could hardly get the carriage up high enough for the fit.

How the faces of all five brightened when they noted the approach of Drizzt and his friends, a well-known company of heroes indeed among the folk of Icewind Dale.

"Well met, I should say, Master Do'Urden!" the merchant Camlaine cried. "Do lend us the strength of your barbarian friend. I will pay you well, I promise. I am to be in Luskan in a fortnight, yet if our luck holds as it has since we left Bremen, I fear that winter will find us still in the dale."

Bruenor handed his axe to Catti-brie and motioned to Wulfgar. "Come on, boy," he said. "Ye'll play come-along and I'll show ye an anvil pose."

With a nonchalant shrug, Wulfgar brought Regis swinging down from his shoulders and set him on the ground. The halfling moaned and rushed to a pile of grass, not wanting to get mud all over his new boots.

"Ye think ye can lift it?" Bruenor asked Wulfgar as the huge man joined him by the wagon. Without a word, without even putting down his magnificent warhammer Aegisfang, Wulfgar grabbed the wagon and pulled hard. The mud slurped loudly in protest, grabbing and clinging, but in the end it could not resist, and the wheel came free of the soupy ground.

The two guards, after a moment of disbelief, found handholds and similarly pulled, hoisting the wagon even higher.

Down to hands and knees went Bruenor, setting his bent back under the axle right beside the wheel. "Go ahead and set the durned thing," he said and then he groaned as the weight came upon him.

Wulfgar took the wheel from the struggling merchant and pulled it into line, then pushed it more securely into place. He took a step back, took up Aegis-fang in both hands, and gave it a good whack, setting it firmly. Bruenor gave a grunt from the suddenly shifting weight, and Wulfgar moved to lift the wagon again, just a few inches, so that Bruenor could slip out from under it. Master Camlaine inspected the work, turning about with a bright smile and nodding his approval.

"You could begin a new career, good dwarf and mighty Wulfgar," he said with a laugh. "Wagon repair."

"There is an aspiration fit for a dwarven king," Drizzt remarked, coming over with Catti-brie and Regis. "Give up your throne, good Bruenor, and fix the carts of wayward merchants."

They all had a laugh at that, except for Wulfgar, who simply seemed detached from it all, and for Regis, still fretting over his muddy boots.

"You are far out from Ten Towns," Camlaine noted, "with nothing to the west. Are you leaving Icewind Dale once more?"

"Briefly," Drizzt replied. "We have business in the south."

"Luskan?"

"Beyond Luskan," the drow explained. "But we will indeed be going through that city, it would seem."

Camlaine brightened, obviously happy to hear that bit of news. He reached to a jingling purse on his belt, but Drizzt held up a hand, thinking it ridiculous that the man should offer to pay.

"Of course," Camlaine remarked, embarrassed, remembering that Bruenor Battlehammer was indeed a dwarven king, wealthy beyond anything a simple merchant could ever hope to achieve. "I wish there was some way I . . . we, could repay you for your help. Or even better, I wish that there was some way I could bribe you into accompanying us to Luskan. I have hired fine and able guards, of course," he added, nodding to the two men. "But Icewind Dale remains a dangerous place, and friendly swords—or warhammers or axes—are always welcomed."

Drizzt looked to his friends and, seeing no objections, nodded. "We will indeed travel with you out of the dale," he said.

"Is your mission urgent?" the scrimshaw merchant asked. "Our wagon has been dragging more than rolling, and our team is weary. We had hoped to repair the wheel and then find a suitable campsite, though there yet remain two or three hours of daylight."

Drizzt looked to his friends and again saw no complaints there. The group, though their mission to go to the Spirit Soaring and destroy Crenshinibon was indeed vital, was in no great hurry. The drow found a campsite, a relatively high bluff not so far away and they all settled down for the night. Camlaine offered his new companions a fine meal of rich venison stew. They passed the meal with idle chatter, with Camlaine and his four companions doing most of the talking, stories about problems in Bremen over the winter, mostly, and about the first catch of the prized knucklehead trout, the fish that provided the bone material for the scrimshaw. Drizzt and the others listened politely, not really interested. Regis, however, who had lived on the banks of Maer Dualdon and had spent years making scrimshaw pieces of his own, begged Camlaine to show him the finished wares he was taking to Luskan. The halfling poured over each piece for a long while, studying every detail.

"Ye think we'll be seeing them giants this night?" Cattibrie asked Drizzt quietly, the two moving off to the side of the main group.

The drow shook his head. "The one who happened upon the tracks turned back for the mountains," he said. "Likely, he was merely checking the route. I had feared that he then went in pursuit of the wagon, but since Camlaine and his crew were not so far away, and since we saw no other sign of any behemoth, I do not expect to see him."

"But he might be bringing trouble to the next wagon along," Catti-brie reasoned.

Drizzt conceded the point with a nod and a smile, a look that grew more intense as he and the beautiful woman locked stares. There had been a notable strain between them since the return of Wulfgar, for in the six years of Wulfgar's absence, Drizzt and Catti-brie had forged a deeper friendship, one bordering on love. But now Wulfgar, who had been engaged to marry Catti-brie at the time of his apparent death, was back, and things between the drow and the woman had become far more complicated.

Not at this moment, though. For some reason that neither of the friends could understand, for this one second, it was as if they were the only two people in all the world, or as if time had stopped all around them, freezing the others in a state of oblivion.

It didn't last, not more than a brief moment, for a commotion at the other side of the encampment drew the two apart. When she looked past Drizzt, Catti-brie found Wulfgar staring at them hard. She locked eyes with the man, but again, it was only for a moment. One of Camlaine's guards standing behind Wulfgar, called to the group, waving his arms excitedly.

"Might be that our giant friend decided to show its ugly face," Catti-brie said to Drizzt. When they joined the others, the guard was pointing out toward another bluff, this one an oozing mud mound pushed up like a miniature volcano by the shifting tundra.

"Behind that," the guard said.

Drizzt studied the mound intently; Catti-brie pulled Taulmaril, the Heartseeker bow, from her shoulder and set an arrow.

"Too small a pimple for a giant to hide behind," Bruenor insisted, but the dwarf clutched his axe tightly as he spoke.

Drizzt nodded his agreement. He looked to Catti-brie and to Wulfgar alternately, motioning that they should cover him. Then he sprinted away, picking a careful and quiet path that brought him right to the base of the mound. With a glance back to ensure that his friends were ready, the drow skipped up the side of the mound, his twin scimitars drawn.

And then he relaxed, and put his deadly blades away, as a man, a huge man wearing a wolf-skin wrap, came out around the base into plain sight.

"Kierstaad, son of Revjak," Catti-brie remarked.

"Following his hero," Bruenor added, looking up at Wulfgar, for it was no secret to any of them, or to any of the barbarians of Icewind Dale, that Kierstaad idolized Wulfgar. The young man had even stolen Aegis-fang and followed the companions along when they had gone out onto the Sea of Moving Ice to rescue Wulfgar from the demon, Errtu. To Kierstaad, Wulfgar symbolized the greatness that the tribes of Icewind Dale might achieve and the greatness that he, too, so desired.

Wulfgar frowned at the sight.

Kierstaad and Drizzt exchanged a few words, then both moved back to the main group. "He has come for a word with Wulfgar," the drow explained.

"To beg for the survival of the tribes," Kierstaad admitted, staring at his barbarian kin.

"The tribes fare well under the care of Berkthgar the Bold," Wulfgar insisted.

"They do not!" Kierstaad replied harshly, and the others took that as their cue to give the two men some space. "Berkthgar understands the old ways, that is true," Kierstaad went on. "But the old ways do not offer the hope of anything greater than the lives we have known for centuries. Only Wulfgar, son of Beornegar, can truly unite the tribes and strengthen our bond with the folk of Ten Towns."

"That would be for the better?" Wulfgar asked skeptically.

"Yes!" Kierstaad replied without hesitation. "No longer should any tribesman starve because the winter is difficult. No longer should we be so completely dependent upon the caribou herd. Wulfgar, with his friends, can change our ways . . . can lead us to a better place."

"You speak foolishness," Wulfgar said, waving his hand and turning from the man. But Kierstaad wouldn't let him get away that easily. The young man ran up behind and grabbed Wulfgar roughly by the arm, turning him about.

Kierstaad started to offer yet another argument, started to explain that Berkthgar still considered the folk of Ten Towns, even the dwarven folk of Wulfgar's own adoptive father, more as enemies than as allies. There were so many things that young Kierstaad wanted to say to Wulfgar, so many arguments to make to the big man, to try and convince him that his place was with the tribes. But all those words went flying away as Kierstaad went flying away, for Wulfgar turned about viciously, following the young man's pull, and brought his free arm swinging about, slugging the young man heavily in the chest and launching him into a short flight and then a backward roll down the side of the bluff.

Wulfgar turned away with a low, feral growl, storming back to his supper bowl. Protests came at him from every side, particularly from Catti-brie. "Ye didn't have to hit the boy," she yelled, but Wulfgar only waved his hand at her and snarled again, then went back to his food.

Drizzt was the first one down to Kierstaad's side. The young barbarian was lying facedown in the muck at the bottom of the bluff. Regis came along right behind, offering one of his many handkerchiefs to wipe some of the mud from Kierstaad's face—and also to allow the man to save some measure of pride and quietly wipe the welling tears from his eyes.

"He must understand," Kierstaad remarked, starting back up the hill, but Drizzt had him firmly by the arm, and the young barbarian did not truly fight against the pull.

"This matter was already resolved," the drow said, "between Wulfgar and Berkthgar. Wulfgar made his choice, and that choice was the road."

"Blood before friends—that is the rule of the tribes," Kierstaad argued. "And Wulfgar's blood kin need him now."

Drizzt tilted his head, and a knowing expression came over his fair, ebon-skinned face, a look that settled

Kierstaad more than any words ever could. "Is it so?" the drow asked calmly. "Do the tribes need Wulfgar, or does Kierstaad need him?"

"What do you mean?" the young man stammered, obviously embarrassed.

"Berkthgar has been angry with you for a long time," the drow explained. "Perhaps you will not find a position that pleases you while Berkthgar rules the tribes."

Kierstaad pulled roughly away; his face screwed up with anger. "This is not about Kierstaad's position within the tribes," he insisted. "My people need Wulfgar, and so I have come for him."

"He'll not follow you," Regis said. "Nor can you drag him, I would guess."

Frustration evident on his face, Kierstaad began clenching and unclenching his fists at his side. He looked up the bluff, then took a step that way, but agile Drizzt moved quickly in front of him.

"He'll not follow," the drow said. "Even Berkthgar begged Wulfgar to remain and to lead, but that, by Wulfgar's own words, is not his place at this time."

"But it is!"

"No!" Drizzt said forcefully, stopping Kierstaad's further arguments cold. "No, and not only because Wulfgar has determined that it is not his place. Truly I was relieved to learn that he did not accept the leadership from Berkthgar, for I, too, care about the welfare of the tribes of Icewind Dale."

Even Regis looked at the drow with surprise at that seemingly illogical reasoning.

"You do not believe Wulfgar to be the rightful leader?" Kierstaad asked incredulously.

"Not at this time," Drizzt replied. "Can any of us appreciate the agony the man has suffered? Or can we measure the lingering effects of Errtu's torments? No, Wulfgar is not now fit to lead the tribes—he is having a difficult enough time leading himself."

"But we are his kin," Kierstaad tried to argue, but as he spoke them the words sounded lame even to him. "If

Wulfgar feels pain, then he should be with us, in our care."

"And how might you tend the wounds that tear at Wulfgar's heart?" Drizzt asked. "No, Kierstaad. I applaud your intentions, but your hopes are false. Wulfgar needs time to remember who he truly is, to remember all that was once important to him. He needs time, and he needs his friends, and though I'll not argue your contention of the importance of blood kin, I tell you now in all honesty that those who love Wulfgar the most are here, not back with the tribes."

Kierstaad started to reply but only huffed and stared emptily back up the bluff, having no practical rebuttal.

"We will return soon enough," the drow explained. "Before the turn of winter, I hope, or in the spring soon after, at the latest. Perhaps Wulfgar will find again his heart and soul on the road with his friends. Perhaps he will return to Icewind Dale ready to assume the leadership that he truly deserves and that the tribes truly deserve."

"And if not?" Kierstaad asked.

Drizzt only shrugged. He was beginning to understand the depth of Wulfgar's pain and could make no guarantees.

"Keep him safe," Kierstaad said.

Drizzt nodded.

"On your word," the young barbarian pressed.

"We care for each other," the drow replied. "It has been that way since before we set out from Icewind Dale to reclaim Bruenor's throne in Mithral Hall nearly a decade ago."

Kierstaad continued to stare up the bluff. "My tribe has camped north of here," he explained, starting slowly away. "It is not far."

"Stay with us through the night," the drow offered.

"Master Camlaine has some fine food," Regis added hopefully. Drizzt knew just from the fact that the halfling was apparently willing to split the portions an extra way that Kierstaad's plight had touched his little friend.

But Kierstaad, obviously too embarrassed to go back up and face Wulfgar, only shook his head and started off to the north, across the empty tundra.

"You should beat him," Regis said, looking back up the hill at Wulfgar.

"How would that help?" the drow asked.

"I think our large friend could use a bit of humility."

Drizzt shook his head. "His reaction to Kierstaad's touch was just that: a reaction," the drow explained. He was beginning to understand Wulfgar's mood a bit more clearly now, for Wulfgar's striking of Kierstaad had been wrought of no conscious thought. Drizzt recalled his days back in Melee-Magthere, the drow school for fighters. In that always dangerous environment, where enemies lurked around every corner, Drizzt had seen such reactions, had reacted similarly on many occasions himself. Wulfgar was back with friends now in a safe enough place, but emotionally he was still the prisoner of Errtu, his constant defenses still in place against the intrusions of the demon and its minions.

"It was instinctual and nothing more."

"He could have apologized," Regis replied.

No, he could not, Drizzt thought, but he kept the notion silent. An idea came over the drow then, one that put a particularly sparkling twinkle in his lavender eyes, a look that Regis had seen many times before.

"What are you thinking?" the halfling prompted.

"About giants," Drizzt replied with a coy smile, "and about the danger to any passing caravans."

"You believe that they will come at us this night?"

"I believe that they are back in the mountains, perhaps planning to bring a raiding party to the trail," Drizzt answered honestly. "And we would be long gone before they ever arrived."

"Would be?" Regis echoed softly, still studying the drow's glowing eyes—no trick of the late-day sun—and the way Drizzt's gaze drifted back toward the snowy peaks shining in the south. "What are you thinking?"

"We cannot wait for the giants' return," the drow said. "Nor do I wish to leave any future caravans in peril. Perhaps Wulfgar and I should go out this night."

44

Regis's jaw dropped open, his dumbfounded expression bringing a laugh to the drow's lips.

"In my days with Montolio, the ranger who trained me, I learned much about horsemanship," Drizzt began to explain.

"You plan to take one or both of the merchant's horses to go to the mountains?" an incredulous Regis asked.

"No, no," Drizzt replied. "Montolio had been quite a rider in his youth, before he lost his vision, of course. And the horses he chose to ride were the strongest and least broken by saddles. But he had a technique—he called it 'running the horse'—to calm the steeds enough so that they would behave. He would bring them out in an open field on a long lead and snap a whip behind them repeatedly to get them running in wide and hard circles, even to get them bucking."

"Would that not only make them less behaved?" the halfling asked, for he knew little about horses.

Drizzt shook his head. "The strongest of horses possesses too much energy, Montolio explained to me. Thus, he would take them out and let them release that extra layer, and when he would then climb on their backs they would ride strong but in control."

Regis shrugged and nodded, accepting the story. "What has that to do with Wulfgar?" he asked, but his expression changed to one of understanding even as the question came out of his mouth. "You plan to run Wulfgar as Montolio ran the horses," he reasoned.

"Perhaps he needs a good fight," Drizzt replied. "And truly I wish to rid the region of any trouble with giants."

"It will take you hours to get to the mountains," Regis estimated, looking to the south. "Perhaps longer if the giants' trail is not clear to follow."

"But we will move much quicker than you three if you stay, as we promised, with Camlaine," the drow replied. "Wulfgar and I will be back beside you within two or three days, long before you've turned the corner around the Spine of the World."

"Bruenor will not like being left out," Regis remarked.

"Then do not tell him," the drow instructed. Then, before

Regis could offer the expected reply, he added, "Nor should you tell Catti-brie. Explain to them only that Wulfgar and I set out in the night, and that I promised to return the day after tomorrow."

Regis gave a frustrated sigh—once before Drizzt had run off, promising Regis to secrecy, and a frantic Catti-brie had nearly beat the information out of the halfling. "Why am I always the one to hold your secrets?" he asked.

"Why are you always sniffing where your nose does not belong?" Drizzt answered with a laugh.

The drow caught up to Wulfgar on the far side of the encampment. The big man was sitting alone, absently tossing stones down to the ground. He did not look up, nor did he offer any apologetic expressions, burying them beneath a wall of anger.

Drizzt sympathized completely and recognized the torment simmering just below the surface. Anger was his friend's only defense against those horrible memories. Drizzt crouched low and looked into Wulfgar's pale blue eyes, even if the huge man did not match the gaze.

"Do you remember our first fight?" the drow asked slyly.

Now Wulfgar did turn his stare up at the drow. "Do you mean to teach me another lesson?" he asked, his tone showing that he was more than ready to accept that challenge.

The words stung Drizzt profoundly. He recalled his last angry encounter with Wulfgar, over the barbarian's treatment of Catti-brie those seven years before in Mithral Hall. They had fought viciously with Drizzt emerging as victor. And he recalled his first fight against Wulfgar, when Bruenor had captured the lad and brought him into the dwarven clan in Icewind Dale after the barbarians had tried to raid Ten Towns. Bruenor had charged Drizzt with training Wulfgar as a fighter, and those first lessons between the two had proven especially painful for the young and overly proud barbarian. But that was not the encounter to which Drizzt was now referring.

"I mean the first time that we fought together side by side against a real enemy," he explained.

Wulfgar's eyes narrowed as he considered the memory, a glimpse at his friendship with Drizzt from many years ago.

"Biggrin and the verbeeg," Drizzt reminded. "You and I and Guenhwyvar charging headlong into a lair full of giants."

The anger melted from Wulfgar's face. He managed a rare smile and nodded.

"A tough one was Biggrin," Drizzt went on. "How many times did we hit the behemoth? It took a final throw from you to drive the dagger—"

"That was a long time ago," Wulfgar interrupted. He couldn't manage to maintain the smile, but at least he did not sink right back into the explosive anger. Wulfgar again found a more even keel, much like his detached, almost ambivalent attitude when they had first started out on this journey.

"But you do remember?" Drizzt pressed, his grin growing across his black face, that telltale twinkle in his lavender eyes.

"Why . . ." Wulfgar started to ask, but stopped short and sat studying his friend. He hadn't seen Drizzt in such a mood in a long, long time, even well before his fateful fight with the handmaiden of the demon queen Lolth back in Mithral Hall. This was a flash of Drizzt from the days before the quest to reclaim the dwarven kingdom, an image of the drow in those times when Wulfgar honestly feared that Drizzt's recklessness would soon put him and the drow in a situation from which they could not escape.

Wulfgar liked the image.

"We have some giants readying to waylay travelers on the road," the drow said. "Our pace will be slower out of the dale, now that we have agreed to accompany Master Camlaine. It seems to me that a side journey to deal with these dangerous marauders might be in order."

It was the first hint of an eager sparkle in Wulfgar's eye that Drizzt had seen since they had been reunited in the ice cave after the defeat of Errtu.

"Have you spoken with the others?" the barbarian asked.

"Just me and you," Drizzt explained. "And Guenhwyvar, of course. She would not appreciate being left out of this fun."

47

The pair left camp long after sunset, waiting for Catti-brie, Regis, and Bruenor to fall asleep. With the drow leading, having no difficulty in seeing under the starry tundra sky, they went straight back to the point where the giant and the wagon tracks intersected. There, Drizzt reached into a pouch and produced the onyx panther figurine, placing it reverently on the ground. "Come to me, Guenhwyvar," he called softly.

A mist came up, swirling about the figurine, growing thicker and thicker, flowing and swirling and taking the shape of the great panther. Thicker and thicker, and then it was no mist circling the onyx likeness, but the panther herself. Guenhwyvar looked up at Drizzt with eyes showing an intelligence far beyond that indicated by her feline form.

Drizzt pointed down to the giant track, and Guenhwyvar, understanding, led them away.

* * * * *

She knew as soon as she opened her eyes that something was amiss. The camp was quiet, the two merchant guards sitting on the bench of the wagon, talking softly.

Catti-brie shifted up to her elbows to better survey the scene. The fire had burned low but was still bright enough to cast shadows from the bedrolls. Closest lay Regis, curled in a ball so near to the fire that Catti-brie was amazed the little fellow hadn't gone up in flames. The mound that was Bruenor lay just a bit further back, right where Catti-brie had said good night to her adoptive father. The woman sat up, then got to one knee, craning her neck, but she could not locate two particular forms among the sleeping.

She started for Bruenor, but changed her mind and went to Regis instead. The halfling always seemed to know. . . .

A gentle shake only made him groan and roll tighter into a ball. A rougher shake and a call of his name only had him spitting curses and tightening even more.

Catti-brie kicked him in the rump.

"Hey!" he protested loudly, coming up suddenly.

"Where'd they go to?" the woman asked.

"What're ye about, girl?" came Bruenor's sleepy voice, the dwarf awakened by Regis's call.

"Drizzt and Wulfgar have gone out from camp," she explained, then turned her penetrating gaze back over Regis.

The halfling squirmed under the scrutiny. "Why would I know?" he argued, but Catti-brie didn't blink. Regis looked to Bruenor for support, but found the half-dressed dwarf ambling over, seeming every bit as perturbed as Catti-brie, and apparently ready, like the woman, to direct his ire the halfling's way.

"Drizzt said that they would return to us, and the caravan, tomorrow, or perhaps the day after that," the halfling admitted.

"And where'd they go off to?" Catti-brie demanded.

Regis shrugged, but Catti-brie had him by the collar, hoisting him to his feet before he ever finished the motion. "Are ye meanin' to play this game again?" she asked.

"To find Kierstaad and apologize, I would guess," the halfling said. "He deserves as much."

"Good enough if the boy's got an apology in his heart," Bruenor remarked. Seemingly satisfied with that, the dwarf turned back for his bedroll.

Catti-brie, though, stood holding Regis roughly and shaking her head. "He's not got it in him," she said, drawing the dwarf back into the conversation. "Not now, and that's not where they're off to." She moved closer to Regis as she spoke, but did let go of him. "Ye need to tell me," she said calmly. "Ye can't be playin' this game. If we're to travel half the length o' Faerûn together, then we're needing a bit o' trust, and that ye're not earning."

"They went after the giants," Regis blurted. He couldn't believe that he had said it, but neither could he deny the logic of Catti-brie's argument nor the plaintive look in her beautiful eyes.

"Bah!" Bruenor snorted, stomping his bare foot—and slamming it so hard that it sounded as if he was wearing boots. "By the brains of a pointed-headed orc-cousin! Why didn't ye tell us sooner?"

"Because you would have made me go," Regis argued, but his voice lost its angry edge when Catti-brie moved right in front of his face.

"Ye always seem to be knowing too much and tellin' too little," she growled. "As when Drizzt left Mithral Hall."

"I listen," Regis replied with a helpless shrug.

"Get dressed," Catti-brie instructed Regis, who just looked back at her incredulously.

"Ye heard her!" Bruenor roared.

"You want to go out there?" the halfling asked, pointing to the black emptiness that was the nighttime tundra. "Now?"

"Won't be the first time I pulled that durned elf from the mouth of a tundra yeti," the dwarf snorted, heading for his bedroll.

"Giants," Regis corrected.

"Even worse, then!" Bruenor roared louder, waking the rest of the camp.

"But we cannot leave," Regis protested, motioning to the three merchants and their guardsmen. "We promised to guard them. What if the giants come in behind us?"

That brought a concerned look to the faces of the five members of the merchant team, but Catti-brie didn't blink at the ridiculous thought. She just kept looking hard at Regis, and at his possessions, including the new unicorn-headed mace one of Bruenor's smithies had forged for him, a beautiful mithral and black steel item with blue sapphires set for the eyes.

With a profound sigh the halfling pulled his tunic on over his head.

They were out within the hour, backtracking to the point where wagon track, giant track, and now drow and barbarian track, intersected. They had much more difficulty finding it than had Wulfgar and Drizzt, with the drow's superior night vision. For even though Catti-brie wore an enchanted circlet that allowed her to see in the dark, she was no ranger and could not match Drizzt's keen senses and training. Bruenor bent low, sniffing the ground, then led on through the darkness.

"Probably get swallowed by waiting yetis," Regis grumbled.

"I'll shoot high, then," Catti-brie answered, holding her deadly bow out. "Above the belly, so ye won't have a hole in ye when we cut ye out."

Of course Regis continued to grumble, but he kept his voice lower, not letting Catti-brie hear clearly so that she could not offer any more sarcastic replies.

* * * * *

They spent the dark hours before the dawn feeling their way over the rocky foothills of the Spine of the World. Wulfgar complained many times that they must have lost the trail, but Drizzt held faith in Guenhwyvar, who kept appearing ahead of them, a darker shadow against the night sky, high on rocky outcroppings.

Soon after the break of day, as they moved along a winding mountain path, the drow's faith in the panther was confirmed as the pair came across a distinctive footprint, a huge boot, along a low and muddy depression on the trail.

"An hour ahead, no more," Drizzt explained, examining the print. He looked back at Wulfgar and smiled widely, lavender eyes sparkling.

The barbarian, more than ready for a fight, nodded.

Following Guenhwyvar's lead, they climbed higher and higher until, above them, the land seemed to suddenly disappear, the trail ending at a sheer cliff face. Drizzt moved up first, shadow to shadow, motioning Wulfgar to follow as he determined the way to be clear. They had come to the side of a canyon, a deep and rocky ravine bordered on all four sides by mountain walls, though the barrier to their right, the south, was not complete, leaving one exit from the valley floor. At first, they surmised that the giant encampment must be down there in the ravine, hidden among the boulders, but then Wulfgar spotted a line of smoke drifting up from behind a wall of boulders on the cliff wall almost directly across the way, some fifty yards from their position.

Drizzt scaled a nearby tree, getting a better angle, and soon confirmed that to be the giants' camp. A pair of behemoths were sitting behind the sheltering stones, eating a meal. The drow surveyed the landscape. He could get around, and so could Guenhwyvar, without going down to the valley floor.

"Can you reach them with a hammer throw from here?" he asked Wulfgar.

The barbarian nodded.

"Lead me in, then," the drow said. With a wink, he started off to the left, moving over the lip of the cliff and edging along its facing. Guenhwyvar also started off, picking a higher route than Drizzt along the cliff face.

The dark elf moved like a spider, crawling from ledge to ledge, while Guenhwyvar went along above him in a series of powerful bounds, clearing twenty feet at a leap. Within half an hour, amazingly, the drow had moved beyond the northern wall, around to the eastern facade and within twenty feet or so of the seemingly oblivious giants. He motioned back to Wulfgar, then set his feet firmly and took a deep breath. Not wanting to be spotted, he had come in slightly below the level of the shelf and the boulder wall, and now he measured the short run he would have, and then the distance of the leap to the giants' shelf. He didn't want to have to use his hands to safely land the jump, preferring to come in with both scimitars drawn and ready.

He could make it, he decided, so he looked up at Guenhwyvar. The cat was perched on a shelf some thirty feet above the giants. Drizzt opened his mouth in a mock roar.

The great panther responded, only her roar was far from silent. It rumbled off the mountain walls, drawing the attention of the giants and of any other creatures for miles around.

With a howl, the giants sprang to their feet. The drow ran silently along the ledge and leaped for their position.

Shouting a call to Tempus, the barbarian god of war, Wulfgar hoisted Aegis-fang . . . but hesitated, stung by the sound of that name. The name of a god he had once worshiped but to whom he had not prayed in so many years. A god he felt had abandoned him in the pits of the Abyss. Waves of emotional turmoil rolled over him, dizzying him, sending him careening back to that awful place of Errtu's darkness.

And leaving Drizzt terribly exposed.

* * * * *

They had been guessing as much as trailing, for though Catti-brie could see well in the dark, her night vision still could not match that of the drow, and Bruenor, though skilled at tracking, could not match the hunting prowess of Guenhwyvar. Still, when they heard the panther's roar echoing off the stones about them, they knew their guess had been a good one.

Off they ran, Bruenor's rolling pace matching Catti-brie's long and graceful strides. Regis didn't even try to catch up, didn't even try to follow the same path. While Bruenor and Catti-brie charged off straight in the direction of the roar, Regis veered north, following an easier trail, smooth but angling upward. The halfling wasn't thrilled with the idea of getting into any fights, let alone one against giants, but he did truly want to help out. Perhaps he might find a higher vantage point from which he could call down directions to his friends. Perhaps he might find a place where he could throw stones (and he was a pretty good shot) at safely distant giants. Perhaps he might find—

A tree trunk, the halfling thought, a bit distracted as he rushed around a bend and bumped into a solid trunk.

No, not a trunk, Regis realized. Trees did not wear boots.

* * * * *

Two giants rose up to search out Guenhwyvar; two giants noted the sudden approach of the leaping drow elf. Drizzt timed and aimed his leap perfectly, coming to the lip of the ledge lightly, in full balance. But he hadn't counted on two opponents waiting for him. He had expected Wulfgar's throw to take one down, or at least to distract the behemoth long enough for the dark elf to find steady footing.

Improvising quickly, the drow summoned his innate magical powers—though few remained after all these years on the surface—and brought forth a globe of impenetrable darkness. He centered it on the back wall ten feet from the ground so that it blocked the sight of the behemoths, but, since the globe's radius was about the same length as Drizzt was tall, it left their lower legs visible to Drizzt. He went in hard and fast, skidding down low and slashing wildly with both his scimitars, Twinkle and the newly named Icingdeath.

The giants kicked and stomped, bent low and swung their clubs frantically, and though they were as likely to hit each other as the drow, a giant could take a solid hit from another giant's club.

Drizzt could not.

* * * * *

Damn Errtu! How many evils had he suffered? How many attacks upon body and soul? He felt again Bizmatec's pincers closing about his neck, felt the dull aches of heavy punches as Errtu beat upon him as he lay in the filth, and then the sharp sting of fire as the demon dragged him into the flames that always surrounded its hideous form. And he felt the touch, gentle and alluring, of the succubus, perhaps the worst tormentor of all.

And now his friend needed him. Wulfgar knew that, could hear the battle being joined. He should have led the way with a throw of Aegis-fang, should have put the giants off balance, perhaps even put one down altogether.

He knew that and wanted desperately to help his friend, and yet his eyes were not seeing the fight between Drizzt and the giants. They were looking again into the swirls of Errtu's prison.

"Damn you!" the barbarian cried, and he built a wall of the sheerest red anger, trying to block the visions with pure rage.

* * * * *

It was easily the largest giant Regis had ever seen, towering twenty feet and as wide as buildings Regis had once called home. Regis looked at his new mace, his pitifully small mace, and doubted that he could even raise a bruise on the giant. Then he looked up to see the monster bending lower, a huge hand—a hand big enough to grab the halfling and squeeze the life out of him—reaching down.

"A bit of a meal, then?" the huge creature said in a voice surprisingly sophisticated for one of its kind. "Not much of one, of course, but little's better than nothing."

Regis sucked in his breath and put his hand over his heart, feeling as if he would faint—and then feeling a familiar lump by his collarbone. He reached into his tunic and pulled out a gemstone, a large ruby dangling at the end of a chain. "A pretty thing, don't you think?" he asked sheepishly.

"I think I like my rodents mashed," the giant replied, and up went its huge foot, and off ran Regis with a squeak. A single long stride put the giant's other foot in front of him, though, and he had nowhere to run.

* * * * *

Drizzt rolled over a kicking giant leg, tucking his shoulder as he hit the stone and coming back over to his feet nimbly, reversing direction and stabbing glowing Twinkle into the huge calf. That brought a roar of pain, and then came another yell. It was Wulfgar. The barbarian's curse was followed by an explosion of stone as something—a relieved Drizzt figured it to be Aegis-fang—slammed hard into the cliff.

The missile bounced from the stone wall into the open air beyond, where the drow could see that it was a boulder—thrown by yet another giant, no doubt—and no warhammer.

Even worse for Drizzt, one of the giants moved out far enough on the ledge to see around the globe of darkness. "Argh, ye black-skinned rat!" it said, lifting its club.

Guenhwyvar soared down thirty feet from her perch to slam the bending behemoth on the shoulders, a six-hundred-pound missile of slashing claws and biting teeth. Caught by surprise and off balance, the giant toppled over the stone wall and out into the air, taking Guenhwyvar with it.

Drizzt, dodging yet another stubborn kick, cried out for the cat, but had to turn away, had to focus on the remaining, kicking giant.

As the plummeting giant rolled over Guenhwyvar sprang again, flying out wide and far, back toward the cliff where Wulfgar stood battling his mental demons. The cat slammed hard against a ledge, far below the barbarian, and there she desperately clung, battered and shaking, while the giant continued its bouncing descent. Down, down the giant fell, a hundred feet and more before it settled, battered and groaning, upon a rocky outcropping.

* * * * *

Another explosion rocked the ledge where Drizzt battled the giant, then a third. The sudden, shocking noise finally broke Wulfgar free of his dark memories. He saw Guenhwyvar struggling to hold her perch on the ledge, nothing but empty air below her all the way to the ravine's floor. He saw Drizzt's globe of darkness, and every now and then a flash of bluish light as the drow sent his scimitar flying fast under the globe but above the blocking boulder wall. He saw the giant's head as it came up straight, and he took aim.

But then another boulder slammed the cliff wall, ricocheting off stone and right into the giant's side, bending it low into the darkness. And then another hit the wall right below Wulfgar's position, nearly shaking him from his feet. The barbarian located the throwers, three more giants on a ledge down and to the right, well concealed behind a barrier of rock, and probably with a cave in the cliff wall behind them. The third threw its rock Wulfgar's way, and the barbarian had to dive aside to avoid being crushed.

He came up and had to scramble again as two more rocks hurtled in.

With a roar—to no god, but just a primal growl—Wulfgar brought Aegis-fang over his head and returned the volley. The mighty warhammer sailed end over end to strike the stone right before the ducking giants. With a thunderous retort it knocked a fair-sized chunk out of the rock wall.

The giants came up staring, obviously impressed with the damage the weapon had inflicted on the stone. When they moved, all three clambered all over each other to retrieve the weapon.

But Aegis-fang disappeared, and when it magically returned to Wulfgar's grasp, the barbarian could see the three giants spread out over the wall in clear view.

* * * * *

Catti-brie and Bruenor came to the lip of the canyon, on the same side as Wulfgar but farther to the south, about halfway between the barbarian and the three giants. They were in time to see the next spinning throw of Aegis-fang. One of the giants managed to get back over the protective wall, and a second was on its way up when the warhammer crashed in, dropping the behemoth onto the back of the third. Solid as the hit was, it didn't kill the giant. Nor did the silver-streaking magical arrow Catti-brie let fly from Taulmaril, scoring a hit on the same giant's back.

"Bah, ye two're to steal all that danged fun!" Bruenor grumbled, skipping off to the south, looking for a way to get at the giants. "Gotta make me a dwarven bow!"

"A bow?" Catti-brie asked skeptically as she set another arrow. "When did you learn to work wood?"

As she finished, Aegis-fang came spinning by once again. Bruenor pointed to it emphatically. "Dwarven bow!" he explained with a wink, then ran off.

Though wounded, the three giants did well to regroup. Up came the first, a huge stone high over its head.

Catti-brie's next arrow drove hard into that stone, cutting right through it, and the two halves slipped down, banging the giant on the head.

The second giant came up fast, throwing hard for Catti-brie, but far wide of the mark. It did get back down in time to dodge her next lightning-streaking arrow, though. The bolt buried itself hard into the cliff wall.

The third giant let fly for Wulfgar even as Aegis-fang returned to the man's hand, and the barbarian had to dive once more to avoid being smashed. Still, the stone rebounded from the back wall at an unexpected angle, clipping Wulfgar painfully on the hip.

Looking up to him, Catti-brie saw that he had an even greater problem, for beyond him, on the north wall and up higher, loomed yet another giant. This one was huge, holding a stone over its head that looked as though it could take down both the barbarian and the ledge he was standing on.

"Wulfgar!" Catti-brie cried in warning, thinking the man doomed.

* * * * *

Drizzt hadn't witnessed any of the missile exchange, though he did get enough of a break from his dodging and slashing to see that Guenhwyvar was all right. The panther had made it onto the lower ledge, and though obviously wounded, seemed more angry at the fact that she could not easily get back into the fight.

The giant's kicks came slower now. As the behemoth tired, its legs stun from many deep cuts. The only trouble the swift drow had now was making sure that he didn't lose his footing in the deepening blood.

Then he heard Catti-brie's cry and was so startled that he slowed too much. The giant's boot caught up to him, hitting him squarely and sending him on a tumbling dive to the far end of the ledge, beyond the edge of the darkness globe. Coming right back to his feet, ignoring the ache, Drizzt ran up the stony wall, climbing a dozen feet before the giant came out in pursuit, bending low, thinking its prey to be on the ground.

Drizzt dropped on the giant's shoulders, wrapping his legs about its neck and double-stabbing his scimitars into the sides of its eyes. The behemoth howled and stood straight. The monster reached for the source of the pain, but the drow was too quick. Rolling over down the giant's back and landing nimbly on his feet, Drizzt cut fast for the lip of the ledge, hopping to the rocky barricade.

The giant batted at its torn eyes, blinded by the cuts and the blood. It waved its hands frantically and turned toward the noise of the drow's movements, lurching to grab him.

But Drizzt was already gone, spinning about the giant and chasing it from behind, prodding hard to keep the behemoth going as it reached for the ledge, overbalancing. Howling with pain, the giant tried to turn around, but that only sent Drizzt in even harder, scimitars biting about the stooping thing's chin.

The giant tried to scramble back but fell into the open air.

* * * * *

Wulfgar turned around at Catti-brie's call but had no time to strike out first or to dodge. Catti-brie got her bow up and level, but the huge giant threw first.

The stone sailed past Wulfgar, past Catti-brie, and Bruenor, down to the ledge in the south. Short-hopping off the stone-blocking wall, it slammed one giant in the chest, throwing it back and to the ground.

Looking down at her drawn arrow, a stunned Catti-brie spotted Regis sitting comfortably on the giant's shoulder. "The little rat," she whispered under her breath, truly impressed.

Now all three—giant, Wulfgar and Catti-brie—turned their attention to the lower ledge. Lightning arrows streaked in one after another, punctuated by a spinning throw of Aegis-fang, or the thunderous report of a huge, giant-hurled boulder. The sheer force of the barrage soon had the three giants dizzy and ducking.

Aegis-fang clipped one on the shoulder as it tried to run out the side down a concealed trail. The force of the hammer blow turned it around in time to see the next streaking arrow, right before the bolt drove through its ugly face. Down it went in a heap. A second giant stepped out, rock high to throw, only to catch a huge boulder in the chest and go flying away.

The third, badly wounded, stayed in a crouch behind the wall, not even daring to creep back the fifteen feet to the cave opening in the wall behind it. Head down, it didn't see the dwarf climb into position on a ledge above it, though it did look up when it heard the roar of a leaping Bruenor.

The dwarf king's axe, buried deep into the giant's brain, sported yet another notch.

Chapter 3
THE UNPLEASANT MIRROR

ell would you do to this one investigate," Giunta the Diviner said to Hand as the man left the wizard's house. "Danger I sense, and we both know who it may be, though to speak the name we fear."

Hand mumbled a reply and continued on his way, glad to be gone from the excitable wizard and Giunta's particularly annoying manner of structuring a sentence, one the wizard claimed came from another plane of existence, but that Hand merely considered Giunta's way of trying to impress those around him. Still, Giunta had his uses, Hand recognized, for of the dozen or so wizards the Basadoni house often utilized, none could unravel mysteries better than Giunta. From simply sensing the emanations of the strange coins Giunta had almost completely reconstructed the conversation between Hand, Kadran, and Sharlotta, as well as the identity of Taddio as the courier of the coins. Looking deeper, Giunta's face had turned into a profound frown, and as he had described the demeanor and general appearance of the one who had given the coins to Taddio, both he and Hand began to put the pieces together.

Hand knew Artemis Entreri. So did Giunta, and it was common knowledge among the street folk that Entreri had left Calimport in pursuit of the dark elf who had brought about the downfall of Pasha Pook, and that the drow was reportedly living in some dwarven city not far from Silverymoon.

Now that his suspicions pointed in a particular direction, Hand knew it was time to turn from magical information gathering to more conventional methods. He went out to the streets, to the many spies, and opened wide the eyes of Pasha Basadoni's powerful guild. Then he started back to the main house to speak with Sharlotta and Kadran but changed his mind. Indeed, Sharlotta had spoken truthfully when she had said that she desired knowledge of her enemies.

Better for Hand that she didn't know.

* * * * *

His room was hardly fitting for a man who had climbed so high among the ranks of the street. This man had been a guildmaster, albeit briefly, and could command huge sums of money from any house in the city simply as a retainer fee for his services. But Artemis Entreri didn't care much about the sparse furnishings of the cheap inn, about the dust piled on the window sills, about the noise of the street ladies and their clients in the adjoining rooms.

He sat on the bed and thought about his options, reconsidering all his movements since returning to Calimport. He had been a bit careless, he realized, particularly in going to the stupid boy who was now claiming rulership of his old shanty town and by showing his dagger to the beggar at Pook's old house. Perhaps, Entreri realized, that journey and encounter had been no coincidence or bad luck, but by subconscious design. Perhaps he had wanted to reveal himself to any who would look closely enough.

But what would that mean? he had to wonder now. How had the guild structures changed, and where in those new hierarchies would Artemis Entreri fit in? Even more importantly, where did Artemis Entreri want to fit in?

Those questions were beyond Entreri at that time, but he realized that he could not afford to sit and wait for others to find him. He should learn some of the answers, at least, before dealing with the more powerful houses of Calimport. The hour was late, well past midnight, but the assassin donned a dark cloak and went out onto the streets anyway.

The sights and sounds and smells brought him back to his younger days, when he had often allied with the dark of night and shunned the light of day. He noticed before he had even left the street that many gazes had settled upon him, and he sensed that they focused with more than a passing interest, more than the attention a foreign merchant might expect. Entreri recalled his own days on these streets, the methods and speed with which information was passed along. He was already being watched, he knew, and probably by several different guilds. Possibly the tavern keeper where he was staying or one of the patrons, perhaps, had recognized him or had recognized enough about him to raise suspicions. These people of Calimport's foul belly lived on the edge of disaster every minute of every day. Thus they possessed a level of alertness beyond anything so many other cultures might know. Like grassland field rats, rodents living in extensive burrow complexes with thousands and thousands of inhabitants, the people of Calimport's streets had designed complex warning systems: shouts and whistles, nods, and even simple body posture.

Yes, Entreri knew as he walked along the quiet street, his practiced footsteps making not a sound, they were watching him.

The time had come for him to do some looking of his own—and he knew where to start. Several turns brought him to Avenue Paradise, a particularly seedy place where potent herbs and weeds were openly traded, as were weapons, stolen goods, and carnal companionship. A mockery of culture itself, Avenue Paradise stood as the pinnacle of hedonism among the underclass. Here a beggar, if he found a few extra coins that day, could, for a few precious moments, feel like a king, could surround himself with perfumed ladies and imbibe enough mind-altering substances to forget the sores that festered on his filthy skin. Here, one like the boy that Entreri had paid in his old shanty town could live, for a few hours, the life of pasha Basadoni.

Of course it was all fake, fancy facades on rat-ridden buildings, fancy clothes on scared little girls or dead-eyed whores, heavily perfumed with cheap smells to hide the months of sweat and dust without a proper bath. But even fake luxury would suffice for most of the street people, whose constant misery was all too real.

Entreri walked slowly along the street, dismissing his introspection and turning his eyes outward, studying every detail. He thought he recognized more than one of the older, pitiful whores, but in truth, Entreri had never succumbed to such unhealthy and tawdry temptations as could be found on Avenue Paradise. His carnal pleasures, on those very few occasions he took them (for he considered them a weakness to one aspiring to be the perfect fighter), came in the harems of mighty pashas, and he had never held any tolerance whatsoever for anything intoxicating, for anything that dulled his keen mind and left him vulnerable. He had come to Avenue Paradise often, though, to find others too weak to resist. The whores had never liked him, nor had he ever bothered with them, though he knew, as did all the pashas, that they could be a very valuable source of information. Entreri simply could not bring himself to ever trust a woman who made her daily life in that particular line of employ.

So now he spent more time looking at the thugs and pickpockets and was amused to learn that one of the pickpockets was also studying him. Hiding a grin, he even changed his course to bring himself closer to the foolish young man.

Sure enough, Entreri was barely ten strides past when the thief came out behind him, walking past and "slipping" at the last moment to cover his reach for Entreri's dangling purse.

A split second later, the would-be thief was off balance, turned in and down, with Entreri's hand clamped over the ends of his fingers, squeezing the most exquisite pain up the man's arm. Out came the jeweled dagger, quietly but quickly, its tip poking a tiny hole in the man's palm as Entreri turned his shoulder in closer to conceal the movement and lessened his paralyzing grip.

Obviously confused at the relief of pressure on his pained hand, the thief moved his free hand to his own belt, pulling aside his cloak and grabbing at a long knife.

Entreri stared hard and concentrated on the dagger, instructing it to do its darker work, using its magic to begin sucking the very life-force out of the foolish thief.

The man weakened, his dagger fell harmlessly to the street, and both his eyes and his jaw opened wide in a horrified, agonized, and ultimately futile attempt at a scream.

"You feel the emptiness," Entreri whispered to him. "The hopelessness. You know that I hold not only your life, but your very soul in my hands."

The man didn't, couldn't move.

"Do you?" Entreri prompted, bringing a nod from the now gasping man.

"Tell me," the assassin bade, "are there any halflings on the street this night?" As he spoke, he let up a bit on the life-stealing process, and the man's expression shifted again, just a bit, to one of confusion.

"Halflings," the assassin explained, punctuating his point by drawing hard on the man's life-force again, so forcefully that the only thing holding the man up was Entreri's body.

With his free hand, trembling violently through every inch of movement, the thief pointed farther down the avenue in the general direction of a few houses that Entreri knew well. He thought to ask the man a more focused question or two but decided against it, realizing that he might have revealed too much of his identity already by the mere hunger of his particular jeweled dagger.

"If I ever see you again, I shall kill you," the assassin said with such complete calm that all the blood ran from the thief's face. Entreri released him, and he staggered away, falling to his knees and crawling on. Entreri shook his head in disgust, wondering, and not for the first time, why he had ever come back to this wretched city.

Without even bothering to look and ensure that the thief continued away, the assassin strode more quickly down the street. If the particular halfling he sought was still about and still alive, Entreri could guess which of those buildings he might be in. The middle and largest of the three, The Copper Ante, had once been a favorite gambling house for many of the halflings in the Calimport dock section, mostly because of the halfling-staffed brothel upstairs and the Thayan brown pipeweed den in the back room. Indeed, Entreri did see many (considering that this was Calimport, where halflings were scarce) of the little folk scattered about the various tables in the common room when he entered. He scanned each table slowly, trying to guess what his former friend might look like now that several years had passed. The halfling would be wider about the belly, no doubt, for he loved rich food and had set himself up in a position to afford ten meals a day if he so chose.

Entreri slipped into an open seat at one table where six halflings tossed dice, each moving so quickly that it was almost impossible for a novice gambler to even tell which call the one at the head of the table was making and which halfling was grabbing which pot as winnings for which throw. Entreri easily sorted it out, though, and found, to his amusement but hardly his surprise, that all six were cheating. It seemed more a contest of who could grab the most coins the fastest than any type of gambling, and all half dozen appeared to be equally suited to the task, so much so that Entreri figured that each of them would likely leave with almost exactly the amount of coins with which he had begun.

The assassin dropped four gold pieces on the table and grabbed up some dice, giving a half-hearted throw. Almost before the dice stopped rolling, the closest halfling reached for the coins, but Entreri was the quicker, slapping his hand over the halfling's wrist and pinning it to the table.

"But you lost!" the little one squeaked, and the flurry of movement came to an abrupt halt, the other five looking at Entreri and more than one reaching for a weapon. The gaming stopped at several other tables, as well, the whole area of the common room focusing on the coming trouble.

"I was not playing," Entreri said calmly, not letting the halfling go.

"You put down money and threw dice," one of the others protested. "That is playing."

Entreri's glare put the complaining halfling back in his seat. "I am playing when I say, and not before," he explained. "And I only cover bets that are announced openly before I throw."

"You saw how the table was moving," a third dared to argue, but Entreri cut him short with an upraised hand and a nod.

He looked to the gambler at his right, the one who had reached for the coins, and waited a moment to let the rest of the room settle down and go back to their own business. "You want the coins? They, and twice that amount above them, shall be yours," he explained, and the greedy halfling's expression went from one of distress to a gleaming-eyed grin. "I came not to play but to ask a simple question. Provide an answer, and the coins are yours." As he spoke, Entreri reached into his purse and brought out more coins—more than twice the number the halfling had grabbed.

"Well, Master . . ." the halfling began.

"Do'Urden," Entreri replied, with hardly a conscious thought, though he had to bite back a chuckle at the irony after he heard the name come out of his mouth. "Master Do'Urden of Silverymoon."

All the halflings at the table eyed him curiously, for the unusual name sounded familiar to them all. In truth, and they came to realize it one by one, they all knew that name. It was the name of the dark elven protector of Regis, perhaps the highest ranking (albeit for a short while!) and most famous halfling ever to walk the streets of Calimport.

"Your skin has—" the halfling pinned under Entreri's grasp started to remark lightheartedly, but he stopped, swallowed hard and blanched as he put the pieces together. Entreri could see the halfling recall the story of Regis and the dark elf, and the one who had subsequently deposed the halfling guildmaster and then gone out after the drow.

"Yes," the halfling said as calmly as he could muster, "a question."

"I seek one of your kind," Entreri explained. "An old friend by the name of Dondon Tiggerwillies."

The halfling put on a confused look and shook his head, but not before a flicker of recognition has crossed his dark eyes, one the sharp Entreri did not miss.

"Everyone of the streets knows Dondon," Entreri stated. "Or once knew of him. You are not a child, and your gaming skills tell me that you have been a regular to the Copper Ante for years. You know, or knew, Dondon. If he is dead, then I wish to hear the story. If not, then I wish to speak with him."

Grave looks passed from halfling to halfling. "Dead," said one across the table, but Entreri knew from the tone and the quick manner in which the diminutive fellow blurted it out that it was a lie, that Dondon, ever the survivor, was indeed alive.

Halflings in Calimport always seemed to stick together, though.

"Who killed him?" Entreri asked, playing along.

"He got sick," another halfling offered, again in that quick, telltale manner.

"And where is he buried?"

"Who gets buried in Calimport?" the first liar replied.

"Tossed into the sea," said another.

Entreri nodded with every word. He was actually a bit amused at how these halflings played off each other, building an elaborate lie and one the assassin knew he could eventually turn against them.

"Well, you have told me much," he said, releasing the halfling's wrist. The greedy gambler immediately went for the coins, but a jeweled dagger jabbed down between the reaching hand and the desired gems in the blink of a startled eye.

"You promised coins!" the halfling protested.

"For a lie?" Entreri calmly asked. "I inquired about Dondon outside and was told that he was in here. I know he is alive, for I saw him just yesterday."

The halflings all glanced at each other, trying to piece together the inconsistencies here. How had they fallen so easily into the trap?

"Then why speak of him in the past tense?" the halfling directly across the table asked, the first to insist that Dondon was dead. This halfling thought himself sly, thought that he had caught Entreri in a lie . . . as indeed he had.

"Because I know that halflings never reveal the whereabouts of other halflings to one who is not a halfling," Entreri answered, his demeanor changing suddenly to a lighthearted, laughing expression, something that had never come easily to the assassin. "I have no fight with Dondon, I assure you. We are old friends, and it has been far too long since we last spoke. Now, tell me where he is and take your payment."

Again the halflings looked around, and then one, licking his lips and staring hungrily at the small pile of coins, pointed to a door at the back of the large room.

Entreri replaced the dagger in its sheath and gave a gesture that seemed a salute as he moved from the table, walking confidently across the room and pushing through the door without even a knock.

There before him reclined the fattest halfling he had ever seen, a creature wider than it was tall. He and the assassin locked stares, Entreri so intent on the fellow that he hardly noticed the scantily clad female halflings flanking him. It was indeed Dondon Tiggerwillies, Entreri realized to his horror. Despite all the years and all the scores of pounds, he knew the halfling, once the slipperiest and most competent confidence swindler in all of Calimport.

"A knock is often appreciated," the halfling said, his voice raspy, as though he could hardly force the sounds from his thick neck. "Suppose that my friends and I were engaged in a more private action."

Entreri didn't even try to figure out how that might be possible.

"Well, what do you want, then?" Dondon asked, stuffing an enormous bite of pie into his mouth as soon as he finished speaking.

Entreri closed the door and walked into the room, halving the distance between him and the halfling. "I want to speak with an old associate," he explained.

Dondon stopped chewing and stared hard. Obviously stunned by recognition, he began violently choking on the pie and wound up spitting a substantial piece of it back onto his plate. His attendants did well to hide their disgust as they moved the plate aside.

"I did not . . . I mean, Regis was no friend of mine. I mean . . ." Dondon stammered, a fairly common reaction from those faced with the spectre of Artemis Entreri.

"Be at ease, Dondon," Entreri said firmly. "I came to speak with you, nothing more. I care not for Regis, nor for any role Dondon might have played in the demise of Pook those years ago. The streets are for the living, are they not, and not the dead?"

"Yes, of course," Dondon replied, visibly trembling. He rolled forward a bit, trying to at least sit up, and only then did Entreri notice a chain trailing a thick anklet he wore about his left leg. Finally, the fat halfling gave up and just rolled back to his previous position. "An old wound," he said with a shrug.

Entreri let the obviously ridiculous excuse slide past. He moved closer to the halfling and went down in a crouch, brushing aside Dondon's robes that he could better see the shackle. "I have only recently returned," he explained. "I hoped that Dondon might enlighten me concerning the current demeanor of the streets."

"Rough and dangerous, of course," Dondon answered with a chuckle that became a phlegm-filled cough.

"Who rules?" Entreri asked in a dead serious tone. "Which houses hold power, and what soldiers champion them?"

"I wish that I could be of help to you, my friend," Dondon said nervously. "Of course I do. I would never withhold information from you. Never that! But you see," he added, lifting up his shackled ankle, "they do not let me out much anymore."

"How long have you been in here?"

"Three years."

Entreri stared incredulously and distastefully at the little wretch, then looked doubtfully at the relatively simple shackle, a lock that the old Dondon could have opened with a piece of hair.

In response, Dondon held up his enormously thick hands, hands so pudgy that he couldn't even bring the higher parts of his fingers together. "I do not feel much with them anymore," he explained.

A burning outrage welled inside Entreri. He felt as if he would simply explode into a murderous fit that would have him physically shaving the pounds from Dondon's fat hide with his jeweled dagger. Instead, he went at the lock, turning it roughly to scan for any possible traps, then reaching for a small pick.

"Do not," came a high-pitched voice behind him. The assassin sensed the presence before he even heard the words. He spun about, rolling into a crouch, dagger in one hand, arm cocked to throw. Another female halfling, this one dressed in a fine tunic and breeches, with thick, curly brown hair and huge brown eyes, stood at the door, hands up and open, her posture completely unthreatening.

"Oh, but that would be a bad thing for me and for you," the female halfling said with a little grin.

"Do not kill her," Dondon pleaded with Entreri, trying to grab for the assassin's arm, but missing far short of the mark and rolling back, gasping for breath.

Entreri, ever alert, noticed then that both the female halflings attending Dondon had slipped hands into secret places, one to a pocket, the other to her generous waist-length hair, both no doubt reaching for weapons of some sort. He understood then that this newcomer was a leader among the group.

71

"Dwahvel Tiggerwillies, at your service," she said with a graceful bow. "At your service, but not at your whim," she added with a smile.

"Tiggerwillies?" Entreri echoed softly, glancing back at Dondon.

"A cousin," the fat halfling explained with a shrug. "The most powerful halfling in all of Calimport and the newest proprietor of the Copper Ante."

The assassin looked back to see the female halfling completely at ease, hands in her pockets.

"You understand, of course, that I did not come in here alone, not to face a man of Artemis Entreri's reputation," Dwahvel said.

That brought a grin to Entreri's face as he imagined the many halflings concealed about the room. It struck him as a half-sized mock-up of another similar operation, that of Jarlaxle the dark elf mercenary in Menzoberranzan. On the occasions when he had to face the always well-protected Jarlaxle, though, Entreri had understood without doubt that if he made even the slightest wrong move, or if Jarlaxle or one of the drow guards ever perceived one of Entreri's movements as threatening, his life would have been at an abrupt end. He couldn't imagine now that Dwahvel Tiggerwillies, or any other halfling for that matter, could command such well-earned respect. Still, he hadn't come here for a fight, even if that old warrior part of him perceived Dwahvel's words as a challenge.

"Of course," he replied simply.

"Several with slings eye you right now," she went on. "And the bullets of those slings have been treated with an explosive formula. Quite painful and devastating."

"How resourceful," the assassin said, trying to sound impressed.

"That is how we survive," Dwahvel replied. "By being resourceful. By knowing everything about everything and preparing properly."

In a single swift movement—one that would surely have gotten him killed in Jarlaxle's court—the assassin spun the dagger over and slipped it into its sheath, then stood up straight and dipped a low and respectful bow to Dwahvel.

"Half the children of Calimport answer to Dwahvel," Dondon explained. "And the other half are not children at all," he added with a wink, "and answer to Dwahvel, as well."

"And of course, both halves have watched Artemis Entreri carefully since he walked back into the city," Dwahvel explained.

"So glad that my reputation preceded me," Entreri said, sounding puffy indeed.

"We did not know it was you until recently," Dwahvel replied, just to deflate the man, who of course, was not at all conceited.

"And you discovered this by. . . . ?" Entreri prompted.

That left Dwahvel a bit embarrassed, realizing that she had just been squeezed for a bit of information she had not intended to reveal. "I do not know why you would expect an answer," she said, somewhat perturbed. "Nor do I begin to see any reason I should help the one who dethroned Regis from the guild of the former Pasha Pook. Regis, was in a position to aid all the other halflings of Calimport."

Entreri had no answer to that, so he offered nothing in reply.

"Still, we should talk," Dwahvel went on, turning sidelong and motioning to the door.

Entreri glanced back at Dondon.

"Leave him to his pleasures," Dwahvel explained. "You would have him freed, yet he has little desire to leave, I assure you. Fine food and fine companionship."

Entreri looked with disgust to the assorted pies and sweets, to the hardly moving Dondon, then to the two females. "He is not so demanding," one of them explained with a laugh.

"Just a soft lap to rest his sleepy head," the other added with a titter that set them both to giggling.

"I have all that I could ever desire," Dondon assured him.

Entreri just shook his head and left with Dwahvel, following the little halfling to a more private—and undoubtedly better guarded—room deeper into the Copper Ante complex. Dwahvel took a seat in a low, plush chair and motioned for the assassin to take one opposite. Entreri was hardly comfortable in the half-sized piece, his legs straight out before him.

"I do not entertain many who are not halflings," Dwahvel apologized. "We tend to be a secretive group."

Entreri saw that she was looking for him to tell her how honored he was. But, of course, he wasn't, and so he said nothing, just keeping a tight expression, eyes boring accusingly into the female.

"We hold him for his own good," Dwahvel said plainly.

"Dondon was once among the most respected thieves in Calimport," Entreri countered.

"Once," Dwahvel echoed, "but not so long after your departure, Dondon drew the anger of a particularly powerful pasha. The man was a friend of mine, so I pleaded for him to spare Dondon. Our compromise was that Dondon remain inside. Always inside. If he ever is seen walking the streets of Calimport again, by the pasha or any of the pasha's many contacts, then I am bound to turn him over for execution."

"A better fate, by my estimation, than the slow death you give him chained in that room."

Dwahvel laughed aloud at that proclamation. "Then you do not understand Dondon," she said. "Men more holy than I have long identified the seven sins deadly to the soul, and while Dondon has little of the primary three, for he is neither proud nor envious nor wrathful, he is possessed of an excess of the last four—sloth, avarice, gluttony, and lust. He and I made a deal, a deal to save his life. I promised to give him, without judgment, all that he desired in exchange for his promise to remain within my doors."

"Then why the chains about his ankle?" Entreri asked.

"Because Dondon is drunk more often than sober," Dwahvel explained. "Likely he would cause trouble within my establishment, or perhaps he would stagger onto the street. It is all for his own protection."

Entreri wanted to refute that, for he had never seen a more pitiful sight than Dondon and would personally prefer a tortured death to that grotesque lifestyle. But when he thought about Dondon more carefully, when he remembered the halfling's personal style those years ago, a style that often included sweet foods and many ladies, he recognized that Dondon's failings now were the halfling's own and nothing forced upon him by a caring Dwahvel.

"If he remains inside the Copper Ante, no one will bother him," Dwahvel said after giving Entreri the moment to think it over. "No contract, no assassin. Though, of course, this is only on the five-year-old word of a pasha. So you can understand why my fellows were a bit nervous when the likes of Artemis Entreri walked into the Copper Ante inquiring about Dondon."

Entreri eyed her skeptically.

"They were not sure it was you at first," Dwahvel explained. "Yet we have known that you were back in town for a couple of days now. Word is fairly common on the streets, though, as you can well imagine, it is more rumor than truth. Some say that you have returned to displace Quentin Bodeau and regain control of Pook's house. Others hint that you have come for greater reasons, hired by the Lords of Waterdeep themselves to assassinate several high-ranking leaders of Calimshan."

Entreri's expression summed up his incredulous response to that preposterous notion.

Dwahvel shrugged. "Such are the trappings of reputation," she said. "Many people are paying good money for any whisper, however ridiculous, that might help them solve the riddle of why Artemis Entreri has returned to Calimport. You make them nervous, assassin. Take that as the highest compliment.

"But also as a warning," Dwahvel went on. "When guilds fear someone or something, they often take steps to erase that fear. Several have been asking very pointed questions about your whereabouts and movements, and you understand this business well enough to realize that to be the mark of the hunting assassin."

Entreri put his elbow on the arm of the small chair and plopped his chin in his hand, considering the halfling carefully. Rarely had anyone spoken so bluntly and boldly to Artemis Entreri, and in the few minutes they had been sitting together, Dwahvel Tiggerwillies had earned more respect from Entreri than most would gather in a lifetime of conversations.

"I can find more detailed information for you," Dwahvel said slyly. "I have larger ears than a Sossalan mammoth and more eyes than a room of beholders, so it is said. And so it is true."

Entreri put a hand to his belt and jiggled his purse. "You overestimate the size of my treasury," he said.

"Look around you," Dwahvel retorted. "What need have I for more gold, from Silverymoon or anywhere else?"

Her reference to the Silverymoon coinage came as a subtle hint to Entreri that she knew of what she was speaking.

"Call it a favor between friends," Dwahvel explained, hardly a surprise to the assassin who had made his life exchanging such favors. "One that you might perhaps repay me one day."

Entreri kept his face expressionless as he thought it over. Such a cheap way to garner information. Entreri highly doubted that the halfling would ever require his particular services, for halflings simply didn't solve their problems that way. And if Dwahvel did call upon him, maybe he would comply, or maybe not. Entreri hardly feared that Dwahvel would send her three-foot-tall thugs after him. No, all that Dwahvel wanted, should things sort out in his favor, was the bragging right that Artemis Entreri owed her a favor, a claim that would drain the blood from the faces of the majority of Calimport's street folk.

The question for Entreri now was, did he really care if he ever got the information Dwahvel offered? He thought it over for another minute, then nodded his accord. Dwahvel brightened immediately.

"Come back tomorrow night, then," she said. "I will have something to tell you."

Outside the Copper Ante, Artemis Entreri spent a long while thinking about Dondon, for he found that every time he conjured an image of the fat halfling stuffing pie into his face he was filled with rage. Not disgust, but rage. As he examined those feelings, he came to recognize that Dondon Tiggerwillies had been about as close to a friend as Artemis Entreri had ever known. Pasha Basadoni had been his mentor, Pasha Pook his primary employer, but Dondon and Entreri had related in a different manner. They acted in each other's benefit without set prices, exchanging information without taking count. It had been a mutually beneficial relationship. Seeing Dondon now, purely hedonistic, having given up on any meaning in life, it seemed to the assassin that the halfling had committed a form of living suicide.

Entreri did not possess enough compassion for that to explain the anger he felt, though, and when he admitted that to himself he came to understand that the sight of Dondon repelled him so much because, given his own mental state lately, it could well be him. Not chained by the ankle in the company of women and food, of course, but in effect, Dondon had surrendered, and so had Entreri.

Perhaps it was time to take down the white flag.

Dondon had been his friend in a manner, and there had been one other similarly entwined. Now it was time to go and see LaValle.

Chapter 4
THE SUMMONS

rizzt couldn't get down to the ledge where Guenhwyvar had landed, so he used the onyx figurine to dismiss the cat. She faded back to the Astral plane, her home, where her wounds would better heal. He saw that Regis and his unexpected giant ally had moved out of sight, and that Wulfgar and Catti-brie were moving to join Bruenor down at the lower ledge to the south, where the last of the enemy giants had fallen. The dark elf began picking his way to join them. At first, he thought he might have to backtrack all the way around to his initial position with Wulfgar, but using his incredible agility and the strength of fingers trained for decades in the maneuvering skills of sword play, he somehow found enough ledges, cracks, and simple angled surfaces to get down beside his friends.

By the time he got there, all three had entered the cave at the back of the shelf.

"Damned things might've kept a bit more treasure if they're meanin' to put up such a fight," he heard Bruenor complaining.

"Perhaps that's why they were scouting out the road,"

Catti-brie replied. "Might it have been better for ye if we went at them on our way back from Cadderly's place? Perhaps then we'd've found more treasure to yer liking. And maybe a few merchant skulls to go along with it."

"Bah!" the dwarf snorted, drawing a wide smile from Drizzt. Few in all the Realms needed treasure less than Bruenor Battlehammer, Eighth King of Mithral Hall (despite his chosen absence from the place) and also leader of a lucrative mining colony in Icewind Dale. But that wasn't the point of Bruenor's ire, Drizzt understood, and he smiled all the wider as Bruenor confirmed his suspicions.

"What kind o' wicked god'd put ye against such powerful foes and not even reward ye with a bit o' gold?" the dwarf grumbled.

"We did find some gold," Catti-brie reminded him. Drizzt, entering the cave, noted that she held a fairly substantial sack that bulged with coins.

Bruenor flashed the drow a disgusted look. "Copper mostly," he grumbled. "Three gold coins, a pair o' silver, and nothing more but stinkin' copper!"

"But the road is safe," Drizzt said. He looked to Wulfgar as he spoke, but the big man would not match his stare. The drow tried hard not to pass any judgment over his tormented friend. Wulfgar should have led Drizzt's charge to the shelf. Never before had he so failed Drizzt in their tandem combat. But the drow knew that the barbarian's hesitance came not from any desire to see Drizzt injured nor, certainly, any cowardice. Wulfgar spun in emotional turmoil, the depths of which Drizzt Do'Urden had never before seen. He had known of these problems before coaxing the barbarian out for this hunt, so he could not rightly place any blame now.

Nor did he want to. He only hoped that the fight itself, after Wulfgar had become involved, had helped the man to rid himself of some of those inner demons, had run the horse, as Montolio would have called it, just a bit.

"And what about yerself?" Bruenor roared, bouncing over to stand before Drizzt. "What're ye about, going off on yer own without a word to the rest of us? Ye thinking all the fun's for yerself, elf? Ye thinking that me and me girl can't be helpin' ye?"

"I did not want to trouble you with so minor a battle," Drizzt calmly replied, painting a disarming smile on his dark face. "I knew that we would be in the mountains, outside and not under them, in terrain not suited for the likes of a short-limbed dwarf."

Bruenor wanted to hit him. Drizzt could see that in the way the dwarf was trembling. "Bah!" he roared instead, throwing up his hands and walking back for the exit to the small cave. "Ye're always doin' that, ye stinkin' elf. Always going about on yer own and taking all the fun. But we'll find more on the road, don't ye doubt! And ye better be hopin' that ye see it afore me, or I'll cut 'em all down afore ye ever get them sissy blades outta their sheaths or that stinkin' cat outta that statue.

"Unless they're too much for us. . . ." he continued, his voice trailing away as he moved out of the cave. "Then I just might let ye have 'em all to yerself, ye stinkin' elf!"

Wulfgar, without a word and without a look at Drizzt, moved out next, leaving the drow and Catti-brie alone. Drizzt was chuckling now as Bruenor continued to grumble, but when he looked at Catti-brie, he saw that she was truly not amused, her feelings obviously hurt.

"I'm thinking that a poor excuse," she remarked.

"I wanted to bring Wulfgar out alone," Drizzt explained. "To bring him back to a different place and time, before all the trouble."

"And ye're not thinkin' that me dad, or meself, might want to be helping with that?" Catti-brie asked.

"I wanted no one here that Wulfgar might fear needed protecting," Drizzt explained, and Catti-brie slumped back, her jaw dropping open.

"I speak only the truth, and you see it clearly," Drizzt went on. "You remember how Wulfgar acted toward you before the fight with the yochlol. He was protective to the point of becoming a detriment to any battle cause. How could I rightly ask you to join us out here now, when that previous scenario might have repeated, leaving Wulfgar, perhaps, in an even worse emotional place than when we set out? That is why I did not ask Bruenor or Regis, either. Wulfgar, Guenhwyvar, and I would fight the giants, as we did that time so long ago in Icewind Dale. And maybe, just maybe, he would remember things the way they had been before his unwelcome tenure with Errtu."

Catti-brie's expression softened, and she bit her lower lip as she nodded her agreement. "And did it work?" she asked.

"Suren the fight went well, and Wulfgar fought well and honestly."

Drizzt's gaze drifted out the exit. "He made a mistake," the drow admitted. "Though surely he compensated as the battle progressed. It is my hope that Wulfgar will forgive himself his initial hesitance and focus on the actual fight where he performed wonderfully."

"Hesitance?" Catti-brie asked skeptically.

"When we first began the battle," Drizzt started to explain, but he waved his hand dismissively as if it did not really matter. "It has been many years since we have fought together. It was an excusable miscue, nothing more." In truth, Drizzt had a hard time dismissing the fact that Wulfgar's hesitance had almost cost him and Guenhwyvar dearly.

"Ye're in a generous mood," the ever-perceptive Catti-brie remarked.

"It is my hope that Wulfgar will remember who he is and who his friends truly are," the drow ranger replied.

"Yer hope," Catti-brie echoed. "But is it your expectation?"

Drizzt continued to stare out the exit. He could only shrug.

* * * * *

The four were out of the ravine and back on the trail shortly after, and Bruenor's grumbling about Drizzt turned into complaining about Regis. "Where in the Nine Hells is Rumblebelly?" the dwarf bellowed. "And how in the Nine Hells did he ever get a giant to throw rocks for him?"

81

Even as he spoke, they felt the vibrations of heavy, heavy footfalls beneath their feet and heard a silly song sung in unison. There was a happy halfling voice, Regis, and a second voice that rumbled like the thunder of a rockslide. A moment later, Regis came around a bend in the northern trail, riding on the giant's shoulder, the two of them singing and laughing with every step.

"Hello," Regis said happily when he steered the giant to join his friends. He noted that Drizzt had his hands on his scimitars, though they were sheathed (and that meant little for the lightning-fast drow), Bruenor clutched tightly to his axe, Catti-brie to her bow, and Wulfgar, holding Aegis-fang, seemed as if he was about to explode into murderous action.

"This is Junger," Regis explained. "He was not with the other band—he says he doesn't even know them. And he is a smart one."

Junger put a hand up to secure Regis's seat, then bowed low before the stunned group.

"In fact, Junger does not even go down to the road, does not go out of the mountains at all," Regis explained. "Says he has no interest in the affairs of dwarves or men."

"He told ye that, did he?" Bruenor asked doubtfully.

Regis nodded, his smile wide. "And I believe him," he said, waggling the ruby pendant, whose magical hypnotizing properties were well known to the friends.

"That don't change a thing," Bruenor said with a growl, looking to Drizzt as if expecting the ranger to start the fight. A giant was a giant, after all, to the dwarf's way of thinking, and any giant looked much better lying down with an axe firmly embedded in its skull.

"Junger is no killer," Regis said firmly.

"Only goblins," the huge giant said with a smile. "And hill giants. And orcs, of course, for who could abide the ugly things?"

His sophisticated dialect and his choice of enemies had the dwarf staring at him wide-eyed. "And yeti," Bruenor said. "Don't ye be forgettin' yeti."

"Oh, not yeti," Junger replied. "I do not kill yeti."

The scowl returned to Bruenor's face.

"Why, one cannot even eat the smelly things," Junger explained. "I do not kill them, I domesticate them."

"Ye what?" Bruenor demanded.

"Domesticate them," Junger explained. "Like a dog or a horse. Oh, but I've quite a selection of yeti workers at my cave back in the mountains."

Bruenor turned an incredulous expression on Drizzt, but the ranger, as much at a loss as the dwarf, only shrugged.

"We've lost too much time already," Catti-brie remarked. "Camlaine and the others'll be halfway out o' the dale afore we catch them. Be rid o' yer friend, Regis, and let us get to the trail."

Regis was shaking his head before she ever finished. "Junger does not usually leave the mountains," he explained. "But he will for me."

"Then I'll not have to carry you anymore," Wulfgar grumbled, walking away. "Good enough for that."

"Ye're not having to carry him anyway," Bruenor replied, then looked back to Regis. "I'm thinking ye can do yer own walking. Ye don't need a giant to act as a horse."

"More than that," Regis said, beaming. "A bodyguard."

The dwarf and Catti-brie both groaned; Drizzt only chuckled and shook his head.

"In every fight, I spend more time trying to keep out of the way," Regis explained. "Never am I any real help. But with Junger—"

"Ye'll still be trying to keep outta the way," Bruenor interrupted.

"If Junger is to fight for you, then he is no more than any of the rest of us," Drizzt added. "Are we, then, merely bodyguards of Regis?"

"No, of course not," the halfling replied. "But—"

"Be rid of him," Catti-brie said. "Wouldn't we look the fine band of friendly travelers walking into Luskan beside a mountain giant?"

"We'll walk in with a drow," Regis answered before he could think about it, then blushed a deep shade of red.

Again, Drizzt only chuckled and shook his head.

"Put him down," Bruenor said to Junger. "I think he's needin' a talk."

"You mustn't hurt my friend Regis," Junger replied. "That I simply cannot allow."

Bruenor snorted. "Put 'im down."

With a look to Regis, who held a stubborn pose for a few moments longer, Junger complied. He set the halfling gently on the ground before Bruenor, who reached as if to grab Regis by the ear, but then glanced up, up, up at Junger and thought the better of it. "Ye're not thinkin', Rumble-belly," the dwarf said quietly, leading Regis away. "What happens if the big damned thing finds its way outta yer ruby spell? He'll squish ye flat afore any o' us can stop him, and I'm not thinking I'd try to stop him if I could, since ye'd be deserving the flattening!"

Regis started to argue, but he remembered the first moments of his encounter with Junger, when the huge giant had proclaimed that he liked his rodents smashed. The little halfling couldn't deny the fact that a single step from Junger would indeed mash him, and the hold of the ruby pendant was ever tentative. He turned and walked back from Bruenor and bade Junger to go back to his home in the deep mountains.

The giant smiled—and shook his head. "I hear it," he said cryptically. "So I shall stay."

"Hear what?" Regis and Bruenor asked together.

"Just a call," Junger assured them. "It tells me that I should go along with you to serve Regis and protect him."

"Ye hit him good with that thing, didn't ye now?" Bruenor whispered at the halfling.

"I need no protecting," Regis said firmly to the giant. "Though we all thank you for your help in the fight. You can go back to your home."

Again Junger shook his head. "Better that I go with you."

Bruenor glowered at Regis, and the halfling had no explanation. As far as he could tell, Junger was still under the spell of the pendant—the fact that Regis was still alive seemed evidence of that—yet the behemoth was clearly disobeying him.

"Perhaps you can come along," Drizzt said to the surprise of them all. "Yes, but if you mean to join us, then perhaps your pet tundra yetis might prove invaluable. How long will it take you to retrieve them?"

"Three days at the most," Junger replied.

"Well, go then, and be quick about it," Regis said, hopping up and down and wriggling the ruby pendant at the end of its chain.

That seemed to satisfy the giant. It bowed low then bounded away.

"We should've killed the thing here and now," Bruenor said. "Now it'll come back in three days and find us long gone, then it'll likely take its damned smelly yetis and go down hunting on the road!"

"No, he told me he never goes out of the mountains," Regis reasoned.

"Enough of this foolishness," Catti-brie demanded. "The thing's gone, and so should we all be." None offered an argument to that, so they set off at once, Drizzt purposely falling into line beside Regis.

"Was it all the call of the ruby pendant?" the ranger asked.

"Junger told me that he was farther from home than he had been in a long, long time," Regis admitted. "He said he heard a call on the wind and went to answer it. I guess he thought I was the caller."

Drizzt accepted that explanation. If Junger continued to fall for the simple ruse, they would be around the edge of the Spine of the World, rushing fast along a better road, before the behemoth ever returned to this spot.

* * * * *

Indeed Junger was running fast in the direction of his relatively lavish mountain home, and it struck the giant as curious, for just a moment, that he had ever left the place.

In his younger days, Junger had been a wanderer, living meal to meal on whatever prey he could find. He snickered now when he considered all that he had told the foolish little halfling, for Junger had indeed once feasted on the meat of humans, and even on a halfling once. The truth was, he shunned such meals now as much because he didn't like the taste as because he thought it better not to make such powerful enemies as humans. Wizards in particular scared him. Of course, to find human or halfling meat, Junger had to leave his mountain home, and that he never liked to do.

He wouldn't have come out at all this time had not a call on the wind, something he still did not quite understand, compelled him.

Yes, Junger had all he wanted at his home: plenty of food, obedient servants, and comfortable furs. He had no desire to ever leave the place.

But he had, and he understood that he would again, and though that seemed an incongruous thought to the not-stupid giant, it was one that he simply couldn't pause to consider. Not now, not with the constant buzzing in his ear.

He would get the yetis, he knew, and then return, following the instructions of the call on the wind.

The call of Crenshinibon.

Chapter 5

STIRRING THE STREETS

aValle walked to his private suite in the guild house late that morning after meeting with Quentin Bodeau and Chalsee Anguaine. Dog Perry was supposed to attend, and he was the one LaValle truly wanted to see, but Dog had sent word that he would not be coming, that he was out on the streets learning more about the dangerous Entreri.

In truth, the meeting proved nothing more than a gathering to calm the nerves of Quentin Bodeau. The guildmaster wanted reassurances that Entreri wouldn't merely show up and murder him. Chalsee Anguaine, in the manner of a cocky young man, promised to defend Quentin with his life. This LaValle knew to be an obvious lie. LaValle argued that Entreri wouldn't work that way, that he would not come in and kill Quentin without first learning all of Quentin's ties and associates and how powerfully the man held the guild.

"Entreri is never reckless," LaValle had explained. "And the scenario you fear would indeed be reckless."

By the time LaValle had turned to leave, Bodeau felt better and expressed his sentiment that he would feel better still if Dog Perry, or someone else, merely killed the dangerous man. It would never be that easy, LaValle knew, but he had kept the thought silent.

As soon as he entered his rooms, a suite of four with a large greeting room, a private study to the right, bedroom directly behind, and an alchemy lab and library to the left, the wizard felt as if something was amiss. He suspected Dog Perry to be the source of the trouble—the man did not trust him and had even privately, though surely subtly, accused him of the intent to side with Entreri should it come to blows.

Had the man come in here when he knew LaValle to be at the meeting with Quentin? Was he still here, hiding, crouched with weapon in hand?

The wizard looked back at the door and saw no signs that the lock—and the door was always locked—had been tripped, or that his traps had been defeated. There was one other way into the place, an outside window, but LaValle had placed so many glyphs and wards upon it, scattering them in several different places, that anyone crawling through would have been shocked with lightning, burned three different times, and frozen solid on the sill. Even if an intruder managed to survive the magical barrage, the explosions would have been heard throughout this entire level of the guild house, bringing soldiers by the score.

Reassured by simple logic and by a defensive spell he placed upon his body to make his skin resistant to any blows, LaValle started for his private study.

The door opened before he reached it, Artemis Entreri standing calmly within.

LaValle did well to stay on his feet, for his knees nearly buckled with weakness.

"You knew that I had returned," Entreri said easily, stepping forward and leaning against the jamb. "Did you not expect that I would pay a visit to an old friend?"

The wizard composed himself and shook his head, looking back at the door. "Door or window?" he asked.

"Door, of course," Entreri replied. "I know how well you protect your windows."

"The door, as well," LaValle said dryly, for obviously he hadn't protected it well enough.

Entreri shrugged. "You still use that lock and trap combination you had upon your previous quarters," he explained, holding up a key. "I suspected as much, since I heard that you were overjoyed when you discovered that the items had survived when the dwarf knocked the door in on your head."

"How did you get a—" LaValle started to ask.

"I got you the lock, remember?" Entreri answered.

"But the guild house is well defended by no soldiers known by Artemis Entreri," the wizard argued.

"The guild house has its secret leaks," the assassin quietly replied.

"But my door," LaValle went on. "There are . . . were other traps."

Entreri put on a bored expression, and LaValle got the point.

"Very well," the wizard said, moving past Entreri into the study and motioning for the assassin to follow. "I can have a fine meal delivered, if you so desire."

Entreri took a seat opposite LaValle and shook his head. "I came not for food, merely for information," he explained. "They know I am in Calimport."

"Many guilds know," LaValle confirmed with a nod. "And yes, I did know. I saw you through my crystal ball as, I am sure, have many of the wizards of the other pashas. You have not exactly been traveling from shadow to shadow."

"Should I be?" Entreri asked. "I came in with no enemies, as far as I know, and with no intent to make any."

LaValle laughed at the absurd notion. "No enemies?" he asked. "Ever have you made enemies. The creation of enemies is the obvious side product of your dark profession." His chuckle died fast when he looked carefully at the not-amused assassin, the wizard suddenly realizing that he was mocking perhaps the most dangerous man in all the world.

"Why did you scry me?" Entreri asked.

LaValle shrugged and held up his hands as if he didn't understand the question. "That is my job in the guild," he answered.

"So you informed the guildmaster of my return?"

"Pasha Quentin Bodeau was with me when your image came into the crystal ball," LaValle admitted.

Entreri merely nodded, and LaValle shifted uncomfortably.

"I did not know it would be you, of course," the wizard explained. "If I had known, I would have contacted you privately before informing Bodeau to learn your intent and your wishes."

"You are a loyal one," Entreri said dryly, and the irony was not lost on LaValle.

"I make no pretensions or promises," the wizard replied. "Those who know me understand that I do little to upset the balance of power about me and serve whoever has weighted his side of the scale the most."

"A pragmatic survivor," Entreri said. "Yet did you not just tell me that you would have informed me had you known? You do make a promise, wizard, a promise to serve. And yet, would you not be breaking that promise to Quentin Bodeau by warning me? Perhaps I do not know you as well as I had thought. Perhaps your loyalty cannot be trusted."

"I make a willing exception for you," LaValle stammered, trying to find a way out of the logic trap. He knew beyond a doubt that Entreri would try to kill him if the assassin believed that he could not be trusted.

And he knew beyond a doubt that if Entreri tried to kill him, he would be dead.

"Your mere presence means that whichever side you serve has weighted the scale in their favor," he explained. "Thus, I would never willingly go against you."

Entreri didn't respond other than to stare hard at the man, making LaValle shift uncomfortably more than once. Entreri, having little time for such games and with no real intention of harming LaValle, broke the tension, though, and quickly. "Tell me of the guild in its present incarnation," he said. "Tell me of Bodeau and his lieutenants and how extensive his street network has become."

"Quentin Bodeau is a decent man," LaValle readily complied. "He does not kill unless forced into such a position and steals only from those who can afford the loss. But many under him, and many other guilds, perceive this compassion as weakness, and thus the guild has suffered under his reign. We are not as extensive as we were when Pook ruled or when you took the leadership from the halfling Regis." He went on to detail the guild's area of influence, and the assassin was indeed surprised at how much Pook's grand old guild had frayed at the edges. Streets that had once been well within Pook's domain were far out of reach now, for those avenues considered borderlands between various operations were much closer to the guild house.

Entreri hardly cared for the prosperity or weakness of Bodeau's operation. This was a survival call and nothing more. He was only trying to get a feeling for the current layout of Calimport's underbelly so that he might not inadvertently bring the wrath of any particular guild down upon him.

LaValle went on to tell of the lieutenants, speaking highly of the potential of young Chalsee and warning Entreri in a deadly serious tone, but one that hardly seemed to stir the assassin, of Dog Perry.

"Watch him closely," LaValle said again, noting the assassin's almost bored expression. "Dog Perry was beside me when we scried you, and he was far from happy to see Artemis Entreri returned to Calimport. Your mere presence poses a threat to him, for he commands a fairly high price as an assassin, and not just for Quentin Bodeau." Still garnering no obvious response, LaValle pressed even harder. "He wants to be the next Artemis Entreri," the wizard said bluntly.

That brought a chuckle from the assassin, not one of doubt concerning Dog Perry's abilities to fulfill his dream or one of any flattery. Entreri was amused by the fact that this Dog Perry hardly understood that which he sought, for if he did, he would turn his desires elsewhere.

"He may see your return as more than an inconvenience," LaValle warned. "Perhaps as a threat, or even worse . . . as an opportunity."

"You do not like him," Entreri reasoned.

"He is a killer without discipline and thus hardly predictable," the wizard replied. "A blind man's flying arrow. If I knew for certain that he was coming after me, I would hardly fear him. It is the often irrational actions of the man that keep us all a bit worried."

"I hold no aspirations for Bodeau's position," Entreri assured the wizard after a long moment of silence. "Nor do I have any intention of impaling myself on the dagger of Dog Perry. Thus you will show no disloyalty to Bodeau by keeping me informed, wizard, and I expect at least that much from you."

"If Dog Perry comes after you, you will be told," LaValle promised, and Entreri believed him. Dog Perry was an upstart, a young hopeful who desired to strengthen his reputation with a single thrust of his dagger. But LaValle understood the truth of Entreri, the assassin knew, and while the wizard might become nervous indeed if he invoked the wrath of Dog Perry, he would find himself truly terrified if ever he learned that Artemis Entreri wanted him dead.

Entreri sat a moment longer, considering the paradox of his reputation. Because of his years of work, many might seek to kill him, but, for the same reasons, many others would fear to go against him and indeed would work for him.

Of course, if Dog Perry did manage to kill him, then LaValle's loyalty to Entreri would come to an abrupt end, transferred immediately to the new king assassin.

To Artemis Entreri it all seemed so perfectly useless.

* * * * *

"You do not see the possibilities here," Dog Perry scolded, working hard to keep his voice calm, though in truth he wanted to throttle the nervous young man.

"Have you heard the stories?" Chalsee Anguaine retorted. "He has killed everything from guildmasters to battle mages. Everyone he has decided to kill is dead."

Dog Perry spat in disgust. "That was a younger man," he

replied. "A man revered by many guilds, including the Basadoni House. A man of connections and protection, who had many powerful allies to assist in his assassinations. Now he is alone and vulnerable, and no longer possessed of the quickness of youth."

"We should bide our time and learn more about him and discover why he has returned," Chalsee reasoned.

"The longer we wait, the more Entreri will rebuild his web," Dog Perry argued without hesitation. "A wizard, a guildmaster, spies on the street. No, if we wait then we cannot go against him without considering the possibility that our actions will begin a guild war. You understand the truth of Bodeau, of course, and recognize that under his leadership we would not survive such a war."

"You remain his principal assassin," Chalsee argued.

Dog Perry chuckled at the thought. "I follow opportunities," he corrected. "And the opportunity I see before me now is one that cannot be ignored. If I—if we—kill Artemis Entreri, we will command his previous position."

"Guildless?"

"Guildless," Dog Perry answered honestly. "Or better described as tied to many guilds. A sword for the highest bidder."

"Quentin Bodeau would not accept such a thing," Chalsee said. "He will lose two lieutenants, thus weakening his guild."

"Quentin Bodeau will understand that because his lieutenants now hire to more powerful guilds, his own position will be better secured," Dog Perry replied.

Chalsee considered the optimistic reasoning for a moment, then shook his head doubtfully. "Bodeau would then be vulnerable, perhaps fearing that his own lieutenants might strike against him at the request of another guildmaster."

"So be it," Dog Perry said coldly. "You should be very careful how tightly you tie your future to the likes of Bodeau. The guild erodes under his command, and eventually another guild will absorb us. Those willing to let the strongest conquer may find a new home. Those tied by foolish loyalty to the loser will have their bodies picked clean by beggars in the gutter."

Chalsee looked away, not enjoying this conversation in the least. Until the previous day, until they had learned that Artemis Entreri had returned, he had thought his life and career fairly secure. He was rising through the ranks of a reasonably strong guild. Now Dog Perry seemed intent on upping the stakes, on reaching for a higher level. While Chalsee could understand the allure, he wasn't certain of the true potential. If they succeeded against Entreri, he did not doubt Dog Perry's prediction, but the mere thought of going after Artemis Entreri . . .

Chalsee had been but a boy when Entreri had last left Calimport, had been connected to no guilds and knew none of the many Entreri had slain. By the time Chalsee had joined the underworld circuit, others had claimed the position of primary assassins in Calimport: Marcus the Knife of Pasha Wroning's Guild; the independent Clarissa and her cohorts who ran the brothels serving the nobility of the region—yes, Clarissa's enemies seemed to simply disappear. Then there was Kadran Gordeon of the Basadoni Guild, and perhaps most deadly of all, Slay Targon, the battle mage. None of them had come near to erasing the reputation of Artemis Entreri, even though the end of Entreri's previous Calimport career had been marred by the downfall of the guildmaster he was supposedly serving and by his reputed inability to defeat a certain nemesis, a drow elf, no less.

And now Dog Perry wanted to catapult himself to the ranks of those four notorious assassins with a single kill, and in truth, the plan sounded plausible to Chalsee.

Except, of course, for the little matter of actually killing Entreri.

"The decision is made," Dog Perry said, seemingly sensing Chalsee's private thoughts. "I am going against him . . . with or without your assistance."

The implicit threat behind those words was not lost on Chalsee. If Dog Perry meant to have any chance against

Entreri, there could be no neutral parties. When he proclaimed his intentions to Chalsee, he was bluntly inferring that Chalsee had to either stand with him or against him, to stand in his court or in Entreri's. Considering that Chalsee didn't even know Entreri and feared the man as much as an ally as an enemy, it didn't seem much of a choice.

The two began their planning immediately. Dog Perry insisted that Artemis Entreri would be dead within two days.

* * * * *

"The man is no enemy," LaValle assured Quentin later that same night as the two walked the corridors leading to the guildmaster's private dining hall. "His return to Calimport was not predicated by any desire to reclaim the guild."

"How can you know?" the obviously nervous leader asked. "How can anyone know the mind-set of that one? Ever has he survived through unpredictability."

"There you are wrong," LaValle replied. "Entreri has ever been predictable because he makes no pretense of that which he desires. I have spoken to him."

The admission had Quentin Bodeau spinning about to face the wizard directly. "When?" he stuttered. "Where? You have not left the guild house all this day."

LaValle smiled and tilted his head as he regarded the man—the man who had just foolishly admitted that he was monitoring LaValle's movements. How frightened Quentin must be to go to such lengths. Still, the wizard knew, Quentin realized that LaValle and Entreri were old companions and that if Entreri did desire a return to power in the guild, he would likely enlist LaValle.

"You have no reason not to trust me," LaValle said calmly. "If Entreri wanted the guild back, I would tell you forthwith, that you might surrender leadership and still retain some high-ranking position."

Quentin Bodeau's gray eyes flared dangerously. "Surrender?" he echoed.

"If I led a guild and heard that Artemis Entreri desired my position, I would surely do that!" LaValle said with a laugh that somewhat dispelled the tension. "But have no such fears. Entreri is back in Calimport, 'tis true, but he is no enemy to you."

"Who can tell?" Bodeau replied, starting back down the corridor. LaValle fell into step beside him. "But understand that you are to have no further contacts with the man."

"That hardly seems prudent. Are we not better off understanding his movements?"

"No further contacts," Quentin Bodeau said more forcefully, grabbing LaValle by the shoulder and turning him so he could look directly into the wizard's eyes. "None, and that is not my choice."

"You miss an opportunity, I fear," LaValle started to argue. "Entreri is a friend, a very valuable—"

"None!" Quentin insisted, coming to an abrupt halt to accentuate his point. "Believe me when I say that it would please me greatly to hire the assassin to take care of a few troublemakers among the sewer wererat guild. I have heard that Entreri particularly dislikes the distasteful creatures and that they hold little love for him."

LaValle smiled at the memory. Pasha Pook had been heavily connected with a nasty wererat leader by the name of Rassiter. After Pook's fall, Rassiter had tried to enlist Entreri into a mutually beneficial alliance. Unfortunately for Rassiter, a very angry Entreri hadn't seen things quite that way.

"But we cannot enlist him," Quentin Bodeau went on. "Nor are we . . . are you, to have any further contact with him. These orders have come down to me from the Basadoni Guild, the Rakers' Guild, and Pasha Wroning himself."

LaValle paused, caught off guard by the stunning news. Bodeau had just listed the three most powerful guilds of Calimport's streets.

Quentin paused at the dining room door, knowing that there were attendants inside, wanting to get this settled privately with the wizard. "They have declared Entreri an untouchable," he went on, meaning that no guildmaster, at the risk of street war, was to even speak with the man, let alone have any professional dealings with him.

LaValle nodded, understanding but none too happy about the prospects. It made perfect sense, of course, as would any joint action the three rival guilds could agree upon. They had iced Entreri out of the system for fear that a minor guildmaster might empty his coffers and hire the assassin to kill one of the more prominent leaders. Those in the strongest positions of power preferred the status quo, and they all feared Entreri enough to recognize that he alone might upset that balance. What a testament to the man's reputation! And LaValle, above all others, understood it to be rightly given.

"I understand," he said to Quentin, bowing to show his obedience. "Perhaps when the situation is better clarified we will find our opportunity to exploit my friendship with this very valuable man."

Bodeau managed his first smile in several days, feeling assured by LaValle's seemingly sincere declarations. He was indeed far more at ease as they continued on their way to share an evening meal.

But LaValle was not. He could hardly believe that the other guilds had moved so quickly to isolate Entreri. If that was the case, then he understood that they would be watching the assassin closely—close enough to learn of any attempts against Entreri and to bring about retaliation on any guild so foolish as to try to kill the man.

LaValle ate quickly, then dismissed himself, explaining that he was in the middle of penning a particularly difficult scroll he hoped to finish that night.

He went immediately to his crystal ball, hoping to locate Dog Perry, and was pleased indeed to learn that the fiery man and Chalsee Anguaine were both still within the guild house. He caught up to them on the street level in the main armory. He could guess easily enough why they might be in that particular room.

"You plan to go out this evening?" the wizard calmly asked as he entered.

"We go out every evening," Dog Perry replied. "It is our job, is it not?"

"A few extra weapons?" LaValle asked suspiciously, noting that both men had daggers strapped to every conceivable retrievable position.

"The guild lieutenant who is not careful is usually dead," Dog Perry replied dryly.

"Indeed," LaValle conceded with a bow. "And, by word of the Basadoni, Wroning, and Rakers' guilds, the guild lieutenant who goes after Artemis Entreri is doing no favors for his master."

The blunt declaration gave both men pause. Dog Perry worked through it quickly and calmly, getting back to his preparations with no discernible trace of guilt upon his blank expression. But Chalsee, less experienced by far, showed some clear signs of distress. LaValle knew he had hit the target directly. They were going after Entreri this very night.

"I would have thought you would consult with me first," the wizard remarked, "to learn his whereabouts, of course, and perhaps see some of the defenses he obviously has set in place."

"You babble, wizard," Dog Perry insisted. "I have many duties to attend and have no time for your foolishness." He slammed the door of the weapons locker as he finished, then walked right past LaValle. A nervous Chalsee Anguaine fell into step behind him, glancing back many times.

LaValle considered the cold treatment and recognized that Dog Perry had indeed decided to go after Entreri and had also decided that LaValle could not be trusted as far as the dangerous assassin was concerned. Now the wizard, in considering all the possibilities, found his own dilemma. If Dog Perry succeeded in killing Entreri the dangerous young man who had just pointedly declared himself no friend of LaValle's would gain immensely in stature and power (if the other guilds did not decide to kill him for his rash actions). But if Entreri won, which LaValle deemed most likely, then he might not appreciate the fact that LaValle had not contacted him with any warning, as they had agreed.

And yet LaValle could not dare to use his magics and contact Entreri. If the other guilds were watching the assassin, such forms of contact would be easily detected and traced.

A very distressed LaValle went back to his room and sat for a long while in the darkness. In either scenario, whether Dog Perry or Entreri proved victorious, the guild might be in for more than a little trouble. Should he go to Quentin Bodeau? he wondered, but then he dismissed the thought, realizing that Quentin would do little more than pace the floor and chew his fingernails. Dog Perry was out in the streets now, and Quentin had no means to recall him.

Should he gaze into his crystal ball and try to learn of the battle? Again, LaValle had to consider that any magical contact, even if it was no more than silent scrying, might be detected by the wizards hired by the more powerful guilds and might then implicate LaValle.

So he sat in the darkness, wondering and worrying, as the hours slipped by.

Chapter 6
LEAVING THE DALE BEHIND

rizzt watched every move the barbarian made—the way Wulfgar sat opposite him across the fire, the way the man went at his dinner—looking for some hint of the barbarian's mind-set. Had the battle with the giants helped? Had Drizzt "run the horse" as he had explained his hopes to Regis? Or was Wulfgar in worse shape now than before the battle? Was he more consumed by this latest guilt, though his actions, or inaction, hadn't really cost them anything?

Wulfgar had to recognize that he had not performed well at the beginning of the battle, but had he, in his own mind, made up for that error with his subsequent actions?

Drizzt was as perceptive to such emotions as anyone alive, but, in truth, he could not get the slightest read of the barbarian's inner turmoil. Wulfgar moved methodically, mechanically, as he had since his return from Errtu's clutches, going through the motions of life itself without any outward sign of pain, satisfaction, relief, or anything else. Wulfgar was existing, but hardly living. If there remained a flicker of passion within those sky-blue orbs, Drizzt could not see it. Thus, the drow ranger was left with the impression that the battle with the giants had been inconsequential, had neither bolstered the barbarian's desire to live nor had placed any further burdens upon Wulfgar. In looking at his friend now, the man tearing a piece of fowl from the bone, his expression unchanging and unrevealing, Drizzt had to admit to himself that he had not only run out of answers but out of places to look for answers.

Catti-brie moved over and sat down beside Wulfgar then, and the barbarian did pause to regard her. He even managed a little smile for her benefit. Perhaps she might succeed where he had failed, the drow thought. He and Wulfgar had been friends, to be sure, but the barbarian and Catti-brie had shared something much deeper than that.

The thought of it brought a tumult of opposing feelings into Drizzt's gut. On the one hand he cared deeply for Wulfgar and wanted nothing more in all the world than for the barbarian to heal his emotional scars. On the other hand, seeing Catti-brie close to the man pained him. He tried to deny it, tried to elevate himself above it, but it was there, and it was a fact, and it would not go away.

He was jealous.

With great effort, the drow sublimated those feelings enough to honestly leave the couple alone. He went to join Bruenor and Regis and couldn't help but contrast the halfling's beaming face as he devoured his third helping with that of Wulfgar, who seemed to be eating only to keep his body alive. Pragmatism against pure pleasure.

"We'll be out o' the dale tomorrow," Bruenor was saying, pointing out the dark silhouettes of the mountains, looming much larger to the south and east. Indeed, the wagon had turned the corner and they were heading south now, no longer west. The wind, which always filled the ears in Icewind Dale, had died to the occasional gust.

"How's me boy?" Bruenor asked when he noticed the dark elf.

Drizzt shrugged.

"Ye could've got him killed, ye durned fool elf," the dwarf huffed. "Ye could've got us all killed. And not for the first time!"

"And not for the last," Drizzt promised with a smile, bowing low. He knew that Bruenor was playing with him here, that the dwarf loved a good fight as much as he did, particularly one against giants. Bruenor had been upset with him, to be sure, but only because Drizzt hadn't included him in the original battle plans. The brief but brutal fight had long since exorcised that grudge from Bruenor, and so now he was just teasing the drow as a means of relieving his honest concerns for Wulfgar.

"Did ye see his face when we battled?" the dwarf asked more earnestly. "Did ye see him when Rumblebelly showed up with his stinkin' giant friend and it appeared as if me boy was about to be squished flat?"

Drizzt admitted that he did not. "I was engaged with my own concerns at the time," he explained. "And with Guenhwyvar's peril."

"Nothing," Bruenor declared. "Nothing at all. No anger as he lifted his hammer to throw it at the giants."

"The warrior sublimates his anger to keep in conscious control," the drow reasoned.

"Bah, not like that," Bruenor retorted. "I saw rage in me boy when we fought Errtu on the ice island, rage beyond anything me old eyes've ever seen. And how I'd like to be seein' it again. Anger, rage, even fear!"

"I saw him when I arrived at the battle," Regis admitted. "He did not know that the new and huge giant would be an ally, and if it was not, if it had joined in on the side of the other giants, then Wulfgar would have easily been killed, for he had no defense against our angle from his open ledge. And yet he was not afraid at all. He looked right up at the giant, and all I saw was . . ."

"Resignation," the drow finished for him. "Acceptance of whatever fate might throw at him."

"I'm not for understanding." Bruenor admitted.

Drizzt had no answers for him. He had his suspicions, of course, that Wulfgar's trauma had been too great and had thus stolen from him his hopes and dreams, his passions and purpose, but he could find no way to put that into words that the ever-pragmatic dwarf might understand. He thought it ironic, in a sense, for the closest example of similar behavior he could recall was Bruenor's own, soon after Wulfgar had fallen to the yochlol. The dwarf had wandered aimlessly through the halls for days on end, grieving.

Yes, Drizzt realized, that was the key word. Wulfgar was grieving.

Bruenor would never understand, and Drizzt wasn't sure that he understood.

"Time to go," Regis remarked, drawing the dark elf from his contemplation. Drizzt looked to the halfling, then to Bruenor.

"Camlaine's invited us to a game o' bones," Bruenor explained. "Come along, elf. Yer eyes see better'n most, and I might be needing ye."

Drizzt glanced back to the fire, to Wulfgar and Catti-brie, sitting very close and talking. He noted that Catti-brie wasn't doing all of the speaking. She had somehow engaged Wulfgar, even had him a bit animated in his discussion. A big part of Drizzt wanted to stay right there and watch their every move, but he wouldn't give in to that weakness, so he went with Bruenor and Regis to watch the game of bones.

* * * * *

"Ye cannot know our pain at seeing the ceiling fall in on ye," Catti-brie said, gently moving the conversation to that fateful day in the bowels of Mithral Hall. Up to now, she and Wulfgar had been sharing happier memories of previous fights, battles in which the companions had overwhelmed monsters and put down threats without so high a price.

Wulfgar had even joined in, telling of his first battle with Bruenor—against Bruenor—when he had broken his standard staff over the dwarf's head, only to have the stubborn little creature swipe his legs out from under him and leave him unconscious on the field. As the conversation wound on, Catti-brie focused on another pivotal event: the crafting of Aegis-fang. What a labor of love that had been, the pinnacle of Bruenor's amazing career as a smith, done purely out of the dwarf's affection for Wulfgar.

"If he hadn't loved ye so, he'd ne'er been able to make so great a weapon," she had explained. When she saw that her words were getting through to the pained man she had shifted the conversation subtly again, to the reverential treatment Bruenor had shown the warhammer after Wulfgar's apparent demise. And that, of course, had brought Catti-brie to the discussion of the day of Wulfgar's fall, to the memory of the evil yochlol.

To her great relief, Wulfgar had not tightened up when she went in this direction, but had stayed with her, hearing her words and adding his own when they seemed relevant.

"All the strength went from me body," Catti-brie went on. "And never have I seen Bruenor closer to breaking. But we went on and started fighting in yer name, and woe to our enemies then."

A distant look came into Wulfgar's light eyes and the woman went silent, giving him time to digest her words. She thought he would respond, but he did not, and the seconds slipped away quietly.

Catti-brie moved closer to him and put her arm about his back, resting her head on his strong shoulder. He didn't push her away, even shifted so they would both be more comfortable. The woman had hoped for more, had hoped to get Wulfgar into an emotional release. But while she hadn't achieved quite that, she recognized that she had gotten more than she could have rightfully expected. The love had not resurfaced, but neither had the rage.

It would take time.

The group did indeed roll out of Icewind Dale the next morning, a distinction made clear by the shifting wind. In the dale, the wind came from the northeast, rolling down off the cold waters of the Sea of Moving Ice. At the juncture to points south, east, and north of the bulk of the mountains, the wind blew constantly no longer, but was more a matter of gusts than the incessant whistle through the dale. And now, moving more to the south, the wind again kicked up, swirling against the towering Spine of the World. Unlike the cold breeze that gave its name to Icewind Dale, this was a gentle blow. The winds wafted up from warmer climes to the south or off the warmer waters of the Sword Coast, hitting against the blocking mountains and swirling back.

Drizzt and Bruenor spent most of the day away from the wagon, both to scout a perimeter about the steady but slow pacing team and to give some privacy to Catti-brie and Wulfgar. The woman was still talking, still trying to bring the man to a better place and time. Regis rode all the day long nestled in the back of the wagon among the generous-smelling foodstuffs.

It proved to be a quiet and uneventful day of travel, except for one point where Drizzt found a particularly disturbing track, that of a huge, booted giant.

"Rumblebelly's friend?" Bruenor asked, bending low beside the ranger as he inspected the footprint.

"So I would guess," Drizzt replied.

"Durned halfling put more of a spell than he should've on the thing," Bruenor grumbled.

Drizzt, who understood the power of the ruby pendant and the nature of enchantments in general, could not agree. He knew that the giant, no stupid creature, had been released from any spell Regis had woven soon after leaving the group. Likely, before they were miles apart, the giant had begun to wonder why in the world he had ever deigned to help the halfling and his strange group of friends. Then, soon after that, he had either forgotten the whole incident or was angry indeed at having been so deceived.

And now the behemoth seemed to be shadowing them, Drizzt realized, noting the general course of the tracks.

Perhaps it was mere coincidence, or perhaps even a different giant—Icewind Dale had no shortage of giants, after all. Drizzt could not be sure, and so, when he and Bruenor returned to the group for their evening meal, they said nothing about the footprints or about increasing the night watch. Drizzt did go off on his own, though, as much to get away from the continuing scene between Catti-brie and

Wulfgar as to scout for any rogue giants. There in the dark of night, he could be alone with his thoughts and his fears, could wage his own emotional wars and remind himself over and over that Catti-brie alone could decide the course of her life.

Every time he recalled an incident highlighting how intelligent and honest the woman had always been, he was comforted. When the full moon began its lazy ascent over the distant waters of the Sword Coast, the drow felt strangely warm. Though he could hardly see the glow of the campfire, he understood that he was truly among friends.

* * * * *

Wulfgar looked deeply into her blue eyes and knew that she had purposefully brought him to this point, had smoothed the jagged edges of his battered consciousness slowly and deliberately, had massaged the walls of anger until her gentle touch had rubbed them into transparency. And now she wanted, she demanded, to look behind those walls, wanted to see the demons that so tormented Wulfgar.

Catti-brie sat quietly, calmly, patiently waiting. She had coaxed some specific horror stories out of the man and then had probed deeper, had asked him to lay bare his soul and his terror, something she knew could not be easy for the proud and strong man.

But Wulfgar hadn't rebuffed her. He sat now, his thoughts whirling, his gaze locked firmly by hers, his breath coming in gasps, his heart pounding in his huge chest.

"For so long I held on to you," he said quietly. "Down there, among the smoke and the dirt, I held fast to an image of my Catti-brie. I kept it right before me at all times. I did."

He paused to catch his breath, and Catti-brie placed a gentle hand on his.

"So many sights that a man was not meant to view," Wulfgar said quietly, and Catti-brie saw a hint of moisture in his light eyes. "But I fought them all with an image of you."

Catti-brie offered a smile, but that did little to comfort Wulfgar.

"He used it against me," the man went on, his tone lowering, becoming almost a growl. "Errtu knew my thoughts and turned them against me. He showed me the finish of the yochlol fight, the creature pushing through the rubble, falling over you and tearing you to pieces. Then it went for Bruenor. . . ."

"Was it not the yochlol that brought you to the lower planes?" Catti-brie asked, trying to use logic to break the demonic spell.

"I do not remember," Wulfgar admitted. "I remember the fall of the stones, the pain of the yochlol's bite tearing into my chest, and then only blackness until I awakened in the court of the Spider Queen.

"But even that image . . . you do not understand! The one thing I could hold onto Errtu perverted and turned against me. The one hope left in my heart burned away and left me empty."

Catti-brie moved closer, her face barely an inch from Wulfgar's. "But hope rekindles," she said softly. "Errtu is gone, banished for a hundred years, and the Spider Queen and her hellish drow minions have shown no interest in Drizzt for years. That road has ended, it seems, and so many new ones lie before us. The road to the Spirit Soaring and Cadderly. From there to Mithral Hall perhaps, and then, if we choose, we might go to Waterdeep and Captain Deudermont, take a wild voyage on *Sea Sprite*, cutting the waves and chasing pirates.

"What possibilities lie before us!" she went on, her smile wide, her blue eyes flashing with excitement. "But first we must make peace with our past."

Wulfgar heard her well, but he only shook his head, reminding her that it might not be as easy as she made it sound. "For all those years you thought I was dead," he said. "And so I thought of you for that time. I thought you killed, and Bruenor killed, and Drizzt cut apart on the altar of some vile drow matron. I surrendered hope because there was none."

"But you see the lie," Catti-brie reasoned. "There is always hope, there must always be hope. That is the lie of Errtu's evil kind. The lie about them, and the lie that is them. They steal hope, because without hope there is no strength. Without hope there is no freedom. In slavery of the heart does a demon find its greatest pleasures."

Wulfgar took a deep, deep breath, trying to digest it all, balancing the logical truths of Catti-brie's words—and of the simple fact that he had indeed escaped Errtu's clutches—against the pervasive pain of memory.

Catti-brie, too, spent a long moment digesting all that Wulfgar had shown to her over the past days. She understood now that it was more than pain and horror that bound her friend. Only one emotion could so cripple a man. In replaying his memories within his own mind, Wulfgar had found some wherein he had surrendered, wherein he had given in to the desires of Errtu or the demon's minions, wherein he had lost his courage or his defiance. Yes, it was obvious to Catti-brie, staring hard at the man now that guilt above all else was the enduring demon of Wulfgar's time with Errtu.

Of course to her that seemed absurd. She could readily forgive anything Wulfgar had said or done to survive the decadence of the Abyss. Anything at all. But it was not absurd, she quickly reminded herself, for it was painted clearly on the big man's pained features.

Wulfgar squinted his eyes shut and gritted his teeth. She was right, he told himself repeatedly. The past was past, an experience dismissed, a lesson learned. Now they were all together again, healthy and on the road of adventure. Now he had learned the errors of his previous engagement to Catti-brie and could look at her with fresh hopes and desires.

She recognized a measure of calm come over the man as he opened his eyes again to stare back at her. And then he came forward, kissing her softly, just brushing his lips against hers as if asking permission.

Catti-brie glanced all around and saw that they were indeed alone. Though the others were not so far away, those who were not asleep were too engaged in their gambling to take note of anything.

Wulfgar kissed her again, a bit more urgently, forcing her to consider her feelings for the man. Did she love him? As a friend, surely, but was she ready to take that love to a different level?

Catti-brie honestly did not know. Once she had decided to give her love to Wulfgar, to marry him and bear his children, to make her life with him. But that was so many years ago, a different time, a different place. Now she had feelings for another, perhaps, though in truth, she hadn't really examined those feelings any deeper than she had her current feelings for Wulfgar.

And she hadn't the time to examine them now, for Wulfgar kissed her again passionately. When she didn't respond in kind, he backed off to arms' length, staring at her hard.

Looking at him then, on the brink of disaster, on a precipice between past and future, Catti-brie came to understand that she had to give this to him. She pulled him back and initiated another kiss, and they embraced deeply, Wulfgar guiding her to the ground, rolling about, touching, caressing, fumbling with their clothes.

She let him lose himself in the passion, let him lead with touches and kisses, and she took comfort in the role she had accepted, took hope that their encounter this night would help bring Wulfgar back to the world of the living.

And it was working. Wulfgar knew it, felt it. He bared his heart and soul to her, threw away his defenses, basked in the feel of her, in the sweet smell of her, in the very softness of her.

He was free! For those first few moments he was free, and it was glorious and beautiful, and so real.

He rolled to his back, his strong hug rolling Catti-brie atop him. He bit softly on the nape of her neck, then, nearing a point of ecstasy, leaned his head back so that he could look into her eyes and share the moment of joy.

A leering succubus, vile temptress of the Abyss, stared back at him.

Wulfgar's thoughts careened back across Icewind Dale,

back to the Sea of Moving Ice, to the ice cave and the fight with Errtu, then back beyond that, back to the swirling smoke and the horrors. It had all been a lie, he realized. The fight, the escape, the rejoining with his friends. All a lie perpetrated by Errtu to rekindle his hope that the demon could then snuff it out once again. All a lie, and he was still in the Abyss, dreaming of Catti-brie while entwining with a horrid succubus.

His powerful hand clamped under the creature's chin and pushed it away. His second hand came across in a vicious punch and then he lifted the beast into the air above his prone form and heaved it away, bouncing across the dirt. With a roar, Wulfgar pulled himself to his feet, fumbling to lift and straighten his pants. He staggered for the fire and, ignoring the pain, reached in to grab a burning branch, then turned back to attack the wicked succubus.

Turned back to attack Catti-brie.

He recognized her then, half-undressed, staggering to her hands and knees, blood dripping freely from her nose. She managed to look up at him. There was no rage, only confusion on her battered face. The weight of guilt nearly buckled the barbarian's strong legs.

"I did not . . ." he stammered. "Never would I . . ." With a gasp and a stifled cry, Wulfgar rushed across the campsite, tossing the burning stick aside, gathering up his pack and warhammer. He ran out into the dark of night, into the ultimate darkness of his tormented mind.

Chapter 7
KELP-ENWALLED

You cannot come in," the squeaky voice said from behind the barricade. "Please, sir, I beg you. Go away."

Entreri hardly found the halfling's nervous tone amusing, for the implications of the shut-out rang dangerously in his mind. He and Dwahvel had cut a deal—a mutually beneficial deal and one that seemed to favor the halfling, if anyone—and yet, now it seemed as if Dwahvel was going back on her word. Her doorman would not even let the assassin into the Copper Ante. Entreri entertained the thought of kicking in the barricade, but only briefly. He reminded himself that halflings were often adept at setting traps. Then he thought he might slip his dagger through the slit in the boards, into the impertinent doorman's arm, or thumb, or whatever other target presented itself. That was the beauty of Entreri's dagger: he could stick someone anywhere and suck the life-force right out of him.

But again, it was a fleeting thought, more of a fantasy wrought of frustration than any action the ever-careful Entreri would seriously consider.

"So I shall go," he said calmly. "But do inform Dwahvel that my world is divided between friends and enemies." He turned and started away, leaving the doorman in a fluster.

"My, but that sounded like a threat," came another voice before Entreri had moved ten paces down the street.

The assassin stopped and considered a small crack in the wall of the Copper Ante, a peep hole, he realized, and likely an arrow slit.

"Dwahvel," he said with a slight bow.

To his surprise, the crack widened and a panel slid aside. Dwahvel walked out in the open. "So quick to name enemies," she said, shaking her head, her curly brown locks bouncing gaily.

"But I did not," the assassin replied. "Though it did anger me that you apparently decided not to go through with our deal."

Dwahvel's face tightened suddenly, stealing the up-to-then lighthearted tone. "Kelp-enwalled," she explained, an expression more common to the fishing boats than the streets, but one Entreri had heard before. On the fishing boats, "kelp-enwalling" referred to the practice of isolating particularly troublesome pincer crabs, which had to be delivered live to market, by building barricades of kelp strands about them. The term was less literal, but with similar meaning, on the street. A kelp-enwalled person had been declared off-limits, surrounded and isolated by barricades of threats.

Suddenly Entreri's expression also showed the strain.

"The order came from greater guilds than mine, from guilds that could, and would, burn the Copper Ante to the ground and kill all of my fellows with hardly a thought," Dwahvel said with a shrug. "Entreri is kelp-enwalled, so they said. You cannot blame me for refusing your entrance."

Entreri nodded. He above many others could appreciate pragmatism for the sake of survival. "Yet you chose to come out and speak with me," he said.

Another shrug from Dwahvel. "Only to explain why our deal has ended," she said. "And to ensure that I do not fall

112

into the latter category you detailed for my doorman. I will offer to you this much, with no charge for services. Everyone knows now that you have returned, and your mere presence has made them all nervous. Old Basadoni still rules his guild, but he is in the shadows now, more a figurehead than a leader. Those handling the affairs of the Basadoni Guild, and the other guilds, for that matter, do not know you. But they do know your reputation. Thus they fear you as they fear each other. Might not Pasha Wroning fear that the Rakers have hired Entreri to kill him? Or even within the individual guilds, might those vying for position before the coming event of Pasha Basadoni's death not fear that one of the others has coaxed Entreri back to assure personal ascension?"

Entreri nodded again but replied, "Or is it not possible that Artemis Entreri has merely returned to his home?"

"Of course," Dwahvel said. "But until they all learn the truth of you, they will fear you, and the only way to learn the truth—"

"Kelp-enwalled," the assassin finished. He started to thank Dwahvel for showing the courage of coming out to tell him this much, but he stopped short. He recognized that perhaps the halfling was only following orders, that perhaps this meeting was part of the surveying process.

"Watch well your back," Dwahvel added, moving for the secret door. "You understand that there are many who would like to claim the head of Entreri for their trophy wall."

"What do you know?" the assassin asked, for it seemed obvious to him that Dwahvel wasn't speaking merely in generalities here.

"Before the kelp-enwalling order, my spies went out to learn what they may about the perceptions concerning your return," she explained. "They were asked more questions than they offered and often by young, strong assassins. Watch well your back." And then she was gone, back through the secret door into the Copper Ante.

Entreri just blew a sigh and walked along. He didn't question his return to Calimport, for either way it simply didn't seem important to him. Nor did he start looking more deeply into the shadows that lined the dark street. Perhaps one or more held his killer. Perhaps not.

Perhaps it simply did not matter.

* * * * *

"Perry," Giunta the Diviner said to Kadran Gordeon as the two watched the young thug steal along the rooftops, shadowing, from a very safe distance, the movements of Artemis Entreri. "A lieutenant for Bodeau."

"Is he watching?" Kadran asked.

"Hunting," the wizard corrected.

Kadran didn't doubt the man. Giunta's entire life had been spent in observation. This wizard was the watcher, and from the patterns of those he observed he could then predict with an amazing degree of accuracy their next movements.

"Why would Bodeau risk everything to go after Entreri?" the fighter asked. "Surely he knows of the kelp-enwalling order, and Entreri has a long alliance with that particular guild."

"You presume that Bodeau even knows of this," Giunta explained. "I have seen this one before. Dog Perry, he is called, though he fancies himself 'the Heart.'"

That nickname rang a chime of recognition in Kadran. "For his practice of cutting a still-beating heart from the chest of his victims," the man remarked. "A brash young killer," he added, nodding, for now it made sense.

"Not unlike one I know," Giunta said slyly, turning his gaze over Kadran.

Kadran smiled in reply. Indeed, Dog Perry was not so unlike a younger Kadran, brash and skilled. The years had taught Kadran some measure of humility, however, though many of those who knew him well thought he was still a bit deficient in that regard. He looked more closely at Dog Perry now, the man moving silently and carefully along the rim of a rooftop. Yes, there seemed a resemblance to the young thug Kadran used to be. Less polished and less wise, obviously, for even in his cocky youth Kadran doubted that he would have gone after the likes of Artemis Entreri so soon after the man's return to Calimport and obviously without too much preparation.

"He must have allies in the region," Kadran remarked to Giunta. "Seek out the other rooftops. Surely the young thug would not be foolish enough to hunt Entreri alone."

Giunta widened his scan. He found Entreri moving easily along the main boulevard and recognized many other characters in the area, regulars who held no known connection to Bodeau's guild or to Dog Perry.

"Him," the wizard explained, pointing to another figure weaving in and out of the shadows, following the same route as Entreri, but far, far behind. "Another of Bodeau's men, I believe."

"He does not seem overly intent on joining the fight," Kadran noted, for the man seemed to hesitate with every step. He was so far behind Entreri and losing ground with each passing second that he could have jumped out and run full speed at the man down the middle of the street without being noticed by the pursued assassin.

"Perhaps he is merely observing," Giunta remarked as he moved the focus of the crystal ball back to the two assassins, their paths beginning to intersect, "following his ally at the request of Bodeau to see how Dog Perry fares. There are many possibilities, but if he does mean to get into the fight beside Dog Perry, then he should run fast. Entreri is not one to drag out a battle, and it seems—"

He stopped abruptly as Dog Perry moved to the edge of a roof and crouched low, muscles tensing. The young assassin had found his spot of ambush, and Entreri turned into the ally, seemingly playing into the man's hand.

"We could warn him," Kadran said, licking his lips nervously.

"Entreri is already on his guard," the wizard explained. "Surely he has sensed my scrying. A man of his talents could not be magically looked at without his knowledge." the wizard gave a little chuckle. "Farewell, Dog Perry," he said.

Even as the words came out of his mouth, the would-be assassin leaped down from the roof, hitting the ground in a rush barely three strides behind Entreri, closing so fast that almost any man would have been skewered before he even registered the noise behind him.

Almost any man.

Entreri spun as Dog Perry rushed in, Perry's slender sword leading. A brush of the spinning assassin's left hand, holding the ample folds of his cloak as further protection, deflected the blow wide. Ahead went Entreri, a sudden step, pushing up with his left hand, lifting Dog Perry's arm as he went. He moved right under the now off-balance would-be killer, stabbing up into the armpit with his jeweled dagger as he passed. Then, so quickly that Dog Perry never had a chance to compensate, so quickly that Kadran and Giunta hardly noticed the subtle turn, he pivoted back, turning to face Dog Perry's back. Entreri tore the dagger free and flipped it to his descending left hand, snapped his right hand around to the chin of the would-be killer, and kicked the man in the back of the knees, buckling his legs and forcing him back and down. The older assassin's left hand stabbed up, driving the dagger under the back of Dog Perry's skull and deep into his brain.

Entreri retracted the dagger immediately and let the dead man fall to the ground, blood pooling under him, so quickly and so efficiently that Entreri didn't even have a drop of blood on him.

Giunta, laughing, pointed to the end of the ally, back on the street, where the stunned companion of Dog Perry took one look at the victorious Entreri, turned on his heel, and ran away.

"Yes, indeed," Giunta remarked. "Let the word go out on the streets that Artemis Entreri has returned."

Kadran Gordeon spent a long while staring at the dead man. He struck his customary pensive pose, pursing his lips so that his long and curvy mustache tilted on his dark face. He had entertained the idea of going after Entreri himself, and now was quite plainly shocked by the sheer skill of the man. It was Gordeon's first true experience with Entreri, and suddenly he understood that the man had come by his reputation honestly.

But Kadran Gordeon was not Dog Perry, was far more skilled than that young bumbler. Perhaps he would indeed pay a visit to this former king of assassins.

"Exquisite," came Sharlotta's voice behind the two. They turned to see the woman staring past them into the image in Giunta's large crystal ball. "Pasha Basadoni told me I would be impressed. How well he moves!"

"Shall I repay the Bodeau guild for breaking the kelpenwalling order?" Kadran asked.

"Forget them," Sharlotta retorted, moving closer, her eyes twinkling with admiration. "Concentrate our attention upon that one alone. Find him and enlist him. Let us find a job for Artemis Entreri."

* * * * *

Drizzt found Catti-brie sitting on the back lip of the wagon. Regis sat next to her, holding a cloth to her face. Bruenor, axe swinging dangerously at his side, pacing back and forth, grumbled a stream of curses. The drow knew at once what had happened, the simple truth of it anyway, and when he considered it, he was not so surprised that Wulfgar had struck out.

"He did not mean to do it," Catti-brie said to Bruenor, trying to calm the volatile dwarf. She, too, was obviously angry, but she, like Drizzt, understood better the truth of Wulfgar's emotional turmoil. "I'm thinking he wasn't seein' me," the woman went on, speaking more to Drizzt. "Looking back at Errtu's torments, by me guess."

Drizzt nodded. "As it was at the beginning of the fight with the giants," he said.

"And so ye're to let it go?" Bruenor roared in reply. "Ye're thinkin' that ye can't hold the boy responsible? Bah! I'll give him a beating that'll make his years with Errtu seem easy! Go and get him, elf. Bring him back that he can tell me girl

117

he's sorry. Then he can tell me. Then he can find me fist in his mouth and take a good long sleep to think about it!" With a growl, Bruenor drove his axe deep into the ground. "I heared too much o' this Errtu," he declared. "Ye can't be livin' in what's already done!"

Drizzt had little doubt that if Wulfgar walked back into camp at that moment, it would take him, Catti-brie, Regis, Camlaine, and all his companions just to pull Bruenor off the man. And in looking at Catti-brie, one eye swollen, her bloody nose bright red, the ranger wasn't sure he would be too quick to hold the dwarf back.

Without another word Drizzt turned and walked away, out of the camp and into the darkness. Wulfgar couldn't have gone far, he knew, though the night was not so dark with the big moon shining bright across the tundra. Just outside the campsite he took out his figurine. Guenhwyvar led the way, rushing into the darkness and growling back to guide the running ranger.

To Drizzt's surprise the trail led neither south nor back to the northeast and Ten Towns, but straight east, toward the towering black peaks of the Spine of the World. Soon Guenhwyvar led him into the foothills, dangerous territory indeed, for the high bluffs and rocky outcroppings provided fine ambush points for lurking monsters or highwaymen.

Perhaps, Drizzt mused, that was exactly why Wulfgar had come this way. Perhaps he was looking for trouble, for a fight, or maybe even for some giant to surprise him and end his pain.

Drizzt skidded to a stop and blew a long and profound sigh, for what seemed most unsettling to him was not the thought that Wulfgar was inviting disaster, but his own reaction to it. For at that moment, the image of hurt Catti-brie clear in his mind, the ranger almost—*almost*—thought that such an ending to Wulfgar's tale would not be such a terrible thing.

A call from Guenhwyvar brought him from his thoughts. He sprinted up a steep incline, leaped to another boulder, then skittered back down to another trail. He heard a growl—from Wulfgar and not the panther—then a crash as Aegis-fang slammed against some stone. The crash was near to Guenhwyvar, Drizzt realized, from the sound of the hit and the cat's ensuing protesting roars.

Drizzt leaped over a stone lip, rushed across a short expanse, and jumped down a small drop to land lightly right beside the big man just as the warhammer magically reappeared in his grasp. For a moment, considering the wild look in Wulfgar's eyes, the drow thought he would have to draw his blades and fight the man, but Wulfgar calmed quickly. He seemed merely defeated, his rage thrown out.

"I did not know," he said, slumping back against the stone.

"I understand," Drizzt replied, holding back his own anger and trying to sound compassionate.

"It was not Catti-brie," Wulfgar went on. "In my thoughts, I mean. I was not with her, but back there, in that place of darkness."

"I know," said Drizzt. "And so does Catti-brie, though I fear we shall have some work ahead of us in calming Bruenor." He ended with a wide and warm smile, but his attempt to lighten the situation was lost on Wulfgar.

"He is right to be outraged," the barbarian admitted. "As I am outraged, in a way you cannot begin to understand."

"Do not underestimate the value of friendship," Drizzt answered. "I once made a similar error, nearly to the destruction of all that I hold dear."

Wulfgar shook his head through every word of it, unable to find any footing for agreement. Black waves of despair washed over him, burying him. What he had done was beyond forgiveness, especially since he realized, and admitted to himself, that it would likely happen again. "I am lost," he said softly.

"And we will all help you to find your way," Drizzt answered, putting a comforting hand on the big man's shoulder.

Wulfgar pushed him away. "No," he said firmly, and then he gave a little laugh. "There is no way to find. The darkness of Errtu endures. Under that shadow, I cannot be who you want me to be."

"We only want you to remember who you once were," the drow replied. "In the ice cave, we rejoiced to find Wulfgar, son of Beornegar, returned to us."

"He was not," the big man corrected. "I am not the man who left you in Mithral Hall. I can never be that man again."

"Time will heal—" Drizzt started to say, but Wulfgar silenced him with a roar.

"No!" he cried. "I do not ask for healing. I do not wish to become again the man that I was. Perhaps I have learned the truth of the world, and that truth has shown me the errors of my previous ways."

Drizzt stared hard at the man. "And the better way is to punch an unsuspecting Catti-brie?" he asked, his voice dripping with sarcasm, his patience for the man fast running out.

Wulfgar locked stares with Drizzt, and again the drow's hands went to his scimitar hilts. He could hardly believe the level of anger rising within him, overwhelming his compassion for his sorely tormented friend. He understood that if Wulfgar did try to strike at him, he would fight the man without holding back.

"I look at you now and remember that you are my friend," Wulfgar said, relaxing his tense posture enough to assure Drizzt that he did not mean to strike out. "And yet those reminders come only with strong willpower. Easier it is for me to hate you, and hate everything around me, and on those occasions when I do not immediately summon the willpower to remember the truth, I will strike out."

"As you did with Catti-brie," Drizzt replied, and his tone was not accusatory, but rather showed a sincere attempt to understand and empathize.

Wulfgar nodded. "I did not even recognize that it was her," he said. "It was just another of Errtu's fiends, the worst kind, the kind that tempted me and defeated my willpower, and then left me not with burns or wounds but with the weight of guilt, with the knowledge of failure. I wanted to resist.... I ..."

"Enough, my friend," Drizzt said quietly. "You shoulder blame where you should not. It was no failure of Wulfgar, but the unending cruelty of Errtu."

"It was both," said a defeated Wulfgar. "And that failure compounds with every moment of weakness."

"We will speak with Bruenor," Drizzt assured him. "We will use this incident as a guide and learn from it."

"You may say to Bruenor whatever you choose," the big man said, his tone suddenly turning ice cold once more. "For I will not be there to hear it."

"You will return to your own people?" Drizzt asked, though he knew in his heart that the barbarian wasn't saying any such thing.

"I will find whatever road I choose," Wulfgar replied. "Alone."

"I once played this game."

"Game?" the big man echoed incredulously. "I have never been more serious in all my life. Now go back to them, back where you belong. When you think of me, think of the man I once was, the man who would never strike Catti-brie."

Drizzt started to reply, but stopped himself and stood studying his broken friend. In truth, he had nothing to say that might comfort Wulfgar. While he wanted to believe that he and the others could help coax the man back to rational behavior, he wasn't certain of it. Not at all. Would Wulfgar strike out again, at Catti-brie, or at any of them, perhaps hurting one of them severely? Would the big man's return to the group facilitate a true fight between him and Bruenor, or between him and Drizzt? Or would Catti-brie, in self-defense, drive Khazid'hea, her deadly sword, deep into the man's chest? On the surface, these fears all rang as preposterous in the drow's mind, but after watching Wulfgar carefully these past few days, he could not dismiss the troublesome possibility.

And perhaps worst of all, he had to consider his own feelings when he had seen the battered Catti-brie. He hadn't been the least bit surprised.

Wulfgar started away, and Drizzt instinctively grabbed him by the forearm.

Wulfgar spun and threw the drow's hand aside. "Farewell, Drizzt Do'Urden," he said sincerely, and those words conveyed many of his unspoken thoughts to Drizzt. A longing to go with the drow back to the group, a plea that things could be as they had once been, the friends, the companions of the hall, running down the road to adventure. And most of all, in that lucid tone, words spoken so clearly and deliberately and thoughtfully, they brought to Drizzt a sense of finality. He could not stop Wulfgar, short of hamstringing the man with a scimitar. And in his heart, at that terrible moment, he knew that he should not stop Wulfgar.

"Find yourself," Drizzt said, "and then find us."

"Perhaps," was all that Wulfgar could offer. Without looking back, he walked away.

For Drizzt Do'Urden, the walk back to the wagon to rejoin his friends was the longest journey of his life.

Part 2

WALKING THE ROADS
OF DANGER

e each have our own path to tread. That seems such a simple and obvious thought, but in a world of relationships where so many people sublimate their own true feelings and desires in consideration of others, we take many steps off that true path.

In the end, though, if we are to be truly happy, we must follow our hearts and find our way alone. I learned that truth when I walked out of Menzoberranzan and confirmed my path when I arrived in Icewind Dale and found these wonderful friends. After the last brutal fight in Mithral Hall, when half of Menzoberranzan, it seemed, marched to destroy the dwarves, I knew that my path lay elsewhere, that I needed to journey, to find a new horizon on which to set my gaze. Catti-brie knew it too, and because I understood that her desire to go along was not in sympathy to my desires but true to her own heart, I welcomed the company.

We each have our own path to tread, and so I learned, painfully, that fateful morning in the mountains, that Wulfgar had found one that diverged from my own. How I wanted to stop him! How I wanted to plead with him or, if that failed, to beat him into unconsciousness and drag him back to the camp. When we parted, I felt a hole in my heart nearly as profound as that which I had felt when I first learned of his apparent death in the fight against the yochlol.

And then, after I walked away, pangs of guilt layered above the pain of loss. Had I let Wulfgar go so easily because of his relationship with Catti-brie? Was there some place within me that saw my barbarian friend's return as a hindrance to a relationship that I had been building with the woman since we had ridden from Mithral Hall together?

The guilt could find no true hold and was gone by the time I rejoined my companions. As I had my road to walk, and now Wulfgar his, so too would Catti-brie find hers. With me? With Wulfgar? Who could know? But whatever her road, I would not try to alter it in such a manner. I did not let Wulfgar go easily for any sense of personal gain. Not at all, for indeed my heart weighed heavy. No, I let Wulfgar go without much of an argument because I knew that there was nothing I, or our other friends, could do to heal the wounds within him. Nothing I could say to him could bring him solace, and if Catti-brie had begun to make any progress, then surely it had been destroyed in the flick of Wulfgar's fist slamming into her face.

Partly it was fear that drove Wulfgar from us. He believed that he could not control the demons within him and that, in the grasp of those painful recollections, he might truly hurt one of us. Mostly, though, Wulfgar left us because of shame. How could he face Bruenor again after striking Catti-brie? How could he face Catti-brie? What words might he say in apology when in truth, and he knew it, it very well might happen again? And beyond that one act, Wulfgar perceived himself as weak because the images of Errtu's legacy were so overwhelming him. Logically, they were but memories and nothing tangible to attack the strong man. To Wulfgar's pragmatic view of the world, being defeated by mere memories equated to great weakness. In his culture, being defeated in battle is no cause for shame, but running from battle is the highest dishonor. Along that same line of reasoning, being unable to defeat a great monster is acceptable, but being defeated by an intangible thing such as a memory equates with cowardice.

He will learn better, I believe. He will come to understand the he should feel no shame for his inability to cope with the persistent horrors and temptations of Errtu and the Abyss. And then, when he relieves himself from the burden of shame, he will find a way to truly overcome those horrors and dismiss his guilt over the temptations. Only then will he return to Icewind Dale, to those who love him and who will welcome him back eagerly.

Only then.

That is my hope, not my expectation. Wulfgar ran off into the wilds, into the Spine of the World, where yetis and giants and goblin tribes make their homes, where wolves will take their food as they find it, whether hunting a deer or a man. I do not honestly know if he means to come out of the mountains back to the tundra he knows well, or to the more civilized southland, or if he will wander the high and dangerous trails, daring death in an attempt to restore some of the courage he believes he has lost. Or perhaps he will tempt death too greatly, so that it will finally win out and put an end to his pain.

That is my fear.

I do not know. We each have our own roads to tread, and Wulfgar has found his, and it is a path, I understand, that is not wide enough for a companion.

—Drizzt Do'Urden

Chapter 8

INADVERTENT SIGNALS

hey moved somberly, for the thrill of adventure and the joy of being reunited and on the road again had been stolen by Wulfgar's departure. When he returned to camp and explained the barbarian's absence, Drizzt had been truly surprised by the reactions of his companions. At first, predictably, Catti-brie and Regis had screamed that they must go and find the man, while Bruenor just grumbled about "stupid humans." Both the halfling and the woman had calmed quickly, though, and it turned out to be Catti-brie's voice above all the others proclaiming that Wulfgar needed to choose his own course. She was not bitter about the attack and to her credit showed no anger toward the barbarian at all.

But she knew. Like Drizzt, she understood that the inner demons tormenting Wulfgar could not be excised with comforting words from friends, or even through the fury of battle. She had tried and had thought that she was making some progress, but in the end it had become painfully apparent to her that she could do nothing to help the man, that Wulfgar had to help himself.

And so they went on, the four friends and Guenhwyvar,

128

keeping their word to guide Camlaine's wagon out of the dale and along the south road.

That night, Drizzt found Catti-brie on the eastern edge of the encampment, staring out into the blackness, and it was not hard for the drow to figure out what she was hoping to spot.

"He will not return to us any time soon," Drizzt remarked quietly, moving to the woman's side.

Catti-brie glanced at him only briefly, then turned her eyes back to the dark silhouettes of the mountains.

There was nothing to see.

"He chose wrong," the woman said softly after several long and silent moments had slipped past. "I'm knowin' that he has to help himself, but he could've done that among his friends, not out in the wilds."

"He did not want us to witness his most personal battles," Drizzt explained.

"Ever was pride Wulfgar's greatest failing," Catti-brie quickly replied.

"That is the way of his people, the way of his father, and his father's father before him," the ranger said. "The tundra barbarians do not accept weakness in others or in themselves, and Wulfgar believes that his inability to defeat mere memories is naught more than weakness."

Catti-brie shook her head. She didn't have to speak the words aloud, for both she and Drizzt understood that the man was purely wrong in that belief, that, many times, the most powerful foes are those within.

Drizzt reached up then and brushed a finger gently along the side of Catti-brie's nose, the area that had swelled badly from Wulfgar's punch. Catti-brie winced at first, but it was only because she had not expected the touch, and not from any real pain.

"It's not so bad," she said.

"Bruenor might not agree with you," the drow replied.

That brought a smile to Catti-brie's face, for indeed, if Drizzt had brought Wulfgar back soon after the assault, it would have taken all of them to pull the vicious dwarf off the man. But even that had changed now, they both knew. Wulfgar had been as a son to Bruenor for many years, and the dwarf had been purely devastated, more so than any of the others, after the man's apparent death. Now, in the realization that Wulfgar's troubles had taken him from them again, Bruenor sorely missed the man, and surely would forgive him his strike against Catti-brie . . . as long as the barbarian was properly contrite. They all would have forgiven Wulfgar, completely and without judgment, and would have helped him in any way they could to overcome his emotional obstacles. That was the tragedy of it all, for they had no help to offer that would be of any real value.

Drizzt and Catti-brie sat together long into the night, staring at the empty tundra, the woman resting her head on the strong shoulder of the drow.

The next two days and nights on the road proved peacefully uneventful, except that Drizzt more than once spotted the tracks of Regis's giant friend, apparently shadowing their movements. Still, the behemoth made no approach near the camp, so the drow did not become overly concerned. By the middle of the third day after Wulfgar's departure, they came in sight of the city of Luskan.

"Your destination, Camlaine," the drow noted when the driver called out that he could see the distinctive skyline of Luskan, including the treelike structure that marked the city's wizard guild. "It has been our pleasure to travel with you."

"And eat your fine food!" Regis added happily, drawing a laugh from everyone.

"Perhaps if you are still in the southland when we return, and intent on heading back to the dale, we will accompany you again," Drizzt finished.

"And glad we will all be for the company," the merchant replied, warmly clasping the drow's hand. "Farewell, wherever your road may take you, though I offer the parting as a courtesy only, for I do not doubt that you shall fare well indeed! Let the monsters take note of your passing and hide their heads low."

The wagon rolled away, down the fairly smooth road to Luskan. The four friends watched it for a long time.

"We could go in with him," Regis offered. "You are known well enough down there, I would guess," he added to the drow. "Your heritage should not bring us any problems . . ."

Drizzt shook his head before the halfling even finished the thought. "I can indeed walk freely through Luskan," he said, "but my course, our course, is to the southeast. A long, long road lies ahead of us."

"But in Luskan—" Regis started.

"Rumblebelly's thinkin' that me boy might be in there," Bruenor bluntly cut in. From the dwarf's tone it seemed that he, too, considered following the merchant wagon.

"He might indeed," Drizzt said. "And I hope that he is, for Luskan is not nearly as dangerous as the wilds of the Spine of the World."

Bruenor and Regis looked at him curiously, for if he agreed with their reasoning, why weren't they following the merchant?

"If Wulfgar's in Luskan, then better by far that we're turning away now," Catti-brie answered for Drizzt. "We're not wanting to find him now."

"What're ye sayin'?" the flustered dwarf demanded.

"Wulfgar walked away from us," Drizzt reminded. "Of his own accord. Do you believe that three days' time has changed anything?"

"We're not for knowin' unless we ask," said Bruenor, but his tone was less argumentative, and the brutal truth of the situation began to sink in. Of course Bruenor, and all of them, wanted to find Wulfgar and wanted the man to recant his decision to leave. But of course that would not happen.

"If we find him now, we'll only push him further from us," Catti-brie said.

"He will grow angry at first because he will see us as meddling," Drizzt agreed. "And then, when his anger at last fades, if it ever does, he will be even more ashamed of his actions."

Bruenor snorted and threw his hands up in defeat.

They all took a last look at Luskan, hoping that Wulfgar was there, then they walked past the place. They headed southeast, flanking the city, then down the southern road with a week's travel before them to the city of Waterdeep. There they hoped to ride with a merchant ship to the south, to Baldur's Gate, and then up river to the city of Iriaebor. There they would take to the open road again, across several hundred miles of the Shining Plains to Caradoon and the Spirit Soaring. Regis had planned the journey, using maps and merchant sources back in Bryn Shander. The halfling had chosen Waterdeep as their best departure point over the closer Luskan because ships left Waterdeep's great harbor every day, with many traveling to Baldur's Gate. In truth, he wasn't sure, nor were any of the others, if this was the best course or not. The maps available in Icewind Dale were far from complete, and far from current. Drizzt and Catti-brie, the only two of the group to have traveled to the Spirit Soaring, had done so magically, with no understanding of the lay of the land.

Still, despite the careful planning the halfling had done, each of them began doubting their ambitious travel plans throughout that day as they passed the city. Those plans had been formed out of a love for the road and adventure, a desire to take in the sights of their grand world, and a supreme confidence in their abilities to get through. Now, though, with Wulfgar's departure, that love and confidence had been severely shaken. Perhaps they would be better off going into Luskan to the notable wizards' guild and hiring a mage to magically contact Cadderly so that the powerful cleric might wind walk to them and finish this business quickly. Or perhaps the Lords of Waterdeep, renowned throughout the lands for their dedication to justice and their power to carry it out, would take the crystal artifact off the companions' hands and, as Cadderly had vowed, find the means to destroy it.

If any of the four had spoken aloud their mounting doubts about the journey that morning, the trip might have been abandoned. But because of their confusion over Wulfgar's departure, and because none of them wanted to admit that they could not focus on another mission while their dear friend was in danger, they held their tongues, sharing thoughts but not words. By the time the sun disappeared into the vast waters to the west, the city of Luskan and the hopes of finding Wulfgar were long out of sight.

Regis's giant friend, though, continued to shadow their movements. Even as Bruenor, Catti-brie, and the halfling prepared the camp, Drizzt and Guenhwyvar came upon the huge tracks, leading down to a copse of trees less than three hundred yards from the bluff they had chosen as a sight. Now the giant's movements could no longer be dismissed as coincidence, for they had left the Spine of the World far behind, and few giants ever wandered into this civilized region where townsfolk would form militias and hunt them down whenever they were spotted.

By the time Drizzt got back to camp, the halfling was fast asleep, several empty plates scattered about his bedroll. "It is time we confront our large shadow," the ranger explained to the other two as he moved over and gave Regis a good shake.

"So ye're meanin' to let us in on yer battle plans this time," Bruenor replied sarcastically.

"I hope there will be no battle," the drow answered. "To our knowledge, this particular giant has posed no threat to wagons rolling along the road in Icewind Dale, and so I find no reason to fight the creature. Better that we convince it to go back to its home without drawing sword."

A sleepy-eyed Regis sat up and glanced around, then rolled back down under his covers—almost, for quick-handed Drizzt caught him halfway back to the comfort zone and roughly pulled him to his feet.

"Not my watch!" the halfling complained.

"You brought the giant to us, and so you shall convince him to leave," the drow replied.

"The giant?" Regis asked, still not catching on to the meaning of it all.

"Yer big friend," Bruenor explained. "He's followin' us, and we're thinking it's past time he goes home. Now, ye come along with yer tricky gem and make him leave, or we'll cut him down where he stands."

Regis's expression showed that he didn't much like that prospect. The giant had served him well in the fight, and he had to admit a certain fondness for the big brute. He shook his head vigorously, trying to clear the cobwebs, then patted his full belly and retrieved his shoes. Even though he was moving as fast as he ever moved, the others were already out of the encampment by the time he was ready to follow.

Drizzt was first into the copse, with Guenhwyvar flanking him. The drow stayed along the ground, picking a clear route away from dried leaves and snapping twigs, silent as a shadow, while Guenhwyvar sometimes padded along the ground and sometimes took to the secure low branches of thick trees. The giant was making no real effort to conceal itself and even had a fairly large fire going. The light guided the two companions and then the other three trailing them.

Still a dozen yards away, Drizzt heard the rhythmic snoring, but then, barely two steps later he heard a loud rustle as the giant apparently woke up and jumped to his feet. Drizzt froze in place and scanned the area, seeking any scouts who might have alerted the behemoth, but there was nothing, no evident creatures and no noise at all save the continuous gentle hissing of the wind through the new leaves.

Convinced that the giant was alone, the drow moved on, coming to a clearing. The fire and the behemoth, and it was indeed Junger, were plainly visible across the way. Out stepped Drizzt, and the giant hardly seemed surprised.

"Strange that we should meet again," the drow remarked, resting his forearms comfortably across the hilts of his sheathed weapons and assuming an unthreatening posture. "I had thought you returned to your mountain home."

"It bade me otherwise," Junger said, and again the drow was taken aback by the giant's command of language and sophisticated dialect.

"It?" the drow asked.

"Some calls cannot be unanswered, you understand," the giant replied.

"Regis," Drizzt called back over his shoulder, and he heard the commotion as his three friends, all of them quiet by the standards of their respective races but clamorous indeed by the standards of the dark elf, moved through the forest behind him. Hardly turning his head, for he did not want to further alert the giant, Drizzt did take note of Guenhwyvar, padding quietly along a branch to the behemoth's left flank. She stopped within easy springing distance of the giant's head. "The halfling will bring it," Drizzt explained. "Perhaps then the call will be better understood and abated."

The giant's big face screwed up with confusion. "The halfling?" he echoed skeptically.

Bruenor crashed through the brush to stand beside the drow, then Catti-brie behind him, her deadly bow in hand, and finally, Regis, coming out complaining about a scratch one branch had just inflicted on his cherubic face.

"It bade Junger to follow us," the drow explained, indicating the ruby pendant. "Show him a better course."

Smiling ear to ear, Regis stepped forward and pulled out the chain and ruby pendant, starting the mesmerizing gem on a gentle swing.

"Get back, little rodent," the giant boomed, averting his eyes from the halfling. "I'll tolerate none of your tricks this time!"

"But it's calling to you," Regis protested, holding the gem out even further and flicking it with a finger of his free hand to set it spinning, its many facets catching the firelight in a dazzling display.

"So it is," the giant replied. "Thus my business is not with you."

"But I hold the gem."

"Gem?" the giant echoed. "What do I care for any such meager treasures when measured against the promises of Crenshinibon?"

That proclamation widened the eyes of the companions, except for Regis, who was so entranced by his own gem-twirling that the behemoth's words didn't even register with him. "Oh, but just look at how it spins!" he said happily. "It calls to you, its dearest friend, and bids you—" Regis ended with a squeaky "Hey!" as Bruenor rushed up and yanked him backward so forcefully that it took him right off the ground. He landed beside Drizzt and skittered backward in a futile attempt to hold his balance, but tripped anyway, tumbling hard into the brush.

Junger came forward in a rush, reaching as if to slap the dwarf aside, but a silver-streaking arrow sizzled past his head, and the giant jolted upright, startled.

"The next one takes yer face," Catti-brie promised.

Bruenor eased back to join the woman and the drow.

"You have foolishly followed an errant call," Drizzt said calmly, trying very hard to keep the situation under control. The ranger held no love for giants, to be sure, but he almost felt sympathy for this poor misguided fool. "Crenshinibon? What is Crenshinibon?"

"Oh, you know well," the giant replied. "You above all others, dark elf. You are the possessor, but Crenshinibon rejects you and has selected me as your successor."

"All that I truly know about you is your name, giant," the drow gently replied. "Ever has your kind been at war with the smaller folk of the world, and yet I offer you this one chance to turn back for the Spine of the World, back to your home."

"And so I shall," the giant replied with a chuckle, crossing his ankles calmly and leaning on a tree for support. "As soon as I have Crenshinibon." The cunning behemoth exploded into motion, tearing a thick limb from the tree and launching it at the friends, mostly to force Catti-brie and that nasty bow to dive aside. Junger strode forward and was stunned to find the drow already in swift motion, scimitars drawn, rushing between his legs and slicing away.

Even as the giant turned to catch Drizzt as he rushed out behind him, Bruenor came in hard. The dwarf's axe chopped for the tendon at the back of the behemoth's ankle, and then, suddenly, six hundred pounds of panther crashed

against the turning giant's shoulder and head, knocking
him off-balance. He would have held his footing, except that
Catti-brie drove an arrow into his lower back. Howling and
spinning, Junger went down. Drizzt, Bruenor and
Guenhwyvar all skittered out of harm's way.

"Go home!" Drizzt called to the brute as he struggled to
his hands and knees.

With a defiant roar, the giant dived out at the drow, arms
outstretched. He pulled his arms in fast, both hands suddenly bleeding from deep scimitar gashes, and then he
jerked in pain as Catti-brie's next arrow drove into his hip.

Drizzt started to call out again, wanting to reason with
the brute, but Bruenor had heard enough. The dwarf rushed
up the prone giant's back, quick-stepping to hold his balance
as the creature tried to roll him off. The dwarf leaped over
the giant's turning shoulder, coming down squarely atop his
collarbone. Bruenor's axe came down fast, quicker to the
strike than the giant's reaching hands. The axe cut deep
into Junger's face.

Huge hands clamped around Bruenor, but they had little
strength left. Guenhwyvar leaped in and caught one of the
giant's arms, bringing it down under her weight, pinning
the hand with claws and teeth. Catti-brie blew the other
arm from the dwarf with a perfectly aimed shot.

Bruenor held his ground, leaning down on the embedded
axe, and at last, the giant lay still.

Regis came out of the brush and gave a kick at the branch
the giant had thrown their way. "Worms in an apple!" he
complained. "Why'd you kill him?"

"Ye're seein' a choice?" Bruenor called back incredulously,
then he braced himself and tugged his axe from the split
head. "I'm not for talking to five thousand pounds of enemy."

"I take no pleasure in that kill," Drizzt admitted. He
wiped his blades on the fallen behemoth's tunic, then slid
them into their sheaths. "Better for all of us that the giant
simply went home."

"And I could have convinced him to do so," Regis argued.

"No," the drow answered. "Your pendant is powerful, I do

not doubt, but it has no strength over one entranced by Crenshinibon." As he spoke, he opened his belt pouch and produced the artifact, the famed crystal shard.

"Ye hold it out, and its call'll be all the louder," Bruenor said grimly. "I'm thinkin' we might be finding a long road ahead of us."

"Let it bring the monsters in," Catti-brie said. "It'll make our task in killing them all the easier."

The coldness of her tone caught them all by surprise, but only for the moment it took them to look back at her and see the bruise on her face and remember the cause of her bad mood.

"Ye notice that the damned thing's not working on any of us," the woman reasoned. "So it seems that any falling under its spell are deservin' what they'll find at our hands."

"It does appear that Crenshinibon's power to corrupt extends only to those already of an evil weal," Drizzt agreed.

"And so our road'll be a bit more exciting," Catti-brie said. She didn't bother to add that in this light, she wished Wulfgar was with them. She knew the others were no doubt thinking the exact same thing.

They searched the giant's camp, then turned back to their own fire. Given the new realization that the crystal shard might be working against them, might be reaching out to any nearby monsters in an attempt to get free of the friends, they decided to double their watches from that point forward, two asleep and two awake.

Regis was not pleased.

Chapter 9

GAINING APPROVAL

rom the shadows he watched the wizard walk slowly through the door. Other voices followed LaValle in from the corridor, but the wizard hardly acknowledged them, just shut the door and moved to his private stock liquor cabinet at the side of the audience room, lighting only a single candle atop it.

Entreri clenched his hands eagerly, torn as to whether he should confront the wizard verbally or merely kill the man for not informing him of Dog Perry's attack.

Cup in one hand, burning taper in the other, LaValle moved from the cabinet to a larger standing candelabra. The room brightened with each touch as another candle flared to life. Behind the occupied wizard, Entreri stepped into the open.

His warrior senses put him on his guard immediately. Something—but what?—at the very edges of his consciousness alerted him. Perhaps it had to do with LaValle's comfortable demeanor or some barely perceptible extraneous noise.

LaValle turned around then and jumped back just a bit upon seeing Entreri standing in the middle of the room.

Again the assassin's perceptions nagged at him. The wizard didn't seem frightened or surprised enough.

"Did you believe that Dog Perry would defeat me?" Entreri asked sarcastically.

"Dog Perry?" LaValle came back. "I have not seen the man—"

"Do not lie to me," Entreri calmly interrupted. "I have known you too long, LaValle, to believe such ignorance of you. You watched Dog Perry, without doubt, as you know all the movements of all the players."

"Not all, obviously," the wizard replied dryly, indicating the uninvited man.

Entreri wasn't so sure of that last claim, but he let it pass. "You agreed to warn me when Dog Perry came after me," he said loudly. If the wizard had guild bodyguards nearby, let them hear of his duplicity. "Yet there he was, dagger in hand, with no prior warning from my friend LaValle."

LaValle gave a great sigh and moved to the side, slumping into a chair. "I did indeed know," he admitted. "But I could not act upon that knowledge," he added quickly, for the assassin's eyes narrowed dangerously. "You must understand. All contact with you is forbidden."

"Kelp-enwalled," Entreri remarked.

LaValle held his hands out helplessly.

"I also know that LaValle rarely adheres to such orders," Entreri went on.

"This one was different," came another voice. A slender man, well dressed and coifed, entered the room from the wizard's study.

Entreri's muscles tensed; he had just checked out that room, along with the other two in the wizard's suite, and no one had been in there. Now he knew beyond doubt that he had been expected.

"My guildmaster," LaValle explained. "Quentin Bodeau."

Entreri didn't blink; he had already guessed that much.

"This kelp-enwalling order came not from any particular guild, but from the three most prominent," Quentin Bodeau clarified. "To go against it would have meant eradication."

"Any magical attempt I might have made would have been detected," LaValle tried to explain. He gave a chuckle, trying to break the tension. "I did not believe it would matter, in any case," he said. "I knew that Dog Perry would prove no real test for you."

"If that is so, then why was he allowed to come after me?" Entreri asked, aiming the question at Bodeau.

The guildmaster only shrugged and said, "Rarely have I been able to control all the movements of that one."

"Let that bother you no more," Entreri replied grimly.

Bodeau managed a weak smile. "You must appreciate our position . . ." he started to say.

"I am to believe the word of the man who ordered me murdered?" Entreri asked incredulously.

"I did not—" Bodeau began to argue before being cut off by yet another voice from the wizard's study, a woman's voice.

"If we believed that Quentin Bodeau, or any other ranking member of his guild knew of and approved of the attack, this guild house would be empty of living people."

A tall, dark-haired woman came through the door, flanked by a muscular warrior with a curving black mustache and a more slender man, if it was a man, for Entreri could hardly make out any features under the cowl of the dark cloak. A pair of armored guards strode in behind the trio, and though the last one through the door shut it behind him, Entreri understood that there was likely another one about, probably another wizard. There was no way such a group could have been concealed in the other room, even from his casual glance, without magical aid. Besides, he knew, this group was too comfortable. Even if they were all skilled with weapons, they could not be confident that they alone could bring Entreri down.

"I am Sharlotta Vespers," the woman said, her icy eyes flashing. "I give you Kadran Gordeon and Hand, my fellow lieutenants in the guild of Pasha Basadoni. Yes, he lives still and is glad to see you well."

Entreri knew that to be a lie. If Basadoni were alive the guild would have contacted him much earlier, and in a less dangerous situation.

"Are you affiliated?" Sharlotta asked.

"I was not when I left Calimport, and I only recently came back to the city," the assassin answered.

"Now you are affiliated," Sharlotta purred, and Entreri understood that he was in no position to deny her claim.

* * * * *

So he would not be killed—not now, at least. He would not have to spend his nights looking over his shoulder for would-be assassins nor deal with the impertinent advances of fools like Dog Perry. The Basadoni Guild had claimed him as their own, and though he would be able to go and take jobs wherever he decided, as long as they did not involve the murder of anyone connected with Pasha Basadoni, his primary contacts would be Kadran Gordeon, whom he did not trust, and Hand.

He should have been pleased at the turn of events, he knew, sitting quietly on the roof of the Copper Ante late that night. He couldn't have expected a better course.

And yet, for some reason that he could hardly fathom, Entreri was not pleased in the least. He had his old life back, if he wanted it. With his skills, he knew he could soon return to the glories he had once known. And yet he now understood the limitations of those glories and knew that while he could easily re-ascend to the highest level of assassin in Calimport, that level would hardly be enough to satisfy the emptiness he felt within.

He simply did not wish to go back to his old ways of murder for money. It was no bout of conscience—nothing like that!—but no thought of that former life sparked any excitement within the man.

Ever the pragmatist, Entreri decided to play it one hour at a time. He went over the side of the roof, silent and surefooted, picking his way down to the street, then entered through the front door.

All eyes focused on him, but he hardly cared as he made his way across the common room to the door at the back. One halfling approached him there, as if to stop him, but a glare from Entreri backed the little one off, and the assassin pushed through.

Again the sight of the enormously fat Dondon assaulted him profoundly.

"Artemis!" Dondon said happily, though Entreri did note a bit of tension creeping into the halfling's voice, a common reaction whenever the assassin arrived unannounced at anyone's doorstep. "Come in, my friend. Sit and eat. Partake of good company."

Entreri looked at the heaps of half-eaten sweets and at the two painted female halflings flanking the bloated wretch. He did sit down a safe distance away, though he moved none of the many platters in front of him narrowing his eyes as one of the female halflings tried to approach.

"You must learn to relax and enjoy those fruits your work has provided," Dondon said. "You are back with Basadoni, so 'tis said, and so you are free."

Entreri noted that the irony of that statement was apparently lost on the halfling.

"What good is all of your difficult and dangerous work if you cannot learn to relax and enjoy those pleasures your labors might buy for you?" Dondon asked.

"How did it happen?" Entreri asked bluntly.

Dondon stared at him, obvious confusion splayed on his sagging face.

In explanation, Entreri looked all around, motioning to the plates, to the whores, and to Dondon's massive belly.

Dondon's expression soured. "You know why I am in here," he remarked quietly, all the bounce having left his tone.

"I know why you came in here . . . to hide . . . and I agree with that decision," Entreri replied. "But why?" Again he let the halfling follow his gaze to all the excess, plate by plate, whore by whore. "Why this?"

"I choose to enjoy . . ." Dondon started, but Entreri would hear none of that.

"If I could offer you back your old life, would you take it?" the assassin asked.

Dondon stared at him blankly.

"If I could change the word on the street so that Dondon could walk free of the Copper Ante, would Dondon be pleased?" Entreri pressed. "Or is Dondon pleased with the excuse?"

"You speak in riddles."

"I speak the truth," Entreri shot back, trying to look the halfling in the eye, though the sight of those drooping, sleepy lids surely revolted him. He could hardly believe his own level of anger in looking at Dondon. A part of him wanted to draw out his dagger and cut the wretch's heart out.

But Artemis Entreri did not kill for passion, and he held that part in check.

"Would you go back?" he asked slowly, emphasizing every word.

Dondon didn't reply, didn't blink, but in the nonresponse, Entreri had his answer, the one he had feared the most.

The room's door swung open, and Dwahvel entered. "Is there a problem in here, Master Entreri?" she asked sweetly.

Entreri climbed to his feet and moved for the open door. "None for me," he replied, moving past.

Dwahvel caught him by the arm—a dangerous move indeed! Fortunately for her, Entreri was too absorbed in his contemplation of Dondon to take affront.

"About our deal," the female halfling remarked. "I may have need of your services."

Entreri spent a long while considering those words, wondering why, for some reason, they so assaulted him. He had enough to think about already without having Dwahvel pressing her ridiculous needs upon him. "And what did you give to me in exchange for these services you so desire?" he asked.

"Information," the halfling replied. "As we agreed."

"You told me of the kelp-enwalling, hardly something I could not have discerned on my own," Entreri replied. "Other than that, Dwahvel was of little use to me, and that measure I surely can repay."

The halfling's mouth opened as if she meant to protest, but Entreri just turned away and walked across the common room.

"You may find my doors closed to you," Dwahvel called after him.

In truth, Entreri hardly cared, for he didn't expect that he would desire to see wretched Dondon again. Still, more for effect than any practical gain, he did turn back to let his dangerous gaze settle over the halfling. "That would not be wise," was all he offered before sweeping out of the room and back onto the dark street, then back to the solitude of the rooftops.

Up there, after many minutes of concentration, he came to understand why he so hated Dondon. Because he saw himself. No, he would never allow himself to become so bloated, for gluttony had never been one of his weaknesses, but what he saw was a creature beaten by the weight of life itself, a creature that had surrendered to despair. In Dondon's case it had been simple fear that had defeated him, that had locked him in a room and buried him in lust and gluttony.

In Entreri's case, would it be simple apathy?

He stayed on the roof all the night, but he did not find his answers.

* * * * *

The knock came in the correct sequence, two raps, then three, then two again, so he knew even as he dragged himself out of his bed that it was the Basadoni Guild come calling. Normally Entreri would have taken precautions anyway—normally he would not have slept through half the day—but he did nothing now, didn't even retrieve his dagger. He just went to the door and, without even asking, pulled it open.

He didn't recognize the man standing there, a young and nervous fellow with woolly black hair cut tight to his head, and dark, darting eyes.

"From Kadran Gordeon," the man explained, handing Entreri a rolled parchment.

"Hold!" Entreri said as the nervous young man turned and started away. The man's head spun back to regard the assassin, and Entreri noted one hand slipping under the folds of his light-colored robes, reaching for a weapon no doubt.

"Where is Gordeon?" Entreri asked. "And why did he not deliver this to me personally?"

"Please, good sir," the young man said in his thick Calimshite accent, bowing repeatedly. "I was only told to give that to you."

"By Kadran Gordeon?" Entreri asked.

"Yes," the man said, nodding wildly.

Entreri shut his door, then heard the running footsteps of the relieved man outside retreating down the hall and then the stairs at full speed.

He stood there, considering the parchment and the delivery. Gordeon hadn't even come to him personally, and he understood why. To do so would have been too much an open show of respect. The lieutenants of the guild feared him—not that he would kill them, but more that he would ascend to a rank above them. Now, by using this inconsequential messenger, Gordeon was trying to show Entreri the true pecking order, one that had him just above the bottom rung.

With a resigned shake of his head, a helpless acceptance of the stupidity of it all, the assassin pulled the tie from the parchment and unrolled it. The orders were simple enough, giving a man's name and last known address, with instructions that he should be killed as soon as it could be arranged. That very night, if possible, the next day at the latest.

At the bottom was a last notation that the targeted man had no known guild affiliation, nor was he in particularly good standing with city or merchant guardsmen, nor did he have any known powerful friends or relatives.

146

Entreri considered that bit of news carefully. Either he was being set up against a very dangerous opponent, or, more likely, Gordeon had given him this pitifully easy hit to demean him, to lessen his credentials. In his former days in Calimport, Entreri's talents had been reserved for the killing of guildmasters or wizards, noblemen, and captains of the guard. Of course, if Gordeon and the other two lieutenants gave him any such difficult tasks and he proved successful, his standing would grow among the community and they would fear his quick ascension through the ranks.

No matter, he decided.

He took one last look at the listed address—a region of Calimport that he knew well—and went to retrieve his tools.

* * * * *

He heard the children crying nearby, for the hovel had only two rooms, and those separated by only a thick drapery. A very homely young woman—Entreri noted as he spied on her from around the edge of the drapery—tended to the children. She begged them to settle down and be quiet, threatening that their father would soon be home.

She came out of the back room a moment later, oblivious to the assassin as he crouched behind another curtain under a side window. Entreri cut a small hole in the drape and watched her movements as she went about her work. Everything was brisk and efficient; she was on edge, he knew.

The door, yet another drape, pushed aside and a young, skinny man entered, his face appearing haggard, eyes sunken back in his skull, several days of beard on his chin and cheeks.

"Did you find it?" the woman asked sharply.

The man shook his head, and it seemed to Entreri that his eyes drooped just a bit more.

"I begged you not to work with them!" the woman scolded. "I knew that no good—"

147

She stopped short as his eyes widened in horror. He saw, looking over her shoulder, the assassin emerging from behind the draperies. He turned as if to flee, but the woman looked back and cried out.

The man froze in place; he would not leave her.

Entreri watched it all calmly. Had the man continued his retreat, the assassin would have cut him down with a dagger throw before he ever got outside.

"Not my family," the man begged, turning back and walking toward Entreri, his hands out wide, palms open. "And not here."

"You know why I have come?" the assassin asked.

The woman began to cry, muttering for mercy, but her husband grabbed her gently but firmly and pulled her back, angling her for the children's room, then pushing her along.

"It was not my fault," the man said quietly when she was gone. "I begged Kadran Gordeon. I told him that I would somehow find the money."

The old Artemis Entreri would not have been intrigued at that point. The old Artemis Entreri would never even have listened to the words. The old Artemis Entreri would have just finished the task and walked out. But now he found that he was interested, mildly, and, as he had no other pressing business, he was in no hurry to finish.

"I will cause no trouble for you if you promise that you will not hurt my family," the man said.

"You believe that you could me cause trouble?" Entreri asked.

The helpless, pitiful man shook his head. "Please," he begged. "I only wished to show them a better life. I agreed to, even welcomed, the job of moving money from Docker's Street to the drop only because in those easy tasks I earned more than a month of labor can bring me in honest work."

Entreri had heard it all before, of course. So many times, fools—camels, they were called—joined into a guild, performing delivery tasks for what seemed to the simple peasants huge amounts of money. The guilds only hired the camels so that rival guilds would not know who was transporting the money. Eventually, though, the other guilds would figure out the routes and the camels, and would steal the shipment.

Then the poor camels, if they survived the ambush, would be quickly eliminated by the guild that had hired them.

"You understood the danger of the company you kept," Entreri remarked.

The man nodded. "Only a few deliveries," he replied. "Only a few, and then I would quit."

Entreri laughed and shook his head, considering the fool's absurd plan. One could not "quit" as a camel. Anyone accepting the position would immediately learn too much to ever be allowed out of the guild. There were only two possibilities: first, that the camel would perform well enough and be lucky enough to earn a higher, more permanent position within the guild structure, and second, that the man or woman (for women were often used) would be slain in a raid or subsequently killed by the hiring guild.

"I beg of you, do not do it here," the man said at length. "Not where my wife will hear my last cries, not where my sons will find me dead."

Bitter bile found its way into the back of Entreri's throat. Never had he been so disgusted, never had he seen a more pitiful human being. He looked around again at the hovel, the rags posing as doors, as walls. There was a single plate, probably used for eating by the entire family, sitting on the single old bench in the room.

"How much do you owe?" he asked, and though he could hardly believe the words as he spoke them, he knew that he would not be able to bring himself to kill this wretch.

The man looked at him curiously. "A king's treasure," he said. "Near to thirty gold pieces."

Entreri nodded, then pulled a pouch from his belt, this one hidden around the back under his dark cloak. He felt the weight as he pulled it free and knew that it held at least fifty gold pieces, but he tossed it to the man anyway.

The stunned man caught it and stared at it so intently that Entreri feared his eyeballs would simply fall out of their sockets. Then he looked back to the assassin, his emotions too twisted and turned about for him to have any revealing expression at all on his face.

149

"On your word that you will not deal with any guilds again once your debt is paid," Entreri said. "Your wife and children deserve better."

The man started to reply, then fell to his knees and started to bow before his savior. Entreri turned about and swept angrily from the hovel, out into the dirty street.

He heard the man's calls following him, cries of thanks and mercy. In truth, and Entreri knew it, there had been no mercy in his actions. He cared nothing for the man or his ugly wife and undoubtedly ugly children. But still he could not kill this pitiful wretch, though he figured he would probably be doing the man a great service if he did put him out of his obvious misery. No, Entreri would not give Kadran Gordeon the satisfaction of putting him through such a dishonorable murder. A camel like this should be work for first year guild members, twelve-year-olds, perhaps, and for Kadran to give such an assignment to one of Entreri's reputation was surely a tremendous insult.

He would not play along.

He stormed down the street to his room at the inn where he collected all his things and set out at once, finally coming to the door of the Copper Ante. He had thought to merely press in, for no better reason than to show Dwahvel how ridiculous her threat to shut him out had been. But then he reconsidered and turned away, in no mood for any dealings with Dwahvel, in no mood for any dealings with anybody.

He found a small, nondescript tavern across town and took a room. Likely he was on the grounds of another guild, and if they found out who he was and who he was affiliated with there might be trouble.

He didn't care.

*　*　*　*　*

A day slipped by unremarkably, but that did little to put Entreri at ease. Much was happening, he knew, and all of it in quiet shadows. He had the wherewithal and understanding of those shadows to go out and discern much, but he hadn't the ambition to do so. He was in a mood to simply let things fall as they might.

He went down to the common room of the little inn that second night, taking his meal to an empty corner, eating alone and hearing nothing of the several conversations going on about the place. He did note the entrance of one character, though, a halfling, and the little folk were not common in this region of the city. Soon enough the halfling found him, taking a seat on the long bench opposite the table from the assassin.

"Good evening to you, fine sir," the little one said. "And how do you find your meal?"

Entreri studied the halfling, understanding that this one held no interest at all in his food. He looked for a weapon on the halfling, though he doubted that Dwahvel would ever be so bold as to move against him.

"Might I taste it?" the halfling said rather loudly, coming forward over the table.

Entreri, picking up the cues, held a spoon of the gruel up but did not extend his arm, allowing the halfling to inconspicuously move even closer.

"I've come from Dwahvel," the little one said as he moved in. "The Basadoni Guild seeks you, and they are in a foul mood. They know where you are and have received permission from the Rakers to come and collect you. Expect them this very night." The halfling took the bite as he finished, then moved back across the table, rubbing his belly.

"Tell Dwahvel that now I am in her debt," Entreri remarked. The little one, with a slight nod, moved back across the room and ordered a bowl of gruel. He took up a conversation with the innkeeper while he was waiting for it and ate it right at the bar, leaving Entreri to his thoughts.

He could flee, the assassin realized, but his heart was not in such a course. No, he decided, let them come and let this be done. He didn't think they meant to kill him in any case. He finished his meal and went back to his room to consider his options. First, he pulled a board from the inner wall, and in the cubby space between that and the outer wall, reaching down to a beam well below the floor in his room, he placed his fabulous jeweled dagger and many of his coins. Then he carefully replaced the board and replaced the dagger on his belt with another from his pack, one that somewhat resembled his signature dagger but without the powerful enchantment. Then, more for appearances than as any deterrent, he wired a basic dart trap about his door and moved across the room, settling into the one chair in the place. He took out some dice and began throwing them on the small night table beside the chair, making up games and passing the hours.

It was late indeed when he heard the first footsteps coming up the stairs—a man obviously trying to be stealthy but making more noise than the skilled Entreri would make even if he were walking normally. Entreri listened more carefully as the walking ceased, and he caught the scrape of a thin slice of metal moving about the crack between the door and the jamb. A fairly skilled thief could get through his impromptu trap in a matter of a couple of minutes, he knew, so he put his hands behind his head and leaned back against the wall.

All the noise stopped, a long and uncomfortable silence.

Entreri sniffed the air; something was burning. For a moment, he thought they might be razing the building around him, but then he recognized the smell, that of burning leather, and as he shifted to look down at his own belt he felt a sharp pain on his collarbone. The chain of a necklace he wore—one that held several lock picks cunningly designed as ornaments—had slipped off his shirt and onto his bare skin.

Only then did the assassin understand that all of his metallic items had grown red hot.

Entreri jumped up and tore the necklace from his neck, then deftly, with a twist of his wrist, dropped his belt and the heated dagger to the floor.

The door burst in, a Basadoni soldier rolling to either side and a third man, crossbow leveled, rushing between them.

He didn't fire, though, nor did the others, their swords in hand, charge in.

Kadran Gordeon walked in behind the bowman.

"A simple knock would have proven as effective," Entreri said dryly, looking down at his glowing equipment. The dagger caused the wood of the floor to send up a trail of black smoke.

In response, Gordeon threw a coin at Entreri's feet, a strange golden coin imprinted with the unicorn head emblem on the side showing to the assassin.

Entreri looked up at Gordeon and merely shrugged.

"The camel was to be killed," Gordeon said.

"He was not worth the effort."

"And that is for you to decide?" the Basadoni lieutenant asked incredulously.

"A minor decision, compared to what I once—"

"Ah!" Gordeon interrupted dramatically. "Therein lies the flaw, Master Entreri. What you once knew, or did, or were told to do, is irrelevant, you see. You are no guildmaster, no lieutenant, not even a full soldier as of yet, and I doubt that ever you will be! You lost your nerve—as I thought you would. You are only gaining approval, and if you survive that time, perhaps, just perhaps, you will find your way back into complete acceptance within the guild."

"Gaining approval?" Entreri echoed with a laugh. "Yours?"

"Take him!" Gordeon instructed the two soldiers who had come in first. As they moved cautiously for the assassin Gordeon added, "The man you tried to save was executed, as were his wife and children."

Entreri hardly heard the words and hardly cared anyway, though he knew that Gordeon had ordered the extended execution merely to throw some pain his way. Now he had a bigger dilemma. Should he allow Gordeon to take him back to the guild, where he would no doubt be physically punished and then released?

No, he would not suffer such treatment by this man or any other. The muscles in his legs, so finely honed, tensed as the two approached, though Entreri seemed perfectly at ease, even held his empty arms out in an unthreatening posture.

The men, swords in hand, came in at his sides, reaching for those arms while the third soldier kept his crossbow steady, aimed at the assassin's heart.

Up into the air went Entreri, a great vertical spring, tucking his legs under him and then kicking out to the sides before the startled soldiers could react, connecting squarely on the faces of both the approaching men and sending them flying away. He did catch the one on his right as he landed, and pulled the man in quickly, just in time to serve as a shield for the firing crossbow. Then he tossed the groaning man to the ground.

"First mistake," he said to Gordeon as the lieutenant drew out a splendid-looking sabre. Off to the side the other kicked soldier climbed back to his feet, but the one on the floor in front of Entreri, a crossbow quarrel deep into his back, wasn't moving. The crossbowman worked hard on the crank, loading another bolt, but even more disturbing for Entreri was the fact that there was obviously a wizard nearby.

"Stay back," Gordeon ordered the man to the side. "I will finish this one."

"To make your reputation?" Entreri asked. "But I have no weapon. How will that sound on the streets of Calimport?"

"After you are dead we will place a weapon in your hand," Gordeon said with a wicked grin. "My men will insist that it was a fair fight."

"Second mistake," Entreri said under his breath, for indeed, it was a fairer fight than the skilled Kadran Gordeon could ever understand. The Basadoni lieutenant came in with a measured thrust, straight ahead, and Entreri slapped his forearm out to intercept, purposely missing the parry but skittering backward out of reach at the same time. Gordeon circle, and so did Entreri. Then the assassin came ahead in a short lunge and was forced back with a slice of the sabre, Gordeon taking care to allow no openings.

But Entreri had no intention of following through his movement anyway. He had only begun it so that he could slightly alter the angle of the circling, putting him in line for his next strike.

On came Gordeon, and Entreri leaped back. When Gordeon kept coming, the assassin went ahead in a short burst, forcing him into a cunning and dangerous parrying maneuver. But again, Entreri didn't follow through. He just fell back to the appropriate spot and, to the surprise of all in the room, stamped his foot hard on the floor.

"What?" Gordeon asked, shaking his head and looking about, for he didn't keep his eyes down at that stamping foot, didn't see the shock of the stamp lift the still-glowing necklace from the floor so that Entreri could hook it about his toe.

A moment later Gordeon came on hard, this time looking for the kill. Out snapped Entreri's foot, launching the necklace at the lieutenant's face. To his credit, the swift-handed Gordeon snapped his free hand across and caught the necklace—as Entreri had expected—but then how he howled, the glowing chain enwrapping his bare hand and digging a fiery line across his flesh.

Entreri was there in the blink of an eye. He slapped the lieutenant's sword arm out wide. Balling both fists, middle knuckles extended forward, he drove his knuckles simultaneously into the man's temples. Clearly dazed, his eyes glossed over, Gordeon's hands slipped to his sides and Entreri snapped his forehead right into the man's face. He caught Gordeon as he fell back and spun him about, then reached through his legs and caught him by one wrist. With a subtle turn to put Gordeon in line with the crossbowman, Entreri pulled hard, through and up, flipping Gordeon right into the startled soldier. The flipped man knocked the crossbow hard enough to dislodge the bolt.

The remaining swordsman came in hard from the side, but he was not a skilled fighter, even by Kadran Gordeon's standards. Entreri easily backed and dodged his awkward, too-far-ahead thrust, then stepped in quickly, before the man could retract and ready the blade. Reaching down and around to catch his sword arm by the wrist, Entreri lifted hard and stepped under that wrist, twisting the arm painfully and stealing the strength from it.

The man came ahead, thinking to grab on for dear life with his free hand. Entreri's palm slapped against the back of his twisted sword hand quicker than he could even comprehend, then bent the hand down low back over the wrist, stealing all strength and sending a wave of pain through the man. A simple slide of the hand had the sword free in Entreri's grasp, and a reversal of grip and deft twist brought it in line.

Entreri retracted his hand, stabbing the blade out and up behind him into the belly and up into the lungs of the hapless soldier.

Moving quickly, not even bothering to pull the sword back out, he spun on the man, thinking to throw him, too, at the crossbowman. And indeed that stubborn archer was once more setting the bolt in place. But a far more dangerous foe appeared, the unseen wizard, rushing down the hallway, robes flapping, across the door. Entreri saw the man lift something slender—a wand, he supposed—but then all he saw was a tumble of arms and legs as the skewered swordsman crashed into the wizard and both went flying away.

"Have I yet gained your approval?" Entreri yelled at the still dazed Gordeon, but he was moving even as he spoke, for the crossbowman had him dead and the wizard was fast regaining his footing. He felt the terrible flash of pain as a quarrel dug through his side, but he gritted his teeth and growled away the pain, putting his arms in front of his face and tucking his legs up defensively as he crashed through the wooden-latticed window, soaring down the ten feet to the street. He turned his legs as he hit, throwing himself into a sidelong roll, and then another to absorb the shock of the fall. He was up and running, not surprised at all when another crossbow quarrel, fired from a completely different direction, embedded itself into the wall right beside him.

All the area erupted with movement as Basadoni soldiers came out of every conceivable hiding place.

Entreri sprinted down one alley, leaped right over a huge man bending low in an attempt to tackle him at the waist, then cut fast around a building. Up to the roof he went, quick as a cat, then across, leaping another alley to another roof, and so on.

He went down the main street, for he knew that his pursuers were expecting him to drop into an alley. He went up fast on the side of one wall, expertly setting himself there, arms and legs splayed wide to find tentative holds and to blend with the contours of the building.

Cries of "Find him!" echoed all about, and many soldiers ran right below his perch, but those cries diminished as the night wore on. Fortunately so for Entreri, who, though he was not losing much blood outwardly, understood that his wound was serious, perhaps even mortal. Finally he was able to slide down from his perch, hardly finding the remaining strength to even stand. He put a hand to his side and felt the warm blood, thick in the folds of his cloak, and felt, too, the very back edge of the deeply embedded quarrel.

He could hardly draw breath now. He knew what that meant.

Luck was with him when he got back to the inn, for the sun had not yet come up, and though there were obviously Basadoni soldiers within the place, few were about the immediate area. Entreri found the window of his room easily enough from the broken wood on the ground and calculated the height of his hidden store. He had to be quiet, for he heard voices, Gordeon's among them, from within his room. Up he went, finding a secure perch, trying hard not to groan, though in truth he wanted to scream from the pain.

He worked the old, weather-beaten wood slowly and quietly until he could pull enough away to retrieve his dagger and small pouch.

"He had to have some magic about him!" he heard Gordeon scream. "Cast your detection again!"

"There is no magic, Master Gordeon," came another voice, the wizard's obviously. "If he had any, then likely he sold it or gave it away before he ever came to this place."

Despite his agony, Entreri managed a smile as he heard Gordeon's subsequent growl and kick. No magic indeed, because they had searched in his room only and not the wall of the room below.

Dagger in hand, the assassin made his way along the still-quiet streets. He hoped to find a Basadoni soldier about, one deserving his wrath, but in truth he doubted he could even muster the strength to beat a novice fighter. What he found instead was a pair of drunks, laying against the side of a building, one sleeping, the other talking to himself.

Silent as death, the assassin stalked in. His jeweled dagger possessed a particularly useful magic, for it could steal the life of a victim and give that energy to its wielder.

Entreri took the talking drunk first, and when he was finished, feeling so much stronger, he bit down hard on a fold of his cloak and yanked the crossbow bolt from his side, nearly fainting as waves of agony assaulted him.

He steadied himself, though, and fell over the sleeping drunk.

He walked out of the alley soon after, showing no signs that he had been so badly wounded. He felt strong again and almost hoped he would find Kadran Gordeon still in the area.

But the fight had only begun, he knew, and despite his supreme skills, he remembered well the extent of the Basadoni Guild and understood that he was sorely overmatched.

* * * * *

They had watched those intent on killing him enter the inn. They had watched him come crashing through the window in full flight, then run on into the shadows. With eyes superior to those of the Basadoni soldiers, they had spotted him splayed on the wall and silently applauded his stealthy trick. And now, with some measure of relief and many nods that their leader had chosen wisely, they watched him exit the alley. And even he, Artemis Entreri, assassin of assassins, had no idea they were about.

Chapter 10

UNEXPECTED AND

UNSATISFYING VENGEANCE

ulfgar moved along the foothills of the Spine of
the World easily and swiftly, sincerely hoping
that some monster would find him and attack
that he might release the frustrating rage boiling
within him. On several occasions he found tracks, and he
followed them, but he was no ranger. Though he could survive well enough in the harsh climate, his tracking skills
were nowhere near as strong as those of his drow friend.

Nor was his sense of direction. When he came over one
ridge the very next day, he was surprised indeed to see that
he had cut diagonally right through the corner of the great
mountain range, for from this high vantage point all the
southland seemed to spread wide before him. Wulfgar
looked back to the mountains, thinking that his chances for
finding a fight would be much better in there, but inevitably
his gaze swung back to the open fields, the dark clusters of
forest, and the many long and unknown roads. He felt a pull
in his heart, a longing for distance and open expanses, a

desire to break the bounds of his boxed-in life in Icewind Dale. Perhaps out there he might find new experiences that would allow him to dismiss all the tumult of images that whirled in his thoughts. Perhaps divorced from the everyday familiar routines he could also find distance from the horrors of his memories of the Abyss.

Nodding to himself, Wulfgar started down the steep southern expanse. He found another set of tracks—orc, most likely—a couple hours later, but this time he passed them by. He was out of the mountains as the sun disappeared below the western horizon. He stood watching the sunset. Great orange and red flames gathered in the bellies of dark clouds, filling the western sky with brilliant striped patterns. The occasional twinkling star became visible against the pale blue wherever the clouds broke apart. He held that pose as all color faded, as darkness crept across the fields and the sky, broken clouds rushing past overhead. Stars seemed to blink on and off. This was the moment of renewal, Wulfgar decided. This was the moment of his rebirth, a clean beginning for a man alone in the world, a man determined to focus on the present and not the past, determined to let the future sort itself out.

He moved away from the mountains and camped under the spreading boughs of a fir tree. Despite his determination, his nightmares found him there.

Still, the next day Wulfgar's stride was long and swift, covering the miles, following the wind or a bird's flight or the bank of a spring creek.

He found plenty of game and plenty of berries. Each passing day he felt as though his stride was less shackled by his past, and each night the terrible dreams seemed to grab a him a bit less.

But then one day he came upon a curious totem, a low pole set in the ground with its top carved to resemble the pegasus, the winged horse, and suddenly Wulfgar found himself vaulted back into a very distinct memory, an incident that had occurred many years before when he was on the road with Drizzt, Bruenor, and Regis seeking the dwarf's ancestral home of Mithral Hall. Part of him wanted to turn away from that totem, to run far from this place, but one particular memory, a vow of vengeance, nagged at him. Hardly registering the movements, Wulfgar found a recent trail and followed it, soon coming to a hillock, and from the top of that bluff he spied the encampment, a cluster of deer-skin tents with people, tall and strong and dark-haired, moving all about.

"Sky Ponies," Wulfgar whispered, remembering well the barbarian tribe that had come into a battle he and his friends had fought against an orc group. After the orcs had been cut down, Wulfgar, Bruenor, and Regis had been taken prisoner. They had been treated fairly well, and Wulfgar had been offered a challenge of strength, which he easily won, against the son of the chieftain. And then, in honorable barbarian tradition, Wulfgar had been offered a place among the tribesmen. Unfortunately, for a test of loyalty Wulfgar had been asked to slay Regis, and that he could never do. With Drizzt's help, the friends had escaped, but then the shaman, Valric High Eye, had used evil magic to transform Torlin, the chieftain's son, into a hideous ghost spirit.

They defeated that spirit. When honorable Torlin's deformed, broken body lay at his feet, Wulfgar, son of Beornegar, had vowed vengeance against Valric High Eye.

The barbarian felt the clamminess in his strong hands—hands subconsciously wringing about the handle of his powerful warhammer. He squinted into the distance, staring hard at the encampment, and discerned a skinny, agitated form that might have been Valric skipping past one tent.

Valric might not even still be alive, Wulfgar reminded himself, for the shaman had been very old those years ago. Again a large part of Wulfgar wanted to sprint down the other side of the hillock, to run far away from this encounter and any other that would remind him of his past.

The image of Torlin's broken, mutilated body, half man, half winged horse, stayed clear in his thoughts, though, and he could not turn away.

Within the hour, he stared at the encampment from a

much closer perspective, close enough to see the individuals.

Close enough to understand that the Sky Ponies had fallen on hard times. And into difficult battles, he realized, for many wounded sat about the camp, and the overall numbers of tents and folk seemed much reduced from what he remembered. Most of the folk in camp were women or very old or very young. A string of more than two-score poles to the south helped to clear up the mystery, for upon them were set the heads of orcs, the occasional carrion bird fluttering down to find a perch in scraggly hair, poking down to find a feast of an eyeball or the side of a nostril.

The sight of the Sky Ponies so obviously diminished pained Wulfgar greatly, for though he had sworn vengeance on their shaman, he knew them to be an honorable people, much like his own in tradition and practice. He thought then that he should leave them, but even as he turned to go, one tent flap at the corner of his line of vision pushed open and out hopped a skinny man, ancient but full of energy, wearing white robes that feathered out like the wings of a bird whenever he raised his arms, and even more telling, an eye patch set with a huge emerald. Barbarians lowered their gazes wherever he passed; one child even rushed up to him and kissed the back of his hand.

"Valric," Wulfgar muttered, for there could be no mistaking the shaman.

Wulfgar came up from the grass in a steady, determined walk, Aegis-fang swinging at the end of one arm. The mere fact that he broke through the camp's perimeter without being assaulted showed him just how disorganized and decimated this tribe truly was, for no barbarian tribe would ever be caught so off guard.

Yet Wulfgar had passed the first tents, had moved close enough to Valric High Eye for the shaman to see him and stare at him incredulously before the first warrior, a tall, older man, strong but very lean, moved to block him.

The warrior came in swinging, not talking, launching a sidelong sweep with a heavy club, but Wulfgar, quicker than the man could anticipate, stepped ahead and caught the club in his free hand before it could gain too much momentum, and then, with strength beyond anything the man had ever imagined, turned his wrist and pulled the weapon free, tossing it far to the side. The warrior howled and charged right in, but Wulfgar got his arm across between himself and the man. With a mighty sweep of his arm, Wulfgar sent the man stumbling away.

All the camp's warriors, not nearly as many as Wulfgar remembered from the Sky Ponies, were out then, flanking Valric, forming a semicircle from the shaman out to the sides of the huge intruder. Wulfgar did turn his gaze from the hated Valric long enough to scrutinize the group, long enough to take note that these were not strong men of prime warrior age. They were too young or too old. The Sky Ponies, he understood, had recently fought a tremendous battle and had not fared well.

"Who are you who comes uninvited?" asked one man, large and strong but very old.

Wulfgar looked hard at the speaker, at the keen set of his eyes, the peppered gray hair in a tousled mop, thick indeed for one his age, at the firm and proud set of his jaw. He reminded Wulfgar of another Sky Pony he had once met, an honorable and brave warrior, and that, combined with the fact that the man had spoken above all others, and even before Valric, confirmed Wulfgar's suspicions.

"Father of Torlin," he said, and gave a bow.

The man's eyes widened with surprise. He seemed as if he wanted to respond but could find no words.

"Jerek Wolf Slayer!" Valric shrieked. "Chieftain of the Sky Ponies. Who are you who comes uninvited? Who are you who speaks of Jerek's long-lost son?"

"Lost?" Wulfgar echoed skeptically.

"Taken by the gods," Valric replied, waving his feathered arms. "A hunting quest, turned to vision quest."

A wry smile made its way onto Wulfgar's face as he came to comprehend the tremendous, decade-old lie. Torlin, mutated into a ghastly and ghostly creature had been sent out by Valric to hunt Wulfgar and his companions and had died horribly on the field at their hands. But Valric, likely not wanting to face Jerek with the horrid news, had somehow manipulated the truth, had concocted a story that would keep Jerek in check. A hunting quest or a vision quest, both god-inspired, might last years, even decades.

Wulfgar realized that he had to handle this delicately now, for any wrong or too-harsh statements might provoke the wrath of Jerek.

"The hunting quest did not last," he said. "For the gods, our gods, recognized the wrongness of it."

Valric's eyes widened indeed, for the first time showing some measure of recognition. "Who are you?" he asked again, a hint of a tremor edging his voice.

"Do you not remember, Valric High Eye?" Wulfgar asked, striding forward, and his movement caused those flanking the shaman to step forward as well. "Have the Sky Ponies so soon forgotten the face of Wulfgar, son of Beornegar?"

Valric tilted his head, his expression showing that Wulfgar had hit a chord of recognition there, but only vaguely.

"Have the Sky Ponies so soon forgotten the northerner they invited to join their ranks, the northerner who traveled with a dwarf, and a halfling, and," he paused, knowing that his next words would bring complete recognition, "a black-skinned elf?"

Valric's eyes nearly rolled out of their sockets. "You!" he said, poking his trembling finger into the air.

The mention of the drow, probably the only dark elf any of these barbarians had ever seen, sparked the memories of many others. Whispered conversations erupted, and many barbarians grasped their weapons tightly, awaiting only a single word to begin their attack and slaughter of the intruder.

Wulfgar calmly held his ground. "I am Wulfgar, son of Beornegar," he repeated firmly, focusing his gaze on Jerek Wolf Slayer. "No enemy of the Sky Ponies. Distant kin to your people and to your ways. I have returned, as I vowed I would, when I saw dead Torlin on the field."

"Dead Torlin?" many voices from warriors and those huddled behind them echoed.

"My friends and I did not come as enemies of the Sky Ponies," Wulfgar went on, using what he expected to be the last few seconds of dialogue. "Indeed we fought beside you against a common foe and won the day."

"You refused us!" Valric screamed. "You insulted my people!"

"What do you know of my son?" Jerek demanded, pushing the shaman aside and stepping forward.

"I know that Valric quested him with the spirit of the Sky Pony to destroy us," Wulfgar said.

"You admit this, and yet you walk openly into our encampment?" Jerek asked.

"I know that your god was not with Torlin on that hunt, for we defeated the creature he had become."

"Kill him!" Valric screamed. "As we destroyed the orcs that came upon us in the dark of night, so shall we destroy the enemy that walks into our camp this day!"

"Hold!" shouted Jerek, throwing his arms out wide. Not a Sky Pony took a step forward, though they seemed eager now, like a pack of hunting dogs straining against their leashes.

Jerek stepped out, walking to stand before Wulfgar.

Wulfgar locked his gaze with the man, but not before he glanced past Jerek to Valric, the shaman fumbling with a leather pouch—a sacred bundle of mystical and magical components—at his side.

"My son is dead?" Jerek, barely a foot from Wulfgar, asked.

"Your god was not with him," Wulfgar replied. "For his cause, Valric's cause, was not just."

He knew before he ever finished that his roundabout manner of telling Jerek had done little to calm the man, that the overriding information, that his son was indeed dead, was too powerful and painful for any explanation or justification. With a roar, the chieftain came at Wulfgar but the younger barbarian was ready, lifting his arm high to raise the intended punch, then snapping his hand down and over Jerek's extended arm, pulling the man off-balance.

Wulfgar dropped Aegis-fang and shoved hard on Jerek's chest, releasing his hold and sending the man stumbling backward into the surprised warriors.

Scooping his warhammer as he went, Wulfgar charged forward, but so did the warriors, and the northern barbarian, to his ultimate frustration, knew that he would get nowhere near to Valric. He hoped for an open throwing path that he might take down the shaman before he, too, was killed, but then Valric surprised him, surprised everybody, by leaping forward through the line, howling a chant and throwing a burst of herbs and powders Wulfgar's way.

Wulfgar felt the magical intrusion. Though the other warriors, Jerek included, backed away a few steps, he felt as if great black walls were closing in on him, stealing his strength, forcing him to hold in place.

Waves and waves of immobilizing magic rolled on, Valric hopping about, throwing more powders, strengthening the spell.

Wulfgar felt himself sinking, felt the ground coming up to swallow him.

He was not unfamiliar with such magics, though. Not at all. In his years in the Abyss, Errtu's minions, particularly the wicked succubi, had used similar spells to render him helpless that they might have their way with him. How many times he had felt such intrusions. He had learned how to defeat them.

He put up a wall of the purest rage, warding every magical suggestion of immobility with ten growls of anger, ten memories of Errtu and the succubi. Outwardly, though, the barbarian took great pains to seem defeated, to hold perfectly still, his warhammer dropping down to his side. He heard the chants of "Valric High Eye" and saw out of the corner of his eye several of the warriors turning in ceremonial dance, giving thanks to their god and to Valric, the human manifestation of that god.

"Of what does he speak?" Jerek said to Valric. "What quest fell upon Torlin?"

"As I told you," the skinny shaman replied, dancing out

from the lines to stand before Wulfgar. "A drow elf! This man, seeming so honorable, traveled beside a drow elf! Could any but Torlin have taken the beast magic and defeated this deadly foe?"

"You said that Torlin was on a vision quest," Jerek argued.

"And so I believed," Valric lied. "And perhaps he is. Do not believe the lies of this one! Did you see how easily the power of Uthgar defeated him, holding him helpless before us? More likely he returned because his friends, all three, were slain by powerful Torlin, and because he knew that he could not hope to find vengeance any other way, could not hope to defeat Torlin even with the aid of the drow."

"But Wulfgar, son of Beornegar, did defeat Torlin in the contest of strength," another man remarked.

"That was before he angered Uthgar!" Valric howled. "See him standing now, helpless and defeated—"

The word barely got out of his mouth before Wulfgar exploded into action, stepping forward and clamping one hand over the shaman's skinny face. With frightening power, Wulfgar lifted Valric into the air and slammed him back down to his feet repeatedly, then shook him wildly.

"What god, Valric?" he roared. "What claim have you of Uthgar above my own as a warrior of Tempus?" To illustrate his point, and still with only one hand, Wulfgar tightened the bulging muscles in his arm and lifted Valric high into the air and held him there, perfectly steady, ignoring the man's flailing arms. "Had Torlin killed my friends in honorable battle, then I would not have returned for vengeance," he said honestly to Jerek. "I came not to avenge them, for they are well, all three. I came to avenge Torlin, a man of strength and honor, used so terribly by this wretch."

"Valric is our shaman!" more than one man yelled.

Wulfgar put him down to his feet with a growl, forcing him down to his knees and bent his head far back. Valric grabbed hard onto the man's forearm, crying out, "Kill him!" but Wulfgar only squeezed all the tighter, and Valric's words became a gurgling groan.

Wulfgar looked around at the ring of warriors. Holding Valric so helpless had bought him some time, perhaps, but they would kill him, no doubt, when he was finished with the shaman. Still, it wasn't that thought that gave Wulfgar pause, for he hardly cared about his own life. Rather, it was the expression he saw upon Jerek's face, a look of a man so utterly defeated. Wulfgar had come in with news that could break the proud chieftain, and he knew that if he killed Valric now, and many others in the ensuing battle before he, too, was finally brought down, then Jerek would not likely recover. And neither, he understood, would the Sky Ponies.

He looked down at the pitiful Valric. While he had been contemplating his next move he had inadvertently pushed back and down. The skinny man was practically bent in half and seemed near to breaking. How easy it would have been for Wulfgar to drive his arm down, snapping the man's spine.

How easy and how empty. With a frustrated roar that had nothing to do with compassion, he lifted Valric from the ground again, clapped his free hand against the man's groin, and brought him high overhead. With a roar, he launched the man a dozen feet and more into the side of a tent, sending Valric, skins, and poles tumbling down.

Warriors came at him, but he quickly had Aegis-fang in hand, and a great swipe drove them back, knocking the weapon from one and nearly tearing the man's arm off in the process.

"Hold!" came Jerek's cry. "And you, Valric!" he emphatically added, seeing the shaman pulling himself from the mess, calling for Wulfgar's death.

Jerek walked past his warriors, right up to Wulfgar. The younger man saw the murderous intent in his eyes.

"I will take no pleasure in killing the father of Torlin," Wulfgar said calmly.

That hit a nerve; Wulfgar saw the softening in the older man's face. Without another word, the barbarian turned about and started walking away, and none of the warriors moved to intercept him.

"Kill him!" Valric cried, but before the words had even left his mouth, Wulfgar whirled about and let fly his warhammer, the spinning weapon covering the twenty feet to the kneeling shaman in the blink of an eye, striking him squarely in the chest and laying him out, quite dead, among the jumble of tent poles and skins.

All eyes turned back to Wulfgar, and more than one Sky Pony made a move his way.

But Aegis-fang was back in his hands, suddenly, dramatically, and they fell back.

"His god Tempus is with him!" one man cried.

Wulfgar turned about and started away once more, knowing in his heart that nothing could be further from the truth. He expected Jerek to run him down or to order his warriors to kill him, but the group behind him remained strangely quiet. He heard no commands, no protests, no movement. Nothing at all. He had so overwhelmed the already battered tribe, had stunned Jerek with the truth of his son's fate, and then had stunned them all by his sudden and brutal vengeance on Valric, that they simply didn't know how to react.

No relief came over Wulfgar as he made his way from the encampment. He stormed down the road, angry at damned Valric, at all the damned Sky Ponies, at all the damned world. He kicked a stone from the path, then picked up another sizable rock and hurled it far through the air, shouting a roar of open defiance and pure frustration behind it. He stomped along with no direction in mind, with no sense of where he should go or where he should be. Soon after, he came upon the trail of a party of orcs, likely the same ones who had battled the Sky Ponies the previous night, an easily discernible track of blood, trampled grass, and broken twigs, veering from the main path into a small forest.

Hardly thinking, Wulfgar turned down that path, still roughly pushing aside trees, growling, and muttering curses. Gradually, though, he calmed and quieted, and replaced his lack of general purpose with a short-term, specific goal. He followed the trail more carefully, paying attention to any side paths where flanking orc scouts might have moved. Indeed, he found one such path and a pair of tracks to confirm it. He went that way quietly, looking for shadows and cover.

The day was late by then, the shadows long, but Wulfgar understood that he would have a hard time finding the scouts before they spotted him if they were on the alert—as they likely would be so soon after a terrific battle.

Wulfgar had spent many years fighting humanoids beside Drizzt Do'Urden, learning of their methods and their motivations. His course now was to make sure that the orcs were not able to warn the larger group. He knew how to do that.

Crouched in some brush by the side, the barbarian wrapped pliable twigs about his warhammer, trying to disguise the weapon as much as possible. Then he smeared mud about his face and pulled his cloak back so that it looked as though it was torn. Dirty and appearing battered, he walked out of the brush and started along the path, limping badly and groaning with every step, and every so often calling out for "my girl."

Just a short time later he sensed that he was being watched. Now he exaggerated his limp, even stumbling down to the ground at one point, using his tumble to allow him a better scan of the area.

He spotted a dark silhouette among the branches, an orc with a spear poised for a throw. Just a few steps more, he realized, and the creature would try to skewer him.

And the other was about, he realized, though he hadn't spotted the wretch. Likely it was on the ground, ready to run in and finish him as soon as the spear took him down. These two should have warned their companions, but they wanted the apparently easy kill for themselves, Wulfgar knew, that they might loot the poor man before informing their leader.

Wulfgar had to take them out quickly, but he didn't dare get much closer to the spear wielder. He pulled himself to his feet, took another staggering step along the trail, then paused and lifted his arm and eyes to the sky, wailing for his missing child. Then, nearly falling over again, shoulders slumped in defeat, he turned around and started back the way he had come, sobbing loudly, shoulders bobbing.

He knew that the orc would never be able to resist that target, despite the range. His muscles tensed, he turned his head just a bit, hearing trained on the distant tree.

Then he spun as the long-flying spear soared in. Deftly, with agility far beyond any man of his size, he caught the missile as he turned, pulling it tight against his side and issuing a profound grunt, then tumbling backward into the dirt, squirming, right hand grasping the spear, left tight about Aegis-fang.

He heard the rustle to the side from an angle above his right shoulder as he lay on his back, waiting patiently.

The second orc came out of the brush, scampering his way. Wulfgar timed the move with near perfection, rolling up and over that right shoulder, letting the spear fall as he went. He came up in a spin, Aegis-fang swiping across. But the orc skidded short, and the mighty weapon swished past harmlessly. Hardly concerned, Wulfgar continued the spin, right around, spotting the spear thrower on the tree branch as he came around and letting fly. He had to continue the spin, couldn't pause and watch the throw, though he heard the crunch and grunt, and the orc's broken body falling through the lower branches.

The orc before him yelped and threw its club, then turned and tried to flee.

Wulfgar accepted the hit as the club bounced off his massive chest. In an instant, he held the creature on its knees as he had held Valric, on its knees, head far back, backbone bowed. He pictured that moment then, conjuring an image of the wicked shaman. Then he drove down, with all his strength, growling and slapping away the orc's flailing arms. He heard the crackle of backbone and those arms stopped slapping at him, stabbing straight up into the air, trembling violently.

Wulfgar let go, and the dead creature fell over.

Aegis-fang came back to his grasp, reminding him of the other orc, and he glanced over and nodded, seeing the thing lying dead at the base of the tree.

Hardly satisfied, his bloodlust rising with each kill, Wulfgar ran, back to the main trail and then down along the clear path. He found the orcish encampment as twilight descended. There were more than a score of the monsters, with others likely out and about, scouting or hunting. He should have waited until long after dark, until the camp had settled and many of the orcs were asleep. He should have waited until he could get a better picture of the group, a better understanding of their structure and strength.

He should have waited, but he could not.

Aegis-fang soared in, right between a pair of smaller orcs, startling them, then on to slam one large creature, taking it and the orc it had been talking to down to the ground.

In charged Wulfgar, roaring wildly. He caught the spear of one startled orc, stabbing it across to impale the orc opposite, then tearing free the tip and spinning back, smashing the spear down across the first orc's head, breaking it in half. Holding both ends, Wulfgar jabbed them into either side of the orc's head, and when it reached up to grab the poles, the barbarian merely heaved it right over his head. A heavy punch dropped the next orc in line even as it moved to draw the sword from its belt, and then, roaring all the louder, Wulfgar crashed into two more, bearing them to the ground. He came up slapping and punching, kicking, anything at all to knock the orcs aside—and in truth, they showed more desire to scramble away than to come at the monstrous man.

Wulfgar caught one, spun it about, and slammed his forehead right into its face, then caught it by the hair as it fell away and drove his fist through its ugly face.

The barbarian leaped about, seeking his next victim. His momentum seemed to be fast waning with the passing seconds, but then Aegis-fang returned to his hand, and he wasted no time in whipping the hammer a dozen feet, its spinning head coming in at just the right angle to drive through the skull of one unfortunate creature.

Orcs charged in, stabbing and clubbing. Wulfgar took one hit, then another, but with each minor gash or bruise the orcs inflicted, the huge and powerful man got his hands on one and tore the life from it. Then Aegis-fang returned again, and the orcish press was shattered, driven back by mighty swipes. Covered in blood, howling wildly, thrashing that terrible hammer, the sheer sight of Wulfgar proved too much for the cowardly creatures. Those who could get away fled into the forest, and those who could not died at the barbarian's strong hands.

Mere minutes later, Wulfgar stomped out of the shattered camp, growling and smacking Aegis-fang against the trees. He knew that many orcs were watching him; he knew that none would dare attack.

Soon after, he came into a clearing on a bluff that afforded him a view of the last moments of sunset, the same fiery lines he had seen on that evening on the southern edges of the Spine of the World.

Now the colors did not touch his heart. Now he knew the thoughts of freedom from his past were a false hope, knew that his memories would follow him wherever he went, whatever he did. He felt no satisfaction at exacting revenge against Valric and no joy in slaughtering the orcs.

Nothing.

He walked on through the night, not even bothering to wash the blood from his clothes or to dress his many minor wounds. He walked toward the sunset, then kept the rising moon at his back, chasing its descent to the western horizon.

Three days later, he found Luskan's eastern gate.

Chapter 11

THE BATTLE-MAGE

o not come here," LaValle cried, and then he added softly, "I beg."

Entreri merely continued to stare at the man, his expression unreadable.

"You wounded Kadran Gordeon," LaValle went on. "In pride more than in body, and that, I warn you, is more dangerous by far."

"Gordeon is a fool," Entreri retorted.

"A fool with an army," LaValle quipped. "No guild is more entrenched in the streets than the Basadonis. None have more resources, and all of those resources, I assure you, have been turned upon Artemis Entreri."

"And upon LaValle, perhaps?" Entreri replied with a grin. "For speaking with the hunted man?"

LaValle didn't answer the obvious question other than to continue to stare hard at Artemis Entreri, the man whose mere presence in his room this night might have just condemned him.

"Tell them everything they ask of you," Entreri instructed. "Honestly. Do not try to deceive them for my sake. Tell them that I came here, uninvited, to speak with you and that

175

I show no wounds for all their efforts."

"You would taunt them so?"

Entreri shrugged. "Does it matter?"

LaValle had no answer to that, and so the assassin, with a bow, moved to the window and, defeating one trap with a flick of the wrist and carefully manipulating his body to avoid the others, slipped out to the wall and dropped silently to the street.

He dared to go by the Copper Ante that night, though only quickly and with no effort to actually enter the place. Still, he did make himself known to the door halflings. To his surprise, a short way down the alley at the side of the building, Dwahvel Tiggerwillies came out a secret door to speak with him.

"A battle-mage," she warned. "Merle Pariso. With a reputation unparalleled in Calimport. Fear him, Artemis Entreri. Run from him. Flee the city and all of Calimshan." And with that, she slipped through another barely detectable crack in the wall and was gone.

The gravity of her words and tone were not lost on the assassin. The mere fact that Dwahvel had come out to him, with nothing to gain and everything to lose—how could he repay the favor, after all, if he took her advice and fled the realm?—tipped him off that she had been instructed to so inform him, or at least, that this battle-mage was making no secret of the hunt.

So perhaps the wizard was a bit too cocksure, he told himself, but that, too, proved of little comfort. A battle-mage! A wizard trained specifically in the art of magical warfare. Cocksure, and with a right to be. Entreri had battled, and killed, many wizards, but he understood the desperate truth of his present situation. A wizard was not so difficult an enemy for a seasoned warrior, as long as the warrior was able to prepare the battlefield favorably. That, too, was usually not difficult, since wizards were often, by nature, distracted and unprepared. Typically a wizard had to anticipate battle far in advance, at the beginning of the day, that he might prepare the appropriate spells. Wizards, distracted by their continual research, rarely prepared such spells. But when a wizard was the hunter and not the hunted he would not be caught off his guard. Entreri knew he was in trouble. He seriously considered taking Dwahvel's advice.

For the first time since he had returned to Calimport, the assassin truly appreciated the danger of being without allies. He considered that in light of his experiences in Menzoberranzan, where unallied rogues could not survive for long.

Perhaps Calimport wasn't so different.

He started for his new room, an empty hovel at the back of an alleyway, but stopped and reconsidered. It wasn't likely that the wizard, with such a reputation as a combat spellcaster, would be overly skilled in divination spells as well. That hardly mattered, Entreri knew. It all came down to connections, and Merle Pariso was acting on behalf of the Basadoni guild. If he wanted to magically locate Entreri, the guild would grant him the resources of their diviners.

Where to go? He didn't want to remain on the open street where a wizard could strike from a long distance, could even, perhaps, levitate high above and rain destructive magic upon him. And so he searched the buildings, looking for a place to hide, an encampment, and knowing all the while that magical eyes might be upon him.

With that rather disturbing thought in mind, Entreri wasn't overly surprised when he slipped quietly into the supposedly empty back room of a darkened warehouse and a robed figure appeared right before him with a puff of orange smoke. The door blew closed behind him.

Entreri glanced all around, noting the lack of exits in the room, cursing his foul luck in finding this place. Again, when he considered it, it came down to his lack of allies and lack of knowledge with present-day Calimport. They were waiting for him, wherever he might go. They were ahead of him, watching his every move and obviously taking a prepared battlefield right with them. Entreri felt foolish for even coming back to this inhospitable city without first probing, without learning all that he would need to survive.

Enough of the doubts and second guesses, he pointedly reminded himself, drawing out his dagger and setting himself low in a crouch, concentrating on the situation at hand. He thought of turning back for the door, but knew without doubt that it would be magically sealed.

"Behold the Merle!" the wizard said with a laugh, waving his arms out wide. The voluminous sleeves of his robes floated out behind his lifting limbs and threw a rainbow of multicolored lights. A second wave and his arms came forward, throwing a blast of lightning at the assassin. But Entreri was already moving, rolling to the side and out of harm's way. He glanced back, hoping the bolt might have blown through the door, but it was still closed and seemed solid.

"Oh, well dodged!" Merle Pariso congratulated. "But really, pitiful assassin, do you desire to make this last longer? Why not stand still and be done with it, quickly and mercifully?" He stopped his taunting and launched into another spellcasting as Entreri charged in, jeweled dagger flashing. Merle made no move to defend against the attack, continuing calmly with his casting as Entreri came in hard, stabbing for his face.

The dagger stopped as surely as if it had struck a stone wall. Entreri wasn't really surprised—any wise wizard would have prepared such a defense—but what amazed him, even as he went flying back, hit by a burst of magical missiles, was Pariso's concentration. Entreri had to admire the man's unflinching spellcasting even as the deadly dagger came at his face, unblinking even as the blade flashed right before his eyes.

Entreri staggered to the side, diving and rolling, anticipating another attack. But now Merle Pariso, supremely confident, merely laughed at him. "Where will you run?" the battle-mage taunted. "How many times will you find the energy to dodge?"

Indeed, if he allowed the wizard's taunts to sink in, Entreri would have found it hard to hold his heart; many lesser warriors might have simply taken the wizard's advice and surrendered to the seemingly inevitable.

But not Entreri. His lethargy fell away. With his very life on the line all the doubts of his life and his purpose flew away. Now he lived completely in the moment, adrenaline pumping. One step at a time, and the first of those steps was to defeat the stoneskin, the magical defense that could turn any blade—but only for a certain number of attacks. Spinning and rolling, the assassin took up a chair and broke free a leg, then rolled about and launched it at the wizard, scoring an ineffective hit.

Another burst of magical missiles slammed into him, following him unerringly in his roll and stinging him. He shrugged through it, though, and came up throwing. A second, then a third chair leg scored two more hits.

The fourth followed in rapid succession. Then Entreri threw the base of the chair. It was a meager missile that would hardly have hurt the wizard even without the magical defense, but one that took yet another layer off the stoneskin.

Entreri paid for the offensive flurry, though, as Merle Pariso's next lightning bolt caught him hard and launched him spinning sidelong. His shoulder burned, his hair danced on end, and his heart fluttered.

Desperate and hurt, the assassin went in hard, dagger slashing. "How many more can you defeat?" he roared, stabbing hard again and again.

His answer came in the form of flames, a shroud of dancing fire covering, but hardly consuming, Merle Pariso. Entreri noted the fire too late to stop short his last attack, and the dagger went through, again hitting harmlessly against the stoneskin—harmlessly to Pariso but not to Entreri. The new spell, the flame shield, replicated the intended bite of that dagger back at Entreri, drawing a deep gash along the already battered man's ribs.

With a howl the assassin fell back, purposely turning

himself in line with the door, then dodging deftly as the predictable lightning bolt came after him.

The rolling assassin looked back as he came around, pleased to see that this time the wooden door had indeed splintered. He grabbed another chair and threw it at the wizard, turning for the door even as he released it.

Merle Pariso's groan stopped him dead and turned him back around, thinking the stoneskin expired.

But then it was Entreri's turn to groan. "Oh, clever," he congratulated, realizing the wizard's groan to be no more than a ruse, buying the man time to cast his next spell.

The assassin turned back for the door but hadn't gone a step before he was forced back, as a wall of huge flames erupted along that wall, blocking escape.

"Well fought, assassin," Merle Pariso said honestly. "I expected as much from Artemis Entreri. But now, alas, you die." He finished by drawing a wand, pointing it at the floor at his feet, and firing a burning seed.

Entreri fell flat, pulling what remained of his cloak over his head as the seed exploded into a fireball, filling all the room, burning his hair and scorching his lungs, but harming Pariso not at all. The wizard was secure within his fiery shield.

Entreri came up dazed, eyes filled with heat and smoke as all the building around him burned. Merle Pariso stood there, laughing wildly.

The assassin had to get out. He couldn't possibly defeat the mage and wouldn't survive for much longer against Pariso's potent magics. He turned for the door, thinking to dive right through the fire wall, but then a glowing sword appeared in midair before him, slashing hard. He had to dodge aside and get his dagger up against the blade to turn it. The invisible opponent—Entreri knew it to be Merle Pariso's will acting through the magical dweomer—came on hard, forcing him to retreat. The sword always stayed between the assassin and the door.

On his balance now, Entreri was more than a match for the slicing weapon, easily dodging and striking back hard.

He knew that no hand guided the blade, that the only way to defeat it was to strike at the sword itself, and that posed no great problem for the warrior assassin. But then another glowing sword appeared. Entreri had never seen this before, had never even heard of a wizard who could control two such magical creations at the same time.

He dived and rolled, and the swords pursued. He tried to dart around them for the doorway but found that they were too quick. He glanced back at Pariso. Barely, through the growing smoke, he could see the wizard still shrouded in defensive flames, tapping his fireball wand against his cheek.

The heat nearly overwhelmed Entreri. The flames were all about, on the walls, the floor, and the ceiling. Wood crackled in protest, and beams collapsed.

"I will not leave," he heard Merle Pariso say. "I will watch until the life is gone from you, Artemis Entreri."

On came the glowing swords, slashing in perfect coordination, and Entreri knew that the wizard almost got what he wanted. The assassin barely, barely, avoiding the hits, dived forward under the blades, coming up in a run for the door. Shielding his face with his arms, he leaped into the fire wall, thinking to break through the battered door.

He hit as solid a barrier as he had ever felt, a magical wall, he knew. He scrambled back out of the flames into the burning room, and the two swords waited for him. Merle Pariso stood calmly pointing the dreaded fireball wand.

But then to the side of the wizard a green-gloved disembodied hand appeared, sliding out of nowhere and holding what appeared to be a large egg.

Merle Pariso's eyes widened in horror. "Wh-who?" he stuttered. "Wha—?"

The hand tossed the egg to the floor, where it exploded into a huge ball of powdery dust, rolling into the air, then shimmering into a multicolored cloud. Entreri heard music then, even above the roar of the conflagration, many different notes climbing the scale, then dropping low and ending in a long, monotonal humming sound.

The glowing swords disappeared. So did the fire wall blocking the door, though the normal flames still burned brightly along door and wall. So did Merle Pariso's defensive fire shield.

The wizard cried out and waved his arms frantically, trying to cast another spell—some magical escape, Entreri realized, for now he was obviously feeling the heat as intensely as was Entreri.

The assassin realized that the magical barrier was likely gone as well, and he could have turned and run from the room. But he couldn't tear his eyes from the spectacle of Pariso, backpedaling, so obviously distressed. To the amazement of both, many of the smaller fires near the wizard then changed shape, appearing as little humanoid creatures, circling Pariso in a strange dance.

The wizard skipped backward, tripped over a loose board, and went down on his back. The little fire humanoids, like a pack of hunting wolves, leaped upon him, lighting his robes and burning his skin. Pariso opened wide his mouth to scream, and one of the fiery animations raced right down his throat, stealing his voice and burning him from the inside.

The green-gloved hand beckoned to Entreri.

The wall behind him collapsed, sparks and embers flying everywhere, stealing his easy escape.

Moving cautiously but quickly, the assassin circled wide of the hand, gaining a better angle as he realized that it was not a disembodied hand at all, but merely one poking through a dimensional gate of some sort.

Entreri's knees went weak at the sight. He nearly bolted back for the blazing door, but a sound from above told him that the ceiling was falling in. Purely on survival instinct, for if he had thought about it he likely would have chosen death, Entreri leaped through the dimensional door.

Into the arms of his saviors.

Chapter 12
FINDING A NICHE

e knew this town, though only vaguely. He'd made a single passage through the place long ago, in the days of hope and future dreams, in the search for Mithral Hall. Little seemed familiar to Wulfgar now as he made his plodding way through Luskan, absorbing the sights and sounds of the many open air markets and the general bustle of a northern city awakening after winter's slumber.

Many, many gazes fell over him as he moved along, for Wulfgar—closer to seven feet tall than to six with a massive chest and shoulders, and the glittering warhammer strapped across his back—was no ordinary sight. Barbarians occasionally wandered into Luskan, but even among the hardy folk Wulfgar loomed huge.

He ignored the looks and the whispers and continued merely to wander the many ways. He spotted the Hosttower of the Arcane, the famed wizard's guild of Luskan, and recognized the building easily enough, since it was in the shape of a huge tree with spreading limbs. But again that one note of recognition did little to guide the man along. It had been so long ago, a lifetime ago it seemed, since he had last been here.

Minutes became an hour, then two hours. The barbarian's vision was turned inward now as much as outward. His mind replayed images of the past few days, particularly the moment of his unsatisfying revenge. The image of Valric High Eye flying back into the jumble of broken tenting, Aegis-fang crushing his chest, was vivid in his mind's eye.

Wulfgar ran his hand through his unkempt hair and staggered along. Clearly he was exhausted, for he had slept only a few scattered hours in three days since the encounter with the Sky Ponies. He had wandered the roads to the west aimlessly until he had spotted the outline of the distant city. The guards at the eastern gate of Luskan had threatened to turn him away, but when he had just swung about with a shrug they called after him and told him he could enter but warned him to keep his weapon strapped across his back.

Wulfgar had no intention of fighting and no intention of following the guards' command should a fight find him. He merely nodded and walked through the gates, then down the streets and through the markets.

He discovered another familiar landmark when the shadows were long, the sun low in the western sky. A signpost named one way Half Moon Street, a place Wulfgar had been before. A short way down the street he saw the sign for the Cutlass, a tavern he knew from his first trip through, a place wherein he had been involved, in some ways had started, a tremendous row. Looking at the Cutlass, at the whole decrepit street now, Wulfgar wondered how he could have ever expected otherwise.

This was the place for the lowest orders of society, for thugs and rogues, for men running from lords. The barbarian put his hand in his nearly empty pouch, fumbling with the few coins, and realized then that this was where he belonged.

He went into the Cutlass half fearing he would be recognized, that he would find himself in another brawl before the door closed behind him.

Of course he was not recognized. Nor did he see any faces

that seemed the least bit familiar. The layout of the place was pretty much the same as he remembered. As he scanned the room, his gaze inevitably went to the wall to the side of the long bar, the wall where a younger Wulfgar had set a brute in his place by driving the man's head right through the planking.

He was so full of pride back then, so ready to fight. Now, too, he was more than willing to put his fists or weapons to use, but his purpose in doing so had changed. Now he fought out of anger, out of the sheerest rage, whether that rage had anything to do with whatever enemy stood before him or not. Now he fought because that course seemed as good as any other. Perhaps, just perhaps, he fought in the hopes that he would lose, that some enemy would end his internal torment.

He couldn't hold that thought, couldn't hold any thought, as he made his way to the bar, taking no care not to jostle the many patrons who crowded before him. He pulled off his traveling cloak and took a seat, not even bothering to ask either of the men flanking the stool if they had a friend who was using it.

And then he watched and waited, letting the myriad of sights and sounds—whispered conversations, lewd remarks aimed at serving wenches more than ready to snap back with their own stinging retort—become a general blur, a welcomed buzz.

His head drooped, and that movement alone woke him. He shifted in his seat and noted then that the barkeep, an old man who still held the hardness of youth about his strong shoulders, stood before him, wiping a glass.

"Arumn Gardpeck," the barkeep introduced himself, extending a hand.

Wulfgar regarded the offered hand but did not shake it.

Without missing a beat the barkeep went back to his wiping. "A drink?" he asked.

Wulfgar shook his head and looked away, desiring nothing from the man, especially any useless conversation.

Arumn came forward, though, leaning over the bar and

drawing Wulfgar's full attention. "I want no trouble in me bar," he said calmly, looking over the barbarian's huge, muscled arms.

Wulfgar waved him away.

Minutes slipped past, and the place grew even more crowded. No one bothered Wulfgar, though, and so he allowed himself to relax his guard, his head inevitably drooping. He fell asleep, his face buried in his arms atop Arumn Gardpeck's clean bar.

"Hey there," he heard, and the voice sounded as if it was far, far away. He felt a shake then, on his shoulder, and he opened his sleepy eyes and lifted his head to see Arumn's smiling face. "Time for leaving."

Wulfgar stared at him blankly.

"Where are ye stayin'?" the barkeep asked. "Might that I could find a couple who'd walk ye there."

For a long while, Wulfgar didn't answer, staring groggily at the man, trying to get his bearings.

"And he weren't even drinking!" one man howled from the side. Wulfgar turned to regard him and noted that several large men, Arumn Gardpeck's security force, no doubt, had formed a semicircle behind him. Wulfgar turned back to eye Arumn.

"Where are ye stayin'?" the man asked again. "And ye shut yer mouth, Josi Puddles," he added to the taunting man.

Wulfgar shrugged. "Nowhere," he answered honestly.

"Well, ye can't be stayin' 'ere!" yet another man growled, moving close enough to poke the barbarian in the shoulder.

Wulfgar calmly swung his head, taking a measure of the man.

"Hush yer mouth!" Arumn was quick to scold, and he shifted about, drawing Wulfgar's gaze. "I could give ye a room for a few silver pieces," he said.

"I have little money," the big man admitted.

"Then sell me yer hammer," said another directly behind Wulfgar. When he turned to regard the speaker he saw that the man was holding Aegis-fang. Now Wulfgar was fully awake and up, hand extended, his expression and posture demanding the hammer's immediate return.

"Might that I will give it back to ye," the man remarked as Wulfgar slid out of the chair and advanced a threatening step. As he spoke, he lifted Aegis-fang, more in an angle to cave in Wulfgar's skull that to hand it over.

Wulfgar stopped short and shifted his dangerous glare over each of the large men, his lips curling up in a confident, wicked, smile. "You wish to buy it?" he asked the man holding the hammer. "Then you should know its name."

Wulfgar spoke the hammer's name, and it vanished from the hands of the threatening man and reappeared in Wulfgar's. The barbarian was moving even before the hammer materialized, closing in on the man with a single long stride and slapping him with a backhand that launched him into the air to land crashing over a table.

The others came at the huge barbarian, but only for an instant, for he was ready now, waving the powerful warhammer so easily that the others understood he was not one to be taken lightly and not one to fight unless they were willing to see their ranks thinned considerably.

"Hold! Hold!" cried Arumn, rushing out from behind the bar and waving his bouncers away. A couple went over to help the man Wulfgar had slapped. So disoriented was he that they had to hoist him and support him.

And still Arumn waved them all away. He stood before Wulfgar, within easy striking distance, but he was not afraid—or if he was, he wasn't showing it.

"I could use one with yer strength," he remarked. "That was Reef ye dropped with an open-handed slap, and Reef's one o' me better fighters."

Wulfgar looked across the room at the man sitting with the other bouncers and scoffed.

Arumn led him back to the bar and sat him down, then went behind and produced a bottle, setting it right before the big man and motioning for him to drink.

Wulfgar did, a great hearty swig that burned all the way down.

"A room and free food," Arumn said. "All ye can eat. And

all that I ask in return is that ye help keep me tavern free o' fights or that ye finish 'em quick if they start."

Wulfgar looked back over his shoulder at the men across the way. "What of them?" he asked, taking another huge swig from the bottle, then coughing as he wiped his bare forearm across his lips. The potent liquor seemed to draw all the coating from his throat.

"They help me when I ask, as they help most o' the inn-keepers on Half Moon street and all the streets about," Arumn explained. "I been thinking o' hiring me own and keeping him on, and I'm thinking that ye'd fit that role well."

"You hardly know me," Wulfgar argued, and his third gulp half drained the bottle. This time the burning seemed to spread out more quickly, until all his body felt warm and a bit numb. "And you know nothing of my history."

"Nor do I care," said Arumn. "We don't get many of yer type in here—northmen, I mean. Ye've got a reputation for fighting, and the way ye slapped Reef aside tells me that reputation's well earned."

"Room and food?" Wulfgar asked.

"And drink," Arumn added, motioning to the bottle, which Wulfgar promptly lifted to his lips and drained. He went to move it back to Arumn, but it seemed to jump from his hand, and when he tried to retrieve it he merely kept pushing it awkwardly along until Arumn deftly scooped it away from him.

Wulfgar sat up straighter, or tried to, and closed his eyes very tightly, trying to find a center of focus. When he opened his eyes once more, he found another full bottle before him, and he wasted no time in bringing that one, too, up to his lips.

An hour later, Arumn, who had taken a few drinks himself, helped Wulfgar up the stairs and into a tiny room. He tried to guide Wulfgar onto the small bed—a cot too small to comfortably accommodate the huge barbarian—but both wound up falling over, crashing across the cot then onto the floor.

They shared a laugh, an honest laugh, the first one Wulfgar had known since the rescue in the ice cave.

"They start coming in soon after midday," Arumn explained, spit flying with every word. "But I won't be needing ye until the sun's down. I'll get ye then, and I'm thinking that ye'll be needin' waking!"

They shared another laugh at that, and Arumn staggered out the door, falling against it to close it behind him, leaving Wulfgar alone in the pitch-black room.

Alone. Completely alone.

That notion nearly overwhelmed him. Sitting there drunk the barbarian realized that Errtu hadn't come in here with him, that everything, every memory, good and bad, was but a harmless blur. In those bottles, under the spell of that potent liquor, Wulfgar found a reprieve.

Food and a room and drink Arumn had promised.

To Wulfgar the last condition of his employment rang out as the most important.

* * * * *

Entreri stood in an alley, not far from his near-disaster with Merle Pariso, looking back at the blazing warehouse. Flames leaped high above the rooftops of the nearest buildings. Three others stood beside him. They were about the same height as the assassin, a bit more slender, perhaps, but with muscles obviously honed for battle.

What distinguished them most was their ebony skin. One wore a huge purple hat, set with a gigantic plume.

"Twice I have pulled you from certain death," the one with the hat remarked.

Entreri looked hard at the speaker, wanting nothing more than to drive his dagger deep into the dark elf's chest. He knew better though, knew that this one, Jarlaxle, was far too protected for any such obvious attacks.

"We have much to discuss," the dark elf said, and he motioned to one of his companions. With a thought, it seemed, the drow brought up another dimensional door, this one leading into a room where several other dark elves had gathered.

"Kimmuriel Oblodra," Jarlaxle explained.

Entreri knew the name—the surname, at least. House Oblodra had once been the third most powerful house in Menzoberranzan and one of the most frightening because of their practice of psionics, a curious and little understood magic of the mind. During the Time of Troubles, the Oblodrans, whose powers were not adversely affected, as were the more conventional magics within the city, used the opportunity to press their advantage, even going so far as to threaten Matron Mother Baenre, the ruling Matron of the ruling house of the city. When the waves of instability that marked that strange time turned again in favor of conventional magics and against the powers of the mind, House Oblodra had been obliterated, the great structure and all its inhabitants pulled into the great gorge, the Clawrift, by a physical manifestation of Matron Baenre's rage.

Well, Entreri thought, staring at the psionicist, not all of the inhabitants.

He went through the psionic door with Jarlaxle—what choice did he have?—and after a long moment of dizzying disorientation took a seat in the small room when the drow mercenary motioned for him to do so. All the dark elf group except for Jarlaxle and Kimmuriel, went out then in practiced order, to secure the area about the meeting place.

"We are safe enough," Jarlaxle assured Entreri.

"They were watching me magically," the assassin replied. "That was how Merle Pariso set the ambush."

"We have been watching you magically for many weeks," Jarlaxle said with a grin. "They watch you no more, I assure you."

"You came for me, then?" the assassin asked. "It seems a bit of trouble to retrieve one *rivvil*," he added, using the drow word, and not a complimentary one, for human.

Jarlaxle laughed aloud at Entreri's choice of that word. It was indeed the word for "human," but one also used to describe many inferior races, which meant any race that was not drow.

"To retrieve you?" the assassin asked incredulously. "Do you wish to return to Menzoberranzan?"

"I would kill you or force you to kill me long before we ever stepped into the drow city," Entreri replied in all seriousness.

"Of course," Jarlaxle said calmly, taking no offense and not disagreeing in the least. "That is not your place, nor is Calimport ours."

"Then why have you come?"

"Because Calimport is your place, and Menzoberranzan is mine," the drow replied, smiling all the wider, as though the simple statement explained everything.

And before he questioned Jarlaxle more deeply, Entreri sat back and took a long while to reflect upon the words. Jarlaxle was, above all else, an opportunist. The drow, along with Bregan D'aerthe, his powerful band of rogues, seemed to find a way to gain from practically every situation. Menzoberranzan was a city ruled by females, the priestesses of Lolth, and yet even there Jarlaxle and his band, almost exclusively males, were far from the underclass. So why now had he come to find Entreri, come to a place that he just openly and honestly admitted was not his place at all?

"You want me to front you," the assassin stated.

"I am not familiar with the term," Jarlaxle replied.

Now Entreri, seeing the lie for what it was, was the one wearing the grin. "You want to extend the hand of Bregan D'aerthe to the surface, to Calimport, but you recognize that you and yours would never be accepted even among the bowel-dwellers of the city."

"We could use magic to disguise our true identity," the drow argued.

"But why bother when you have Artemis Entreri?" the assassin was quick to reply.

"And do I?" asked the drow.

Entreri thought it over for a moment, then merely shrugged.

"I offer you protection from your enemies," Jarlaxle

stated. "No, more than that, I offer you power over your enemies. With your knowledge and reputation and the power of Bregan D'aerthe secretly behind you, you will soon rule the streets of Calimport."

"As Jarlaxle's puppet," Entreri said.

"As Jarlaxle's partner," the drow replied. "I have no need of puppets. In fact, I consider them a hindrance. A partner truly profiting from the organization is one working harder to reach higher goals. Besides, Artemis Entreri, are we not friends?"

Entreri laughed aloud at that notion. The words "Jarlaxle" and "friend" seemed incongruous indeed when used in the same sentence, bringing to mind an old street proverb that the most dangerous and threatening words a Calimshite street vendor could ever say to someone were "trust me."

And that is exactly what Jarlaxle had just said to Entreri.

"Your enemies of the Basadoni Guild will soon call you pasha," the drow went on.

Entreri showed no reaction.

"Even the political leaders of the city, of all the realm of Calimshan, will defer to you," said Jarlaxle.

Entreri showed no reaction.

"I will know now, before you leave this room, if my offer is agreeable," Jarlaxle added, his voice sounding a bit more ominous.

Entreri understood well the implications of that tone. He knew about Bregan D'aerthe being within the city now, and that alone meant that he would either play along or be killed outright.

"Partners," the assassin said, poking himself in the chest. "But I direct the sword of Bregan D'aerthe in Calimport. You strike when and where I decide."

Jarlaxle agreed with a nod. Then he snapped his fingers and another dark elf entered the room, moving beside Entreri. This was obviously the assassin's escort.

"Sleep well," Jarlaxle bade the human. "For tomorrow begins your ascent."

Entreri didn't bother to reply but just walked out of the room.

Yet another drow came out from behind a curtain then. "He was not lying," he assured Jarlaxle, speaking in the tongue common to dark elves.

The cunning mercenary leader nodded and smiled, glad to have the services of so powerful an ally as Rai'gy Bondalek of Ched Nasad, formerly the high priest of that other drow city, but ousted in a coup and rescued by the ever-opportunistic Bregan D'aerthe. Jarlaxle had settled his sights on Rai'gy long before, for the drow was not only powerful in the god-given priestly magics, but was well-versed in the ways of wizards as well. How lucky for Bregan D'aerthe that Rai'gy had suddenly found himself an outcast.

Rai'gy had no idea that Jarlaxle had been the one to incite that coup.

"Your Entreri did not seem thrilled with the treasures you dangled before him," Rai'gy dared to remark. "He will do as he promised, perhaps, but with little heart."

Jarlaxle nodded, not the least bit surprised by Entreri's reaction. He had come to understand Artemis Entreri quite well in the months the assassin had lived with Bregan D'aerthe in Menzoberranzan. He knew the man's motivations and desires—better, perhaps, than Entreri knew them.

"There is one other treasure that I did not offer," he explained. "One that Artemis Entreri does not even yet realize that he wants." Jarlaxle reached into the folds of his cloak and produced an amulet dangling at the end of a silver chain. "I took it from Catti-brie," he explained. "Companion of Drizzt Do'Urden. It was given to her adoptive father, the dwarf Bruenor Battlehammer, by the High Lady Alustriel of Silverymoon long ago as a means of tracking the rogue drow."

"You know much," Rai'gy remarked.

"That is how I survive," Jarlaxle replied.

"But Catti-brie knows it is gone," reasoned Kimmuriel Oblodra. "Thus, she and her companion have likely taken steps to defeat any further use of it."

Jarlaxle was shaking his head long before the psionicist ever finished. "Catti-brie's was returned to her cloak before she left the city. This one is a copy in form and in magic, created by a wizard associate. Likely the woman returned the original to Bruenor Battlehammer, and he gave it back to Lady Alustriel. I should think she would want it back or at least want it out of Catti-brie's possession, for it seems the two had somewhat of a rivalry growing concerning the affections of the rogue Drizzt Do'Urden."

Both the others crinkled their faces in disgust at the thought that any drow so beautiful could find passion with a non-drow, a creature, by that simple definition, who was obviously *iblith*, or excrement.

Jarlaxle, himself intrigued by the beautiful Catti-brie, didn't bother to refute their racist feelings.

"But if that is a copy, is the magic strong enough?" Kimmuriel asked, and he emphasized the word "magic" as if to prompt Jarlaxle to explain how it might prove useful.

"Magical dweomers create pathways of power," Rai'gy Bondalek explained. "Pathways that I know how to enhance and to replicate."

"Rai'gy spent many of his earlier years perfecting the technique," Jarlaxle added. "His ability to recover the previous powers of ancient Ched Nasad relics proved pivotal in his ascension to the position as the city's high priest. And he can do it again, even enhancing the previous dweomer to new heights."

"That we might find Drizzt Do'Urden," Kimmuriel said.

Jarlaxle nodded. "What a fine trophy for Artemis Entreri."

Part 3

CLIMBING TO THE TOP

OF THE BOTTOM

watched the miles roll out behind me, whether walking down a road or sailing fast out of Waterdeep for the southlands, putting distance between us and the friend we four had left behind. The friend?

Many times during those long and arduous days, each of us in our own little space came to wonder about that word "friend" and the responsibilities such a label might carry. We had left Wulfgar behind in the wilds of the Spine of the World no less and had no idea if he was well, if he was even still alive. Could a true friend so desert another? Would a true friend allow a man to walk alone along troubled and dangerous paths?

Often I ponder the meaning of that word. Friend. It seems such an obvious thing, friendship, and yet often it becomes so very complicated. Should I have stopped Wulfgar, even knowing and admitting that he had his own road to walk? Or should I have gone with him? Or should we all four have shadowed him, watching over him?

I think not, though I admit that I know not for certain. There is a fine line between friendship and parenting, and when that line is crossed, the result is often disastrous. A parent who strives to make a true friend of his or her child may well sacrifice authority, and though that parent may be comfortable with surrendering the dominant position, the unintentional result will be to steal from that child the necessary guidance and, more importantly, the sense of security the parent is supposed to impart. On the opposite side, a friend who takes a role as parent forgets the most important ingredient of friendship: respect.

197

R. A. Salvatore

For respect is the guiding principle of friendship, the light-house beacon that directs the course of any true friendship. And respect demands trust.

Thus, the four of us pray for Wulfgar and intend that our paths will indeed cross again. Though we'll often look back over our shoulders and wonder, we hold fast to our understanding of friendship, of trust, and of respect. We accept, grudgingly but resolutely, our divergent paths.

Surely Wulfgar's trials have become my trials in many ways, but I see now that the friendship of mine most in flux is not the one with the barbarian—not from my perspective, anyway, since I understand that Wulfgar alone must decide the depth and course of our bond—but my relationship with Catti-brie. Our love for each other is no secret between us, or to anyone else watching us (and I fear that perhaps the bond that has grown between us might have had some influence in Wulfgar's painful decisions), but the nature of that love remains a mystery to me and to Catti-brie. We have in many ways become as brother and sister, and surely I am closer to her than I could ever have been to any of my natural siblings! For several years we had only each other to count on and both learned beyond any doubt that the other would always be there. I would die for her, and she for me. Without hesitation, without doubt. Truly in all the world there is no one, not even Bruenor, Wulfgar, or Regis, or even Zaknafein, with whom I would rather spend my time. There is no one who can view a sunrise beside me and better understand the emotions that sight always stirs within me. There is no one who can fight beside me and better compliment my movements. There is no one who better knows all that is in my heart and thoughts, though I had not yet spoken a word.

But what does that mean?

Surely I feel a physical attraction to Catti-brie as well. She is possessed of a combination of innocence and a playful wickedness. For all her sympathy and empathy and compassion, there is an edge to Catti-brie that makes potential enemies tremble in fear and potential lovers tremble in anticipation. I believe that she feels similarly toward me, and yet we both understand the dangers of this uncharted territory, dangers more frightening than any physical enemy we have ever known. I am drow, and young, and with the dawn and twilight of several centuries ahead of me. She is human and, though young, with merely decades of life ahead of her. Of course, Catti-brie's life is complicated enough merely having a drow elf as a traveling companion and friend. What troubles might she find if she and I were more than that? And what might the world think of our children, if ever that path we walked? Would any society in all the world accept them?

I know how I feel when I look upon her, though, and believe that I understand her feelings as well. On that level, it seems such an obvious thing, and yet, alas, it becomes so very complicated.

—Drizzt Do'Urden

Chapter 13
SECRET WEAPON

ou have found the rogue?" Jarlaxle asked Rai'gy Bondalek. Kimmuriel Oblodra stood beside the mercenary leader, the psionicist appearing unarmed and unarmored, seeming perfectly defenseless to one who did not understand the powers of his mind.

"He is with a dwarf, a woman, and a halfling," Rai'gy answered. "And sometimes they are joined by a great black cat."

"Guenhwyvar," Jarlaxle explained. "Once the property of Masoj Hun'ette. A powerful magical item indeed."

"But not the greatest magic that they carry," Rai'gy informed. "There is another, stored in a pouch on the rogue's belt, that radiates magic stronger than all their other magics combined. Even through the distance of my scrying it beckoned to me, almost as if it were asking me to retrieve it from its present unworthy owner."

"What could it be?" the always opportunistic mercenary asked.

Rai'gy shook his head, his shock of white hair flying from side to side. "Like no dweomer I have seen before," he admitted.

"Is that not the way of magic?" Kimmuriel Oblodra put in with obvious distaste. "Unknown and uncontrollable."

Rai'gy shot the psionicist an angry glare, but Jarlaxle, more than willing to utilize both magic and psionics, merely smiled. "Learn more about it and about them," he instructed the wizard-priest. "If it beckons to us, then perhaps we would be wise to heed its call. How far are they, and how fast can we get to them?"

"Very," Rai'gy answered. "And very. They had begun an overland route but were accosted by giantkind and goblinkin at every bend in the path."

"Perhaps the magical item is not particular about who it calls for a new owner," Kimmuriel remarked with obvious sarcasm.

"They turned about and took ship," Rai'gy went on, ignoring the comment. "Out of the great northern city of Waterdeep, I believe, far, far up the Sword Coast."

"But sailing south?" Jarlaxle asked hopefully.

"I believe," Rai'gy answered. "It does not matter. There are magics, of course, and mind powers," he added, nodding deferentially to Kimmuriel, "that can get us to them as easily as if they were standing in the next room."

"Back to your searching, then," Jarlaxle said.

"But are we not to visit a guild this very night?" Rai'gy asked.

"You will not be needed," Jarlaxle replied. "Minor guilds alone will meet this night."

"Even minor guilds would be wise to employ wizards," the wizard-priest remarked.

"The wizard of this one is a friend of Entreri," Jarlaxle explained with a laugh that made it sound as if it were all too easy. "And the other guild is naught but halflings, hardly versed in the ways of magic. Tomorrow night you will be needed, perhaps. This night continue your examination of Drizzt Do'Urden. In the end he will likely prove the most important cog of all."

"Because of the magical item?" Kimmuriel asked.

"Because of Entreri's lack of interest," Jarlaxle replied.

The wizard-priest shook his head. "We offer him power and riches beyond his comprehension," he said. "And yet he leads us onward as if he were going into hopeless battle against the Spider Queen herself."

"He cannot appreciate the power or the riches until he has resolved an inner conflict," explained Jarlaxle, whose greatest gift of all was the ability to get into the minds of enemies and friends alike, and not with prying powers, such as Kimmuriel Oblodra might use, but with simple empathy and understanding. "But fear not his present lack of motivation. I know Artemis Entreri well enough to understand that he will prove more than effective whether his heart is in the fight or not. As humans go I have never met one more dangerous or more devious."

"A pity his skin is so light," Kimmuriel remarked.

Jarlaxle only smiled. He knew well enough that if Artemis Entreri had been born drow in Menzoberranzan the man would have been among the greatest of weapon masters, or perhaps he would have even exceeded that claim. Perhaps he would have been a rival to Jarlaxle for control of Bregan D'aerthe.

"We will speak in the comfortable darkness of the tunnels when the shining hellfire rises into the too-high sky," he said to Rai'gy. "Have more answers for me."

"Fare well with the guilds," Rai'gy answered, and with a bow he turned and left.

Jarlaxle turned to Kimmuriel and nodded. It was time to go hunting.

* * * * *

With their cherubic faces, halflings were regarded by the other races as creatures with large eyes, but how much wider those eyes became for the four in the room with Dwahvel when a magical portal opened right before them (despite the usual precautions against such magical intrusion), and Artemis Entreri stepped into the room. The assassin cut an impressive figure in a layered black coat and a black bolero, banded about the base of its riser in blacker silk.

Entreri assumed a strong, hands-on-hips pose just as Kimmuriel had taught him, holding steady against the waves of disorientation that always accompanied such psionic dimensional travel.

Behind him, in the chamber on the other side of the door, a room lightless save that spilling in through the gate from Dwahvel's chamber, huddled a few dark shapes. When one of the halfling soldiers moved to meet the intruder, one of those dark shapes shifted slightly, and the halfling, with hardly a squeak, toppled to the floor.

"He is sleeping and otherwise unharmed," Entreri quickly explained, not wanting a fight with the others, who were scrambling about for weapons. "I did not come here for a fight, I assure you, but I can leave all of you dead in my wake if you insist upon one."

"You could have used the front door," Dwahvel, the only one appearing unshaken, remarked dryly.

"I did not wish to be seen entering your establishment," the assassin, fully oriented once more, explained. "For your protection."

"And what form of entrance is this?" Dwahvel asked. "Magical and unbidden, yet none of my wards—and I paid well for them, I assure you—offered resistance."

"No magic that will concern you," Entreri replied, "but that will surely concern my enemies. Know that I did not return to Calimport to lurk in shadows at the bidding of others. I have traveled the Realms extensively and have brought back with me that which I have learned."

"So Artemis Entreri returns as the conqueror," Dwahvel remarked. Beside her the soldiers bristled, but Dwahvel did well to hold them in check. Now that Entreri was among them, to fight him would cost her dearly, she realized.

Very dearly.

"Perhaps," Entreri conceded. "We shall see how it goes."

"It will take more than a display of teleportation to convince me to throw the weight of my guild behind you,"

Dwahvel said calmly. "To choose wrongly in such a war would prove fatal."

"I do not wish you to choose at all," Entreri assured her.

Dwahvel eyed him suspiciously, then turned to each of her trusted guards. They, too, wore doubting expressions.

"Then why bother to come to me?" she asked.

"To inform you that a war is about to begin," Entreri answered. "I owe you that much, at least."

"And perhaps you wish for me to open wide my ears that you may learn how goes the fight," the sly halfling reasoned.

"As you wish," Entreri replied. "When this is finished, and I have found control, I will not forget all that you have already done for me."

"And if you lose?"

Entreri laughed. "Be wary," he said. "And, for your health, Dwahvel Tiggerwillies, be neutral. I owe you and see our friendship as to the benefit of both, but if I learn that you betray me by word or by deed, I will bring your house down around you." With that, he gave a polite bow, a tip of the black bolero and slipped back through the portal.

One globe of darkness after another filled Dwahvel's chamber, forcing her and the three standing soldiers to crawl about helplessly until one found the normal exit and called the others to him.

Finally the darkness abated, and the halflings dared to re-enter, to find their sleeping companion snoring contentedly, and then to find, upon searching the body, a small dart stuck into his shoulder.

"Entreri has friends," one of them remarked.

Dwahvel merely nodded, not surprised and glad indeed at that moment that she had previously chosen to help the outcast assassin. He was not a man Dwahvel Tiggerwillies wished for an enemy.

* * * * *

"Ah, but you make my life so dangerous," LaValle said with an exaggerated sigh when Entreri, unannounced and uninvited, walked from thin air, it seemed, into LaValle's private room.

"Well done—on your escape from Kadran Gordeon, I mean," LaValle went on when Entreri didn't immediately respond. The wizard was trying hard to appear collected. Hadn't Entreri slipped into his guarded room twice before, after all? But this time—and the assassin recognized it splayed on LaValle's face—he had truly surprised the wizard. Bodeau had sharpened up the defenses of his guild house amazingly well against both magical and physical intrusion. As much as he respected Entreri, LaValle had obviously not expected the assassin to get through so easily.

"Not so difficult a task, I assure you," the assassin replied, keeping his voice steady so that his words sounded as simple fact and not a boast. "I have traveled the world, and under the world and have witnessed powers very different from anything experienced in Calimport. Powers that will bring me that which I desire."

LaValle sat on an old and comfortable chair, planting one elbow on the worn arm and dropping his head sidelong against his open palm. What was it about this man, he wondered, that so mocked all the ordinary trappings of power? He looked all around at his room, at the many carved statues, gargoyles, and exotic birds, at the assortment of finely carved staves, some magical, some not, at the three skulls grinning from the cubbies atop his desk, at the crystal ball set upon the small table across the way. These were his items of power, items gained through a lifetime of work, items that he could use to destroy or at least to defend against, any single man he had ever met.

Except for one. What was it about this one? The way he stood? The way he moved? The simple aura of power that surrounded him, as tangible as the gray cloak and black bolero he now wore?

"Go and bring Quentin Bodeau," Entreri instructed.

"He will not appreciate becoming involved."

"He already is," Entreri assured the wizard. "Now he must choose."

205

"Between you and . . . ?" LaValle asked.

"The rest of them," Entreri replied calmly.

LaValle tilted his head curiously. "You mean to do battle with all of Calimport then?" he asked skeptically.

"With all in Calimport who oppose me," Entreri said, again with the utmost calm.

LaValle shook his head, not knowing what to make of it all. He trusted Entreri's judgment—never had the wizard met a more cunning and controlled man—but the assassin spoke foolishness, it seemed, if he honestly believed he could stand alone against the likes of the Basadonis, let alone the rest of Calimport's street powers.

But still . . .

"Shall I bring Chalsee Anguaine, as well?" the wizard asked, standing and heading for the door.

"Chalsee has already been shown the futility of resistance," Entreri replied.

LaValle stopped abruptly, turning on the assassin as if betrayed.

"I knew you would go along," Entreri explained. "For you have come to know and love me as a brother. The lieutenant's mind-set, however, remained a mystery. He had to be convinced, or removed."

LaValle just stared at him, awaiting the verdict.

"He is convinced," Entreri remarked, moving to fall comfortably into LaValle's comfortable chair. "Very much so.

"And so," he continued as the wizard again started for the door, "will you find Bodeau."

LaValle turned on him again.

"He will make the right choice," Entreri assured the man.

"Will he have a choice?" LaValle dared to ask.

"Of course not."

Indeed, when LaValle found Bodeau in his private quarters and informed him that Artemis Entreri had come again the guildmaster blanched white and trembled so violently that LaValle feared he would simply fall over dead on the floor.

"You have spoken with Chalsee then?" LaValle asked.

"Evil days," Bodeau replied, and moving as if he had to battle mind with muscle through every pained step, he headed for the corridor.

"Evil days?" LaValle echoed incredulously under his breath. What in all the Realms could prompt the master of a murderous guild to make such a statement? Suddenly taking Entreri's claims more seriously, the wizard fell into step behind Bodeau. He noted, his intrigue mounting ever higher, that the guildmaster ordered no soldiers to follow or even to flank.

Bodeau stopped outside the wizard's door, letting LaValle assume the lead into the room. There in the study sat Entreri, exactly as the wizard had left him. The assassin appeared totally unprepared had Bodeau decided to attack instead of parlay, as if he had known without doubt that Bodeau wouldn't dare oppose him.

"What do you demand of me?" Bodeau asked before LaValle could find any opening to the obviously awkward situation.

"I have decided to begin with the Basadonis," Entreri calmly replied. "For they, after all, started this fight. You, then, must locate all of their soldiers, all of their fronts, and a complete layout of their operation, not including the guild house."

"I offer to tell no one that you came here and to promise that my soldiers will not interfere," Bodeau countered.

"Your soldiers could not interfere," Entreri shot back, a flash of anger crossing his black eyes.

LaValle watched in continued amazement as Quentin Bodeau fought so very hard to control his shaking.

"And we will not," the guildmaster offered.

"I have told you the terms of your survival," Entreri said, a coldness creeping into his voice that made LaValle believe that Bodeau and all the guild would be murdered that very night if the guildmaster didn't agree. "What say you?"

"I will consider—"

"Now."

Bodeau glared at LaValle, as if blaming the wizard for

ever allowing Artemis Entreri into his life, a sentiment that LaValle, as unnerved as Bodeau, could surely understand.

"You ask me to go against the most powerful pashas of the streets," Bodeau said, trying hard to find some courage.

"Choose," Entreri said.

A long, uncomfortable moment slipped past. "I will see what my soldiers may discern," Bodeau promised.

"Very wise," said Entreri. "Now leave us. I wish a word with LaValle."

More than happy to be away from the man, Bodeau turned on his heel and after another hateful glare at LaValle, swiftly exited the room.

"I do not begin to guess what tricks you have brought with you," LaValle said to Entreri.

"I have been to Menzoberranzan," Entreri admitted. "The city of the drow."

LaValle's eyes widened, his mouth drooping open.

"I returned with more than trinkets."

"You have allied with . . ."

"You are the only one I have told and the only one I shall tell," Entreri announced. "Understand the responsibility that goes with such knowledge. It is one that I shan't take lightly."

"But Chalsee Anguaine?" LaValle asked. "You said he had been convinced."

"A friend found his mind and there put images too horrible for him to resist," Entreri explained. "Chalsee knows not the truth, only that to resist would bring about a fate too terrible to consider. When he reported to Bodeau his terror was sincere."

"And where do I stand in your grand plans?" the wizard asked, trying very hard not to sound sarcastic. "If Bodeau fails you, then what of LaValle?"

"I will show you a way out should that come to pass," Entreri promised, walking over to the desk. "I owe you that much at least." He picked up a small dagger LaValle had set there to cut seals on parchments or to prick a finger when a spell called for a component of blood.

LaValle understood then that Entreri was being pragmatic, not merciful. If the wizard was indeed spared should Bodeau fail the assassin, it would only be because Entreri had some use for him.

"You are surprised that the guildmaster so readily complied," Entreri said evenly. "You must understand his choice: to risk that I will fail and the Basadonis will win out and then exact revenge on my allies . . . or to die now, this very night, and horribly, I assure you."

LaValle forced an expressionless set to his visage, playing the role of complete neutrality, even detachment.

"You have much work ahead of you, I assume," Entreri said, and he flicked his wrist, sending the dagger soaring past the wizard to knock heavily into the outside wall. "I take my leave."

Indeed, as the signal knock against the wall sounded, Kimmuriel Oblodra went into his contemplation again and brought up another dimensional pathway for the assassin to make his exit.

LaValle saw the portal open and thought for a moment out of sheer curiosity to leap through it beside Entreri to unmask this great mystery.

Good sense overruled curiosity.

And then the wizard was alone and very glad of it.

* * * * *

"I do not understand," Rai'gy Bondalek said when Entreri rejoined him, Jarlaxle, and Kimmuriel in the complex of tunnels beneath the city that the drow had made their own. He remembered then to speak more slowly, for Entreri, while fairly proficient in the drow language, was not completely fluent, and the wizard-priest didn't want to bother with the human tongue at all, either by learning it or by wasting the energy necessary to enact a spell that would allow them all to understand each other, whatever language each of them chose to speak. In truth, Bondalek's decision to force the discussion to continue in the drow language, even when Entreri was with them, was more a choice to keep the human assassin somewhat off-balance. "It seems, from all you previously said that the halflings would be better suited and more easily convinced to perform the services you just put upon Quentin Bodeau."

"I doubt not Dwahvel's loyalty," Entreri replied in the human Calimport tongue, and he eyed Rai'gy with every word.

The wizard turned a curious and helpless look over Jarlaxle, and the mercenary, with a laugh at the pettiness of it all, produced an orb from an inside fold of his cloak, held it aloft, and spoke a word of command. Now they would all understand.

"To herself and her well-being, I mean," Entreri said, again in the human tongue, though Rai'gy heard it in drow. "She is no threat."

"And pitiful Quentin Bodeau and his lackey wizard are?" Rai'gy asked incredulously, Jarlaxle's enchantment reversing the effect, so that, while the drow spoke in his native tongue, Entreri heard it in his own.

"Do not underestimate the power of Bodeau's guild," Entreri warned. "They are firmly entrenched, with eyes ever outward."

"So you force his loyalty early," Jarlaxle agreed, "that he cannot later claim ignorance whatever the outcome."

"And where from here?" Kimmuriel asked.

"We secure the Basadoni Guild," Entreri explained. "That then becomes our base of power, with both Dwahvel and Bodeau watching to make certain that the others aren't aligning against us."

"And from there?" Kimmuriel pressed.

Entreri smiled and looked to Jarlaxle, and the mercenary leader recognized that Entreri understood that Kimmuriel was asking the questions as Jarlaxle had bade him to ask.

"From there we will see what opportunities present themselves," Jarlaxle answered before Entreri could reply. "Perhaps that base will prove solid enough. Perhaps not."

Later on, after Entreri had left them, Jarlaxle, with some pride, turned to his two cohorts. "Did I not choose well?" he asked.

"He thinks like a drow," Rai'gy replied, offering as high a compliment as Jarlaxle had ever heard him give to a human or to anyone else who was not drow. "Though I wish he would better learn our language and our sign language."

Jarlaxle, so pleased with the progress, only laughed.

Chapter 14
REPUTATION

he man felt strange indeed. Alcohol dimmed his senses so that he could not register all the facts about his current situation. He felt light, floating, and felt a burning in his chest.

Wulfgar clenched his fist more tightly, grasping the front of the man's tunic and pulling chest hairs from their roots in the process. With just that one arm the barbarian easily held the two hundred pound man off the ground. Using his other arm to navigate the crowd in the Cutlass, he made his way for the door. He hated taking this roundabout route—previously he had merely tossed unruly drunks through a window or a wall—but Arumn Gardpeck had quickly reigned in that behavior, promising to take the cost of damages out of Wulfgar's pay.

Even a single window could cost the barbarian a few bottles, and if the frame went with it Wulfgar might not find any drink for a week.

The man, smiling stupidly, looked at Wulfgar and finally managed to find some focus. Recognition of the bouncer and of his present predicament at last showed on his face. "Hey!" he complained, but then he was flying, flat out in the air, arms and legs flailing. He landed facedown in the muddy road, and there he stayed. Likely a wagon would have run him over had not a couple of passersby taken pity on the poor slob and dragged him into the gutter . . . taking the rest of his coins from him in the process.

"Fifteen feet," Josi Puddles said to Arumn, estimating the length of the drunk's flight. "And with just one arm."

"I told ye he was a strong one," Arumn replied, wiping the bar and pretending that he was hardly amazed. In the weeks since the barkeep had hired Wulfgar, the barbarian had made many such throws.

"Every man on Half Moon Street's talking about that," Josi added, the tone of his voice somewhat grim. "I been noticing that your crowd's a bit tougher every night this week."

Arumn understood the perceptive man's less than subtle statement. There was a pecking order in Luskan's underbelly that resisted intrusion. As Wulfgar's reputation continued to grow, some of those higher on that pecking order would find their own reputations at stake and would filter in to mend the damage.

"You like the barbarian," Josi stated as much as asked.

Arumn, staring hard at Wulfgar as the huge man filtered through the crowd once more, gave a resigned nod. Hiring Wulfgar had been a matter of business, not friendship, and Arumn usually took great pains to avoid any personal relationships with his bouncers—since many of those men, drifters by nature, either wandered away of their own accord or angered the wrong thug and wound up dead at Arumn's doorstep. With Wulfgar, though, the barkeep had lost some of that perspective. Their late nights together when the Cutlass was quiet, Wulfgar drinking at the bar, Arumn preparing the place for the next day's business, had become a pleasant routine. Arumn truly enjoyed Wulfgar's companionship. He discovered that once the drink was in the man, Wulfgar let down his cold and distant facade. Many nights they stayed together until the dawn, Arumn listening intently as Wulfgar wove tales of the frigid northland, of

Icewind Dale, and of friends and enemies alike that made the barkeep's hair stand up on the back of his neck. Arumn had heard the story of Akar Kessel and the crystal shard so many times that he could almost picture the avalanche at Kelvin's Cairn that took down the wizard and buried the ancient and evil relic.

And every time Wulfgar recounted tales of the dark tunnels under the dwarven kingdom of Mithral Hall and the coming of the dark elves, Arumn later found himself shivering under his blankets, as he had when he was a child and his father had told him similarly dark stories by the hearth.

Indeed, Arumn Gardpeck had come to like his newest employee more than he should and less than he would.

"Then calm him," Josi Puddles finished. "He'll be bringing in Morik the Rogue and Tree Block Breaker anytime soon."

Arumn shuddered at the thought and didn't disagree. Particularly concerning Tree Block. Morik the Rogue, he knew, would be a bit more cautious (and thus, would be much more dangerous), would spend weeks, even months, sizing up the new threat before making his move, but brash Tree Block, arguably the toughest human—if he even was human, for many stories said that he had more than a little orc, or even ogre, blood in him—ever to step into Luskan, would not be so patient.

"Wulfgar," the barkeep called.

The big man sifted through the crowd to stand opposite Arumn.

"Did ye have to throw him out?" Arumn asked.

"He put his hand where it did not belong," Wulfgar replied absently. "Delly wanted him gone."

Arumn followed Wulfgar's gaze across the room to Delly . . . Delenia Curtie. Though not yet past her twentieth birthday, she had worked in the Cutlass for several years. She was a wisp of a thing, barely five feet tall and so slender that many thought she had a bit of elven blood in her—though it was more the result of drinking elven spirits, Arumn knew. Her blond hair hung untrimmed and unkempt and often not very clean. Her brown eyes had long ago lost their soft innocence and taken on a harder edge, and her pale skin had not seen enough of the sun in years, nor proper nutrition, and was now dry and rough. Her step had replaced the bounce of youth with the caution of a woman often hunted. But still there remained a charm about Delly, a sensual wickedness that many of the patrons, particularly after a few drinks, found too tempting to resist.

"If ye're to be killing every man who's grabbing Delly's bottom, I'll have no patrons left within the week," Arumn said dryly.

"Just push them out," Arumn continued when Wulfgar offered no response, not even a change of expression. "Ye don't have to be throwing them halfway to Waterdeep." He motioned back to the crowd, indicating that he was done with the barbarian.

Wulfgar walked away, back to his duties sifting through the boisterous bunch.

Within an hour another man, bleeding from his nose and mouth, took the aerial route, this time a two-handed toss that put him almost to the other side of the street.

* * * * *

Wulfgar held up his shirt, revealing the jagged line of deep scars. "Had me up in its mouth," he explained grimly, slurring the words. It had taken more than a little of the potent spirits to bring him to a level of comfort where he could discuss this battle, the fight with the yochlol, the fight that had brought him to Lolth, and she to Errtu for his years of torment. "A mouse in the cat's mouth." He gave a slight chuckle. "But this mouse had a kick."

His gaze drifted to Aegis-fang, lying on the bar a couple of feet away.

"Prettiest hammer I've ever seen," remarked Josi Puddles. He reached for it tentatively, staring at Wulfgar as his hand inched in, for he, like all the others, had no desire to anger the frightfully dangerous man.

But Wulfgar, usually very protective of Aegis-fang, his

sole link to his past life, wasn't even watching. His recounting of the yochlol fight had sent his thoughts and his heart careening back across the years, had locked him into a replay of the events that had put him in living hell.

"And how it hurt," he said softly, voice quavering, one hand subconsciously running the length of the scar.

Arumn Gardpeck stood before him staring, but though Wulfgar's eyes aimed at those of the barkeep, their focus was far, far away. Arumn slid another drink before the man, but Wulfgar didn't notice. With a deep and profound sigh the barbarian dropped his head into his huge arms, seeking the comfort of blackness.

He felt a touch on his bare arm, gentle and soft, and turned his head so that he could regard Delly. She nodded to Arumn, then gently pulled Wulfgar, coaxing him to rise and leading him away.

Wulfgar awoke later that night, long and slanted rays of moonlight filtering into the room through the western window. It took him a few moments to orient himself and to realize that this was not his room, for his room had no windows.

He glanced around and then to the blankets beside him, to the lithe form of Delly amidst those blankets, her skin seeming soft and delicate in the flattering light.

Then he remembered. Delly had taken him from the bar to bed—not to his own, but to hers—and he remembered all they had done.

Fearful, recalling his less-than-tender parting with Cattibrie, Wulfgar gently reached over and put his hand about the woman's neck, sighing in profound relief to find that she still had a pulse. Then he turned her over and scanned her bare body, not in any lustful way, but merely to see if she showed any bruises, any signs that he had brutalized her.

Her sleep was quiet and sound.

Wulfgar turned to the side of the bed, rolling his legs off the edge. He started to stand, but his throbbing head nearly knocked him backward. Reeling, he fought to control his balance and then ambled over to the window, staring out at the setting moon.

Catti-brie was likely watching that same moon, he thought, and somehow knew it to be true. After a while he turned to regard Delly again, all soft and snuggled amidst mounds of blankets. He had been able to make love to her without the anger, without the memories of the succubi balling his fists in rage. For a moment he felt as if he might be free, felt as if he should burst out of the house, out of Luskan altogether, running down the road in search of his old friends. He looked back at the moon and thought of Catti-brie and how wonderful it would be to fall into her arms.

But then he realized the truth of it all.

The drink had allowed him to build a wall against those memories, and behind that protective barrier he had been able to live in the present and not the past.

"Come on back to bed," came Delly's voice behind him, a gentle coax with a subtle promise of sensual pleasure. "And don't you be worrying over your hammer," she added, turning so that Wulfgar could follow her gaze to the opposite wall, against which Aegis-fang rested.

Wulfgar spent a long moment regarding the woman, caretaker of his emotions and his possessions. She was sitting up, the covers bundled about her waist, and making no move to cover her nakedness. Indeed she seemed to flaunt it a bit to entice the man back into her bed.

A large part of Wulfgar did want to go to her. But he resisted, realizing the danger, realizing that the drink had worn off. In a fit of passion, a fit of remembered rage, how easy it would be for him to squeeze her birdlike neck.

"Later," he promised, moving to gather his clothes. "Before we go to work this night."

"But you don't have to leave."

"I do," he said briskly, and he saw the flash of pain across her face. He moved to her immediately, very close. "I do," he repeated in a softer tone. "But I will come back to you. Later."

He kissed her gently on the forehead and started for the door.

"You are thinking that I'll want you back," came a harsh call behind him, and he turned to see Delly staring at him, her gaze ice cold, her arms folded defensively across her chest.

At first surprised, Wulfgar only then realized that he wasn't the only one in this room carrying around personal demons.

"Go," Delly said to him. "Maybe I'll take you back, and maybe I'll find another. All the same to me."

Wulfgar sighed and shook his head, then pushed out into the hall, more than happy to be out of that room.

The sun peeked over the eastern rim before the barbarian, an empty bottle at his side, found his way back into the void of sleep. He didn't see the sunrise, though, for his room had no windows.

He preferred it that way.

Chapter 15
THE CALL OF CRENSHINIBON

he prow cut swiftly through the azure blanket of the Sword Coast, shooting great fins of water and launching spray high into the air. At the forward rail, Catti-brie felt the stinging, salty droplets, so cold in contrast to the heat of the brilliant sun on her fair face. The ship, *Quester*, sailed south, and so south the woman looked. Away from Icewind Dale, away from Luskan, away from Waterdeep, from which they had sailed three days previous.

Away from Wulfgar.

Not for the first time, and she knew not for the last, the woman reconsidered their decision to let the beleaguered barbarian go off on his own. In his present state of mind, a state of absolute tumult and confusion, how could Wulfgar not need them?

And yet she had no way to get to him now, sailing south along the Sword Coast. Catti-brie blinked away moisture that was not sea spray and set her gaze firmly on the wide waters before them, taking some heart at the sheer speed of the vessel. They had a mission to complete, a vital mission, for during their days crossing by land they had come to learn beyond doubt that Crenshinibon remained a potent foe, sentient and intelligent. It was able to call in creatures to serve as its minions, monsters of dark heart eager to grasp at the promises of the relic. Thus the friends had gone to Waterdeep and had taken passage on the sturdiest available ship in the harbor, believing that enemies would be fewer at sea and far easier to discern. Both Drizzt and Catti-brie greatly lamented that Captain Deudermont and his wondrous *Sea Sprite* were not in.

Less than two hours out from port one of the crewmen had come after Drizzt, thinking to steal the crystal. Battered by the flat sides of flashing twin scimitars, the man, bound and gagged, had been handed off to another ship passing by, heading to the north to Waterdeep, with instructions to turn him over to the dock authorities in that lawful city for proper punishment.

Since then, though, the voyage had been uneventful, just swift sailing and empty waters, flat horizons dotted rarely by the sails of another distant ship.

Drizzt moved to join Catti-brie at the rail. Though she didn't turn around, she knew by the footsteps that followed the near-silent drow that Bruenor and Regis had come too.

"Only a few more days to Baldur's Gate," the drow said.

Catti-brie glanced over at him, noting that he kept the cowl of his traveling cloak low over his face—not to block any of the stinging spray, she knew, for Drizzt loved that feel as much as she, but to keep him in comfortable shade. Drizzt and Catti-brie had spent years together aboard Deudermont's *Sea Sprite*, and still the high sun of midday glittering off the waters bothered the drow elf, whose heritage had designed him for walking lightless caverns.

"How fares Bruenor?" the woman asked quietly, pretending not to know that the dwarf was standing behind her.

"Grumbling for solid ground and all the enemies in the world to stand against him, if necessary, to get him off this cursed floating coffin," the ranger replied, playing along.

Catti-brie managed a slight grin, not surprised at all. She had journeyed the seas with Bruenor farther to the south. While the dwarf had kept a stoic front on that occasion, his relief had been obvious when they had at last docked and returned again to solid ground. This time Bruenor was having an even worse time of it, spending long stretches at the rail—and not for the view.

"Regis seems unbothered," Drizzt went on. "He makes certain that no food remains on Bruenor's plate soon after Bruenor declares that he cannot eat."

Another smile found its way onto Catti-brie's face. Again it was short-lived. "Do ye think we'll be seeing him again?" she asked.

Drizzt sighed and turned his gaze out to the empty waters. Though they were both looking south, the wrong direction, they were both, in a manner of speaking, looking for Wulfgar. It was as if, against all logic and reason, they expected the man to come swimming toward them.

"I do not know," the drow admitted. "In his mood, it is possible that Wulfgar has found many enemies and has flung himself against them with all his heart. No doubt many of them are dead, but the north is a place of countless foes, some, I fear, too powerful even for Wulfgar."

"Bah!" Bruenor snorted from behind. "We'll find me boy, don't ye doubt. And the worst foe he'll be seeing'll be meself, paying him back for slapping me girl and for bringing me so much worry!"

"We shall find him," Regis declared. "And Lady Alustriel will help, and so will the Harpells."

The mention of the Harpells brought a groan from Bruenor. The Harpells were a family of eccentric wizards known for blowing themselves and their friends up, turning themselves—quite by accident and without repair—into various animals and all other manner of self-inflicted catastrophes.

"Alustriel, then," Regis agreed. "She will help if we cannot find him on our own."

"Bah! And how tough're ye thinking that to be?" Bruenor argued. "Are ye knowin' many rampaging seven-footers then? And them carrying hammers that can knock down a giant or the house it's living in with one throw?"

"There," Drizzt said to Catti-brie. "Our assurances that we will indeed find our friend."

The woman managed another smile, but it, too, was a strained thing and could not last. And what would they find when they at last located their missing friend? Even if he was physically unharmed, would he wish to see them? And even if he did, would he be in a better humor? And most important of all, would they—would she—really wish to see him? Wulfgar had hurt Catti-brie badly, not in body, but in heart, when he had struck her. She could forgive him that, she knew, to some extent at least.

But only once.

She studied her drow friend, saw his shadowed profile under the edge of his cowl as he stared vacantly to the empty waters, his lavender eyes glazed, as if his mind were looking elsewhere. She turned to consider Bruenor and Regis then and found them similarly distracted. All of them wanted to find Wulfgar again—not the Wulfgar who had left them on the road but the one who had left them those years ago in the tunnels beneath Mithral Hall, taken by the yochlol. They all wanted it to be as it had once been, the Companions of the Hall adventuring together without the company of brooding internal demons.

"A sail to the south," Drizzt remarked, drawing the woman from her contemplation. Even as Catti-brie looked out from the rail, squinting in a futile attempt to spot the too-distant ship, she heard the cry from the crow's nest confirming the drow's claim.

"What's her course?" Captain Vaines called from somewhere near the middle of the deck.

"North," Drizzt answered quietly so that only Catti-brie, Bruenor, and Regis could hear.

"North," cried the crewman from the crow's nest a few seconds later.

"Yer eyes've improved in the sunlight," Bruenor remarked.

"Credit Deudermont," Catti-brie explained.

"My eyes," Drizzt added, "and my perceptions of intent."

"What're ye babbling about?" Bruenor asked, but the ranger held up his hand, motioning for silence. He stood staring intently at the distant ship whose sails now appeared to the other three as tiny black dots, barely above the horizon.

"Go and tell Captain Vaines to turn us to the west," Drizzt instructed Regis.

The halfling stood staring for just a moment, then rushed back to find Vaines. Just a minute or so later the friends felt the pull as *Quester* leaned and turned her prow to the left.

"Ye're just making the trip longer," Bruenor started to complain, but again Drizzt held up his hand.

"She is turning with us, keeping her course to intercept," the drow explained.

"Pirates?" Catti-brie asked, a question echoed by Captain Vaines as he moved up to join the others.

"They are not in trouble, for they cut the water as swiftly as we, perhaps even more so," Drizzt reasoned. "Nor are they a ship of a king's fleet, for they fly no standard, and we are too far out for any coastal patrollers."

"Pirates," Captain Vaines spat distastefully.

"How can ye know all that?" an unconvinced Bruenor demanded.

"Comes from hunting 'em," Catti-brie explained. "And we've hunted more than our share."

"So I heard in Waterdeep," said Vaines, which was why he had agreed to take them aboard for a swift run to Baldur's Gate in the first place. Normally a woman, a dwarf, and a halfling would find no easy—and surely no cheap—passage out of Waterdeep Harbor when accompanied by a dark elf, but among the honest sailors of Waterdeep the names Drizzt Do'Urden and Catti-brie rang out as sweet music.

The approaching ship showed bigger on the horizon now, but it was still too small for any detailed images—except to Drizzt, and to Captain Vaines and the man in the crow's nest, both holding rare and expensive spyglasses. The captain put his to his eye now and recognized the telltale triangular sails. "She's a schooner," he said. "And a light one. She cannot hold more than twenty or so and is no match for us."

Catti-brie considered the words carefully. *Quester* was a caravel, and a large one at that. She held three strong banks of sails and had a front end long and tapered to aid in her run, but she carried a pair of ballistae, and had thick and strong sides. A slender schooner did not seem much of a match for *Quester*, to be sure, but how many pirates had said the same about another schooner, Deudermont's *Sea Sprite*, only to wind up fast filling with sea water?

"Back to the south with us!" the captain called, and *Quester* creaked and leaned to the right. Soon enough, the approaching schooner corrected her course to maintain her intercepting route.

"Too far to the north," Vaines remarked, striking a pensive pose, one hand coming up to stroke the gray hairs of his beard. "Pirates should not be this far north and should not deign to approach us."

The others, particularly Drizzt and Catti-brie, understood his trepidation. Concerning brute force at least, the schooner and her crew of twenty, perhaps thirty, would seem no match for the sixty of Vaines's crew. But such odds could often be overcome at sea by use of a single wizard, Catti-brie and Drizzt both knew. They had seen *Sea Sprite*'s wizard, a powerful invoker named Robillard, take down more than one ship single-handedly long before conventional weapons had even been used.

"Shouldn't and aren't ain't the same word," Bruenor remarked dryly. "I'm not knowing if they're pirates or not, but they're coming, to be sure."

Vaines nodded and moved back to the wheel with his navigator.

"I'll get me bow and go up to the nest," Catti-brie offered.

"Pick your shots well," Drizzt replied. "Likely there is one, or maybe a couple, who are guiding this ship. If you can find them and down them, the rest might flee."

"Is that the way of pirates?" Regis asked, seeming more than a little confused. "If they even are pirates?"

"That is the way of a lesser ship coming after us because of the crystal shard," Drizzt replied, and then the other two caught on.

"Ye're thinking the damned thing's calling them?" Bruenor asked.

"Pirates take few chances," Drizzt explained. "A light schooner coming after *Quester* is taking a great chance."

"Unless they got wizards," Bruenor reasoned, for he, too, had understood Captain Vaines's concerns.

Drizzt was shaking his head before the dwarf ever finished. Catti-brie would have been, too, except that she had already run off to retrieve Taulmaril. "A pirate running with enough magical aid to destroy *Quester* would have long ago been marked," the drow explained. "We would have heard of her and been warned of her before we ever left Waterdeep."

"Unless she is new to the trade or new of the power," Regis reasoned.

Drizzt conceded the point with a nod, but he remained unconvinced, believing that Crenshinibon had brought this new enemy in, as it had brought in so many others in a desperate attempt to wrest the relic away from those who would see it destroyed. The drow looked back across the deck, spotting the familiar form of Catti-brie with Taulmaril, the wondrous Heartseeker, strapped across her back as she made her nimble way up the knotted rope.

Then he opened his belt pouch and gazed upon the wicked relic, Crenshinibon. How he wished he could hear its call to better understand the enemies it would bring before them.

Quester shuddered suddenly as one of its great ballistae let fly. The huge spear leaped away, skipping a couple times across the water far short of the out-of-range schooner, but close enough to let the sailors aboard her recognize that *Quester* had no intention of parlay or surrender.

But the schooner flew on without the slightest course change, splitting the water right beside the spent ballista bolt, even clipping the metal-tipped spear as it hung buoy-like in the swelling sea. Smooth and swift was its run, seeming more like an arrow cutting the air than a ship cutting the water. The narrow hull had been built purely for speed. Drizzt had seen pirates such as this; often similar ships had led *Sea Sprite*, also a schooner, but a three-master and much larger, on long pursuits. The drow had enjoyed those chases most of all during his time with Deudermont, sails full of wind, spray rushing past, his white hair flowing out behind him as he stood poised at the forward rail.

He was not enjoying this scenario, though. There were many pirates along the Sword Coast well capable of destroying *Quester*, larger and better armed and armored than the well-structured caravel, truly the hunting lions of the region. But this approaching ship was more a bird of prey, a swift and cunning hunter designed for smaller quarry, for fishing boats wandering too far from protected harbors or the luxury barges of wealthy merchants who let their warship escorts get a bit too far away from them. Or pirate schooners would work in conjunction, several on a target, a fleet hunting pack.

But no other sails were to be seen on any horizon.

From a different pouch, Drizzt took out his onyx figurine. "I will bring in Guenhwyvar soon," he explained to Regis and Bruenor. Captain Vaines came up again, a nervous expression stamped on his face—one that told the drow that, despite his many years at sea, Vaines had not seen much battle. "With a proper run the panther can leap fifty feet or more to gain the deck of our enemies' ship. Once there she will make more than a few call for a retreat."

"I have heard of your panther friend," Vaines said. "She was much the talk of Waterdeep Harbor."

"Ye better bring the damned cat up soon then," Bruenor grumbled, looking out over the rail. Indeed, the schooner already seemed much closer, speeding over the waves.

To Drizzt the image struck him as purely out of control; suicidal, like the giant that had followed them out of the Spine of the World. He put the figurine on the ground and called softly for the panther, watching as the telltale gray mist began to swirl about the statue, gradually taking shape.

* * * * *

Catti-brie wiped her eyes, then lifted the spyglass once again, scanning the deck, hardly believing what she saw. But again she saw the truth of it all: that this was no pirate, at least none of the kind she had ever before seen. There were women aboard, and not warrior women, not even sailors, and surely not prisoners. And children! Several she had seen, and none of them dressed as cabin boys.

She winced as a ballista spear grazed the schooner's deck, skipping off a turnstile and cracking through the side rail, only missing a young boy by a hands' breadth.

"Get ye down, and be quick," she instructed the lookout sharing the crow's nest. "Tell yer captain to load chain and take her in her high sails."

The man, obviously impressed with the tales he had heard of Drizzt and Catti-brie, turned without hesitation and started down the rope, but the woman knew that the task for stopping this coming travesty had fallen squarely upon her shoulders.

Quester had dropped to battle sail, but the schooner kept at full, kept its run straight and swift, and seemed as if it meant to smash right through the larger caravel.

Catti-brie put up the spyglass again, scanning slowly, searching, searching. She knew now that Drizzt's guess about the schooner's course and intent had been correct, knew that this was Crenshinibon's doing, and that truth made her blood boil with rage. One, or two, perhaps, would be the key, but where . . .

She spotted the man at the forward rail of the flying bridge, his form mostly obscured by the mainmast. She held her sights on him for a long while, resisting the urge to shift and observe damage as *Quester*'s ballistae let fly again, this time in accord with Catti-brie's orders. Spinning chains ripped high through the schooner's top sails. This sight, this man at the rail, one hand gripping the wood so tightly that it was white for lack of blood, was more important.

The schooner flinched, the ship veering slightly, unintentionally, until the crew could work the ballista-altered sails to put her in line again. In that turn, the image of the man at the rail drifted clear of the obstructing mast, and Catti-brie saw him clearly, saw the crazed look upon his face, saw the line of drool running from the corner of his mouth.

And she knew.

She dropped the spyglass and took up Taulmaril, lining her shot with great care, using the mainmast as a guide, for she could hardly even see the target.

* * * * *

"If they've a wizard, he should have acted by now," a frantic Captain Vaines cried. "For what do they wait? To tease us, as a cat to a mouse?"

Bruenor looked at the man and snorted derisively.

"They've no wizard," Drizzt assured the captain.

"Do they mean to simply ram us, then?" the captain asked. "We'll take her down, then!" He turned to yell new instructions to the ballista crews, to instruct his archers to rake the deck. But before he uttered a word a silver streak from the nest above startled him. He spun around to see the streak cut across the schooner's deck, then angle sharply to the right and fly out over the open sea.

Before he could begin to question it another streak shot out, following nearly the same course, except that this one didn't deflect. It soared right past the schooner's mainmast.

Everything seemed to come to a stop, a tangible pause from caravel and schooner alike.

"Hold the cat!" Catti-brie called down to Drizzt.

Vaines looked at the drow doubtfully, but Drizzt didn't doubt, not at all. He put his hand up and called Guenhwyvar—who had moved back on the deck to get a running start—back to his side.

"It is ended," the dark elf announced.

The captain's doubting expression melted as the schooner's mainsail dropped, the ship's prow also dropping instantly, deeper into the sea. Her back beam swung out wide, turning the triangular back sail. She leaned far to the side, turning her prow back toward the east, back toward the far-distant shore.

* * * * *

Through the spyglass, Catti-brie saw a woman kneeling over the dead man while another man cradled his head. An emptiness settled in Catti-brie's breast, for she never enjoyed such an action, never wanted to kill anyone.

But that man had been the antagonist, the driving force behind a battle that would have left many innocents on the schooner dead. Better that he pay for his failings with his own life alone than with the lives of others.

She told herself that repeatedly.

It helped but a little.

* * * * *

Certain that the fight had indeed been avoided, Drizzt looked down at the crystal shard once more with utter contempt. A single call to a single man had nearly brought ruin to so many.

He could not wait to be rid of the thing.

Chapter 16

BROTHERS OF MIND AND MAGIC

he dark elf leaned back in a chair, settling comfortably, as he always seemed to do, and listening with more than a passing amusement. Jarlaxle had planted a device of clairaudience on the magnificent wizard's robe he had given to Rai'gy Bondalek, one of many enchanted gemstones sewn into the black cloth. This one had a clever aura, deceiving any who would detect it into thinking it was a stone the wizard wearing the robe could use to cast the clairaudience spell. And indeed it was, but it possessed another power, one with a matching stone that Jarlaxle kept, allowing the mercenary to listen in at will upon Rai'gy's conversations.

"The replica was well made and holds much of the original's dweomer," Rai'gy was saying, obviously referring to the magical, Drizzt-seeking locket.

"Then you should have no trouble in locating the rogue again and again," came the reply, the voice of Kimmuriel Oblodra.

"They are still aboard the ship," Rai'gy explained. "And

from what I have heard they mean to be aboard for many more days."

"Jarlaxle demands more information," the Oblodran psionicist said, "else he will turn the duties over to me."

"Ah, yes, given to my principal adversary," the wizard said in mock seriousness.

In that distant room, Jarlaxle chuckled. The two thought it important to keep him believing that they were rivals and thus no threat to him, though in truth they had forged a tight and trusted friendship. Jarlaxle didn't mind that—in fact, he rather preferred it—because he understood that even together the psionicist and the wizard, dark elves of considerable magical talents and powers but little understanding of the motivations and nature of reasoning beings, would never move against him. They feared not so much that he would defeat them, but rather that they would prove victorious and then be forced to shoulder the responsibility for the entire volatile band.

"The best method to discern more about the rogue would be to go to him in disguise and listen to his words," Rai'gy went on. "Already I have learned much of his present course and previous events."

Jarlaxle came forward in his chair, listening intently as Rai'gy began a chant. He recognized enough of the words to understand that the wizard-priest was enacting a scrying spell, a reflective pool.

"That one there," Rai'gy said a few moments later.

"The young boy?" came Kimmuriel's response. "Yes, he would be an easy target. Humans do not prepare their children well, as do the drow."

"You could take his mind?" Rai'gy asked.

"Easily."

"Through the scrying pool?"

There came a long pause. "I do not know that it has ever been done," Kimmuriel admitted, and his tone told Jarlaxle that he was not afraid of the prospect, but rather intrigued.

"Then our eyes and ears would be right beside the outcast," Rai'gy went on. "In a form Drizzt Do'Urden would not think to distrust. A curious child, one who would love to hear his many tales of adventure."

Jarlaxle took his hand from the gemstone, and the clairaudience spell went away. He settled back into his chair and smiled widely, taking comfort in the ingenuity of his underlings.

That was the truth of his power, he realized, the ability to delegate responsibility and allow others to rightfully take their credit. The strength of Jarlaxle lay not in Jarlaxle, though even alone he could be formidable indeed, but in the competent soldiers with whom the mercenary surrounded himself. To battle Jarlaxle was to battle Bregan D'aerthe, an organization of free-thinking, amazingly competent drow warriors.

To battle Jarlaxle was to lose.

The guilds of Calimport would soon recognize that truth, the drow leader knew, and so would Drizzt Do'Urden.

* * * * *

"I have contacted another plane of existence and from the creatures there, beings great and wise, beings who can see into the humble affairs of the drow with hardly a thought, I have learned of the outcast and his friends, of where they have been and where they mean to go," Rai'gy Bondalek proclaimed to Jarlaxle the next day.

Jarlaxle nodded and accepted the lie, seeing Rai'gy's proclamation of some otherworldly and mysterious source as inconsequential.

"Inland, as I earlier told you," Rai'gy explained. "They took to a ship—the *Quester*, it is called—in Waterdeep, and now sail south for a city called Baldur's Gate, which they should reach in a matter of three days."

"Then back to land?"

"Briefly," Rai'gy answered, for indeed, Kimmuriel had learned much in his half day as a cabin boy. "They will take to ship again, a smaller craft, to travel along a river that will bring them far from the great water they call the Sword

Coast. Then they will take to land travel again, to a place called the Snowflake Mountains and a structure called the Spirit Soaring, wherein dwells a mighty priest named Cadderly. They go to destroy an artifact of great power," he went on, adding details that he and not Kimmuriel had learned through use of the reflecting pool. "This artifact is Crenshinibon by name, though often referred to as the crystal shard."

Jarlaxle's eyes narrowed at the mention. He had heard of Crenshinibon before in a story concerning a mighty demon and Drizzt Do'Urden. Pieces began to fall into place then, the beginnings of a cunning plan creeping into the corners of his mind. "So that is where they shall go," he said. "As important, where have they been?"

"They came from Icewind Dale, they say," Rai'gy reported. "A land of cold ice and blowing wind. And they left behind one named Wulfgar, a mighty warrior. They believe him to be in the city of Luskan, north of Waterdeep along the same seacoast."

"Why did he not accompany them?"

Rai'gy shook his head. "He is troubled, I believe, though I know not why. Perhaps he has lost something or has found tragedy."

"Speculation," Jarlaxle said. "Mere assumptions. And such things will lead to mistakes that we can ill afford."

"What part plays Wulfgar?" Rai'gy asked with some surprise.

"Perhaps no part, perhaps a vital one," Jarlaxle answered. "I cannot decide until I know more of him. If you cannot learn more, then perhaps it is time I go to Kimmuriel for answers." He noted the way the wizard-priest stiffened at his words, as though Jarlaxle had slapped him.

"Do you wish to learn more of the outcast or of this Wulfgar?" Rai'gy asked, his voice sharp.

"More of Cadderly," Jarlaxle replied, drawing a frustrated sigh from his off-balance companion. Rai'gy didn't even move to answer. He just turned about, threw his hands up in the air and walked away.

Jarlaxle was finished with him anyway. The names of Crenshinibon and Wulfgar had him deep in thought. He had heard of both; of Wulfgar, given by a handmaiden to Lolth and from Lolth to Errtu, the demon who sought the Crystal Shard. Perhaps it was time for the mercenary leader to go and pay a visit to Errtu, though truly he hated dealing with the unpredictable and ultimately dangerous creatures of the Abyss. Jarlaxle survived by understanding the motivations of his enemies, but demons rarely held any definite motivations and could certainly alter their desires moment by moment.

But there were other ways with other allies. The mercenary drew out a slender wand and with a thought teleported his body back to Menzoberranzan.

His newest lieutenant, once a proud member of the ruling house, was waiting for him.

"Go to your brother Gromph," Jarlaxle instructed. "Tell him that I wish to learn of the story of the human named Wulfgar, the demon Errtu, and the artifact known as Crenshinibon."

"Wulfgar was taken in the first raid on Mithral Hall, the realm of Clan Battlehammer," Berg'inyon Baenre answered, for he knew well the tale. "By a handmaiden, and given to Lolth."

"But where from there?" Jarlaxle asked. "He is back on our plane of existence, it would seem, on the surface."

Berg'inyon's expression showed his surprise at that. Few ever escaped the clutches of the Spider Queen. But then, he admitted silently, nothing about Drizzt Do'Urden had ever been predictable. "I will find my brother this day," he assured Jarlaxle.

"Tell him that I wish to know of a mighty priest named Cadderly," Jarlaxle added, and he tossed Berg'inyon a small amulet. "It is imbued with the emanations of my location," he explained, "that your brother might find me or send a messenger."

Again Berg'inyon nodded.

"All is well?" Jarlaxle asked.

"The city remains quiet," the lieutenant reported, and Jarlaxle was not surprised. Ever since the last assault upon Mithral Hall several years before, when Matron Baenre, the figurehead of Menzoberranzan for centuries, had been killed, the city had been outwardly quiet above the tumult of private planning. To her credit, Triel Baenre, Matron Baenre's oldest daughter, had done a credible job of holding the house together. But despite her efforts it seemed likely that the city would soon know interhouse wars beyond the scope of anything previously experienced. Jarlaxle had decided to strike out for the surface, to extend his grasp, thus making his mercenary band invaluable to any house with aspirations for greater power.

The key to it all now, Jarlaxle understood, was to keep everyone on his side even as they waged war with each other. It was a line he had learned to walk with perfection centuries before.

"Go to Gromph quickly," he instructed. "This is of utmost importance. I must have my answers before Narbondel brightens a hands' pillars," he explained, using a common expression to mean before five days had passed. The expression "hands' pillars" represented the five fingers on one hand.

Berg'inyon departed, and with a silent mental instruction to his wand Jarlaxle was back in Calimport. As quickly as his body moved, so too moved his thoughts to another pressing issue. Berg'inyon would not fail him, nor would Gromph, nor would Rai'gy and Kimmuriel. He knew that with all confidence, and that knowledge allowed him to focus on this very night's work: the takeover of the Basadoni Guild.

* * * * *

"Who is there?" came the old voice, a voice full of calmness despite the apparent danger.

Entreri, having just stepped through one of Kimmuriel Oblodra's dimensional portals, heard it as if from far, far away, as the assassin fought to orient himself to his new surroundings. He was in Pasha Basadoni's private room, behind a lavish dressing screen. Finally finding his center of balance and consciousness, the assassin spent a moment studying his surroundings, his ears pricked for the slightest of sounds: breathing or the steady footfalls of a practiced killer.

But of course he and Kimmuriel had properly scouted the room and the whereabouts of the pasha's lieutenants, and they knew that the old and helpless man was quite alone.

"Who is there?" came another call.

Entreri walked out around the screen and into the candlelight, shifting his bolero back on his head that the old man might see him clearly, and that the assassin might gaze upon Basadoni.

How pitiful the old man looked, a hollow shell of his former self, his former glory. Once Pasha Basadoni had been the most powerful guildmaster in Calimport, but now he was just an old man, a figurehead, a puppet whose strings could be pulled by several different people at once.

Entreri, despite himself, hated those string pullers.

"You should not have come," Basadoni rasped at him. "Flee the city, for you cannot live here. Too many, too many."

"You have spent two decades underestimating me," Entreri replied lightly, taking a seat on the edge of the bed. "When will you learn the truth?"

That brought a phlegm-filled chuckle from Basadoni, and Entreri flashed a rare smile.

"I have known the truth of Artemis Entreri since he was a street urchin killing intruders with sharpened stones," the old man reminded him.

"Intruders you sent," said Entreri.

Basadoni conceded the point with a grin. "I had to test you."

"And have I passed, Pasha?" Entreri considered his own tone as he spoke the words. The two were speaking like old friends, and in a manner they were indeed. But now, because of the actions of Basadoni's lieutenants, they were also mortal enemies. Still the pasha seemed quite at ease here, alone and helpless with Entreri. At first, the assassin had thought that the man might be better prepared than he had assumed, but after carefully inspecting the room and the partially upright bed that held the old man, he was secure in the fact that Basadoni had no tricks to play. Entreri was in control, and that didn't seem to bother Pasha Basadoni as much as it should.

"Always, always," Basadoni replied, but then his smile dissipated into a grimace. "Until now. Now you have failed, and at a task too easy."

Entreri shrugged as if it did not matter. "The targeted man was pitiful," he explained. "Truly. Am I, the assassin who passed all of your tests, who ascended to sit beside you though I was still but a young man, to murder wretched peasants who owe a debt that a novice pickpocket could cover in half a day's work?"

"That was not the point," Basadoni insisted. "I let you back in, but you have been gone a long time, and thus you had to prove yourself. Not to me," the pasha quickly added, seeing the assassin's frown.

"No, to your foolish lieutenants," Entreri reasoned.

"They have earned their positions."

"That is my fear."

"Now it is Artemis Entreri who underestimates," Pasha Basadoni insisted. "Each of the three have their place and serve me well."

"Well enough to keep me out of your house?" Entreri asked.

Pasha Basadoni gave a great sigh. "Have you come to kill me?" he asked, and then he laughed again. "No, not that. You would not kill me, because you have no reason to. You know, of course, that if you somehow succeed against Kadran Gordeon and the others, I will take you back in."

"Another test?" Entreri asked dryly.

"If so, then one you created."

"By sparing the life of a wretch who likely would have preferred death?" Entreri said, shaking his head as if the whole notion was purely ridiculous.

R. A. Salvatore

A flicker of understanding sharpened Basadoni's old gray eyes. "So it was not sympathy," he said, grinning.

"Sympathy?"

"For the wretch," the old man explained. "No, you care nothing for him, care not that he was subsequently murdered. No, no, and I should have understood. It was not sympathy that stayed the hand of Artemis Entreri. Never that! It was pride, simple, foolish pride. You would not lower yourself to the level of street enforcer, and thus you started a war you cannot win. Oh, fool!"

"Cannot win?" Entreri echoed. "You assume much." He studied the old man for a long moment, locking gazes. "Tell me, Pasha, who do you wish to win?" he asked.

"Pride again," Basadoni replied with a flourish of his skinny arms that stole much of his strength and left him gasping. "But the point," he continued a moment later, "in any case, is moot. What you truly ask is if I still care for you, and of course I do. I remember well your ascent through my guild, as well as any father recalls the growth of his son. I do not wish you ill in this war you have begun, though you understand that there is little I can do to prevent these events that you and Kadran, prideful fools both, have put in order. And of course, as I said before, you cannot win."

"You do not understand everything."

"Enough," the old man said. "I know that you have no allegiance among the other guilds, not even with Dwahvel and her little ones or Quentin Bodeau and his meager band. Oh, they swear neutrality—we would have it no other way—but they will not aid you in your fight, and neither will any of the other truly powerful guilds. And thus are you doomed."

"And you know of every guild?" Entreri asked slyly.

"Even the wretched wererats of the sewers," Pasha Basadoni said with confidence, but Entreri noted a hint at the edges of his tone that showed he was not as smug as he outwardly pretended. There was a sadness here, Entreri knew, a weariness and, obviously, a lack of control. The lieutenants ran the guild.

"I tell you this out of admission for all that you did for me," the assassin said, and he was not surprised to see the wise old pasha's eyes narrow warily. "Call it loyalty, call it a last debt repaid," Entreri went on, and he was sincere—about the forewarning, at least—"you do not know all, and your lieutenants shall not prevail against me."

"Ever the confident one," the pasha said with another phlegm-filled laugh.

"And never wrong," Entreri added, and he tipped his bolero and walked behind the dressing screen, back to the waiting dimensional portal.

* * * * *

"You have made every defense?" Pasha Basadoni asked with true concern, for the old man knew enough about Artemis Entreri to take the assassin's warning seriously. As soon as Entreri had left him, Basadoni had gathered his lieutenants. He didn't tell them of his visitor, but he wanted to ensure that they were ready. The time was near, he knew, very near.

Sharlotta, Hand, and Gordeon all nodded—somewhat condescendingly, Basadoni noted. "They will come this night," he announced. Before any of the three could question where he might have garnered that information, he added, "I can feel their eyes upon us."

"Of course, my Pasha," purred Sharlotta, bending low to kiss the old man's forehead.

Basadoni laughed at her and laughed all the louder when a guard shouted from the hallway that the house had been breached.

"In the sub-cellar!" the man cried. "From the sewers!"

"The wererat guild?" Kadran Gordeon asked incredulously. "Domo Quillilo assured us that he would not—"

"Domo Quillilo stayed out of Entreri's way, then," Basadoni interrupted.

"Entreri has not come alone," Kadran reasoned.

239

"Then he will not die alone," Sharlotta said, seeming unconcerned. "A pity."

Kadran nodded, drew his sword, and turned to leave. Basadoni, with great effort, grabbed his arm. "Entreri will come in separately from his allies," the old man warned. "For you."

"More to my pleasure, then," Kadran growled in reply. "Go lead our defenses," he told Hand. "And when Entreri is dead, I will bring his head to you that we may show it to those stupid enough to join with him."

Hand had barely exited the room when he was nearly run over by a soldier coming up from the cellars. "Kobolds!" the man cried, his expression showing that he hardly believed the claim as he spoke it. "Entreri's allies are smelly rat kobolds."

"Lead on, then," said Hand, much more confidently. Against the power of the guild house, with two wizards and two hundred soldiers, kobolds—even if they poured in by the thousands—would prove no more than a minor inconvenience.

Back in the room, the other two lieutenants heard the claim and stared at each other in disbelief, then broke into wide smiles.

Pasha Basadoni, lying on the bed and watching them, didn't share that mirth. Entreri was up to something, he knew, something big, and kobolds would hardly be the worst of it.

* * * * *

Kobolds indeed led the way into the Basadoni guild house, up from the sewers where frightened wererats—as per their agreement with Entreri—stayed hidden in shadows, out of the way. Jarlaxle had brought a considerable number of the smelly little creatures with him from Menzoberranzan. Bregan D'aerthe was housed primarily along the rim of the great Clawrift that rent the drow city, and in there the kobolds bred and bred, thousands and thousands of the things. Three hundred had accompanied the forty drow to Calimport, and they now led the charge, running wildly through all the lower corridors of the guild house, inadvertently setting off the traps, both mechanical and magical, and marking the locations of the Basadoni soldiers.

Behind them came the drow host, silent as death.

Kimmuriel Oblodra, Jarlaxle, and Entreri moved up one slanting corridor, flanked by a foursome of drow warriors holding hand crossbows readied with poison-tipped darts. Up ahead the corridor opened into a wide room, and a group of kobolds scrambled across, chased by a threesome of archers.

"Click, click, click," went the crossbows, and the three archers stumbled, staggered, and slumped to the floor, deep in sleep.

An explosion to the side sent the kobolds, half the previous number, scrambling back the other way.

"Not a magical blast," Kimmuriel remarked.

Jarlaxle sent a pair of his soldiers out wide the other way, flanking the human position. Kimmuriel took a more direct route, opening a dimensional door diagonally across the wide floor to the open edge of the corridor from which the explosion had come. As soon as the door appeared, leading into another long, ascending corridor, he and Entreri spotted the bombers. There was a group of men rushing behind a barricade, flanked by several large kegs.

"Drow elf!" one of the men shouted, pointing to the open door. Kimmuriel stood across the dimensional space behind the other door.

"Light it! Light it!" cried another man. A third brought a torch over to light the long rag hanging off the top of one keg.

Kimmuriel reached into his mind yet again, focusing on the keg, on the latent energy within the wood planking. He touched that energy, exciting it. Before the men could even begin to roll the barrel out from behind the barricade it blew apart, then exploded again as the burning wick hit the oil.

A flaming man tumbled out from the barricade, rolling frantically down the corridor, trying to douse the flames. A second, less injured, staggered into the open, and one of the remaining drow soldiers put a hand crossbow dart into his face.

Kimmuriel dropped the dimensional door—better to run through the room—and the group set off, rushing past the burning corpse and the sleeping and badly injured man, past the third victim of the explosion, curled in death in a fetal position in the corner of the small cubby, then down a side passage. There they found three more men, two asleep and a third lying dead before the feet of the two soldiers Jarlaxle had sent out to flank.

And so it went throughout the lower levels, with the dark elves overrunning all obstacles. Jarlaxle had taken only his finest warriors with him to the surface: renegade, houseless dark elves who had once belonged to noble houses, who had trained for decades, centuries even, for just this kind of close-quartered, room-to-room, tunnel-to-tunnel combat. A brigade of knights in shining mail and with wizard supporters might prove a credible enemy to the dark elves on an open field of battle. These street thugs, though, with their small daggers, short swords, and minor magics, and with no foreknowledge of the enemy that had come against them, fell systematically to Jarlaxle's steadily moving band. Basadoni's men surrendered position after position, retreating higher and higher into the guild house proper.

Jarlaxle found Rai'gy Bondalek and half a dozen warriors moving along the street level of the house.

"They had two wizards," the wizard-priest explained. "I put them in a globe of silence and—"

"Pray tell me you did not destroy them," said the mercenary leader, who knew well the value of wizards.

"We hit them with darts," Rai'gy explained. "But one had a stoneskin enchantment about him and had to be destroyed."

Jarlaxle could accept that. "Finish the business at hand," he said to Rai'gy. "I will take Entreri to claim his place in the higher rooms."

"And him?" Rai'gy asked sourly, motioning toward Kimmuriel.

Knowing their little secret, Jarlaxle did well to hide his smile. "Lead on," he instructed Entreri.

They encountered another group of heavily armed soldiers, but Jarlaxle used one of his many wands to entrap them all within globs of goo. Another one did slip away—or would have, except that Artemis Entreri knew well the tactics of such men. He saw the shadow lengthening against the wall and directed the shot well.

* * * * *

Kadran Gordeon's eyes widened when Hand stumbled into the room, gasping and clutching at his hip. "Dark elves," the man explained, slumping in the arms of his comrade. "Entreri. The bastard brought dark elves!"

Hand slipped to the floor, fast asleep.

Kadran Gordeon let him fall and ran on, out the back door of the room, across the wide ballroom of the second floor, and up the sweeping staircase.

Entreri and his friends noted every movement.

"That is the one?" Jarlaxle asked.

Entreri nodded. "I will kill him," he promised, starting away, but Jarlaxle grabbed his shoulder. Entreri turned to see the mercenary leader looking slyly at Kimmuriel.

"Would you like to fully humiliate the man?" Jarlaxle asked.

Before Entreri could respond, Kimmuriel came up to stand right before him. "Join with me," the drow psionicist said, lifting his fingers for Entreri's forehead.

The ever-wary assassin brushed the reaching hand away.

Kimmuriel tried to explain, but Entreri knew only the basics of drow language, not the subtleties. The psionicist's words sounded more like the joining of lovers than anything Entreri understood. Frustrated, Kimmuriel turned to Jarlaxle and started talking so fast that it seemed to Entreri as if he was saying one long word.

"He has a trick for you to play," Jarlaxle explained in the common surface tongue. "He wishes to get into your mind, but only briefly, to enact a kinetic barrier and show you how to maintain it."

"A kinetic barrier?" the confused assassin asked.

"Trust him this one time," Jarlaxle bade. "Kimmuriel Oblodra is among the greatest practitioners of the rare and powerful psionic magic and is so skilled with it that he can often lend some of his power to another, albeit briefly."

"He will teach me?" Entreri asked skeptically.

Kimmuriel laughed at the absurd notion.

"The mind magic is a gift, a rare gift, and not a lesson to be taught," Jarlaxle explained. "But Kimmuriel can lend you a bit of the power, enough to humiliate Kadran Gordeon."

Entreri's expression showed that he wasn't so sure of any of this.

"We could kill you at any time by more conventional means if we so decided," Jarlaxle reminded him. He nodded to Kimmuriel, and Artemis Entreri did not back away.

And so Entreri got his first personal understanding of psionics and walked up the sweeping staircase unafraid. Across the way a concealed archer let fly, and Entreri took the arrow right in the back—or would have, except that the kinetic barrier stopped the arrow's flight, fully absorbing its energy.

* * * * *

Sharlotta heard the ruckus in the outer rooms of the royal complex and figured that Gordeon had returned. She still had no idea of the rout in the lower halls, though, and so she decided to move quickly, to use this opportunity well. From one of the long sleeves of her alluring gown she drew out a slender knife, moving with purpose for the door that would lead into a larger room, with the door of Pasha Basadoni across the way.

Finally she would be done with the man, and it would look as if Entreri or one of his associates had completed the assassination.

Sharlotta paused at the door, hearing another slam beyond and the sound of running feet. Gordeon was on the move, as was another.

Had Entreri gained this level?

The thought assaulted her but did not dissuade her. There were other ways, more secret ways, though the route would be longer. She went to the back of her room, removed a specific book from her bookshelf, then slipped into the corridor that opened behind the case.

* * * * *

Entreri caught up to Kadran Gordeon soon after in a complex of many small rooms. The man rushed out the side, sword slashing. He hit Entreri a dozen times at least and the assassin, focusing his thoughts with supreme concentration, didn't even try to block. Instead he just took them and stole their energy, feeling the power building, building within him.

Eyes wide, mouth agape, Kadran Gordeon backpedaled. "What manner of demon are you?" the man gasped, falling back through a door into the room where Sharlotta, small dagger in hand, had just come out of another concealed passage, standing along a wall to the side of Pasha Basadoni's bed.

Entreri, brimming with confidence, strode in.

On came Gordeon again, sword slashing. This time Entreri drew the sword Jarlaxle had given him and countered, parrying each slash perfectly. He felt his mental concentration waning and knew that he had to react soon or be consumed by the pent-up energy, so when Gordeon came with a sidelong slash, Entreri dipped the tip of his blade below the angle of the cut, then brought it up and over quickly, stepping under, turning about, and rolling his sword around. He took Gordeon off balance and crashed into the man, knocking him to the floor and coming down atop him, weapon pinning weapon.

* * * * *

Sharlotta lifted her arm to throw her knife into Basadoni but then shifted, seeing the too-tempting target of Artemis

Entreri's back as the man went down atop Kadran Gordeon.

But then she shifted again as another, darker form entered the room. She cocked to throw, but the drow was quicker. A dagger sliced her wrist, pinning her arm to the wall. Another dagger stuck in the wall to the right of her head, then another to the left. Another grazed the side of her chest, and then another as Jarlaxle pumped his arm rapidly, sending a seemingly endless stream of steel her way.

Gordeon punched Entreri in the face.

That, too, was absorbed.

"I do grow tired of your foolishness," said Entreri, putting his hand on Gordeon's chest, ignoring the man's free hand as it pumped punch after punch at his face.

With a thought Entreri released the energy, all of it, the arrow, the many sword hits, the many punches. His hand sank into Gordeon's chest, melting the skin and ribs below it. A rolling fountain of blood erupted, spewing into the air and falling back on Gordeon's surprised expression, filling his mouth as he tried to scream in horror.

And then he was dead.

Entreri got up to see Sharlotta standing against the wall, hands in the air—one pinned to the wall—facing Jarlaxle, who had yet another dagger ready. Several other drow, including Kimmuriel and Rai'gy, had come into the room behind their leader. The assassin quickly moved between her and Basadoni, noting the dagger Sharlotta had obviously dropped on the floor right beside the bed. He turned his sly gaze on the dangerous woman.

"It would seem that I arrived just in time, Pasha," Entreri explained, picking up the weapon. "Sharlotta, thinking the guild house secure, had apparently decided to use the battle to her advantage, finally ridding herself of you."

Both Entreri and Basadoni looked at Sharlotta. She stood impassive, obviously caught, though she finally managed to extract the material of her sleeve from the sticking dagger.

"She did not know the truth of her enemies," Jarlaxle explained.

Entreri looked at him and nodded. The dark elves all

stepped back, allowing the assassin his moment.

"Should I kill her?" Entreri asked Basadoni.

"Why ask my permission?" the pasha replied, obviously none too pleased. "Am I then to credit you for this? For bringing dark elves to my house?"

"I acted as I needed to survive," Entreri replied. "Most of the house survives, neutralized but not killed. Kadran Gordeon is dead—never could I have trusted that one—but Hand survives. And so we will go on under the same arrangement as before, with three lieutenants and one guildmaster." He looked to Jarlaxle, then back to Sharlotta. "Of course, my friend Jarlaxle desires a position of lieutenant," he said. "One well-earned, and that I cannot deny."

Sharlotta stiffened, expecting then to die, for she could do simple math.

Indeed Entreri did originally mean to kill her, but when he glanced back to Basadoni, when he looked again upon the feeble old man, such a shadow of his former glory, he reversed the direction of his sword and put it through Pasha Basadoni's heart instead.

"Three lieutenants," he said to the stunned Sharlotta. "Hand, Jarlaxle, and you."

"So Entreri is guildmaster," the woman remarked with a crooked grin. "You said you could not trust Kadran Gordeon, yet you recognize that I am more honorable," she said seductively, coming forward a step.

Entreri's sword came out and about too fast for her to follow, its tip stopping against the tender flesh of her throat. "Trust you?" the assassin balked. "No, but neither do I fear you. Do as you are instructed, and you will live." He shifted the angle of his blade slightly so that it tucked under her chin, and he nicked her there. "Exactly as instructed," he warned, "else I will take your pretty face from you, one cut at a time."

Entreri turned to Jarlaxle.

"The house will be secured within the hour," the dark elf assured him. "Then you and your human lieutenants can decide the fate of those taken and put out on the streets

247

whatever word suits you as guildmaster."

Entreri had thought that this moment would bring some measure of satisfaction. He was glad that Kadran Gordeon was dead and glad that the old wretch Basadoni had been given a well-deserved rest.

"As you wish, my Pasha," Sharlotta purred from the side.

The title turned his stomach.

Chapter 17
EXORCISING DEMONS

here was indeed something appealing about the fighting, about the feeling of superiority and the element of control. Between the fact that the fights were not lethal—though more than a few patrons were badly injured—and the conscience-dulling drinks, no guilt accompanied each thunderous punch.

Just satisfaction and control, an edge that had been too long absent.

Had he stopped to think about it, Wulfgar might have realized that he was substituting each new challenger for one particular nemesis, one he could not defeat alone, one who had tormented him all those years.

He didn't bother with contemplation, though. He simply enjoyed the sensation of his fist colliding with the chest of this latest troublemaker, sending the tall, thin man reeling back in a hopping, staggering, stumbling quickstep, finally to fall backward over a bench some twenty feet from the barbarian.

Wulfgar methodically waded in, grabbing the decked man by the collar (and taking out more than a few chest hairs in the process) and the groin (and similarly extracting hair).

249

With one jerk the barbarian brought the horizontal man level with his waist. Then a rolling motion snapped the man up high over his head.

"I just fixed that window," Arumn Gardpeck said dryly, helplessly, seeing the barbarian's aim.

The man flew through it to bounce across Half Moon Street.

"Then fix it again," Wulfgar replied, casting a glare over Arumn that the barkeep did not dare to question.

Arumn just shook his head and went back to wiping his bar, reminding himself that, by keeping such complete order in the place Wulfgar was attracting customers—many of them. Folk now came looking for a safe haven in which to waste a night, and then there were those interested in the awesome displays of power. These came both as challengers to the mighty barbarian or, more often, merely as spectators. Never had the Cutlass seen so many patrons, and never had Arumn Gardpeck's purse been so full.

But how much more full it would be, he knew, if he didn't have to keep fixing the place.

"Shouldn't've done that," a man near the bar remarked to Arumn. "That's Rossie Doone, he throwed, a soldier."

"Not wearing any uniform," Arumn remarked.

"Came in unofficial," the man explained. "Wanted to see this Wulfgar thug."

"He saw him," Arumn replied in the same resigned and dry tones.

"And he'll be seein' him again," the man promised. "Only next time with friends."

Arumn sighed and shook his head, not out of any fear for Wulfgar, but because of the expenses he anticipated if a whole crew of soldiers came in to fight the barbarian.

Wulfgar spent that night—half the night—in Delly Curtie's room again, taking a bottle with him from the bar, then grabbing another one on his way outside. He went down to the docks and sat on the edge of a long wharf, watching the sparkles grow on the water as the sun rose behind him.

* * * * *

Josi Puddles saw them first, entering the Cutlass the very next night, a half-dozen grim-faced men including the one the patron had identified as Rossie Doone. They moved to the far side of the room, evicting several patrons from tables, then pulling three of the benches together so they could all sit side by side with their backs to the wall.

"Full moon tonight," Josi remarked.

Arumn knew what that meant. Every time the moon was full the crowd was a bit rowdier. And what a crowd had come in this evening, every sort of rogue and thug Arumn could imagine.

"Been the talk of the street all the day," Josi said quietly.

"The moon?" Arumn asked.

"Not the moon," Josi replied. "Wulfgar and that Rossie fellow. All have been talking of a coming brawl."

"Six against one," Arumn remarked.

"Poor soldiers," Josi said with a snicker.

Arumn nodded to the side then, to Wulfgar, who, sitting with a foaming mug in hand, seemed well aware of the group that had come in. The look on the barbarian's face, so calm and yet so cold, sent a shiver along Arumn's spine. It was going to be a long night.

* * * * *

On the other side of the room, in a corner opposite where sat the six soldiers, another man, quiet and unassuming, also noted the tension and the prospective combatants with more than a passing interest. The man's name was well known on the streets of Luskan, though his face was not. He was a shadow stalker by trade, a man cloaked in secrecy, but a man whose reputation brought trembles to the hardiest of thugs.

Morik the Rogue had been hearing quite a bit about Arumn Gardpeck's new strong-arm; too much, in fact. Story after story had come to him about the man's incredible feats

251

of strength. About how he had been hit squarely in the face with a heavy club and had shaken it away seemingly without care. About how he lifted two men high into the air, smashed their heads together, then simultaneously tossed them through opposite walls of the tavern. About how he had thrown one man out into the street, then rushed out and blocked a team of two horses with his bare chest to stop the wagon from running down the prone drunk. . . .

Morik had been living among the street people long enough to understand the exaggerated nonsense in most of these tales. Each storyteller tried to outdo the previous one. But he couldn't deny the impressive stature of this man Wulfgar. Nor could he deny the many wounds showing about the head of Rossie Doone, a soldier Morik knew well and whom he had always respected as a solid fighter.

Of course Morik, his ears so attuned to the streets and alleyways, had heard of Rossie's intention to return with his friends and settle the score. Of course Morik had also heard of another's intention to put this newcomer squarely in his place. And so Morik had come in to watch, and nothing more, to measure this huge northerner, to see if he had the strength, the skills, and the temperament to survive and become a true threat.

Never taking his gaze off Wulfgar, the quiet man sipped his wine and waited.

* * * * *

As soon as he saw Delly moving near to the six men, Wulfgar drained his beer in a single swallow and tightened his grip on the table. He saw it coming, and how predictable it was, as one of Rossie Doone's sidekicks reached out and grabbed Delly's bottom as she moved past.

Wulfgar came up in a rush, storming in right before the offender, and right beside Delly.

"Oh, but 'tis nothing," the woman said, pooh-poohing Wulfgar away. He grabbed her by the shoulders, lifted her, and turned, depositing her behind him. He turned back, glaring at the offender, then at Rossie Doone, the true perpetrator.

Rossie remained seated, laughing still, seeming completely relaxed with three burly fighters on his right, two more on his left.

"A bit of fun," Wulfgar stated. "A cloth to cover your wounds, deepest of all the wound to your pride."

Rossie stopped laughing and stared hard at the man.

"We have not yet fixed the window," Wulfgar said. "Do you prefer to leave by that route once more?"

The man next to Rossie bristled, but Rossie held him back. "In truth, northman, I prefer to stay," he answered. "In my own eyes it's yourself who should be leaving."

Wulfgar didn't blink. "I ask you a second time, and a last time, to leave of your own accord," he said.

The man farthest from Rossie, down to Wulfgar's left, stood up and stretched languidly. "Think I'll get me a bit o' drink," he said calmly to the man seated beside him, and then, as if going to the bar, he took a step Wulfgar's way.

The barbarian, already a seasoned veteran of barroom brawls, saw it coming. He understood that the man would grab at him to hold and slow him so that Rossie and the others could pummel him. He kept his apparent focus directly on Rossie and waited. Then, as the man came within two steps, as his hands started coming up to grab at Wulfgar, the barbarian spun suddenly, stepping inside the other's reach. The barbarian snapped his back muscles, launching his forehead into the man's face, crushing his nose and sending him staggering backward.

Wulfgar turned back fast, fist flying, and caught Rossie across the jaw as he started to rise, slamming the man back against the wall. Hardly slowing, Wulfgar grabbed the stunned Rossie by the shoulders and yanked him hard to the side, flipping him to the left to deflect the coming rush of the two men remaining there. Then around went the barbarian again, growling, fists flying, to swap heavy punches with the two men leaping at him from that direction.

A knee came up for his groin, but Wulfgar recognized the

move and reacted fast. He turned his leg in to catch the blow with his thigh, then reached down under the bent leg. The attacker instinctively grabbed at Wulfgar, catching shoulder and hair, trying to use him for balance. But the powerful barbarian, simply too strong, drove on, heaving him up and over his shoulder, turning as he went to again deflect the attack from the two men coming in at his back.

The movement cost Wulfgar several punches from the man who had been standing next to the latest human missile. Wulfgar accepted them stoically, hardly seeming to care. He came back hard, legs pumping, to drive the puncher into the wall, wrestling him around.

The desperate soldier grabbed on with all his strength, and the man's friends fast approached from behind. A roar, a wriggle, and a stunning punch extracted Wulfgar from the man's grasp. He skittered back away from the wall and the pursuers, instinctively ducking a punch as he went and grabbing a table by the leg.

Wulfgar spun back, facing the group, and halted the swinging momentum of the table so fully that the item snapped apart. The bulk of the table flew into the chest of the closest man, leaving Wulfgar standing with a wooden table leg in hand, a club he wasted no time in putting to good use. The barbarian smacked it below the table at the exposed legs of the man he had hit with the missile, cracking the side of the soldier's knee once and then again. The man howled in pain and shoved the table back out at Wulfgar, but he accepted the missile strike with merely a shrug, concentrating instead on turning the club in line and jabbing the man in the eye with its narrow end.

A half turn and full swing caught another across the side of the head, splitting the club apart and dropping the attacker like a sack of ground meal. Wulfgar ran right over him as he fell—the barbarian understood that mobility was his only defense against so many. He barreled into the next man in line, carrying him halfway across the room to slam into a wall, a journey that ended with a wild flurry of fists from both. Wulfgar took a dozen blows and gave a like number, but his were by far the heavier, and the dazed and defeated man crumbled to the floor—or would have, had not Wulfgar grabbed him as he slumped. The barbarian turned about fast and let his latest human missile fly, spinning him in low across the ankles of the closest pursuer, who tripped headlong, both arms reaching out to grab the barbarian. Wulfgar, still in his turn, using the momentum of that spin, dived forward, punch leading, stretching right between those arms. His force combined with the momentum of the stumbling man, and he felt his fist sink deep into the man's face, snapping his head back violently.

That man, too, went down hard.

Wulfgar stood straight, facing Rossie and his one standing ally, who had blood rolling freely from his nose. Another man holding his torn eye tried to stand beside them, but his broken knee wouldn't support his weight. He stumbled away to the side to slam into a wall and sink there into a sitting position.

In the first truly coordinated attack since the chaos had begun, Rossie and his companion came in slow and then leaped together atop Wulfgar, thinking to bear him down. But though the two were both large men, Wulfgar didn't fall, didn't stumble in the least. The barbarian caught them as they soared in and held his footing. His thrashing had them both holding on for dear life. Rossie slipped away, and Wulfgar managed to get both arms on the other, dragging the clutching man horizontally across in front of his face. The man's arms flailed about Wulfgar's head, but the angle of attack was all wrong, and the blows proved ineffectual.

Wulfgar roared again and bit the man's stomach hard, then started a full-out, blind run across the tavern floor. Gauging the distance, Wulfgar dipped his head at the last moment to put his powerful neck muscles in proper alignment, then rammed full force into the wall. He bounced back, holding the man with just one arm hooked under his shoulder, and kept it there long enough to allow the man to come down on his feet.

The man stood, against the wall, watching in confusion as Wulfgar ran back a few steps, and then his eyes widened indeed when the huge barbarian turned about, roared, and charged, dipping his shoulder as he came.

The man put his arms up, but that hardly mattered, for Wulfgar shoulder-drove him against the planking—right into the planking, which cracked apart. Louder than the splitting wood came the sound of a groan and a sigh from resigned Arumn Gardpeck.

Wulfgar bounced back again but leaned in fast, slamming left and right repeatedly, each thunderous blow driving the man deeper into the wall. The poor man, crumbled and bloody, splinters deep in his back, his nose already broken and half his body feeling the same way, held up a feeble arm to show that he had had enough.

Wulfgar smashed him again, a vicious left hook that came in over the upraised arm and shattered his jaw, throwing him into oblivion. He would have fallen except that the broken wall held him fast in place.

Wulfgar didn't even notice, for he had turned around to face Rossie, the lone enemy still showing any ability to fight. One of the others, the man Wulfgar had traded blows with against the wall, crawled about on hands and knees, seeming as if he didn't even know where he was. Another, the side of his head split wide by the vicious club swing, kept trying to stand and kept falling over, while a third still sat against the wall, clutching his torn eye and broken knee. The fourth of Rossie's companions, the one Wulfgar had hit with the single, devastating punch, lay very still with no sign of consciousness.

"Gather your friends and be gone," a tired Wulfgar offered to Rossie. "And do not return."

In answer, the outraged man reached down to his boot and drew out a long knife. "But I want to play," Rossie said wickedly, approaching a step.

"Wulfgar!" came Delly's cry from across the way, from behind the bar, and both Wulfgar and Rossie turned to see the woman throwing Aegis-fang out toward her friend, though she couldn't get the heavy warhammer half the distance.

That hardly mattered, though, for Wulfgar reached for it with his arm and with his mind, telepathically calling to the hammer.

The hammer vanished, then reappeared in the barbarian's waiting grasp. "So do I," Wulfgar said to an astonished and horrified Rossie. To accentuate his point, he swung Aegis-fang, one armed, out behind him. The swing hit and split a beam, which drew another profound groan from Arumn.

Rossie, his eager expression long gone, glanced about and backed away liked a trapped animal. He wanted to back out, to find some way to flee—that much was apparent to everybody in the room.

And then the outside door banged open, turning all heads—those that weren't broken open—Rossie Doone's and Wulfgar's included, and in strode the largest human, if he was indeed a human, that Wulfgar had ever seen. He was a giant man, taller than Wulfgar by a foot at least, and almost as wide, weighing perhaps twice the barbarian's three hundred pounds. Even more impressive was the fact that very little of the giant's bulk jiggled as he stormed in. He was all muscle, and gristle, and bone.

He stopped inside the suddenly hushed tavern, his huge head turning slowly to scan the room. His gaze finally settled on Wulfgar. He brought his arms out slowly from under the front folds of his cloak to reveal that he held a heavy length of chain in one hand and a spiked club in the other.

"Ye too tired for me, Wulfgar the dead?" Tree Block Breaker asked, spittle flying with each word. He finished with a growl, then brought his arm across powerfully, slamming the length of chain across the top of the nearest table and splitting the thing neatly down the middle. The three patrons sitting at that particular table didn't scamper away. They didn't dare to move at all.

A smile widened across Wulfgar's face. He flipped Aegis-fang into the air, a single spin, to catch it again by the handle.

257

Arumn Gardpeck groaned all the louder; this would be an expensive night.

Rossie Doone and those of his friends who could still move scrambled across the room, out of harm's way, leaving the path between Wulfgar and Tree Block Breaker clear.

In the shadows across the room, Morik the Rogue took another sip of wine. This was the fight he had come to see.

"Well, ye give me no answer," Tree Block Breaker said, whipping his chain across again. This time it did not connect solidly but whipped about one angled leg of the fallen table. Then, after slapping the leg of one sitting man, its tip got a hold on the man's chair. With a great roar, Tree Block yanked the chain back, sending table and chair flying across the room and dropping the unfortunate patron on his bum.

"Tavern etiquette and my employer require that I give you the opportunity to leave quietly," Wulfgar calmly replied, reciting Arumn's creed.

On came Tree Block Breaker, a great, roaring monster, a giant gone wild. His chain flailed back and forth before him, his club raised high to strike.

Wulfgar realized that he could have taken the giant out with a well-aimed throw of Aegis-fang before Tree Block had gone two steps, but he let the creature come on, relishing the challenge. To everyone's surprise he dropped Aegis-fang to the floor as Tree Block closed. When the chain swished for his head, he dropped into a sudden squat but held his arm vertically above him.

The chain hooked around, and Wulfgar reached over it and grabbed on, giving a great tug that only increased Tree Block's charge. The huge man swung with his club, but he was too close and still coming. Wulfgar went down low, driving his shoulder against the man's legs. Tree Block's momentum carried his bulk across the bent barbarian's back.

Amazingly, stunningly, Wulfgar stood up straight, bringing Tree Block up above him. Then, to the astonished gasps of all watching, he bent at the knees quickly and jerked back up straight. Pushing with all his strength, he lifted Tree Block into the air above his head.

Before the huge man could wriggle about and bring his club to bear, Wulfgar ran back the way Tree Block had charged, and with a great roar of his own, threw the man right through the door, taking it and the jamb out completely and depositing the huge man in a jumble of kindling outside the Cutlass. His arm still enwrapped by the chain, Wulfgar gave a huge tug that sent Tree Block spinning about in the pile of wood before he surrendered the chain altogether.

The stubborn giant thrashed about, finally extricating himself from the wood heap. He stood roaring, his face and neck cut in a dozen places, his club whirling about wildly.

"Turn and leave," Wulfgar warned. The barbarian reached behind him and with a thought brought Aegis-fang back to his hand.

If Tree Block even heard the warning, he showed no indication. He smacked his club against the ground and came forward in a rush, snarling.

And then he was dead. Just like that, caught by surprise as the barbarian's arm came forward, as the mighty warhammer twirled out, too fast for his attempted deflection with the club, too powerfully for Tree Block's massive chest to absorb the hit.

He stumbled backward and went down with more a whisper than a bang and lay very still.

Tree Block Breaker was the first man Wulfgar had killed in his tenure at Arumn Gardpeck's bar, the first man killed in the Cutlass in many, many months. All the tavern, Delly and Josi, Rossie Doone and his thugs, seemed to stop in pure amazement. The place went perfectly silent.

Wulfgar, Aegis-fang returned to his grasp, calmly turned about and walked over to the bar, paying no heed to the dangerous Rossie Doone. He placed Aegis-fang on the bar before Arumn, indicating that the barkeep should replace it on the shelves behind the counter, then casually remarked, "You should fix the door, Arumn, and quickly, else someone walks in and steals your stock."

And then, as if nothing had happened, Wulfgar walked back across the room, seemingly oblivious to the silence and the open-mouthed stares that followed his every stride.

Arumn Gardpeck shook his head and lifted the warhammer, then stopped as a shadowy figure came up opposite him.

"A fine warrior you have there, Master Gardpeck," the man said. Arumn recognized the voice, and the hairs on the back of his neck stood up.

"And Half Moon Street is a better place without that bully Tree Block running about," Morik went on. "I'll not lament his demise."

"I have never asked for any quarrel," Arumn said. "Not with Tree Block and not with you."

"Nor will you find one," Morik assured the innkeeper as Wulfgar, noting the conversation, came up beside the man— as did Josi Puddles and Delly, though they kept a more respectful distance from the dangerous rogue.

"Well fought, Wulfgar, son of Beornegar," Morik said. He slid a glass of drink along the bar before Wulfgar, who looked down at it, then back at Morik suspiciously. After all, how could Morik know his full name, one he had not used since his entry into Luskan, one that he had purposely left far, far behind.

Delly slipped in between the two, calling for Arumn to fetch her a couple of drinks for other patrons, and while the two stood staring at each other, she slyly swapped the drink Morik had placed with one from her tray. Then she moved out of the way, rolling back behind Wulfgar, wanting the security of his massive form between her and the dangerous man.

"Nor will you find one," Morik said again to Arumn. He tapped his forehead in salute and walked away, out of the Cutlass.

Wulfgar eyed him curiously, recognizing the balanced gait of a warrior, then moved to follow, pausing only long enough to lift and drain the glass.

"Morik the Rogue," Josi Puddles remarked to Arumn and Delly, moving opposite the barkeep. Both he and Arumn noted that Delly was holding the glass Morik had offered to Wulfgar.

"And likely this'd kill a fair-sized minotaur," she said, reaching over to dump the contents into a basin.

Despite Morik's assurances, Arumn Gardpeck did not disagree. Wulfgar had solidified his reputation a hundred times over this night, first by absolutely humbling Rossie Doone and his crowd—there would be no more trouble from them—and then by downing—and oh, so easily—the toughest fighter Half Moon Street had known in years.

But with such fame came danger, all three knew. To be in the eyes of Morik the Rogue was to be in the sights of his deadly weapons. Perhaps the man would keep his promise and let things lay low for a time, but eventually Wulfgar's reputation would grow to become a distraction, and then, perhaps, a threat.

Wulfgar seemed oblivious to it all. He finished his night's work with hardly another word, not even to Rossie Doone and his companions, who chose to stay—mostly because several of them needed quite a bit of potent drink to dull the pain of their wounds—but quietly so. And then, as was his growing custom, he took two bottles of potent liquor, took Delly by the arm, and retired to her room for half the night.

When that half a night had passed he, the remaining bottle in hand, went to the docks to watch the reflection of the sunrise.

To bask in the present, care nothing about the future, and forget the past.

Chapter 18

OF IMPS AND PRIESTS AND A GREAT QUEST

our name and reputation have preceded you," Captain Vaines explained to Drizzt as he led the drow and his companions to the boarding plank. Before them loomed the broken skyline of Baldur's Gate, the great port city halfway between Waterdeep and Calimport. Many structures lined the impressive dock areas, from low warehouses to taller buildings set with armaments and lookout positions, giving the region an uneven, jagged feel.

"My man found little trouble in gaining you passage on a river runner," Vaines went on.

"Discerning folk who'd take a drow," Bruenor said dryly.

"Less so if they'd take a dwarf," Drizzt replied without the slightest hesitation.

"Captained and crewed by dwarves," Vaines explained. That brought a groan from Drizzt and a chuckle from Bruenor. "Captain Bumpo Thunderpuncher and his brother, Donat, and their two cousins thrice removed on their mother's side."

"Ye know them well," Catti-brie remarked.

"All who meet Bumpo meet his crew, and admittedly they are a hard foursome to forget," Vaines said. "My man had little trouble in gaining your passage, as I said, for the dwarves know well the tale of Bruenor Battlehammer and the reclamation of Mithral Hall. And of his companions, including the dark elf."

"Bet ye'd never see the day when ye'd become a hero to a bunch o' dwarves," Bruenor remarked to Drizzt.

"Bet I'd never see the day when I'd want to," the ranger replied.

The group came to the rail then, and Vaines moved aside, holding his arm out toward the plank. "Farewell, and may your journey return you safely to your home," he said. "If I am in port or nearby when you return to Baldur's Gate, perhaps we will sail together again."

"Perhaps," Regis politely replied, but he, like all the others, understood that, if they did get to Cadderly and get rid of the Crystal Shard, they meant to ask for Cadderly's help in bringing them magically to Luskan. They had approximately another two weeks of travel before them if they moved swiftly, but Cadderly could wind walk all the way back to Luskan in a matter of minutes. So said Drizzt and Catti-brie, who had taken such a walk with the powerful priest before. Then they could get on with the pressing business of finding Wulfgar.

They entered Baldur's Gate without incident, and though Drizzt felt many stares following him, they were not ominous glares but looks of curiosity. The drow couldn't help contrast this experience with his other visit to the city, when he'd gone in pursuit of Regis who had been whisked away to Calimport by Artemis Entreri. On that occasion, Drizzt, with Wulfgar beside him, had entered the city under the disguise of a magical mask that had allowed him to appear as a surface elf.

"Not much like the last time ye came through?" Catti-brie, who knew well the tale of the first visit asked, seeing Drizzt's gaze.

"Always I wished to walk freely in the cities of the Sword Coast," Drizzt replied. "It appears that our work with Captain Deudermont has granted me that privilege. Reputation has freed me from some of the pains of my heritage."

"Ye thinking that's a good thing?" the so perceptive woman asked, for she had noted clearly the slight wince at the corner of Drizzt's eye when he made the claim.

"I do not know," Drizzt admitted. "I like that I can walk freely now in most places without persecution."

"But it pains ye to think that ye had to earn the right," Catti-brie finished perfectly. "Ye look at me, a human, and know that I had to earn no such thing. And at Bruenor and Regis, dwarf and halfling, and know that they can walk anywhere without earnin' a thing."

"I do not begrudge any of you that," Drizzt replied. "But see their gazes?" He looked around at the many people walking the streets of Baldur's Gate, almost every one turning to regard the drow curiously, some with admiration in their eyes, some with disbelief.

"So even though ye're walking free, ye're not walking free," the woman observed, and her nod told Drizzt that she understood then. Given the choice between facing the hatred of prejudice or the similarly ignorant looks of those viewing him as a curiosity piece, the latter seemed the better by far. But both were traps, both prisons, jailing Drizzt within the confines of the preceding reputation of a drow elf, of any drow elf, and thus limiting Drizzt to his heritage.

"Bah, they're just a stupid lot," Bruenor interrupted.

"Those who know you, know better," Regis added.

Drizzt took it all in stride, all with a smile. Long ago he had abandoned any futile hopes of truly fitting in among the surface-dwellers—his kinfolk's well-earned reputation for treachery and catastrophe would always prevent that—and had learned instead to focus his energy on those closest to him, on those who had learned to see him beyond his physical trappings. And now here he was with three of his most trusted and beloved friends, walking freely, easily booking passage, and presenting no problems to them other than those created by the relic they had to carry. That was truly what Drizzt Do'Urden had desired from the time he had come to know Catti-brie and Bruenor and Regis, and with them beside him how could the stares, be they of hatred or of ignorant curiosity, bother him?

No, his smile was sincere; if Wulfgar was beside them, then all the world would be right for the drow, the king's treasure at the end of his long and difficult road.

* * * * *

Rai'gy rubbed his black hands together as the smallish creature began to form in the center of the magical circle he had drawn. He didn't know Gromph Baenre by anything more than reputation, but despite Jarlaxle's insistence that the archmage would be trustworthy on this issue, the mere fact that Gromph was drow and of the ruling house of Menzoberranzan worried Rai'gy profoundly. The name Gromph had given him was supposedly of a minor denizen, easily controlled, but Rai'gy couldn't know for certain until the creature appeared before him.

A bit of treachery from Gromph could have had him opening a gate to a major demon, to Demogorgon himself, and the impromptu magical circle Rai'gy had drawn here in the sewers of Calimport would hardly prove sufficient protection.

The wizard-priest relaxed a bit as the creature took shape—the shape, as Gromph had promised, of an imp. Even without the magical circle, a wizard-priest as powerful as Rai'gy would have little trouble in handling a mere imp.

"Who is it that calls my name?" asked the imp in the guttural language of the Abyss, obviously more than a little perturbed and, both Rai'gy and Jarlaxle noted, a bit trepidatious—and even more so when he noted that his summoners were drow elves. "You should not bother Druzil. No, no, for he serves a great master," Druzil went on, speaking fluently in the drow tongue.

"Silence!" Rai'gy commanded, and the little imp was compelled to obey. The wizard-priest looked to Jarlaxle.

"Why do you protest?" Jarlaxle asked Druzil. "Is it not the desire of your kind to find access to this world?"

Druzil tilted his head and narrowed his eyes, a pensive yet still apprehensive pose.

"Ah, yes," the mercenary leader went on. "But of late, you have been summoned not by friends, but by enemies, so I have been told. By Cadderly of Caradoon."

Druzil bared his pointy teeth and hissed at the mention of the priest. That brought a smile to the faces of both dark elves. Gromph Baenre, it seemed, had not steered them wrong.

"We would like to pain Cadderly," Jarlaxle explained with a wicked grin. "Would Druzil like to help?"

"Tell me how," the imp eagerly replied.

"We need to know everything about the human," Jarlaxle explained. "His appearance and demeanor, his history and present place. We were told that Druzil, above all others in the Abyss, knows the man."

"Hates the man," the imp corrected, and he seemed eager indeed. But suddenly he backed off, staring suspiciously at the two. "I tell you, and then you dismiss me," he remarked.

Jarlaxle looked to Rai'gy, for they had anticipated such a reaction. The wizard-priest stood up, walked to the side in the tiny room, and pulled aside a screen, revealing a small kettle, bubbling and boiling.

"I am without a familiar," Rai'gy explained. "An imp would serve me well."

Druzil's coal black eyes flared with red fires. "Then we can pain Cadderly and so many other humans together," the imp reasoned.

"Does Druzil agree?" Jarlaxle asked.

"Does Druzil have a choice?" the imp retorted sarcastically.

"As to serving Rai'gy, yes," the drow replied, and the imp was obviously surprised, as was Rai'gy. "As to revealing all that you know about Cadderly, no. It is too important, and if we must torment you for a hundred years, we shall."

"Then Cadderly would be dead," Druzil said dryly.

"The torment would remain pleasurable to me," Jarlaxle

was quick to respond, and Druzil knew enough about dark elves to understand that this was no idle threat.

"Druzil wishes to pain Cadderly," the imp admitted, dark eyes sparkling.

"Then tell us," Jarlaxle said. "Everything."

Later on that day, while Druzil and Rai'gy worked the magic spells that would bind them as master and familiar, Jarlaxle sat alone in the room he had taken in the subbasement of House Basadoni. He had indeed learned much from the imp, most important of all that he had no desire to bring his band anywhere near the one named Cadderly Bonaduce. This was to Druzil's ultimate dismay. The leader of the Spirit Soaring, armed with magic far beyond even Rai'gy and Kimmuriel, might prove too great a foe. Even worse, Cadderly was apparently rebuilding an order of priests, surrounding himself with young and strong acolytes, enthusiastic idealists.

"The worst kind," Jarlaxle said as Entreri entered the room. "Idealists," he explained to the assassin's perplexed expression. "Above all else, I hate idealists."

"They are blind fools," Entreri agreed.

"They are unpredictable fanatics," Jarlaxle explained. "Blind to danger and blind to fear as long as they think their path is according to the tenets of their particular god-figure."

"And the leader of this other guild is an idealist?" a confused Entreri asked, for he thought he had been summoned to discuss his upcoming meeting with the remaining guilds of Calimport, to stop a war before it ever began.

"No, no, it is another matter," Jarlaxle explained, waving his hand dismissively. "One that concerns my activities in Menzoberranzan and not here in Calimport. Let it not trouble you, for you have business more important by far."

And Jarlaxle, too, put it out of his mind then, focusing on the more immediate problem. He had been surprised by Druzil's accounting of Cadderly, never imagining that this human would present such a problem. Though he held firm to his determination to keep his minions away from

Cadderly, he was not dismayed, for he understood that Drizzt and his friends were still a long way from the great library known as the Spirit Soaring.

It was a place Jarlaxle had no intention of ever allowing them to see.

* * * * *

"Yes, a pleasure meetin' ye! Oh, a pleasure, King Bruenor, and to yer kin, me blessin's," Bumpo Thunderpuncher, a rotund and short little dwarf with a fiery orange beard and a huge and flat nose that was pushed over to one side of his ruddy face, said to Bruenor for perhaps the tenth time since *Bottom Feeder* had put out of Baldur's Gate. The dwarven vessel was a square-bottomed, shallow twenty-footer with two banks of oars—though only one was normally in use—and a long aft pole for steering and for pushing off the bottom. Bumpo and his equally rotund and bumbling brother Donat had fallen all over themselves at the sight of the Eighth King of Mithral Hall. Bruenor had seemed honestly surprised that his name had grown to such proportions, even among his own race.

Now, though, that surprise was turning to mere annoyance, as Bumpo and Donat and their two oar-pulling cousins, Yipper and Quipper Fishsquisher, continued to rain compliments, promises of fealty, and general slobber all over him.

Sitting back from the dwarves, Drizzt and Catti-brie smiled. The ranger alternated his looks between Catti-brie—how he loved to gaze upon her when she wasn't looking—and the tumult of the dwarves. Then Regis—who was lying on his belly at the prow, head hanging over the front of the boat, his hands drawing pictures in the water—and back behind them to the diminishing skyline of Baldur's Gate.

Again he thought about his passage through the city, as easy a time of it as the drow had ever known, including those occasions when he had worn the magical mask. He had earned this peace; they all had. Once this mission was completed and the crystal shard was safely in the hands of Cadderly, and once they had recovered Wulfgar and helped him through his darkness, then perhaps they could journey the wide world again, for no better reason than to see what lay over the next horizon and with no troubles beyond the fawning of bumbling dwarves.

Truly Drizzt wore a contented smile, finding hope again, for Wulfgar and for them all. He could never have dreamed that he would ever find such a life on that day decades before when he had walked out of Menzoberranzan.

It occurred to him then that his father, Zaknafein, who had died to give him this chance, was watching him at that moment from another plane, a goodly place for one as deserving as Zak.

Watching him and smiling.

Part 4

KINGDOMS

hether a king's palace, a warrior's bastion, a wizard's tower, an encampment for nomadic barbarians, a farmhouse with stone-lined or hedge-lined fields, or even a tiny and unremarkable room up the back staircase of a ramshackle inn, we each of us spend great energy in carving out our own little kingdoms. From the grandest castle to the smallest nook, from the arrogance of nobility to the unpretentious desires of the lowliest peasant, there is a basic need within the majority of us for ownership, or at least for stewardship. We want to—need to—find our realm, our place in a world often too confusing and too overwhelming, our sense of order in one little corner of a world that oft looms too big and too uncontrollable.

And so we carve and line, fence and lock, then protect our space fiercely with sword or pitchfork.

The hope is that this will be the end of that road we chose to walk, the peaceful and secure rewards for a life of trials. Yet, it never comes to that, for peace is not a place, whether lined by hedges or by high walls. The greatest king with the largest army in the most invulnerable fortress is not necessarily a man at peace. Far from it, for the irony of it all is that the acquisition of such material wealth can work against any hope of true serenity. But beyond any physical securities there lies yet another form of unrest, one that neither the king nor the peasant will escape. Even that great king, even the simplest beggar will, at times, be full of the unspeakable anger we all sometimes feel. And I do not mean a rage so great that it cannot be verbalized but rather a frustration so elusive and permeating that one can find no words for it. It is the quiet source of irrational outbursts against

273

*friends and family, the perpetrator of temper. True freedom
from it cannot be found in any place outside one's own mind
and soul.*

*Bruenor carved out his kingdom in Mithral Hall, yet
found no peace there. He preferred to return to Icewind Dale,
a place he had named home not out of desire for wealth, nor
out of any inherited kingdom, but because there, in the frozen
northland, Bruenor had come to know his greatest measure
of inner peace. There he surrounded himself with friends,
myself among them, and though he will not admit this—I
am not certain he even recognizes it—his return to Icewind
Dale was, in fact, precipitated by his desire to return to that
emotional place and time when he and I, Regis, Catti-brie,
and yes, even Wulfgar, were together. Bruenor went back in
search of a memory.*

*I suspect that Wulfgar now has found a place along or at
the end of his chosen road, a niche, be it a tavern in Luskan
or Waterdeep, a borrowed barn in a farming village, or even
a cave in the Spine of the World. Because what Wulfgar does
not now have is a clear picture of where he emotionally
wishes to be, a safe haven to which he can escape. If he finds
it again, if he can get past the turmoil of his most jarring
memories, then likely he, too, will return to Icewind Dale in
search of his soul's true home.*

*In Menzoberranzan I witnessed many of the little king-
doms we foolishly cherish, houses strong and powerful and
barricaded from enemies in a futile attempt at security. And
when I walked out of Menzoberranzan into the wild Underdark, I, too, sought to carve out my niche. I spent time in a
cave talking only to Guenhwyvar and sharing space with
mushroomlike creatures that I hardly understood and who
hardly understood me. I ventured to Blingdenstone, city of
the deep gnomes, and could have made that my home, perhaps, except that staying there, so close to the city of drow,
would have surely brought ruin upon those folk.*

*And so I came to the surface and found a home with Mon-
tolio deBrouchee in his wondrous mountain grove, perhaps
the first place I ever came to know any real measure of inner*

peace. And yet I came to learn that the grove was not my home, for when Montolio died I found to my surprise that I could not remain there.

Eventually I found my place and found that the place was within me, not about me. It happened when I came to Icewind Dale, when I met Catti-brie and Regis and Bruenor. Only then did I learn to defeat the unspeakable anger within. Only there did I learn true peace and serenity.

Now I take that calm with me, whether my friends accompany me or not. Mine is a kingdom of the heart and soul, defended by the security of honest love and friendship and the warmth of memories. Better than any land-based kingdom, stronger than any castle wall, and most importantly of all, portable.

I can only hope and pray that Wulfgar will eventually walk out of his darkness and come to this same emotional place.

—Drizzt Do'Urden

Chapter 19
CONCERNING WULFGAR

elly pulled her coat tighter about her, more trying to hide her gender than to fend off any chill breezes. She moved quickly along the street, skipping fast to try and keep up with the shadowy figure turning corners ahead of her, a man one of the other patrons of the Cutlass had assured her was indeed Morik the Rogue, no doubt come on another spying mission.

She turned into an alleyway, and there he was. He was standing right before her, waiting for her, dagger in hand.

Delly skidded to a stop, hands up in a desperate plea for her life. "Please Mister Morik!" she cried. "I'm just wantin' to talk to ye."

"Morik?" the man echoed, and his hood slipped back revealing a dark-skinned face—too dark for the man Delly sought.

"Oh, but I'm begging yer pardon, good sir," Delly stammered, backing away. "I was thinking ye were someone else." The man started to respond, but Delly hardly heard him, for she turned about and sprinted back toward the Cutlass.

When she got safely away, she calmed and slowed enough to consider the situation. Ever since the fight with Tree

276

Block Breaker, she and many other patrons had seen Morik the Rogue in every shadow, had heard him skulking about every corner. Or had they all, in their fears, just thought they had seen the dangerous man? Frustrated by that thought, knowing that there was indeed more than a little truth to her reasoning, Delly gave a great sigh and let her coat droop open.

"Selling your wares, then, Delly Curtie?" came a question from the side.

Delly's eyes widened as she turned to regard the shadowy figure against the wall, the figure belonging to a voice she recognized. She felt the lump grow in her throat. She had been looking for Morik, but now that he had found her on his terms she felt foolish indeed. She glanced down the street, back toward the Cutlass, wondering if she could make it there before a dagger found her back.

"You have been asking about me and looking for me," Morik casually remarked.

"I've been doing no such—"

"I was one of those whom you asked," Morik interrupted dryly. His voice changed pitch and accent completely as he added, "So be tellin' me, missy, why ye're wantin' to be seein' that nasty little knife-thrower."

That set Delly back on her heels, remembering well her encounter with an old woman who had said those very words in that very voice. And even if she hadn't recognized the phrasing or the voice, she wouldn't for a moment doubt the man who was well-known as Luskan's master of disguise. She had seen Morik on several occasions, intimately, many months before. Every time he had appeared differently to her, not just in physical features but in demeanor and attitude as well, walking differently, talking differently, even making love differently. Rumors circulating through Luskan for years had claimed that Morik was, in fact, several different men, and while Delly thought them exaggerated, she realized just then that if they turned out to be correct, she wouldn't be surprised.

"So you have found me," Morik said firmly.

Delly paused, not sure how to proceed. Only Morik's obvious agitation and impatience prompted her to blurt out, "I'm wanting ye to leave Wulfgar alone. He gave Tree Block what Tree Block asked for and wouldn't've gone after the man if the man didn't go after him."

"Why would I care for Tree Block Breaker?" Morik asked, still using a tone that seemed to say that he had hardly given it a thought. "An irritating thug, if ever I knew one. Half Moon Street seems a better place without him."

"Well, then ye're not for avenging that one," Delly reasoned. "But word's out that ye're none too fond o' Wulfgar and looking to prove—"

"I have nothing to prove," Morik interrupted.

"And what of Wulfgar then?" Delly asked.

Morik shrugged noncommittally. "You speak as if you love the man, Delly Curtie."

Delly blushed fiercely. "I'm speaking for Arumn Gardpeck, as well," she insisted. "Wulfgar's been good for the Cutlass, and as far as we're knowing, he's been not a bit o' trouble outside the place."

"Ah, but it seems as if you do love him, Delly, and more than a bit," Morik said with a laugh. "And here I thought that Delly Curtie loved every man equally."

Delly blushed again, even more fiercely.

"Of course, if you do love him, then I, out of obligation to all other suitors, would have to see him dead," Morik reasoned. "I would consider that a duty to my fellows of Luskan, you see, for a treasure such as Delly Curtie is not to be hoarded by any one man."

"I'm not loving him," Delly said firmly. "But I'm asking ye, for meself and for Arumn, not to kill him."

"Not in love with him?" Morik asked slyly.

Delly shook her head.

"Prove it," Morik said, reaching out to pull the tie string on the neck of Delly's dress.

The woman teetered for just a moment, unsure. And then—for Wulfgar only, for she did not wish to do this—she nodded her agreement.

Later on, Morik the Rogue lay alone in his rented bed, Delly long gone—to Wulfgar's bed, he figured. He took a deep draw on his pipe, savoring the intoxicating aroma of the exotic and potent pipeweed.

He considered his good fortune this night, for he hadn't been with Delly Curtie in more than a year and had forgotten how marvelous she could be.

Especially when it didn't cost him anything, and on this nigh, it most certainly had not. Morik had indeed been watching Wulfgar but had no intention of killing the man. The fate of Tree Block Breaker had shown him well how dangerous a proposition that attempt could prove.

He did plan to have a long talk with Arumn Gardpeck, though, one that Delly would surely make easier now. There was no need to kill the barbarian, as long as Arumn kept the huge man in his place.

* * * * *

Delly fumbled with her dress and cloak, all in a fit after her encounter with Morik, as she stumbled through the upstairs rooms of the inn. She turned a corner in the hallway and was surprised indeed to see the street looming in front of her, right in front of her, and before she could even stop herself, she was outside. And then the world was spinning all about.

When she at last re-oriented herself, she glanced back behind her, seeing the open street under the moonlight, and the inn where she had left Morik many yards away. She didn't understand, for hadn't she been walking inside just a moment ago? And in an upstairs hallway? Delly merely shrugged. For this woman, not understanding something was not so uncommon an occurrence. She shook her head, figured that Morik had really set her thoughts to spinning that night, and headed back for the Cutlass.

On the other side of the dimensional door that had transported the woman out of the inn, Kimmuriel Oblodra almost laughed aloud at the bumbling spectacle. Glad of his camouflaging *piwafwi* cloak, for Jarlaxle had insisted that he leave no traces of his ever being in Luskan, and Jarlaxle considered murdered humans as traces, the drow turned the corner in the hallway and lined up his next spatial leap.

He winced at the notion, reminding himself that he had to handle this one delicately; he and Rai'gy had done some fine spying on Morik the Rogue, and Kimmuriel knew the man to be dangerous, for a human, at least. He brought up his kinetic barrier, focused all his thoughts on it, then enacted the dimensional path down the corridor and beyond Morik's door.

There lay the man on his bed, bathed in the soft glow of his pipe and the embers from the hearth across the room. Morik sat up immediately, obviously sensing the disturbance, and Kimmuriel went through the portal, focusing his thoughts more strongly on the kinetic barrier. If the disorientation of the spatial walk defeated his concentration, he would likely be dead before his thoughts ever unscrambled.

Indeed, the drow felt Morik come into him hard, felt the jab of a dagger against his belly. But the kinetic barrier held, and he absorbed the blow. As he found again his conscious focus and took two more hits, he pushed back against the man and wriggled out to the side, standing facing Morik and laughing at him.

"You can not hurt me," he said haltingly, his command of the common tongue less than perfect, even with the magics Rai'gy had bestowed upon him.

Morik's eyes widened considerably as he recognized the truth of the intruder, as his mind came to grips with the fact that a drow elf had come into his room. He glanced about, apparently seeking an escape route.

"I come to talk, Morik," Kimmuriel explained, not wanting to have to chase this one all across Luskan. "Not to hurt you."

Morik hardly seemed to relax at the assurance of a dark elf.

"I bring gifts," Kimmuriel went on, and he tossed a small

box onto the bed, its contents jingling. "Belaern, and pipe-weed from the great cavern of Yoganith. Very good. You must answer questions."

"Questions about what?" the still nervous thief asked, remaining in his defensive crouch, one hand turning his dagger over repeatedly. "Who are you?"

"My master is . . ." Kimmuriel paused, searching for the right word. "Generous," he decided. "And my master is merciless. You deal with us." He stopped there and held up his hand to halt any reply before Morik could respond. Kimmuriel felt the energy tingling within him, and holding it had become a drain he could ill afford. He focused on a small chair, sending his thoughts into it, animating it and having it walk right past him.

He touched it as it crossed before him, releasing all the energy of Morik's hits, shattering the wooden chair completely.

Morik eyed him skeptically, without comprehension. "A warning?" he asked.

Kimmuriel only smiled.

"You did not like my chair?"

"My master wishes to hire you," Kimmuriel explained. "He needs eyes in Luskan."

"Eyes and a sword?" Morik asked, his own eyes narrowing.

"Eyes and no more," Kimmuriel came back. "You tell me of the one called Wulfgar now, and then you will watch him closely and tell me about him when occasions have me return to you."

"Wulfgar?" Morik muttered under his breath, fast growing tired of the name.

"Wulfgar," answered Kimmuriel, who shouldn't have been able to hear, but of course, with his keen drow ears, certainly did. "You watch him."

"I would rather kill him," Morik remarked. "If he is trouble—" He stopped abruptly as murderous intent flashed across Kimmuriel's dark eyes.

"Not that," the drow explained. "Kyorlin . . . watch him. Quietly. I return with more belaern for more answers."

He motioned to the box on the bed and repeated the drow word, "Belaern," with great emphasis.

Before Morik could ask anything else the room darkened utterly, a blackness so complete that the man couldn't see his hand if he had waved it an inch before his eyes. Fearing an attack, he went lower and skittered forward, dagger slashing.

But the dark elf was long gone, was back through his dimensional door into the hallway, then through that onto the street, then back through Rai'gy's teleportation gate, walking all that way back to Calimport before the globe of darkness even dissipated in Morik's room. Rai'gy and Jarlaxle, both of whom had watched the exchange, nodded their approval.

Jarlaxle's grasp on the surface world widened.

* * * * *

Morik came out from under his bed tentatively when the embers of the hearth at last reappeared. What a strange night it had been! he thought. First with Delly, though that was not so unexpected, since she obviously loved Wulfgar and knew that Morik could easily kill him.

But now . . . a drow elf! Coming to Morik to talk about Wulfgar! Was everything on Luskan's street suddenly about Wulfgar? Who was this man, and why did he attract such amazing attention?

Morik looked at the blasted chair—an impressive feat—then, frustrated, threw his dagger across the room so that it sank deep into the opposite wall. Then he went to the bed.

"Belaern," he said quietly, wondering what that might mean. Hadn't the dark elf said something about pipeweed?

He gingerly inspected the unremarkable box, looking for any traps. Finding none and reasoning that the dark elf could have used a more straightforward method of killing him if that had been the drow's intent, he set the box solidly on a night table and gently pulled its latch back and opened the lid.

Gems and gold stared back at him, and packets of a dark weed.

"Belaern," Morik said again, his smile gleaming as did the treasure before him. So he was to watch Wulfgar, something he had planned to do anyway, and he would be rewarded handsomely for his efforts.

He thought of Delly Curtie; he looked at the contents of the opened box and the rumpled sheets.

Not a bad night.

* * * * *

Life at the Cutlass remained quiet and peaceful for several days, with no one coming in to challenge Wulfgar after the demise of the legendary Tree Block Breaker. But when the peace finally broke, it did so in grand fashion. A new ship put in to Luskan harbor with a crew too long on the water and looking for a good row.

And they found one in the form of Wulfgar, in a tavern they nearly pulled down around them.

Finally, after many minutes of brawling, Wulfgar lifted the last squirming sailor over his head and tossed the man out through the hole in the wall created by the four previous men the barbarian had thrown out. Another stubborn sea dog tried to rush back in through the hole, and Wulfgar hit him in the face with a bottle.

Then the big man wiped a bloody forearm across his bloody face, took up another bottle—this one full—and staggered to the nearest intact table. Falling into a chair and taking a deep swig, Wulfgar grimaced as he drank, as the alcohol washed over his torn lip.

At the bar, Josi and Arumn sat exhausted and also beaten. Wulfgar had taken the brunt of it, though; these two had minor cuts and bruises only.

"He's hurt pretty bad," Josi remarked, motioning to the big man—to his leg in particular, for Wulfgar's pants were soaked in blood. One of the sailors had struck him hard with a plank. The board had split apart and torn fabric and skin, leaving many large slivers deeply embedded in the barbarian's leg.

Even as Arumn and Josi regarded him, Delly moved beside him, falling to her knees and wrapping a clean cloth about the leg. She pushed hard on the deep slivers and made Wulfgar growl in agony. He took another deep drink of the pain-killing liquor.

"Delly will see to him again," Arumn remarked. "That's become her lot in life."

"A busy lot, then," Josi agreed, his tone solemn. "I'm thinking that the last crew Wulfgar dumped, Rossie Doone and his thugs, probably pointed this bunch in our direction. There'll always be another to challenge the boy."

"And one day he will find his better. As did Tree Block Breaker," Arumn said quietly. "He'll not die comfortably in bed, I fear."

"Nor will he outlive either of us," Josi added, watching as Delly, supporting the barbarian, led him out of the room.

Just then another pair of rowdy sailors came rushing through the broken wall, running straight for the staggering Wulfgar's back. Just before they got to him, the huge barbarian found a surge of energy. He pushed Delly safely away, then spun, fist flying between the reaching arms of one man to slam him in the face. He dropped as though his legs had turned to liquid beneath him.

The other sailor barreled into Wulfgar, but the big man didn't move an inch, just grunted and accepted the man's left and right combination.

But then Wulfgar had him, grabbing tight under his arms and squeezing hard, lifting the man right from the floor. When the sailor tried to punch and kick at him, the barbarian shook him so violently that the man bit the tip right off his tongue.

Then he was flying, Wulfgar taking two running steps and launching him for the hole in the wall. Wulfgar's aim wasn't true, though, and the man crashed against the wall a foot or so to the left.

"I'll push him out for ye," Josi Puddles called from the bar.

Wulfgar nodded, accepted Delly's arm again, and ambled away.

"But he will take his share down with him, now won't he?" Arumn Gardpeck remarked with a chuckle.

Chapter 20

DANGLING A LOCKET

y dear Domo," Sharlotta Vespers purred, moving over seductively to put her long fingers on the wererat leader's shoulders. "Can you not see the mutual gain to our alliance?"

"I see Basadonis moving into my sewers," Domo Quillilo replied with a snarl. He was in human form now, but still carried characteristics—such as the way he twitched his nose—that seemed more fitting to a rat. "Where is the old wretch?"

Artemis Entreri started to respond, but Sharlotta shot him a plaintive look, begging him to follow her lead. The assassin sat back in his chair, more than content to let Sharlotta handle the likes of Domo.

"The old wretch," the woman began, imitating Domo's less-than-complimentary tone, "is even now securing a partnership with an even greater ally, one whom Domo would not wish to cross."

The wererat's eyes narrowed dangerously; he was not accustomed to being threatened. "Who?" he asked. "Those smelly kobolds we found running through our sewers?"

"Kobolds?" Sharlotta echoed with a laugh. "Hardly them.

No, they are just fodder, the leading edge of our new ally's forces."

The wererat leader pulled away from the woman, rose out of his chair, and strode across the room. He knew that a fight had occurred in the sewers and subbasement of the Basadoni House. He knew that it concerned many kobolds and the Basadoni soldiers and also, so his spies had told him, some other creatures. These were unseen but obviously powerful, with cunning magics and tricks. He also knew, simply from the fact that Sharlotta still lived, that the Basadonis, some of them at least, had survived. Domo suspected that a coup had occurred with these two, Sharlotta and Entreri, masterminding it. They claimed that old man Basadoni was still alive, though Domo wasn't sure he believed that, but had admitted that Kadran Gordeon, a friend of Domo's, had been killed. Unfortunately, so said Sharlotta, but Domo understood that luck, good or bad, had nothing to do with it.

"Why does he speak for the old man?" the wererat asked Sharlotta, nodding toward Entreri, and with more than a bit of distaste in his tone. Domo held no love for Entreri. Few wererats did since Entreri had murdered one of the more legendary of their clan in Calimport, a conniving and wicked fellow named Rassiter.

"Because I choose to," Entreri cut in sharply before Sharlotta could intervene. The woman cast a sour look the assassin's way, then mellowed her visage as she turned back to Domo. "Artemis Entreri is well skilled in the ways of Calimport," she explained. "A proper emissary."

"I am to trust him?" Domo asked incredulously.

"You are to trust that the deal we offer you and yours is the best one you shall find in all the city," Sharlotta replied.

"You are to trust that if you do not take the deal," Entreri added, "you are thus declaring war against us. Not a pleasant prospect, I assure you."

Domo's rodent's eyes narrowed again as he considered the assassin, but he was respectful enough, and wise enough, not to push Artemis Entreri any farther.

"We will talk again, Sharlotta," he said. "You, me, and old man Basadoni." With that, the wererat took his leave with two Basadoni guards flanking him as soon as he exited the room and escorting him back to the subbasement where he could then find his way back into his sewer lair.

He was hardly gone before a secret door opened on the wall behind Sharlotta and Entreri, and Jarlaxle strode into the room.

"Leave us," the drow mercenary instructed Sharlotta, his tone showing that he wasn't overly pleased with the results.

Sharlotta gave another sour look Entreri's way and started out of the room.

"You performed quite admirably," Jarlaxle said to her, and she nodded.

"But I failed," Entreri said as soon as the door closed behind the woman. "A pity."

"These meetings mean everything to us," Jarlaxle said to him. "If we can secure our power and assure the other guilds that they are in no danger, I will have completed my first order of business."

"And then trade can begin between Calimport and Menzoberranzan," Entreri said dramatically, sarcastically, sweeping his arms out wide. "All to the gain of Menzoberranzan."

"All to the profit of Bregan D'aerthe," Jarlaxle corrected.

"And for that, I am to care?" Entreri bluntly asked.

Jarlaxle paused for a long moment to consider the man's posture and tone. "There are those among my group who fear that you do not have the will to carry this through," he said, and though the mercenary leader had allowed no hint of a threatening tone into his voice, Entreri understood the practices of the dark elves well enough to recognize the dire implications.

"Have you no heart for this?" the mercenary leader asked. "Why, you are on the verge of becoming the most influential pasha ever to rule the streets of Calimport. Kings will bow before you and pay you homage and treasures."

"And I will yawn in their ugly faces," Entreri replied.

"Yes, it all bores you," Jarlaxle remarked. "Even the fighting. You have lost your goals and desires, thrown them away. Why? Is it fear? Or is it simply that you believe there is nothing left to attain?"

Entreri shifted uncomfortably. Of course, he had known for a long time exactly the thing about which Jarlaxle was now speaking, but to hear another verbalize the emptiness within him struck him profoundly.

"Are you a coward?" Jarlaxle asked.

Entreri laughed at the absurdity of the remark, even considered leaping from his chair in a full attack upon the drow. He understood Jarlaxle's techniques and knew that he would likely be dead before he ever reached the taunting mercenary, but still he seriously considered the move. Then Jarlaxle hit him with a preemptive strike that put him back on his heels.

"Or is it that you have witnessed Menzoberranzan?" he asked.

That was indeed a huge part of it, Entreri knew, and his expression showed Jarlaxle clearly that he had struck a nerve.

"Humbled?" the drow asked. "Did you find the sights of Menzoberranzan humbling?"

"Daunting," Entreri corrected, his voice full of force and venom. "To see such stupidity on so grand a scale."

"Ah, and you know it to be a stupidity that mirrors your own existence," Jarlaxle remarked. "All that Artemis Entreri strove to achieve he found played out before him on a grand scale in the city of drow."

Still sitting, Entreri wrung his hands and bit his lip, edging closer, closer, to an attack.

"Is your life, then, a lie?" an unperturbed Jarlaxle went on, and then he sent a verbal dagger flying for Entreri's heart. "That is what Drizzt Do'Urden claimed to you, is it not?"

For just an instant, a flash of seething rage crossed Entreri's stoic face, and Jarlaxle laughed loudly. "At last, a sign of life from you!" he said. "A sign of desire, even if that desire was to tear out my heart." He gave a great sigh and lowered his voice. "Many of my companions do not think you worth the trouble," he admitted. "But I know better, Artemis Entreri. We are friends, you and I, and more alike than either of us wish to admit. You have greatness before you, if only I can show you the way."

"You speak foolishness," Entreri said evenly.

"That way lies through Drizzt Do'Urden," Jarlaxle continued without hesitation. "That is the hole in your heart. You must fight him again on terms of your choosing, because your pride will not allow you to go on with any other facet of your life until that business is settled."

"I have fought him too many times already," Entreri retorted, his anger rising. "Never do I wish to see that one again."

"So you may profess to believe," Jarlaxle said. "But you lie, to me and to yourself. Twice have you and Drizzt Do'Urden battled fairly, and twice has Entreri been sent running."

"In these very sewers he was mine!" the assassin insisted. "And would have been, had not his friends come to his aid."

"And on the cliff overlooking Mithral Hall it was he who proved the stronger."

"No!" Entreri insisted, losing his calm edge for just a moment. "No. I had him beaten."

"So you honestly believe, and thus you are trapped by the pain of the memories," Jarlaxle reasoned. "You told me of that fight in detail, and I did watch some of it from afar. We both know that either of you could have won that duel. And that is your turmoil. If Drizzt had cleanly beaten you and yet you had managed to survive, you could have gone on with your life. And if you had beaten him, whether he had lived or not, you would think no more about him. It is the not knowing that so gnaws at you, my friend. The pain of recognizing that there is one challenge that has not been decided, one challenge blocking all other aspirations you might find, be they a desire for greater power or merely for hedonistic pleasure, both easily within your reach."

Entreri sat back, seeming more intrigued than angry then.

"And that, too, I can give to you," Jarlaxle explained. "That which you desire most of all, if you'll only admit what is in your heart. I can continue my plans for Calimport without you now; Sharlotta is a fine front, and I am too firmly entrenched to be uprooted. Yet I do not desire such an arrangement. For my ventures to the surface, I want Artemis Entreri leading Bregan D'aerthe, the real Artemis Entreri and not this shell of your former self, too absorbed by this futile and empty challenge with the rogue Drizzt to concentrate on those skills that elevate you above all others."

"Skills," Entreri echoed skeptically and turned away.

But Jarlaxle knew he had gotten to the man, knew that he had dangled a treat before Entreri's eyes that the assassin could not resist. "There is one meeting remaining, the most important of the lot," Jarlaxle explained. "My drow associates and I will watch you closely when you speak with the leaders of the Rakers, Pasha Wroning's emissaries, Quentin Bodeau, and Dwahvel Tiggerwillies. Perform your duties well, and I will deliver Drizzt Do'Urden to you."

"They will demand to see Pasha Basadoni," Entreri reasoned, and the mere fact that he was giving any thought at all to the coming meeting told Jarlaxle that his bait had been taken.

"Have you not the mask of disguise?" Jarlaxle asked.

Entreri halted for a moment, not understanding, but then he realized what Jarlaxle was speaking of: a magical mask he had taken from Catti-brie in Menzoberranzan. The mask he had used to impersonate Gromph Baenre, the archmage of the drow city, to sneak right into Gromph's quarters to secure the valuable Spider Mask that had allowed him to get into House Baenre in search of Drizzt. "I do not have it," he said brusquely, obviously not wanting to elaborate.

"A pity," said Jarlaxle. "It would make things much simpler. But not to worry, for it will all be arranged," the drow promised, and with a sweeping bow he left the room, left Artemis Entreri sitting there, wondering.

"Drizzt Do'Urden," the assassin said, and there was no

venom in his voice now, just an emotionless resignation. Indeed, Jarlaxle had tempted him, had shown him a different side of his inner turmoil that he had not considered—not honestly, at least. After the escape from Menzoberranzan, the last time he had set eyes upon Drizzt, Entreri had told himself with more than a little convictio, that he was through with the rogue drow, that he hoped never to see wretched Drizzt Do'Urden again.

But was that the truth?

Jarlaxle had spoken correctly when he had insisted that the issue as to who was the better swordsman had not been decided between the two. They had fought against each other in two razor-close battles and other minor skirmishes, and had fought together on two separate occasions, in Menzoberranzan and in the lower tunnels of Mithral Hall before Bruenor's clan had reclaimed the place. All those encounters had shown them was that with regard to fighting styles and prowess they were practically mirrors of each other.

In the sewers the fight had been even until Entreri spat dirty water in Drizzt's face, gaining the upper hand. But then that wretched Catti-brie with her deadly bow had arrived, chasing the assassin away. The fight on the ledge had been Entreri's, he believed, until the drow used an unfair advantage, using his innate magics to drop a globe of darkness over them both. Even then, Entreri had maintained a winning edge until his own eagerness had caused him to forget his enemy.

What was the truth between them, then? Who would win?

The assassin gave a great sigh and rested his chin in his palm, wondering, wondering. From a pocket inside his cloak he took out a small locket, one that Jarlaxle had taken from Catti-brie and that Entreri had recovered from the mercenary leader's own desk in Menzoberranzan, a locket that could lead him to Drizzt' Do'Urden.

Many times over the past few years Artemis Entreri had stared at this locket, wondering over the whereabouts of the rogue, wondering what Drizzt might be doing, wondering what enemies he had recently battled.

Many times the assassin had stared at the locket and wondered, but never before had he seriously considered using it.

* * * * *

A noticeable spring enhanced Jarlaxle's always fluid step as he went from Entreri. The mercenary leader silently congratulated himself for the foresight of spending so much energy in hunting Drizzt Do'Urden and for his cunning in planting so powerful a seed within Entreri.

"But that is the thing," he said to Rai'gy and Kimmuriel when he found them in Rai'gy's room, Jarlaxle finishing aloud his silent pondering. "Foresight, always."

The two looked at him quizzically.

Jarlaxle dismissed those looks with a laugh. "And where are we with our scouting?" the mercenary leader asked, and he was pleased to see that Druzil was still with the mage; Rai'gy's intentions to make the imp his familiar seemed to be well on course.

The other two dark elves looked to each other, and it was their turn to laugh. Rai'gy began a quiet chant, moving his arms in slow and specified motions. Gradually he increased the speed of his waving, and he began turning about, his flowing robes flying behind him. A gray smoke arose about him, obscuring him and making it seem as if he were moving and twirling faster and faster.

And then it stopped, and Rai'gy was gone. Standing in his place was a human dressed in a tan tunic and trousers, a light blue silken cape, and a curious—curiously like Jarlaxle's own—wide-brimmed hat. The hat was blue and banded in red, plumed on the right side, and with a porcelain and gold pendant depicting a candle burning above an open eye set in its center.

"Greetings, Jarlaxle, I am Cadderly Bonaduce of Caradoon," the impostor said, bowing low.

Jarlaxle didn't miss the fact that this supposed human spoke fluently in the tongue of the drow, a language rarely heard on the surface.

"The imitation is perfect," the imp Druzil rasped. "So much does he look like the wretch Cadderly that I want to stick him with my poisoned tail!" Druzil finished with a flap of his little leathery wings that sent him up into a short flight, clapping his clawed hands and feet as he went.

"I doubt that Cadderly Bonaduce of Caradoon speaks drow," Jarlaxle said dryly.

"A simple spell will correct that," Rai'gy assured his leader, and indeed Jarlaxle knew of such a spell, had often employed it in his travels and meetings with varied races. But that spell had its limitations, Jarlaxle knew.

"I will look as Cadderly looks and speak as Cadderly speaks," Rai'gy went on, smiling at his cleverness.

"Will you?" Jarlaxle asked in all seriousness. "Or will our perceptive adversary hear you transpose a subject and verb, more akin to the manner of our language, and will that clue him that all is not as it seems?"

"I will be careful," Rai'gy promised, his tone showing that he did not appreciate anyone doubting his prowess.

"Careful may not prove to be enough," Jarlaxle replied. "As magnificent as your work has been we can take no chances here."

"If we are to go to Drizzt, as you said, then how?" Rai'gy asked.

"We shall need a professional impersonator," Jarlaxle said, drawing a groan from both his drow companions.

"What does he mean?" Druzil asked nervously.

Jarlaxle looked to Kimmuriel. "Baeltimazifas is with the illithids," he instructed. "You can go to them."

"Baeltimazifas," Rai'gy said with obvious disgust, for he knew the creature and hated it profoundly, as did most. "The illithids control the creature and set his fees exorbitantly high."

"It will be expensive," added Kimmuriel, who had the most experience in dealing with the strange illithids, the mind flayers.

"The gain is worth the price," Jarlaxle assured them both.

"And the possibility of treachery?" Rai'gy asked. "Those

kinds, both Baeltimazifas and the illithids, have never been known to follow through with bargains nor to fear the drow or any other race."

"Then we will be the first and best at treachery," Jarlaxle insisted, nodding, smiling, and seeming completely unafraid.

"And what of this Wulfgar who was left behind?"

"In Luskan," Kimmuriel replied. "He is of no consequence. A minor player and nothing more, unconnected to the rogue at this time."

Jarlaxle assumed a pensive posture, putting all the pieces together. "Minor in fact but not in tale," he decided. "If you went to Drizzt in the guise of Cadderly would you have enough remaining power—clerical powers and not wizardly—to magically bring them all to Luskan?"

"Not I and not Cadderly," Rai'gy replied. "They are too many for any clerical transport spell. I could take one or two, but not four. Nor could Cadderly, unless he is possessed of powers I do not understand."

Again Jarlaxle paused, thinking, thinking. "Not Luskan, then," he remarked, more thinking aloud than talking to his companions. "Baldur's Gate, or even a village near that city, will suit our needs." It all fell into place for the cunning mercenary leader then, the lure that would help separate Drizzt and friends from the crystal shard. "Yes, this could be rather enjoyable."

"And profitable?" Kimmuriel asked.

Jarlaxle laughed. "I cannot have one without the other."

Chapter 21

TIMELY WOUNDS

e always put in here," Bumpo Thunderpuncher explained as *Bottom Feeder* bumped hard against a fallen tree overhanging the river. The jarring shock nearly sent Regis and Bruenor tumbling off the side of the boat. "Don't like carrying too many supplies all at once," the rotund dwarf explained. "Me brother and cousins eat 'em to dangnabbit fast!"

Drizzt nodded—they did indeed need some food, mostly because of the gluttonous dwarves—and glanced warily at the trees clustered about the river. Several times over the previous two days the friends had noted movements shadowing their journey, and once Regis had seen the pursuers clearly enough to identify them as a band of goblins. By the dogged pursuit, and any pursuit longer than a few hours would be considered dogged by goblin standards, it seemed as if Crenshinibon was calling out yet again.

"How long to resupply and get back out?" the drow asked.

"Oh, not more'n an hour," Bumpo replied.

"Half that time," Bruenor bade him. "And me and me halfling friend'll help." He nodded to Drizzt and Catti-brie then, and they took the signal; Bruenor hadn't included

296

them because he knew they had to go out and do a bit of scouting.

It didn't take the seasoned pair of hunters long to find goblin sign, the tracks of at least a score of the wicked little creatures. And not far away. The goblins had apparently veered from the river at this point, and when Drizzt and Catti-brie moved to higher ground, looking east to see more of the silvery snake that was the river bending about up ahead, the two understood the goblins' reasoning. *Bottom Feeder* had been going generally north for the past hour, for the river hooked at this juncture, but the boat would soon turn back east, then south, then back to the east once more. Crossing the fairly open ground moving directly to the east, the goblin band would get to the banks in the east far ahead of the dwarves' boat.

"Ah, they're knowing the river then," Bumpo said when Drizzt and Catti-brie returned to report their findings. "They'll be beatin' us to the spot, and the river's narrower there, not wide enough for us to avoid a fight."

Bruenor turned a serious gaze upon Drizzt. "How many're ye figuring, elf?" he asked.

"A score," Drizzt replied. "Perhaps as many as thirty."

"Let's be picking our place for fighting, then," Bruenor said. "If we're to fight, then let it be on ground of our own choosing."

Everyone around noted the lack of dismay in Bruenor's tone.

"They'll be seein' the boat a long way off," Bumpo explained. "If we're to keep it here, tied up, they might be catching on."

Drizzt was shaking his head before the dwarf ever finished. "*Bottom Feeder* will go along as planned," he explained, "but without we three." He indicated Bruenor and Catti-brie, then moved near to Regis, unstrapping his belt so that he could slide off the pouch that held the Crystal Shard. "This remains on the boat," he explained to the halfling. "Above all else, keep it safe."

"So they will come after the boat, and you three will come after them," Regis reasoned, and Drizzt nodded.

"Be quick, if you please," the halfling added.

"What're ye grumbling over, Rumblebelly?" Bruenor asked with a chuckle. "Ye just loaded a ton o' food on the boat, and knowing ye the way I do I'm figuring there won't be much left for me when we get back aboard!"

Regis looked down doubtfully at the pouch, but his face did brighten as he turned to regard the supply-laden boat.

They parted company then, Bumpo, his crew, and Regis pushed off from the impromptu tree landing back into the swift currents. Before they had gone far Drizzt, on the riverbank, took out his onyx figurine, set it down, and called for his panther companion. Then he and his three companions set off, running straight to the east, following the same course as the goblin troupe.

Guenhwyvar took the point position, blending into the brush, barely seeming to stir the grasses and bushes as she passed. Drizzt came along next, working as liaison between the cat and the other two, who brought up the rear, Bruenor with his axe comfortably across his shoulder and Catti-brie with Taulmaril in hand, arrow notched and ready.

* * * * *

"Well, if we're to be fightin', then this'll be the place," Donat said a short while later as *Bottom Feeder* rounded a bend in the river, crossing into a region of narrower banks and swifter current and with many tree limbs overhanging the water.

Regis took one look at the area and groaned, not liking the prospects at all. Goblins could be anywhere, he realized, taking a good measure of the many bushes and hillocks. He took little comfort in the apparent giddiness of the four dwarves, for he had been around dwarves long enough to know that they were always happy before a fight, no matter the prospects.

And even more disconcerting to the halfling came a voice within his head, a tempting, teasing voice, reminding him that with a word he could construct a crystalline tower—a tower that a thousand goblins couldn't breach—if Regis just took control of the crystal shard. The goblins wouldn't even try to take the tower, Regis knew, for Crenshinibon would work with him to control the little wretches.

They could not resist.

* * * * *

Drizzt, looking back with his back against a tree some distance ahead of Bruenor and Catti-brie, motioned for the woman to hold her shot. He, too, had seen the goblin on the branch above, a goblin intent on the river ahead and taking no note of the approaching friends. No need to tell the whole troupe that danger was about, the ranger decided, and Catti-brie's thunderous bow would certainly raise the general alarm.

So up the tree went the drow ranger, one scimitar in hand. With amazing stealth and equal agility, he made a branch level with the goblin. Then, balancing perfectly without using his free hand, he closed suddenly in five quick steps. The drow clamped his empty hand around the creature's side, through bow and bowstring and over the surprised goblin's mouth, and drove his scimitar into the creature's back, hooking the blade upward as he went to slice smoothly through heart and lung. He held the goblin for a few seconds, letting it descend into the complete blackness of death, then carefully set it down over the branch, laying the crude bow atop it.

Drizzt looked all around for Guenhwyvar, but the panther was nowhere to be seen. He had instructed the cat to hold back until the main fighting started and trusted that Guenhwyvar would do as told.

That fight fast approached, Drizzt knew, for the goblins were all about, huddled in bushes and in trees near to the riverbank. He didn't like the prospects for a quick victory here; the region was too jumbled, with too many physical barriers and too many hiding holes. He would have liked the luxury of spending an hour or more locating all the goblins.

But then *Bottom Feeder* came into sight, rounding a bend not so far away.

Drizzt looked back to his waiting friends, motioning strongly for them to come on fast.

A roar from Bruenor and a sizzling arrow from Taulmaril led the way, Catti-brie's missile cutting by the base of Drizzt's tree, diving through some underbrush and taking a goblin in the hip, dropping it squirming to the ground.

Three other goblins emerged from that same brush, running out and screaming wildly.

Those screams fast diminished as the drow, now holding both his deadly blades, leaped down atop them. He struck hard as he crashed in, stabbing one to the side, and felling the one under him by tucking the hilt of his second blade tight against his torso and using his momentum to drive it halfway through the unfortunate creature.

And he nearly collided in midair with another soaring, dark form. Guenhwyvar, leaping strong, crossed by the descending drow and crashed into yet another bush atop a shadowy goblin form.

The one goblin of the three to escape Drizzt's initial leap staggered to the side against the trunk of the same tree from which Drizzt had jumped and turned about, spear raised to throw.

It heard the cursing howl and tried to turn its angle to the newest foe, but Bruenor came in too quick, moving within the sharpened tip of the long weapon and transferring his momentum into his overhead axe with a skidding stop, every muscle in his body snapping forward.

"Damn!" the dwarf grumbled, realizing that it might take him some time to extricate the embedded weapon from the split skull.

Even as the dwarf tugged and twisted, Catti-brie came running by, dropping to one knee and letting fly another arrow. This one blasted a goblin from a tree. She dropped her bow and in one fluid motion drew out Khazid'hea, her powerfully enchanted sword. The blade glowing fiercely, she ran on.

Still Bruenor tugged.

Drizzt, both the other two goblins quite dead, leaped up and ran on, disappearing through a small cluster of trees.

Up ahead, Guenhwyvar ran up the side of a tree, and the terrified goblins on the lowest branches both threw their spears errantly and tried to leap to the ground. One made it; the other got caught in midair by a swiping panther claw and was pulled, squirming wildly, back up to its death.

"Damn," Bruenor said again, tugging and tugging, missing all the fun. "I gotta hit the stinkin' things softer!"

* * * * *

He couldn't raise the crystal tower on the boat, of course, but right over the side, even in the river. Yes, the bottom levels of the structure might be under the water, but Crenshinibon would still show him a way in.

"They got spears!" Bumpo Thunderpuncher cried. "To the wall! To the wall!" On cue, the dwarf captain and his three kinsfolk dived down to the deck and rolled up against the blocking side wall closest to the goblin-infested shore. Donat, who got there first, quickly broke open a wooden locker, each dwarf taking up a crossbow and huddling tight against the shielding planking while loading.

All of the movement finally caught Regis's eye, and he shook away his visions of a crystal tower, hardly believing that he could have even considered raising the thing, and looked, quite startled, at the dwarves. He looked up as the boat drifted beneath an overhanging limb and saw a goblin there, its arm poised to throw.

The four dwarves rolled in unison to their backs, lining up their crossbows and letting fly. Each bolt hit its mark, driving into the goblin and jerking it up and over so that it tumbled into the river behind the floating craft.

But not before it had thrown the spear and thrown it well.

Regis yelped and tried to dodge, but too late. He felt the spear dive into the back of his shoulder. The halfling heard, with sickening clarity, the tip of it prodding right through him to knock against the deck. He was down, facedown, and he heard himself howling, though his voice came from no conscious act.

Then he felt the uneven edges of the decking planks as the dwarves pulled him to the side, and he heard, as if from a great distance, Donat crying, "They killed him! They killed him to death!"

And then he was alone, and so cold, and he heard the splashing of water as swimming goblins made the edge of the boat.

* * * * *

Down from a high branch came the panther, graceful and beautiful, a soaring black arrow. She went past one goblin, one paw kicking out swiftly enough to rake out the oblivious creature's throat, and then crashed upon another pair, bearing one down under her great weight and ripping the life from it in an instant, then skipping on to the next before it could rise and flee.

The goblin rolled to its back, flailed its arms wildly to try to fend off the great cat. But Guenhwyvar was too strong and too fast and soon got her maw clamped about the creature's throat.

Not far to the side, Drizzt and Catti-brie, independently in pursuit of goblins, discovered each other in a small clearing and found that they had become ringed by goblins, who, seeing a sudden advantage, leaped out of the brush and encircled the pair.

"A bit o' good luck, I'd say," Catti-brie remarked with a wink to her friend, and they fell together defensively, back-to-back.

The goblins tried to coordinate their attacks, calling to each other, opposite ones coming in at the same time, while those beside them waited to see if the first attack might leave the two humans vulnerable.

They simply didn't understand.

Drizzt and Catti-brie rolled about each other's back, thus

changing their angles of attack, the drow going after those goblins that had come in at Catti-brie and vice versa. Out Drizzt came, scimitars flashing in circling motions, hooking inside spear shafts and turning them harmlessly aside. A subtle shift in wrist angle, a quick step forward, and both goblins staggered backward, guts torn.

Across the way Catti-brie went down low under the high thrust of one spear and sent Khazid'hea slashing across, the wickedly edged blade taking the goblin's leg off cleanly at the knee. A goblin to the side tried to adjust its spear angle down at the woman, but she caught the weapon shaft with her free hand and turned it aside, using it as leverage to propel her up and out, a single thrust taking the creature in the chest.

"Straight on!" Drizzt yelled, rushing by and hooking Catti-brie under the shoulder, helping her to her feet and pushing her along in his charge, their momentum shattering the line of the frightened creatures.

Those behind didn't dare follow that charge, except for one, and thus Drizzt knew that Crenshinibon had crazed this one.

In the span of three heartbeats it lay dead.

* * * * *

Still behind the main fighting, Bruenor heard the commotion, and that made him madder than ever. Twisting and pulling, tugging with all his strength, the dwarf nearly toppled as his axe came free—almost free, he realized with revulsion, for instead of pulling the heavy blade from the creature's skull he had torn the dead goblin's head right off.

"Well, that's pretty," he said with disgust, and then he had no more time to complain as a pair of goblins crashed out of the brush near to him. He hit the closest hard, a roundabout throw that slammed its kin's head right into its belly and sent it staggering backward.

Weaponless, Bruenor took a hit from the second goblin, a

club smash across his shoulders that stung but hardly slowed him. He leaped in close, moving right before the goblin, and snapped his forehead into the creature's face, sending it reeling and taking its club from its weakened grasp as it staggered.

Before the goblin could retrieve its bearings, that club smashed down hard once, twice, thrice, and left the thing twitching helplessly on the ground.

Bruenor spun about and launched the club into the legs of the first goblin as it tried to charge at his back, tripping the creature and sending it headlong to the ground. Bruenor quickstepped over it, back to the brush to retrieve his axe.

"Enough playin'!" the dwarf roared. Finesse aside, he slammed his axe against the nearest tree trunk, shattering away the remnants of the head.

Up and spinning, the goblin took one look at the ferocious dwarf and his axe, took one look at the decapitated remains of Bruenor's first kill, and turned and ran.

"No ye don't!" the dwarf howled, and he let fly an overhead throw that sent his axe spinning hard into the goblin's back, dropping it facedown into the dirt.

Bruenor ran by, thinking to pull the axe free in full stride, heading to rejoin his companions.

It was stuck again, this time hooked on the dying goblin's spine.

"Orc-brained, troll-smellin', bug-eater!" Bruenor cursed.

* * * * *

Donat worked hard over Regis, trying to hold the spear shaft steady so the embedded weapon wouldn't do any more damage, while his three kinfolk rushed about frantically, working furiously themselves to keep *Bottom Feeder* free of goblins. One creature nearly made the deck, but Bumpo smashed his crossbow across its face, shattering the weapon and the goblin's jaw.

The dwarf howled in glee, lifted the stunned creature above his head and threw it into two others that were trying to come over the side, dropping all three back into the water.

His two cousins proved equally effective and equally damaging to expensive crossbows, but the boat stayed clear of goblins, soon outdistancing those giving stubborn pursuit in the swift current.

That allowed Bumpo to take up Donat's crossbow, the only one still working, and pluck a few in the water.

Most of the creatures did make the other bank but had seen enough of the fight—too much, actually—and simply ran off into the underbrush.

* * * * *

Bruenor planted his heavy boots on the back of the still-groaning goblin, spat in both his hands, took up his axe handle, and gave a great tug, ripping the head and half the goblin's backbone free.

The dwarf went over in a backward roll to wind up sitting in the dirt.

"Oh, even prettier," he remarked, noting the torn creature and the length of spine lying across his extended legs. He shook his head and hopped to his feet, running fast to join his friends, but by the time he arrived the battle had ended. Drizzt and Catti-brie stood amidst several dead creatures, and Guenhwyvar circled about, searching for any others.

But those held in Crenshinibon's mental grasp were already dead, and those still of free will were long gone.

"Tell the stupid crystal shard to call in thicker-skinned creatures," Bruenor grumbled. He gave Drizzt a sidelong glance as they headed for the riverbank. "Ye're sure we got to get rid of that thing?"

Drizzt only smiled and ran along. One goblin did come out of the river on this side, but Guenhwyvar buried it before the friends ever got close.

Up ahead, Bumpo maneuvered *Bottom Feeder* into a small side pool out of the main current. The three friends laughed all the way, replaying the battle and talking light-heartedly about how good it was to be back on the road.

Their expressions changed abruptly when they saw Regis lying on the deck, pale and very still.

* * * * *

From a dark room in the subbasement of House Basadoni, Jarlaxle and his wizard-priest assistant watched it all.

"This could not be any easier," the mercenary leader remarked with a laugh. He turned to Rai'gy. "Find yourself a human persona in the guise of a priest much like Cadderly and in the same ceremonial dress. Not his hat, though," the mercenary added after a short pause. "That might constitute rank, I believe, or prove more a matter of Cadderly's personal taste."

"But Kimmuriel has gone for Baeltimazifas," Rai'gy protested.

"And you shall accompany the doppleganger to Drizzt and his companions," Jarlaxle explained, "as a student of Cadderly Bonaduce's Spirit Soaring library. Prepare spells of powerful healing."

Rai'gy's eyes widened with surprise. "I am to pray to Lady Lolth for spells with which to heal a halfling?" he asked incredulously. "And you believe that she will grant me such spells, given that intent?"

Jarlaxle, supremely confident, nodded. "She will, because bestowing such spells shall further the cause of her drow," he explained, and he smiled widely, knowing that the outcome of the battle had just made his life a lot easier and much more interesting.

Chapter 22
SAVING GRACE

egis gasped and groaned in agony, squirming just a bit, which only made things worse for the poor halfling. Every movement made the spear shaft quiver, sending waves of burning pain through his body.

Bruenor brushed aside any soft emotions and blinked away any tears, realizing that he would be doing his grievously injured friend no favors by showing any sympathy at all. "Do it quick," he said to Drizzt. The dwarf knelt down over Regis, setting himself firmly, pressing the halfling by the shoulders and putting one knee on his back to hold him perfectly still.

Drizzt wasn't sure how to proceed. The spear was barbed, that much he recognized, but to push it all the way through and out the other side seemed too brutal a technique for Regis to possibly survive. Yet, how could Drizzt cut the spear quickly enough and smoothly enough so that Regis did not have to endure such unbearable agony? Even a minor shift in the long shaft had the halfling groaning in pain. What might the jarring of the shaft being hacked by a scimitar do to him?

R. A. Salvatore

"Take it in both yer hands," Catti-brie instructed. "One hand on the wound, t'other on the spear, right above where ye want the thing broken."

Drizzt looked at her and saw that she had Taulmaril in hand again, an arrow readied. He looked from the bow to the spear and understood her intent. While he doubted the potential of such a technique, he simply had no other answers. He gripped the spear shaft tightly just above the entry wound, then again two handsbreadths up. He looked to Bruenor, who secured his hold on Regis even more—drawing another whimper from the poor halfling—and nodded grimly.

Drizzt then nodded to Catti-brie who bent low, lining up her shot and the angle of the arrow after it passed through, so that it would not hit one of her friends. If she was not perfect, she realized, or even if she simply was not lucky, the arrow might deflect badly, and then they'd have another seriously wounded companion lying on the deck beside Regis. With that thought in mind Catti-brie relaxed her bowstring a bit, but then Regis whimpered again, and she understood that her poor little friend was fast running out of time.

She drew back, took perfect aim, and left fly, the blinding, lightning-streaking arrow sizzling right through the shaft cleanly, and soaring into, and through the opposite deck wall and off across the river.

Drizzt, stunned by the sudden flash even though he had expected the shot, held in place for just a moment. After allowing his senses to catch up with the scene he handed the broken piece of the shaft to Bumpo.

"Lift him gently," the drow instructed Bruenor, who did so, raising the halfling's injured shoulder slowly from the deck.

Then, with a plaintive and helpless look to all about, the drow grasped the remaining piece of shaft firmly and began to push.

Regis howled and screamed and wriggled too much for sympathetic Drizzt to continue. At a loss, he let go of the shaft and held his hands out helplessly to Bruenor.

"The ruby pendant," Catti-brie remarked suddenly, dropping to her knees beside her friends. "We'll get him thinking of better things." She moved quickly as Bruenor lifted the groaning Regis a bit higher, reaching into the front of the halfling's shirt and pulling forth the dazzling ruby pendant.

"Watch it close," Catti-brie said to Regis several times. She held the gemstone, spinning alluringly at the end of its chain before the halfling's half-closed eyes. Regis's head started to droop, but Catti-brie grabbed him by the chin and forced him steady.

"Ye remember the party after we rescued ye from Pook?" she asked calmly, forcing a wide smile across her face.

Gradually she brought him into her words with more coaxing, more reminding of that enjoyable affair, one in which Regis had become quite intoxicated. And intoxicated was what the halfling seemed to be now. He was groaning no more, his gaze locked on the spinning gemstone.

"Ah, but didn't ye have the fun of it in the pillowed room?" the woman said, speaking of the harem in Pook's house. "We thought ye'd never come forth!" As she spoke, she looked to Drizzt and nodded. The drow took up the remaining piece of embedded shaft once more and, with a look to Bruenor to make certain that the dwarf had Regis properly secured and braced, he slowly began to push.

Regis winced as the rest of the wide-bladed head tore through the front of his shoulder but offered no real resistance and no screaming. Drizzt soon had the spear fully extracted.

It came out with a gush of blood, and both Drizzt and Bruenor had to work fast and furiously to stem the flow. Even then, as they lay Regis gently on his back, they saw his arm discoloring.

"He's bleeding inside," Bruenor said through gritted teeth. "We'll be taking the arm off if we can't fix it!"

Drizzt didn't respond, just went back to work on his small friend, moving aside the bandages and trying to reach his nimble fingers right into the wound to pinch the blood flow.

Catti-brie kept up her soothing talk, doing a marvelous job of distracting the halfling, concentrating so fully on the task before her that she managed to minimize her nervous glances Drizzt's way.

Had Regis seen the drow's face the spell of the ruby pendant might have shattered. For Drizzt understood the trouble here and understood that his little friend was in real danger. He couldn't stop the flow. Bruenor's drastic measure of amputating the arm might be necessary, and even that, Drizzt understood, would likely kill the halfling.

"Ye got it?" Bruenor asked again and again. "Ye got it?"

Drizzt grimaced, looking pointedly at Bruenor's already bloodstained axe blade, and went at his work more determinedly. Finally, he relaxed his grip on the vein just a bit, easing, easing, breathing a bit easier as he lessened the pressure and felt no more blood spurting from the tear.

"I'm taking the damned arm!" Bruenor declared, misinterpreting Drizzt's resigned look.

The drow held up his hand and shook his head. "It is stemmed," he announced.

"But for how long?" Catti-brie asked, genuinely concerned.

Again Drizzt shook his head helplessly.

"We should be going," Bumpo Thunderpuncher remarked, seeing that the commotion about Regis had subsided. "Them goblins might not be far."

"Not yet," Drizzt insisted. "We cannot move him until we're sure the wound will not reopen."

Bumpo gave a concerned look to his brother. Then both of them glanced nervously at their thrice-removed cousins.

But Drizzt was right, of course, and Regis could not be immediately moved. All three friends stayed close to him; Catti-brie kept the ruby pendant in hand, should its calming hypnosis prove necessary. For the time being, though, Regis knew nothing at all, nothing beyond the relieving blackness of unconsciousness.

* * * * *

"You are nervous," Kimmuriel Oblodra remarked, obviously taking great pleasure in seeing the normally unshakable Jarlaxle pacing the floor.

Jarlaxle stopped and stared at the psionicist incredulously. "Nonsense," he insisted. "Baeltimazifas performed his impersonation of Pasha Basadoni perfectly."

It was true enough. At the important meeting that same morning, the doppleganger had impersonated Pasha Basadoni perfectly, no small feat considering that the man was dead and Baeltimazifas could not probe his mind for the subtle details. Of course, his role in the meeting was minor—hindered, so Sharlotta had explained to the other guildmasters, by the fact that he was very old and not in good health. Pasha Wroning had been convinced by the doppelganger's performance. With the powerful Wroning satisfied, Domo Quillilo of the wererats and the younger and more nervous leaders of the Rakers could hardly protest. Calm had returned to Calimport's streets, and all, as far as the others were concerned, was as it had been.

"He told the other guildmasters that which they desired to hear," Kimmuriel said.

"And so we shall do the same with Drizzt and his friends," Jarlaxle assured the psionicist.

"Ah, but you know that the target this time is more dangerous," said the ever-observant Kimmuriel. "More alert, and more . . . drow."

Jarlaxle stopped and stared hard at the Oblodran, then laughed aloud, admitting his edginess. "Ever has it proven interesting where Drizzt Do'Urden is concerned," he explained. "This one has again and again outrun, outsmarted, or merely out-lucked the most powerful enemies one can imagine. And look at him," he added, motioning to the magical reflective pool Rai'gy had left in place. "Still he survives, nay, thrives. Matron Baenre herself wanted to make a trophy of that one's head, and she, not he, has passed from this world."

"We do not desire his death," Kimmuriel reminded. "Though that, too, might prove quite profitable."

Jarlaxle shook his head fiercely. "Never that," he said determinedly.

Kimmuriel spent a long while studying the mercenary leader. "Could it be that you have come to like this outcast?" he asked. "That is the way of Jarlaxle, is it not?"

Jarlaxle laughed again. " 'Respect' would be a better word."

"He would never join Bregan D'aerthe," the psionicist reminded.

"Not knowingly," the opportunistic mercenary replied. "Not knowingly."

Kimmuriel didn't press the point but rather motioned to the reflective pool excitedly. "Pray that Baeltimazifas lives up to his fees," he said.

Jarlaxle, who had witnessed the catastrophe of many futile attempts against the likes of Drizzt Do'Urden, certainly was praying.

Artemis Entreri entered the room then, as Jarlaxle had bade him. He took one look at the two dark elves, then moved cautiously to the side of the reflecting pool—and his eyes widened when he saw the image displayed within, the image of his greatest adversary.

"Why are you so surprised?" Jarlaxle asked. "I told you I can deliver to you that which you most desire."

Entreri worked hard to keep his breathing steady, not wanting the mercenary to draw too much enjoyment from his obvious excitement. He recognized the truth of it all now, that Jarlaxle—damned Jarlaxle!—had been right. There in the pool stood the source of Entreri's apathy, the symbol that his life had been a lie. There stood the one challenge yet facing the master assassin, the one remaining uneasiness that so prevented him from enjoying his present life.

Right there, Drizzt Do'Urden. Entreri looked back at Jarlaxle and nodded.

The mercenary, hardly surprised, merely smiled.

* * * * *

Regis squirmed and groaned, resisting Catti-brie's attempts with the pendant this time, for as the emergency had dictated, she had not begun the charming process until after Drizzt's fingers were already working furiously inside the halfling's torn shoulder.

Bruenor, his axe right beside him, did well to hold the halfling steady, but Drizzt kept growling and shaking his head in frustration. The wound had reopened, and badly, and this time the nimble-fingered drow could not possibly close it.

"Take the damned arm!" Drizzt finally cried in ultimate frustration, falling back, his own arm soaked in blood. The four dwarves behind him gave a unified groan, but Bruenor, always steady and reliable, understood the truth and moved methodically for his axe.

Catti-brie continued to talk to Regis, but he was no longer listening to her or to anything, his consciousness long flown.

Bruenor leveled the axe, lining up the stroke. Catti-brie, having no logical arguments, understanding that they had to stem the bleeding even if that meant cutting off the arm and cauterizing the wound with fire, hesitantly extended the torn arm.

"Take it," Drizzt instructed, and the four dwarves groaned again.

Bruenor spat in his hands and took up the axe, but doubt crossed his face as he looked down at his poor little friend.

"Take it!" Drizzt demanded.

Bruenor lifted the axe and brought it down again slowly, lining up the hit.

"Take it!" Catti-brie said.

"Do not!" came a voice from the side, and all the friends turned to see two men walking toward them.

"Cadderly!" Catti-brie cried, and so it seemed to be. So surprised and pleased was she, and was Drizzt, that neither noticed that the man seemed older than the last time they had seen him, though they knew the priest was not aging,

313

but was rather growing more youthful as his health returned. The great effort of raising the magical Spirit Soaring library from the rubble had taken its toll on the young man.

Cadderly nodded to his companion, who rushed over to Regis. "Good it is that beside you we arrived," the other priest said, a curious comment and in a dialect that none of the others had heard before.

They didn't question him about it, though, not with their friend Cadderly standing beside him, and certainly not while he bent over and began a quiet chant over the prone halfling.

"My associate, Arrabel, will see to the wound," Cadderly explained. "Truly I am surprised to see you out here so far from home."

"Coming to see yerself," Bruenor explained.

"Well, turn about," Baeltimazifas, in the guise of Cadderly, said dramatically, exactly as Jarlaxle had instructed. "I will welcome you indeed in a grand manner, when you arrive at the Spirit Soaring, but your road now is in the other direction, for you've a friend in dire need."

"Wulfgar," Catti-brie breathed, and the others were surely thinking the same.

Cadderly nodded. "He tried to follow your course, it would seem, and has come into a small hamlet east of Baldur's Gate. The downstream currents will take you there quickly."

"What hamlet?" Bumpo asked.

The doppleganger shrugged, having no name. "Four buildings behind a bluff and trees. I know not its name."

"That'd be Yogerville," Donat insisted, and Bumpo nodded his agreement.

"Get ye there in a day," the dwarf captain told Drizzt.

The drow looked questioningly to Cadderly.

"It would take me a day to pray for such a spell of transport," the phony priest explained. "And even then I could take but one of you along."

Regis groaned then, drawing the attention of all, and to the companions' amazement and absolute joy the halfling sat up, looking much better already, and even managed to flex the fingers at the end of his torn arm.

Beside him, Rai'gy, in the uncomfortable mantle of a human, smiled and silently thanked Lady Lolth for being so very understanding.

"He can travel, and immediately," the doppleganger explained. "Now be off. Your friend is in dire need. It would seem that his temper has angered the farmers, and they have him prisoner and plan to hang him. You have time to save him, for they'll not act until their leader returns, but be off at once."

Drizzt nodded, then reached down and took his pouch from Regis's belt. "Will you join us?" he asked, and even then, eager Catti-brie, Bruenor, Regis, and the dwarves began readying the boat for departure. Drizzt and Cadderly's associate moved out of the craft to join the priest.

"No," the doppleganger replied, perfectly mimicking Cadderly's voice, according to the imp who had supplied the strange, creature with most of the details and insights. "You'll not need me, and I have other urgent matters to attend."

Drizzt nodded and handed the pouch over. "Take care with it," he explained. "It has the ability to call in would-be allies."

"I will be back in the Spirit Soaring in a matter of minutes," the doppleganger replied.

Drizzt paused at that curious comment—hadn't Cadderly just proclaimed that he needed a day to memorize a spell of transport?

"Word of recall," Rai'gy, picking up the uneasiness, put in quickly. "Get us home to the Spirit Soaring will the spell, but not to any other place."

"Come on, elf!" Bruenor cried. "Me boy's waiting."

"Go," Cadderly bade Drizzt, taking the pouch and in the same movement, putting his hand on Drizzt's shoulder and turning him back to the boat, pushing him gently along. "Go at once. You've not a moment to spare."

Silent alarms continued to ring out in Drizzt's head, but

he had no time then to stop and consider them. *Bottom Feeder* was already sliding back out into the river, the four crew working to turn her about. With a nimble leap Drizzt joined them, then turned back to see Cadderly waving and smiling, his associate already in the throes of spellcasting. Before the craft had gone very far the friends watched the pair dissipate into the wind.

"Why didn't the durned fool just take one of us to me boy now?" Bruenor asked.

"Why not, indeed?" Drizzt replied, staring back at the empty spot and wondering.

Wondering.

Bright and early the next morning, *Bottom Feeder* put in against the bank a couple hundred yards short of Yogerville and the four friends, including Regis, who was feeling much better, leaped ashore.

They had all agreed that the dwarves would remain with the boat, and also, on the suggestion of Drizzt, had decided that Bruenor, Regis, and Catti-brie would go in to speak with the townsfolk alone while the ranger circumvented the hamlet, getting a full lay of the region.

The three were greeted by friendly farm folk, by wide smiles, and then, when asked about Wulfgar, by expressions of confusion.

"Ye thinking that we'd forget one of that description?" one old woman asked with a cackle.

The three friends looked at each other with confusion.

"Donat picked the wrong town," Bruenor said with a great sigh.

* * * * *

Drizzt harbored troubling thoughts. A magical spell had obviously brought Cadderly to him and his companions, but if Wulfgar was in such dire need, why hadn't the cleric just gone to him first instead? He could explain it, of course, considering that Regis was in more dire peril, but why hadn't Cadderly gone to one, while his associate went to the other?

Again, logical explanations were there. Perhaps the priests had only one spell that could bring them to one place and had been forced to choose. Yet there was something else nagging at Drizzt, and he simply could not place it.

But then he understood his inner turmoil. How had Cadderly even known to look for Wulfgar, a man he had never met and had only heard about briefly?

"Just good fortune," he told himself, trying logically to trace Cadderly's process, one that had obviously brought him onto Drizzt's trail, and there he had discovered Wulfgar, not so far behind. Luck alone had informed the priest of whom this great man might be.

Still, there seemed holes in that logic, but ones that Drizzt hoped might be filled in by Wulfgar when at last they managed to rescue him. With all that in mind Drizzt made his way around the back side of the hamlet, moving behind the blocking ridge south of the town, out of sight of his friends and their surprising exchange with the townsfolk, who honestly had no idea who Wulfgar might be.

But Drizzt could have guessed as much anyway when he came around that ridgeline, to see a crystalline tower, an image of Crenshinibon, sparkling in the morning light.

Chapter 23

THE LAST CHALLENGE

rizzt stood transfixed as a line appeared on the unblemished side of the crystalline tower, widening, widening, until it became an open doorway.

And inside the door, beckoning to Drizzt, stood a drow elf wearing a great plumed hat that Drizzt surely recognized. For some reason he could not immediately discern, Drizzt was not as surprised as he should have been.

"Well met again, Drizzt Do'Urden," Jarlaxle said, using the common surface tongue. "Please do come in and speak with me."

Drizzt put one hand to a scimitar hilt, the other to the pouch holding Guenhwyvar—though he had only recently sent the panther back to her astral home and knew she would be weary if recalled. He tensed his leg muscles and measured the distance to Jarlaxle, recognizing that he, with the enchanted ankle bracers he wore, could cover the ground in the blink of an eye, perhaps even get a solid strike in against the mercenary.

But then he would be dead, he knew, for if Jarlaxle was here, then so was Bregan D'aerthe, all about him, weapons trained upon him.

"Please," Jarlaxle said again. "We have business we must discuss to the benefit of us both and to our friends."

That last reference, coupled with the fact that Drizzt had come back this way on the word of an impostor—who was obviously working for the mercenary leader or was, perhaps the mercenary leader—that Wulfgar was in some danger, made Drizzt relax his grip on his weapon.

"I guarantee that neither I nor my associates shall strike against you," Jarlaxle assured him. "And furthermore the friends who accompanied you to this village will walk away unharmed as long as they take no action against me."

Drizzt held a fair understanding of the mysterious mercenary, enough to trust Jarlaxle's word, at least. Jarlaxle had held all the cards in previous meetings, times when the mercenary could have easily killed Drizzt, and Catti-brie as well. And yet he had not, despite the fact that bringing the head of Drizzt Do'Urden back to Menzoberranzan at that time might have proven quite profitable. With a look back to the direction of the town, blocked from view by the high ridge, Drizzt moved to the door.

Many memories came to Drizzt as he followed Jarlaxle into the structure, the magical door sliding closed behind them. Though this ground level was not as the ranger remembered it, he could not help but recall the first time he entered a manifestation of Crenshinibon, when he had gone after the wizard Akar Kessell back in Icewind Dale. It was not a pleasant memory to be sure, but a somewhat comforting one, for within those recollections came to Drizzt an understanding of how he could defeat this tower, of how he could sever its power and send it crumbling down.

Looking back at Jarlaxle, though, as the mercenary settled comfortably into a lavish chair beside a huge upright mirror, Drizzt understood he wouldn't likely get any such chance.

Jarlaxle motioned to a chair opposite him, and again Drizzt moved to comply. The mercenary was as dangerous as any creature Drizzt had ever know, but he was not reckless and not vicious.

One thing Drizzt did notice, though, as he moved for the seat: his feet seemed just a bit heavier to him, as though the dweomer of his bracers had diminished.

"I have followed your movements for many days," Jarlaxle explained. "A friend of mine requires your services, you see."

"Services?" Drizzt asked suspiciously.

Jarlaxle only smiled and continued. "It became important for me to bring the two of you together again."

"And important for you to steal the crystal shard," Drizzt reasoned.

"Not so," the mercenary honestly answered. "Not so. Crenshinibon was not known to me when this began. Acquiring it was merely a pleasant extra in seeking that which I most needed: you."

"What of Cadderly?" Drizzt asked with some concern. He still was not certain whether it really had been Cadderly who had come to Regis's aid. Had Jarlaxle subsequently garnered Crenshinibon from the priest? Or had the entire episode with Cadderly been merely a clever ruse?

"Cadderly remains quite comfortable in the Spirit Soaring, oblivious to your quest," Jarlaxle explained. "Much to the dismay of my wizard friend's new familiar, who holds a particular hatred for Cadderly."

"Promise me that Cadderly is safe," Drizzt said in all seriousness.

Jarlaxle nodded. "Indeed, and you are quite welcome for our actions to save your halfling friend."

That caught Drizzt off guard, but he had to admit that it was true enough. Had not Jarlaxle's cronies come in the guise of Cadderly and enacted great healing upon Regis, the halfling likely would have died, or at the very least would have lost an arm.

"Of course, for the minor price of a spellcasting you gained much of our confidence," Drizzt did remark, reminding Jarlaxle that he understood the mercenary rarely did anything that did not bring some benefit to him.

"Not so minor a spellcasting," Jarlaxle bantered. "And we could have faked it all, providing only the illusion of healing, a spell that would have temporarily healed the halfling's wounds, only to have them reopen later on to his ultimate demise.

"But I assure you that we did not," he quickly added, seeing Drizzt's eyes narrow dangerously. "No, your friend is nearly fully healed."

"Then I do thank you," Drizzt replied. "Of course, you understand that I must take Crenshinibon back from you?"

"I do not doubt that you are brave enough to try," Jarlaxle admitted. "But I do understand that you are not stupid enough to try."

"Not now, perhaps."

"Then why ever?" the mercenary asked. "What care is it to Drizzt Do'Urden if Crenshinibon works its wicked magic upon the dark elves of Menzoberranzan?"

Again, the mercenary had put Drizzt somewhat off his guard. What care, indeed? "But does Jarlaxle remain in Menzoberranzan?" he asked. "It would seem not."

That brought a laugh from the mercenary. "Jarlaxle goes where Jarlaxle needs to go," he answered. "But think long and hard on your choice before coming for the crystal shard, Drizzt Do'Urden. Are there truly any hands in all the world better suited to wield the artifact than mine?"

Drizzt did not reply but was indeed considering the words carefully.

"Enough of that," Jarlaxle said, coming forward in his chair, suddenly more intent. "I have brought you here that you might meet an old acquaintance, one you have battled beside and battled against. It seems as if he has some unfinished business with Drizzt Do'Urden, and that uncertainty is costing me precious time with him."

Drizzt stared hard at the mercenary, having no idea what Jarlaxle might be talking about—for just a moment. Then he remembered the last time he had seen the mercenary, right before Drizzt and Artemis Entreri had parted ways. His expression showed his disappointment clearly as he came to suspect the truth of it all.

* * * * *

"Ye picked the wrong durned town," Bruenor said to Bumpo and Donat when he and the other two returned to *Bottom Feeder*.

The two dwarven brothers looked curiously at each other, Donat scratching his head.

"Had to be this one," Bumpo insisted. "By yer friend's description, I mean."

"The townsfolk might have been lying to us," Regis put in.

"They're good at it, then," said Catti-brie. "Every one o' them."

"Well, I know a way to find out for certain," the halfling said, a mischievous twinkle in his eye. When Bruenor and Catti-brie, recognizing that tone in his voice, turned to regard him, they found him dangling his hypnotic ruby pendant.

"Back we go," Bruenor said, starting away from the boat once more. He paused and looked back at the four dwarves. "Ye're sure, are ye?" he asked.

All four heads began wagging enthusiastically.

Just before the threesome arrived back among the cluster of houses, a small boy ran out to meet them. "Did you find your friend?" he asked.

"Why no, we haven't," Catti-brie replied, holding back both Bruenor and Regis with a wave of her hand. "Have ye seen him?"

"He might be in the tower," the youngster offered.

"What tower?" Bruenor asked gruffly before Catti-brie could reply.

"Over there," the young boy answered, unruffled by the dwarf's stern tone. "Out back." He pointed to the ridge that rose up behind the small village, and as the friends followed that line they noted several villagers ascending the ridge. About halfway up the villagers began gasping in astonishment, some pointing, others falling to the ground, and still others running back the way they had come.

The three friends began running, too, to the ridge and up.

Then they too skidded to abrupt stops, staring incredulously at the tower image of Crenshinibon.

"Cadderly?" Regis asked incredulously.

"I'm not thinkin' so," said Catti-brie. Crouching low, she led them on cautiously.

* * * * *

"Artemis Entreri wishes this contest between you two at last resolved," Jarlaxle confirmed.

"And why would I go along?" Drizzt asked, coming right out of his chair. "I have no desire ever to see the likes of Artemis Entreri again, let alone do battle with the wretch. If his inability to fight with me brings him discomfort, then all the better, I say!"

Drizzt's uncharacteristic outburst made it quite obvious to Jarlaxle just how much he despised Entreri and just how sincere he was in his claim to never want to go against the man again.

"Never do you disappoint me," Jarlaxle said with a chuckle. "Your lack of hubris is commendable, my friend. I applaud you for it and do wish, in all sincerity, that I could grant you your desire and send you and your friends on your way. But that I cannot do, I fear, and I assure you that you must settle your relationship with Entreri. For your friends, if not for yourself."

Drizzt chewed on that threat for a long moment. While he did, Jarlaxle waved his hand in front of the mirror beside his chair, which clouded over immediately. As Drizzt watched the fog swirled away, leaving a clear image of Catti-brie, Bruenor, and Regis making their way up to the base of the tower. Catti-brie was in the lead, moving in a staggered manner, trying to utilize the little cover available.

"I could kill them with a thought," the mercenary assured Drizzt.

"But why would you?" Drizzt asked. "You gave me your word."

"And so I shall keep it," Jarlaxle replied. "As long as you cooperate."

Drizzt paused, digesting the information. "What of Wulfgar?" he asked suddenly, thinking that Jarlaxle must have some information regarding the man since he'd used Wulfgar's name to lure Drizzt and his friends to this place.

Now it was Jarlaxle's turn to pause and think, but just for a moment. "He is alive and well from what I can discern," the mercenary admitted. "I have not spoken with him, but looked in on him long enough to find out how his present situation might benefit me."

"Where?" Drizzt asked.

Jarlaxle smiled widely. "There will be time for such talk later," he said, looking back over his shoulder to the one staircase ascending from the room.

"You will find that your magics will not work in here," the mercenary went on, and Drizzt understood then why his feet seemed heavier. "None of them, not your scimitars, the bracers you took from Dantrag Baenre when you killed him, nor even your innate drow powers."

"Yet a new and wondrous aspect of the crystal shard," Drizzt remarked sarcastically.

"No," Jarlaxle admitted, smiling. "More the help of a friend. It was necessary to defeat all magic, you see, because this last meeting between you and Artemis Entreri must be on perfectly equal footing, with no possible unfair advantages to be gained by either party."

"Yet your mirror worked," Drizzt reasoned, as much trying to buy himself some time as out of any curiosity. "Is that not magic?"

"It is yet another piece of the tower, nothing I brought in, and all the tower is impervious to my associate's attempts to defeat the magic," Jarlaxle explained. "What a marvelous gift you gave to me—or to my associate—in handing over Crenshinibon. It has told me so much about itself . . . how to raise the towers and how to manipulate them to fit my needs"

"You know that I cannot allow you to keep it," Drizzt said again.

"And you know well that I would never have invited you here if I thought there was anything at all you could do to take Crenshinibon away from me," Jarlaxle said with a laugh. He ended the sentence by looking again at the mirror to his side.

Drizzt followed that gaze to the mirror, to see his friends moving about the base of the tower then, searching for a door—a door that Drizzt knew they would not find unless Jarlaxle willed it to be so. Catti-brie did find something of interest, though: Drizzt's tracks.

"He's in there!" she cried.

"Please be Cadderly," both dark elves heard Regis remark nervously. That brought a chuckle from Jarlaxle.

"Go to Entreri," the mercenary said more seriously, waving his hand so that the mirror clouded over again, the image dissipating. "Go and satisfy his curiosity, and then you and your friends will go your way, and I will go mine."

Drizzt spent a long while staring at the mercenary. Jarlaxle didn't press him for many moments, just locked stares with him. In that moment they came to a silent understanding.

"Whatever the outcome?" Drizzt asked again, just to be sure.

"Your friends walk away unharmed," Jarlaxle assured him. "With you, or with your body."

Drizzt turned his gaze back to the staircase. He could hardly believe that Artemis Entreri, his nemesis for so long, awaited him just up those steps. His words to Jarlaxle had been sincere and heartfelt; he never wanted to see the man again, let alone fight with him. That was Entreri's emotional pain, not Drizzt's. Even now, with the fight so close and obviously so necessary, the drow ranger did not look forward to his climb up those stairs. It wasn't that he was afraid of the assassin. Not at all. While Drizzt respected Entreri's fighting prowess, he didn't fear the challenge.

He rose from his chair and started for the stairs, silently

recounting all the good he might accomplish in this fight. In addition to satisfying Jarlaxle, Drizzt might well be ridding the world of a scourge.

Drizzt stopped and turned about. "This counts as one of my friends," he said, producing the onyx figurine from his pouch.

"Ah, yes, Guenhwyvar," Jarlaxle said, his face brightening.

"I will not see Guenhwyvar in Entreri's hands," Drizzt said. "Nor in yours. Whatever the outcome, she is to be returned to me or to Catti-brie."

"A pity," Jarlaxle remarked with a laugh. "I had thought you might forget to include the magnificent panther in your conditions. How much I would love a companion such as Guenhwyvar."

Drizzt stood up straighter, lavender eyes narrowing.

"You would never trust me with such a treasure," Jarlaxle said. "Nor could I blame you. I do indeed have a weakness for things magical!" The mercenary was laughing, but Drizzt was not.

"Give it to them yourself," Jarlaxle offered, motioning for the door. "Just toss the figurine at the wall, above where you entered. Watch the results for yourself," he added, motioning to the mirror, which cleared again of fog and produced an image of Drizzt's friends.

The ranger looked back to the door to see a small opening appear right above it. He rushed over. "Be gone from this place!" he cried, hoping his friends would hear, and tossed the onyx figurine through the portal. Thinking suddenly that the whole episode might be just one of Jarlaxle's tricks, he swung about and scrambled to watch in the mirror.

To his relief he saw the trio, Catti-brie calling for him and Regis picking up the panther from the ground. The halfling wasted no time in setting the thing down and calling to Guenhwyvar, and the cat soon appeared beside Drizzt's friends, growling out to the trapped drow even as the other three called for him.

"You know they'll not leave," Jarlaxle said dryly. "But go

on and be done with this. You have my word that your friends, all four, will not be harmed."

Drizzt hesitated just one more time, glancing back at the mercenary who still sat comfortably in his chair as though Drizzt presented no threat to him whatsoever. For a moment Drizzt considered calling that bluff, drawing his weapons enchanted or not, and rushing over to cut the mercenary down. But he could not, of course, not when the safety of his friends hung in the balance.

Jarlaxle, so smug in his chair, knew that implicitly.

Drizzt took a deep breath, trying to throw away all the confusion of this last day, the craziness that had handed the mighty artifact over to Jarlaxle and brought Drizzt to this place, to fight Artemis Entreri, no less.

He took a second deep breath, stretched out his fingers and arms, and started up the stairs.

* * * * *

Artemis Entreri paced the room nervously, studying the many contours, staircases, and elevated planks. No simple circular, empty chamber for Jarlaxle. The mercenary had constructed this, the second floor of the tower, with many ups and downs, places where strategy could play in to the upcoming fight. At the center of the room was a staircase of four steps, rising to a landing large enough for only one man. The back side mirrored the front, another four steps back down to the floor level. More steps completely bordered the room, five up to the wall, where another landing ran all the way around. From these, on Entreri's left, went a plank, perhaps a foot wide, connecting the fourth step to the top landing of the center case.

Yet another obstacle, a two-sided ramp, loomed near the back wall beside where Entreri paced. Two others, low, circular platforms, were set about the room by the door across the way, the door through which Drizzt Do'Urden would enter.

But how to make all of these props work for him? Entreri pondered, and he realized that his thoughts mattered little, for Drizzt was too unpredictable a foe, was too quick and quick thinking for Entreri to lay out a plan of attack. No, he would have to improvise every step and roll of the way, to counter and anticipate, and fight in measured thrusts.

He drew out his weapons then, dagger and sword. At first he had considered coming in with two swords to offset Drizzt's twin scimitars. In the end he decided to go with the style he knew best, and with the weapon, though its magic would not work in here, that he loved best.

Back and forth he paced, stretching his muscles, arms, and neck. He talked quietly to himself, reminding himself of all that he had to do, warning himself to never, not for a single instant, underestimate his enemy. And then he stopped suddenly, and considered his own movements, his own thoughts.

He was indeed nervous, anxious and, for the first time since he had left Menzoberranzan, excited. A slight sound turned him around.

Drizzt Do'Urden stood on the landing.

Without a word the drow ranger entered, then flinched not at all as the door slid closed behind him.

"I have waited for this for many years," Entreri said.

"Then you are a bigger fool than I supposed," Drizzt replied.

Entreri exploded into motion, rushing up the back side of the center stairs, brandishing dagger and sword as he came over the lip, as if he expected Drizzt to meet him there, battling for the high ground.

The ranger hadn't moved, hadn't even drawn his weapons.

"And a bigger fool still if you believe that I will fight you this day," Drizzt said.

Entreri's eyes widened. After a long pause he came down the front stairs slowly, sword leading, dagger ready, moving to within a couple of steps of Drizzt.

Who still did not draw his weapons.

"Ready your scimitars," Entreri instructed.

"Why? That we might play as entertainment for Jarlaxle and his band?" Drizzt replied.

"Draw them!" Entreri growled. "Else I'll run you through."

"Will you?" Drizzt calmly asked, and he slowly drew out his blades. As Entreri came on another measured step, the ranger dropped those scimitars to the ground.

Entreri's jaw dropped nearly as far.

"Have you learned nothing in all the years?" Drizzt asked. "How many times must we play this out? Must all of our lives be dedicated to revenge upon whichever of us won the last battle?"

"Pick them up!" Entreri shouted, rushing in so that his sword tip came in at Drizzt's breastbone.

"And then we shall fight," Drizzt said nonchalantly. "And one of us will win, but perhaps the other will survive. And then, of course, we will have to do this all over again, because you believe that you have something to prove."

"Pick them up," Entreri said through gritted teeth, prodding his sword just a bit. Had that blade still been carrying the weight of its magic, the prod surely would have slid it through Drizzt's ribs. "This is the last challenge, for one of us will die this day. Here it is, laid out for us by Jarlaxle, as fair a fight as we might ever find."

Drizzt didn't move.

"I will run you through," Entreri promised.

Drizzt only smiled. "I think not, Artemis Entreri. I know you better than you believe, and surely better than you are comfortable with. You would take no pleasure in killing me in such a manner and would hate yourself for the rest of your life for doing so, for stealing from yourself the only chance you might ever have to know the truth. Because that is what this is about, is it not? The truth, your truth, the moment when you hope to either validate your miserable existence or put an end to it."

Entreri growled loudly and came forward, but he did not, could not, press his arm forward and impale the drow. "Damn you!" he cried, spinning away, growling and slashing, back around the stairs, cursing with every step. "Damn you!"

Behind him Drizzt nodded, bent, and retrieved his

scimitars. "Entreri," he called, and the change in his tone told the assassin that something was suddenly very different.

Entreri, on the other side of the room now, turned about to see Drizzt standing ready, blades in hand, to see the vision he so desperately craved.

"You passed my test," Drizzt explained. "Now I'll take yours."

* * * * *

"Are we to watch or just wait to see who shall walk out victorious?" Rai'gy asked as he and Kimmuriel walked out from a small chamber off to the side of the first floor's main room.

"This show will be worth the watching," Jarlaxle assured the pair. He motioned to the stairs. "We will ascend to the landing, and I will make the door translucent."

"An amazing artifact," Kimmuriel said, shaking his head. In only a day of communing with the crystal shard Jarlaxle had learned so very much. He had learned how to shape and design the tower reflection of the shard, to make doors appear and seemingly vanish, to create walls, transparent or opaque, and to use the tower as one great scrying device, as he was now. Both Kimmuriel and Rai'gy noted this as they came around to see the image of Catti-brie, Regis, Bruenor, and the great cat showing in the mirror.

"We shall watch, and they should as well," Jarlaxle said. He closed his eyes, and all three drow heard a scraping sound along the outside of Crenshinibon. "There," Jarlaxle announced a moment later. "Now we may go."

* * * * *

Catti-brie, Bruenor, and Regis stood dumbfounded as the crystalline tower seemed to snake to life, one edge rolling out wide, releasing a hidden fold. Then, amazingly, a stairway appeared, circling down along the tower from a height of about twenty feet.

The three hesitated, looking to each other for answers, but Guenhwyvar waited not at all, bounding up the stairs, roaring with every mighty leap.

* * * * *

They stared at each other for some time, looks of respect more than hatred, for they had come past hatred, these two, losing a good deal of their enmity by the sheer exertions of their running battle.

So now they stared from opposite sides of the thirty-foot diameter room, across the central stairs, each waiting for the other to make the first move, or rather, for the other to show that he was about to move.

They broke as one, both charging for the center stairs, both seeking the higher ground. Even without the aid of the magical bracers Drizzt gained a step advantage, perhaps because though he was twice the assassin's actual age, he was much younger in terms of a drow lifetime than Entreri was for a human.

Always the improviser, Entreri took one step on the staircase, then dived to the side, headlong in a roll that brought him harmlessly past Drizzt's swishing blades. He went right under the raised plank, using it as a barrier against the scimitars.

Drizzt turned completely around, falling into a ready crouch at the top of the stairs and preventing Entreri from coming back in.

But Entreri knew that the ranger would protect his high-ground position, and so the assassin never slowed, coming out of his roll back to his feet and running to the side of the room, up the five steps, then moving along that higher ground to the end of the raised plank. When Drizzt did not pursue, neither by following Entreri's course nor rushing across the plank, Entreri hopped down to that narrow walkway and moved halfway along it toward the center stair.

Drizzt held his ground on the wider platform of the staircase apex.

"Come along," Entreri bade him, indicating the walkway. "Even footing."

* * * * *

They feared climbing that stair, for how vulnerable they would all be perched on the side of Crenshinibon, but when Guenhwyvar, at the landing and looking into the tower, roared louder and began clawing at the wall they could not resist. Again Catti-brie arrived first to find a translucent wall at the top of the stairs, a window into the room where Drizzt and Entreri faced off.

She banged on the unyielding glass. So did Bruenor when he arrived, with the back of his axe, but to no avail, for they could not even scratch the thing. If Drizzt and Entreri heard them, or even saw them, neither showed it.

* * * * *

"You should have made the room smaller," Rai'gy remarked dryly when he, Jarlaxle, and Kimmuriel arrived at their landing, similarly watching the action—or lack thereof—within.

"Ah, but the play's the thing," Jarlaxle replied. He pointed across the way then, to Catti-brie and the others. "We can see the combatants and Drizzt's friends across the way, and those friends can see us," he explained, and even as he did so the three drow saw Catti-brie pointing their way, screaming something that they could not hear but could well imagine. "But Drizzt and Entreri can see only each other."

"Quite a tower," Rai'gy had to admit.

* * * * *

Drizzt wanted to hold the secure position, but Entreri showed patience now, and the ranger knew that if he did not go out, this fight that he desperately wanted to be done with could take a long, long time. He hopped onto the narrow walkway easily and came out toward Entreri slowly, inch by inch, setting each foot firmly before taking the next small step.

He snapped into sudden motion as he neared, a quick-step thrust of his right blade. Entreri's dagger, his left-hand weapon, wove inside the thrust perfectly and pushed the scimitar out wide. In the same fluid movement the assassin turned his shoulder and moved ahead, sword tip leading.

Drizzt's second scimitar was halfway into the parry before the thrust ever began, turning a complete circle in the air, then ascending inside the angle of the thrust on the second pass, deflecting the rushing sword, rolling right over it and around as his first blade did the same with the dagger. Into the dance fully he went, his curving blades accentuating the spinning circular motions, cutting over and around, reversing the direction of one, then both, then one again. Spinning, seeking opening, thrusting ahead, slashing down.

And Entreri matched every movement, his actions in straighter lines, straight to the side or above or straight ahead, picking off the blades, forcing Drizzt to parry. The metal screamed continuously, hit after hit after hit.

But then Drizzt's left hand came in cleanly and cleanly swished through the air, for the assassin did not try to parry but dived into a forward roll instead, his sword knocking one scimitar at bay, his movement causing the other to miss, and his dagger, leading the ascent out of the roll, aimed for Drizzt's heart with no chance for the ranger to bring his remaining scimitar in to block.

So up went Drizzt, up and out, a great leap to the left side, tucking and turning to avoid the strike, landing on the floor in a roll that brought him back to his feet. He took two running steps away as he spun about, knowing that Entreri, slight advantage gained, would surely pursue. He came around just in time to meet a furious attack from dagger and sword.

Again the metal rang out repeatedly in protest, and Drizzt was forced back by the sheer momentum of Entreri's charge.

He accepted that retreat, though, quickstepping all the way to maintain perfect balance, his hands working in a blur.

* * * * *

At the interior landing the three drow, who had lived all their lives around expert swordsmen and had witnessed many, many battles, watched every subtle movement with mounting amazement.

"Did you arrange this for Entreri's benefit or ours?" Rai'gy remarked, his tone surely different, surely without hint of sarcasm.

"Both," Jarlaxle admitted. As he spoke, Drizzt darted past Entreri up the center stairs and did not stop, but rather leaped off, turning in midair as he went, then landing in a rush back to the side toward the plank. Entreri took a shorter route instead of a direct pursuit, leaping up to the plank ahead of Drizzt, stealing the advantage the dark elf had hoped to achieve.

As much the improviser as his opponent, Drizzt dived down low, skittering under the plank even as Entreri got his footing, and slashing back up and over his head, an amazingly agile move that would have hamstrung the assassin had Entreri not anticipated just that and continued on his way, leaping off the plank back to the floor and turning around.

Still, Drizzt had scored a hit, tearing the back of Entreri's trousers and a line across the back of his calf.

"First blood to Drizzt," Kimmuriel observed. He looked to Jarlaxle, who was smiling and looking across the way. Following the mercenary's gaze Rai'gy saw that Drizzt's friends, including even the panther, were similarly entranced, watching the battle with open-mouthed admiration.

And so it was well-earned, Kimmuriel silently agreed, turning his full attention back to the dance, brutal and beautiful all at once.

* * * * *

Now they came in at floor level, rushing together in a blur of swords and flying capes, their routines neither attack nor defense, but somewhere in between. Blade scraped along blade, throwing sparks, the metal shrieking in protest.

Drizzt's left blade swished across at neck level. Entreri dropped suddenly below it into a squat from which he seemed to gain momentum, coming back up with a double thrust of sword and dagger. But Drizzt didn't stop his turn with the miss. The dark elf went right around, a complete circuit, coming back with a right-handed, backhand down-and-over parry. The inside hook of his curving blade caught both the assassin's blades and turned them aside. Then Drizzt altered the angle of his left before it swished overhead, the blade screaming down for Entreri's head.

But the assassin, his hands even closer together because of Drizzt's block, switched blades easily, then extracted the dagger by bringing his right arm in suddenly, pumping it back out, dagger tip rising as scimitar descended.

Then they both howled in pain, Drizzt leaping back with a deep puncture in his wrist, Entreri falling back with a gash along the length of his forearm.

But only for a second, only for the time it took each to realize that he could continue, that he would not drop a weapon. Both Drizzt's scimitars started out wide, closing like the jaws of a wolf as he and Entreri came together. The assassin, though his blades had the inside track, found himself a split second behind and had to double block, throwing his own blades, and the scimitars they caught, out wide and coming forward with the momentum. He hesitated just an instant to see if he could possibly bring one of his blades back in.

Drizzt hadn't hesitated at all, though, dipping his forehead just ahead of Entreri's similar movement, so that when they came smacking together, head to head, Entreri got the brunt of it.

But the assassin, dazed, punched out straight with his right hand, knuckles and dagger crosspiece slamming into Drizzt's face.

They fell apart again, one of Entreri's eyes fast swelling, Drizzt's cheek and nose bleeding.

The assassin pressed the attack fiercely then, before his eye closed and gave Drizzt a huge advantage. He went in hard, stabbing his sword down low.

Drizzt's scimitar crossed down over it, and he pivoted perfectly, launching a kick that got Entreri in the face.

The kick hardly slowed him, for the assassin had anticipated that exact move indeed, he had counted on it. He ducked as the foot came in, a grazing blow, but one that nonetheless stung his already injured eye. Skittering forward he launched his dagger in a roundabout manner, the edge coming in at the back of Drizzt's knee.

Drizzt could have struck with his second blade, hoping to get it past the already engaged sword, but if he tried and Entreri somehow managed to parry, he knew that the fight would be all but over, that the dagger would tear the back out of his leg.

He knew all of that, instinctively, without thinking at all, so instead he just kicked his one supporting leg forward, falling backward over the dagger. Drizzt was scraped but not skewered. He meant to go all the way around in the roll and come right back up to his feet, but before he even really started he saw that the growling Entreri was fast pursuing and would catch him defenseless halfway around.

So he stopped and set himself on his back as the assassin came in.

On both sides of the room, dark elves and Drizzt's friends alike gasped, thinking the contest at its end. But Drizzt fought on, scimitars whirling, smacking, and stabbing to somehow, impossibly, hold Entreri at bay. And then the ranger managed to tuck one foot under him and come up in a wild rush, fighting ferociously, hitting each of Entreri's blades and hitting them hard, driving, driving to gain an equal footing.

Now they were in it, face to face, blades working too quickly for the onlookers to even discern individual moves, but rather to watch the general flow of the battle. A gash appeared here on one combatant, a gash appeared there on the other, but neither warrior found the opportunity to bring any cut to completion. They were superficial nicks, torn clothes and skin. It went on and on, up one side of the staircase and down the other, and any misgivings that Drizzt might have had about this fight had long flown, and any doubts Entreri had ever had about desiring to battle Drizzt Do'Urden again had been fully erased. They fought with passion and fury, their blades striking so rapidly that the ring came as constant.

They were out on the plank then, but they didn't know it. They came down together, each knocking the other from his perch, on opposite sides, then went under the plank together, battling in a crouch. They moved past each other, coming up on either side, then leaping back atop the narrow walkway in perfect balance to begin anew.

On and on it went, and the seconds became minutes, and sweat mixed with blood and stung open wounds. One of Drizzt's sleeves got sliced so badly that it interfered with his movements, and he had to launch an explosive flurry to drive Entreri back long enough so he could flip his blade in the air and pull the remnants of the sleeve from his arm, then catch his blade as it descended, just in time to react to the assassin's charge. A moment later Entreri lost his cape as Drizzt's scimitar came in for his throat, cutting the garment's drawstring and tearing a gash under Entreri's chin as it rose.

Both labored for breath; neither would back off.

But for all the nicks and blood, for all the sweat and bruises, one injury alone stood out, for Entreri's vision on his right side was indeed blurring. The assassin switched weapon hands, dagger back in left and the longer, better blocking sword back in his right.

Drizzt understood. He launched a feint, a right, left, right combination that Entreri easily picked off, but the attacks had not been designed to score any definitive hit anyway, just to allow Drizzt to put his feet in line.

To the side of the room cunning Jarlaxle saw it and understood that the fight was about to end.

Now Drizzt came in again with a left, but he stepped into the blow and launched his scimitar from far out to the side, from a place where Entreri's closed eye could hardly make out the movement. The assassin did instinctively parry with the sword and counter with the dagger, but Drizzt rolled his scimitar right over the intended parry, then snapped it back out, slashing Entreri's wrist and launching the sword away. At the same time, the ranger dropped his blade from his right hand and caught Entreri's stabbing dagger arm at the wrist. Stepping in and rolling his wrist and turning his weapon hand, Drizzt twisted Entreri's dagger arm back under itself, holding it out wide while before the assassin's free hand could hold Drizzt's arm back the dark elf's scimitar tip came in at Entreri's throat.

All movement stopped suddenly. The assassin, with one arm twisted out wide and the other behind Drizzt's scimitar arm, was helpless to stop the ranger's momentum if Drizzt decided to plunge the blade through Entreri's throat.

Growling and trembling, as close to the very edge of control as he had ever been, Drizzt held the blade back. "So what have we proven?" he demanded, voice full of venom, his lavender orbs locked in a wicked stare with Entreri's dark eyes. "Because my head connected in a favorable place with yours, limiting your vision, I am the better fighter?"

"Finish it!" Entreri snarled back.

Drizzt growled again and twisted Entreri's dagger arm more, bending the assassin's wrist so that the dagger fell to the floor. "For all those you have killed, and all those you surely will, I should kill you," Drizzt said, but he knew even as he said the words, and Entreri did, too, that he could not press home his blade, not now. In that awful moment Drizzt lamented not going through with the move in the first instant, before he had found the time to consider his actions.

But now he could not, so with a sudden explosion of motion he let go of Entreri's arm and drove his open palm hard into the assassin's face, disengaging them and knocking Entreri staggering backward.

"Damn you, Jarlaxle, have you had your pleasure?" Drizzt

cried, turning about to see the mercenary and his companions, for Jarlaxle had opened the door.

Drizzt came forward determinedly, as if he meant to run right over Jarlaxle, but a noise behind him stopped him, for Entreri came on, yelling.

Yelling. The significance of that was lost on Drizzt in that moment as he spun about, right to left, his free right arm brushing out and across, lifting Entreri's leading arm, which held again that awful dagger. And around came Drizzt's left arm, scimitar leading, in a stab as Entreri crashed in, a stab that should have plunged the weapon into the assassin's chest to its hilt.

The two came together and Drizzt's eyes widened indeed, for somehow, somehow, Entreri's very skin had repelled the blow.

But Artemis Entreri, his body tingling with the energy of the absorbed hit, with the psionics Kimmuriel had suddenly given back to him, surely understood, and in a purely reactive move, without any conscious thought—for if the tormented man had considered it he would have loosed the energy back into himself—Entreri reached out and clasped Drizzt's chest and gave him back his blow with equal force.

His hand sank into Drizzt's chest even as Drizzt, blood bubbling from the wound, fell to the ground.

* * * * *

Out on the landing time seemed to freeze, stuck fast in that awful, awful moment. Guenhwyvar roared and leaped into the translucent wall, but merely bounced away. Outraged, roaring wildly, the cat went back at the wall, claws screeching against the unyielding pane.

Bruenor, too, went into a fighting frenzy, hacking futilely with his axe while Regis stood dumbfounded, saying, "No, it cannot be," over and over.

And there stood Catti-brie, wavering back and forth, her jaw drooping open, her eyes locked on that horrible sight. She suffered through every agonizing second as Entreri's empowered hand melted into Drizzt's chest, as the lifeblood of her dearest friend, of the ranger she had come to love so dearly, spurted from him. She watched the strength leave his legs, the buckling knees, and the sinking, sinking as Entreri guided him to the floor, and the sinking, sinking, of her own heart, an emptiness she had felt before, when she had seen Wulfgar fall with the yochlol.

And even worse it seemed for her this time.

* * * * *

"What have I done?" the assassin wailed, falling to his knees beside the drow. He turned an evil glare over Jarlaxle. "What have you done?"

"I gave you your fight and showed you the truth," Jarlaxle calmly replied. "Of yourself and your skills. But I am not finished with you. I came to you for my own purposes, not your own. Having done this for you, I demand that you perform for me."

"No! No!" the assassin cried, reaching down furiously to try to stem the spurting blood. "Not like this!"

Jarlaxle looked to Kimmuriel and nodded. The psionicist gripped Entreri with a mental hold, a telekinetic force that lifted Entreri from Drizzt and dragged him behind Kimmuriel as the psionicist headed out of the room, back down the stairs.

Entreri thrashed and cursed, aiming his outrage at Jarlaxle but eyeing Drizzt, who lay very still on the floor. Indeed he had been granted his fight and, indeed, as he should have foreseen, it had proven nothing. He had lost— or would have, had not Kimmuriel intervened—yet he was the one who had lived.

Why, then, was he so angry? Why did he want at that moment, to put his dagger across Jarlaxle's slender throat?

Kimmuriel hauled him away.

"He fought beautifully," Rai'gy remarked to Jarlaxle, indicating Drizzt, the blood flowing much lighter now, a pool of it all about his prone and very still form. "I understand now why Dantrag Baenre is dead."

Jarlaxle nodded and smiled. "I have never seen Drizzt Do'Urden's equal," he admitted, "unless it is Artemis Entreri. Do you understand now why I chose that one."

"He is drow in everything but skin color," Rai'gy said with a laugh.

An explosion rocked the tower.

"Catti-brie and her marvelous bow," Jarlaxle explained, looking to the landing where only Guenhwyvar remained, roaring and clawing futilely at the unyielding glass. "They saw, of course, every bit of it. I should go and speak with them before they bring the place down around us."

With a thought to the crystal shard, Jarlaxle turned that wall in front of Guenhwyvar opaque once more.

Then he nodded to the still form of Drizzt Do'Urden and walked out of the room.

EPILOGUE

e is sulking," Kimmuriel remarked, joining Jarlaxle sometime later in the main chamber of the lower floor. "But at least he has stopped swearing to cut off your head."

Jarlaxle, who had just witnessed one of the most enjoyable days of his long life, laughed yet again. "He will come to his senses and will at last be free of the shadow of Drizzt Do'Urden. For that Artemis Entreri will thank me openly." He paused and considered his own words. "Or at least," the mercenary corrected, "he will . . . silently thank me."

"He tried to die," Kimmuriel stated flatly. "When he went at Drizzt's back with the dagger he led the way with a shout that alerted the outcast. He tried to die and we, and I, at your bidding, stopped that."

"Artemis Entreri will no doubt find other opportunities for stupidity if he holds that course," the mercenary leader replied with a shrug. "And we will not need him forever."

Drizzt Do'Urden came down the stairs then in tattered clothing, stretching his sore arm, but otherwise seeming not too badly injured.

"Rai'gy will have to pray to Lady Lolth for a hundred

years to regain her favor after using one of her bestowed healing spells upon your dying form," Jarlaxle remarked with a laugh. He nodded to Kimmuriel, who bowed and left the room.

"May she take him to her side for those prayers," Drizzt replied dryly. His witty demeanor did not hold, though, could not hold, in the face of all that he had just come through. He eyed Jarlaxle with all seriousness. "Why did you save me?"

"Future favors?" Jarlaxle asked more than stated.

"Forget it."

Yet again Jarlaxle found himself laughing. "I envy you, Drizzt Do'Urden," he replied honestly. "Pride played no part in your fight, did it?"

Drizzt shrugged, not quite understanding.

"No, you were free of that self-defeating emotion," Jarlaxle remarked. "You did not need to prove yourself Artemis Entreri's better. Indeed, I do envy you, to have found such inner peace and confidence."

"You still have not answered my question."

"A measure of respect, I suppose," Jarlaxle answered with a shrug. "Perhaps I did not believe that you deserved death after your worthy performance."

"Would I have deserved death if my performance did not measure up to your standards, then?" Drizzt asked. "Why does Jarlaxle decide?"

Jarlaxle wanted to laugh again but held it to a smile in deference to Drizzt. "Or perhaps I allowed my cleric to save you as a favor to your dead father," he said, and that put Drizzt on his heels, catching him completely by surprise.

"Of course I knew Zaknafein," Jarlaxle explained. "He and I were friends, if I can be said to have any friends. We were not so different, he and I."

Drizzt screwed up his face with obvious doubts.

"We both survived," Jarlaxle explained. "We both found a way to thrive in a hostile land, in a place we despised but could not find the courage to leave."

"But you have left now," Drizzt said.

343

"Have I?" came the reply. "No, by building my empire in Menzoberranzan I have inextricably tied myself to the place. I will die there, I am sure, and probably by the hands of one of my own soldiers—perhaps even Artemis Entreri."

Somehow Drizzt doubted the claim, suspecting that Jarlaxle would die of old age centuries hence.

"I respected him greatly," the mercenary went on, his tone steady and serious. "Your father, I mean, and I believe it was mutual."

Drizzt considered the words carefully and found that he couldn't disagree with Jarlaxle's claims. For all Jarlaxle's capacity for cruelty, there was indeed a code of honor about the mercenary leader. Jarlaxle had proven that when he had held Catti-brie captive and had not taken advantage of her, though he had even professed to her that he wanted to. He had proven it by allowing Drizzt, Catti-brie, and Entreri to walk out of the Underdark after their escape from House Baenre, though surely he could have captured or killed them and such an act would have brought him great favor of the ruling house.

And now, by not letting Drizzt die in such a manner, he had proven it again.

"He'll not bother you ever again," Jarlaxle remarked, drawing Drizzt from his contemplation.

"So I dared to hope once before."

"But now it is settled," the mercenary leader explained. "Artemis Entreri has his answer, and though it is not what he had hoped it will suffice."

Drizzt considered it for a moment then nodded, hoping Jarlaxle, who seemed to understand so very much about everyone, was right yet again.

"Your friends await you in the village," Jarlaxle explained. "And it was no easy task getting them to go there and wait. I feared that I would taste the axe of Bruenor Battlehammer, and given the fate of Matron Baenre, that I did not wish at all."

"But you persuaded them without injuring any of them," Drizzt said.

"I gave you my word, and that word I honor . . . sometimes."

Now Drizzt, despite himself, couldn't hold back a grin. "Perhaps, then, I owe you yet again."

"Future favors?"

"Forget it."

"Surrender the panther then," Jarlaxle teased. "How I would love to have Guenhwyvar at my side!"

Drizzt understood that the mercenary was just teasing, that his promise concerning the panther, too, would hold. "Already you will have to look over your shoulder as I come for the crystal shard," the ranger replied. "If you take the cat, I will not only have to retrieve her but will have to kill you, as well."

Those words surely raised the eyebrows of Rai'gy as he came onto the top of the stairs, but the two were merely bantering. Drizzt would not come for Crenshinibon, and Jarlaxle would not take the panther.

Their business was completed.

Drizzt left the crystalline tower then to rejoin his friends, all together and waiting for him in the village, unharmed as Jarlaxle had promised.

After many tears and many hugs they left the village. But they did not go straight to the waiting *Bottom Feeder* but rather, back up the ridge.

The crystalline tower was gone. Jarlaxle and the other drow were gone. Entreri was gone.

"Good enough for them, if they bring the foul artifact back to yer old home and it brings all the ceiling down atop 'em!" Bruenor snorted. "Good enough for them!"

"And now we need not go to Cadderly," Catti-brie said. "Where then?"

"Wulfgar?" Regis reminded.

Drizzt paused a moment to consider Jarlaxle's words— trustworthy words—about their missing friend. He shook his head. It wasn't time for that road just yet. "We have the whole world open before us," he said. "And any direction will prove as good as another."

"And now we don't have the damned crystal shard bringing monsters in on us at every turn," Catti-brie noted.

"Won't be as much fun then," said Bruenor.

And off they went to catch the sunset . . . or the sunrise.

* * * * *

Back in Calimport Artemis Entreri, possibly the most powerful man on the streets, mulled over the titanic events of the last days, the amazing twists and turns his life's road had shown him.

Drizzt Do'Urden was dead, he believed, and by his hand, though he had not proven the stronger.

Or hadn't he? For wasn't it Entreri, and not Drizzt, who had befriended the more powerful allies?

Or did it even matter?

For the first time in many months a sincere smile found its way onto Artemis Entreri's face as he walked easily down Avenue Paradise, assured that none would dare move against him. He found the halfling door guards at the Copper Ante more than happy to see and admit him, and he found his way into Dondon's room without the slightest hindrance, without even questioning stares.

He emerged a short while later to find an angry Dwahvel waiting for him.

"You did it, didn't you?" she accused.

"It had to be done," was all Entreri bothered to reply, wiping his bloodstained dagger on the cloak of one of the guards flanking Dwahvel, as if daring them to make a move against him. They did not, of course, and Entreri moved unhindered to the outside door.

"Our arrangement is still in force?" he heard a plaintive Dwahvel call from behind. With a grin that nearly took in his ears, the ruler of House Basadoni left the inn.

* * * * *

Wulfgar left Delly Curtie that night, as he did every night, bottle in hand. He went down to the wharves where his newest drinking buddy, a man of some repute, waited for him.

"Wulfgar, my friend," Morik the Rogue said happily, taking the bottle and a deep, deep swallow of the burning liquid. "Is there anything that we two cannot accomplish together?"

Wulfgar considered the words with a dull smile. Indeed, they were the kings of Half Moon Street, the two men who rated deferential nods from everyone they passed, the two men in all of Luskan's belly who could part a crowd merely by walking through it.

Wulfgar took the bottle from Morik and, though it was more than half full, drained it in one swallow.

He just had to.